Light My Fire

Precious air hit her scorched face, but when Kat tried to suck in a deep breath, a cruel, unseen fist twisted her lungs. She coughed again, clutching her chest. Her head spun. So did the two big trucks pulling up the drive.

A hand grabbed her upper arm.

"Ma'am? Are you all right?"

The deep baritone voice sent a thrill to every nerve ending. A smooth shot of Jack Daniel's after a long dry spell, warming her fingers and toes. Other places, too. *Good God, Katherine Frances, get real.* Raising her head, she found herself gazing at the broadest chest she'd ever seen, even allowing for the bulk of his coat.

"Ma'am?" He pressed close, his worry evident.

Kat tilted her chin up. *Way* up. A giant of a man roughly the size of an aircraft carrier towered over her, saying something else. Shadowed under the wide brim of his hat, she noted the line of his strong, square jaw. Full, sensual lips. Dark eyes.

"I'm . . . fine," she croaked. And promptly ruined the assertion by hacking up a lung. The black edges spiraled inward, dizziness winning out, the mountainous man disappearing.

In spite of her best efforts, Kat did something she'd never done in her twenty-nine years. She collapsed into a total stranger's arms.

TRIAL BY FIRE

THE FIREFIGHTERS OF STATION FIVE

JO DAVIS

A SIGNET ECLIPSE BOOK

SIGNET ECLIPSE
Published by New American Library, a division of
Penguin Group (USA) Inc., 375 Hudson Street,
New York, New York 10014, USA
Penguin Group (Canada), 90 Eglinton Avenue East, Suite 700, Toronto,
Ontario M4P 2Y3, Canada (a division of Pearson Penguin Canada Inc.)
Penguin Books Ltd., 80 Strand, London WC2R 0RL, England
Penguin Ireland, 25 St. Stephen's Green, Dublin 2,
Ireland (a division of Penguin Books Ltd.)
Penguin Group (Australia), 250 Camberwell Road, Camberwell, Victoria 3124,
Australia (a division of Pearson Australia Group Pty. Ltd.)
Penguin Books India Pvt. Ltd., 11 Community Centre, Panchsheel Park,
New Delhi - 110 017, India
Penguin Group (NZ), 67 Apollo Drive, Rosedale, North Shore 0632,
New Zealand (a division of Pearson New Zealand Ltd.)
Penguin Books (South Africa) (Pty.) Ltd., 24 Sturdee Avenue,
Rosebank, Johannesburg 2196, South Africa

Penguin Books Ltd., Registered Offices:
80 Strand, London WC2R 0RL, England

First published by Signet Eclipse, an imprint of New American Library,
a division of Penguin Group (USA) Inc.

First Printing, August 2008
10 9 8 7 6 5 4 3 2 1

To my parents, Bryan and Trena.

Dad, your example of quiet strength and perseverance, and the respect you command from others, continues to be the most valuable gift a father can give. When I looked for a role model to instill these qualities in Lieutenant Howard Paxton, I turned to you. And now the whole world knows it.

Mom, your unwavering faith in me, and your infectious optimism and encouragement, has picked me up off the floor more times than I can count. You're proof that a mom can truly be a daughter's best friend.

I love you both.

ACKNOWLEDGMENTS

Thank you to:

My family, who freed me to follow my dream: my wonderful husband, Paul, you are forever my hero. Also, our two terrific children, my parents, my in-laws, and far too many family members to list. I love you all.

My fantastic agent, Roberta Brown. Your faith in me never wavered. I'm proud to know you, and to call you a friend.

My savvy editor, Tracy Bernstein, for believing in my work and giving the boys of Fire Station Five a home. I'll always be grateful for the day Howard crossed your path.

Debra Stevens, my best friend of nearly forty years. You've always believed I could achieve anything, and encouraged me to go for it—especially when it involved getting us both in hot water! You are my sister, my lifeline.

Diana Dittman, my sister-in-law and best friend of almost thirty years. You've encouraged me every step of my journey. The miles may separate us, but the path always leads us home.

My fabulous critique partners, Tracy Garrett and Suzanne Welsh. I couldn't do it without you. Girlfriends, life is good.

The Foxes: Tracy Garrett, Suzanne Welsh, Jane Graves, Sandy Blair, Franny Karkosak, Kay Thomas, Julie Benson, Lorraine Heath, and Alice Fairbanks-Burton. You guys are my cheering section, my margarita buddies, my sanity.

The NAL art department for the fabulous cover of my dreams.

Stonecreek Media for my awesome Web site. Amy and Justin, your gorgeous custom designs and awesome client relations set the bar for the rest.

Special thanks to:

These brave, real-life heroes who inspired the Fire-fighters of Station Five series: Captain Steve Deutsch, David Lewis, Wally Harris, Nick Franco, and Ken Marston. Steve, thank you for putting up with my endless questions and welcoming me into your world. I appreciate you more than you know. Ken, you have my eternal gratitude for inspiring Howard.

Peggy Harrell and the guys at the Plano Fire Department: Captain Forest Harrell, Brian Askew, and James Henry. Thank you all for your generosity, and for the saying printed on the window of the door to your bay, EVERYBODY GOES HOME. Those words still give me goose bumps, and I had to include them in the book.

Sean Hughes, division chief and emergency management/homeland security coordinator, North Richland Hills Fire Department, for a unique look into the very difficult job of protecting citizens from all manner of threats.

Lieutenant Steve Voltmann, Arlington Fire Department. Bless you for answering pages of my questions, and on your vacation, no less!

AUTHOR'S NOTE

Station Five's hometown of Sugarland, Tennessee, is a fictional city, existing only in my imagination. In addition, any mistakes I've made or liberties I've taken in regard to fire department procedure are completely my own, for story line purposes. That's my story and I'm stickin' to it.

1

Lieutenant Howard Paxton gritted his teeth against the burn, every muscle straining as he pumped three hundred pounds of iron from his bare, sweaty chest.

This, friends and neighbors, is where you wind up when you're cursed with insomnia and a drunken screwup for a bunkmate. As far back as he recalled, he'd never slept through the night. The odds of running across a miraculous cure for night-owl syndrome after thirty-six years? Forget it. No help for that, except working himself until he dropped.

As for Julian Party-Like-You're-Gonna-Die Salvatore . . .

Recalling the nasty scene on shift today between Jules and Zack, Howard tightened his grip on the bar and started another series of reps. Of all things to target with his asinine practical jokes, Jules had to pick Engine 171, for God's sake? Zack's baby, his pride and joy. Took a biggie to trip Zack's trigger, and Salvatore knew exactly how to flip the switch. They'd almost come to blows before he'd stepped between them, yanking apart a couple of snarling junkyard dogs.

Quiet, nerdy Zack Knight? Who knew?

Hands down, Salvatore was the most immature, self-absorbed team member he'd ever taken under his wing. Wasn't first time he'd dealt with a weak link like Salvatore, wouldn't be the last. If the guy didn't grow up, he'd get somebody hurt one of these days. Case in point: today's fireworks. Slowly, his lack of discipline in his personal life was bleeding into the job. Pray to Jesus the captain fired him first. And yet . . .

Tense with frustration, Julian had defended himself later, keeping his anger in check, his tone respectful. They'd been holed up in the privacy of the office Howard shared with the captain. "Lieutenant, if the joke had come from anybody but me, we wouldn't be standing here. Can you deny that?"

He couldn't.

In spite of having the personality of a horny jackrabbit with ADD, Salvatore was an excellent firefighter and paramedic. Coolheaded in a tough situation, good at calming accident victims. If only he'd get a handle on the cocky attitude and get serious, maybe the team would bond with him.

Okay, give Jules a chance. Can't fix the guy overnight. Think about something else.

Another rep, and another. He ought to stop, but he needed to exhaust his body enough to sleep without shadows crowding his mind, forming the strange images that always began in confusion.

Night after night for the past few months. Always the same. A bunch of fragments ending in murky terror.

Shouting. Anxiety. Why?

The vegetable garden in the moonlight. Tomatoes ripening on the curling vines. Fresh dirt under the little boy's toes.

The cool night air whispering on his skin.

Fear. Horror. The crushing pressure on his chest. Can't get away . . .

Howard!

No escape. Don't understand—

"Howard! God, what are you doing?"

At the moment? Suffocating. His lapse in focus had caused him to push past his limit. Lose control. More than three hundred pounds bore down on his chest, pressing the silver bar into his skin, fingers trapped underneath.

Captain Sean Tanner's worried face appeared above his. Sean grabbed the bar with both hands and heaved upward, helping to set the weights into the holder with a metallic clang.

Gasping, Howard struggled to sit up. Sean knelt, steadying him with one hand on his back, the other on his shoulder.

"Thanks, pal." Howard coughed, sucked in several more breaths.

"Are you all right, Six-Pack?"

"I'm fine."

"How many times do I have to tell you not to bench press without a goddamned spotter?"

Wiping the sweat off his face, he glanced at Sean. Yep, his friend was rattled, judging by the reproach in his startling green eyes.

"Sorry, hoss. Can't find the sandman tonight." He paused, taking in Tanner's haggard appearance. "Looks like I'm not the only one."

"Shit, yeah." Sean pushed to his feet, backed up a few steps, and parked his butt on the seat of the stationary exercise bike. With a loud sigh, he raked a hand through his dark brown hair.

Studying him, Howard felt his gut knot. Purple smudges under his friend's eyes and the hollows in his pale cheeks testified to just how little rest he'd been getting. He'd lost so much weight, his stomach was concave and the blue warm-up pants hung off his hips. And, Christ, when had his hair started to turn silver at the temples?

Then again, they all knew the tragic answer to that one.

"The medication's not helping?" he asked carefully.

"I'm not taking it anymore."

"Jesus, Sean—"

"Don't start with me, Howard." His face hardened. "The station doesn't need a captain zoned out on anti-depressants."

"The guys need a *leader* who's not gonna pick up a gun and blow his brains out."

The blood drained from Sean's face. "My God, is that what you think? That I want to die?"

"Seems like you already have. Now you're just waiting to bury yourself with Blair and the kids." *Bull's-eye.*

Tanner clenched his fists so hard his knuckles turned as white as the grooves around his mouth. "You push too far, old friend."

"Not nearly far enough. You're no quitter, so prove it. Keep taking the pills," he urged gently. "Just for a while longer. Promise me."

Sean gave a bitter laugh. "And then what? Tell me what I'm supposed to do with the rest of my life."

Without my family. The unspoken truth hung heavy between them.

Howard shook his head and opened his mouth to reply, but three loud, high tones sounded over the up-dated intercom system, interrupting whatever he was about to say.

The captain had began sprinting for the bay and Howard had pulled his discarded T-shirt over his head by the time a pleasant, computerized female voice announced a house fire in one of Sugarland's older, more exclusive subdivisions. A jolt of adrenaline recharged the exhaustion he'd worked so hard to achieve. When was the last call to a residence fire they'd received in Station Five's sector? Months, at least.

He jogged from the weight room, hitting the door to the bay on Tanner's heels. As always, he glanced at the statement embossed on the square glass window of the door in bold, black-and-white lettering: EVERYBODY GOES HOME. And, as always, the familiar chill zinged down his spine.

A potentially dangerous call—the ever-present ticking bomb. Sixteen years in the Sugarland Fire Department, in this building, and he'd never asked whether the words on the window affected the rest of the team the same way. He didn't have to.

The other members of A-shift spilled into the bay behind him, silent and alert, well used to being jerked from a dead sleep. With quick movements, they bunked out in their gear, slipping the heavy, flame-resistant pants and coats on over jeans and warm-ups, stepping into boots. Last, they slapped on hard fire hats and climbed onto the vehicles.

As the fire apparatus operator, Zack's job was to drive the quint, the city's largest and best-equipped engine. This was a privilege afforded his rank, second only to a captain and lieutenant. He hauled himself into his seat, hitting the opener to raise the huge door of the bay. Tanner climbed into the front passenger's seat, the place of the commanding officer, next to Knight. Tommy Skyler, the team's youngest member, and Eve Marshall, Station Five's only female firefighter, took places in the backseat.

Howard slid into the driver's seat of the ambulance, Julian jumping in the front beside him. Zack pulled the quint out of the bay onto the deserted, moonlit street, activating the lights and siren. Eerie, the wail and the crimson light, pulsing in the darkness like a heartbeat. Howard suppressed a shiver and eased the ambulance out, following Zack.

Done. The whole team on the road in seconds, without one word. Fast and efficient, like a well-oiled machine. Nothing like those stupid television shows where everybody's running around shouting and beating their breasts. Nope, when it's showtime, dramatics have no place in the real world. Not in a firefighter's world, anyway. It's all about working together. Giving aid to those in need and keeping the team safe.

Everybody goes home.

As he followed the quint into the upscale neighborhood, saw the orange glow dancing in the night sky like an angry dragon, something occurred to him. His brows drew together in a troubled frown. He'd asked Sean for a promise.

A promise his old friend, a man at the end of his rope, had never made.

"Please hurry!"

Kat McKenna ended the call to 911, shoved the tiny flip cell phone into her back jeans pocket, and clapped a hand over her mouth in disbelief. *Jeez. Oh, jeez.*

The Hargraves' house on fire! While vacationing on a cruise with her own parents, no less. Oh, God, how in the hell had this *happened?* She'd checked both homes, brought in the mail and newspapers, and watered the plants for the past three days.

Her heart jackhammered against her ribs. Was this her fault? Had she left any appliances on? Bulbs burning? No, she was positive everything had been fine. Until now. And how long would it take the firemen to get here?

Too damned long. Through the large arched windows, she saw the flames already spreading through the living room and the upper floor, as well. *Both levels at the same time? How was that possible?* Bouncing from one foot to the other, she stood in the middle of the street, debating what to do.

Until she heard the scream. Distant, fading into the cool breeze.

She gasped, staring at the house. Strained to hear it

again. The faint wail of sirens reached her ears, giving her goose bumps. Maybe that was the sound she'd heard. Probably.

Still, she ran. Across the street, up the long brick pavestone drive. Plunging into the artfully sculpted hedges near the front door, she found the water spigot, hose still attached from spraying the hanging baskets yesterday. *Joan's petunias will be fried.* She shook her head. How frigging stupid to think of flowers.

Even more stupid to fight a fire with an effing garden hose, Katherine Frances. But, dammit, the stubborn, take-charge side of her personality demanded she *do* something! Unfortunately, listening to the evil twin usually landed her ass in hot water.

She cranked the faucet to full blast and wrestled the hose out of the bushes, onto the porch. Momentary panic seized her. The house key? Her fingers dug into her front pocket, searching. There!

Tucking the hose under one arm, she flipped through the ring to the key the Hargraves had given her, plunged it into the lock with shaking hands, and turned. Testing the knob with her fingertips, she winced. Damn. Using the edge of her shirt, she grabbed and turned the knob, then threw the door wide. A rush of heat and smoke seared her face in greeting, stinging her eyes.

Blinking, she stepped into the wide marble foyer and took in the scene at a glance. She'd never seen a house fire up close and personal, didn't know the first thing about the technicalities, but it seemed a fire shouldn't start in the middle of the room. On the furniture. *What, like the sofa just spontaneously combusted?*

Strange, but there wasn't time to stand around analyzing the situation. Flames were crawling across the carpet from the center of the room outward, chewing a path of destruction. The sofas, draperies, and staircase were fully engulfed, fire licking toward the ceiling.

Kat squeezed the spray nozzle, pointing the stream at the carpet first, sweeping back and forth in hopes of saturating the material enough to stop the spread of flames along the floor. Not good enough. Thick smoke billowed around her, the fire consuming lamps, framed photos. Frantic, she turned the water toward the drapes. More smoke, and the inferno leapt, hissing and sizzling like a furious beast. Mocking her puny efforts.

"Shit!"

From outside, the shrill scream grew louder. Thank God! The heat was unbearable. Stifling. She coughed, glancing around to the open door, now hardly visible through the smoke. Flashing red lights approached, cutting into the murky pea soup. She could've wept with relief. Admitting defeat, she dropped the hose and stumbled outside onto the porch.

Precious air hit her scorched face, but when she tried to suck in a deep breath, a cruel, unseen fist twisted her lungs. She coughed again, clutching her chest. Her head spun. So did the big truck and ambulance pulling up the drive.

Men spilled from the vehicles like ants, a couple scurrying to grab and unroll a hose. Their images blurred through the tears welling in her eyes as she sputtered. Bodies ran toward the house. She wiped her face, took a step forward. Blackness threatened, curling the edges of her vision.

Two firefighters, maneuvering the large hose, rushed past and into the burning house. A hand grabbed her upper arm.

"Ma'am? Are you all right?"

The deep baritone voice sent a thrill to every nerve ending. A smooth shot of Jack Daniel's after a long dry spell, warming her fingers and toes. Other places, too. *Good God, Katherine Frances, get real.* Raising her head, she found herself gazing at the broadest chest she'd ever seen, even allowing for the bulk of his coat.

"Ma'am?" He pressed close, worry evident in his tone.

Kat tilted her chin up. *Way* up. A giant of a man roughly the size of an aircraft carrier towered over her, saying something else. Shadowed under the wide brim of his hat, she noted the line of his strong, square jaw. Full, sensual lips. Dark eyes.

"I'm . . . fine," she croaked. And promptly ruined the assertion by hacking up a lung. The black edges spiraled inward, dizziness winning out, the mountainous man disappearing. *Oh, no!*

In spite of her best efforts, Kat did something she'd never done in her twenty-nine years.

She collapsed into a total stranger's arms.

"Whoa!"

Howard lunged, catching the woman as her knees buckled. He scooped her up with little effort, cradling her soft body against his chest. Fear spiked, along with irritation. Jesus, when would people learn to leave the dangerous stuff to the professionals?

Her cheek lay against his coat as he carried her quickly to the back of the ambulance, her hair tickling his nose and chin. She wore the silky blond mass on top of her head in some little scrunchie doodad, the hair a fountain sprouting every which way, slapping his face with every step, making him want to sneeze. And nuzzle it, too.

He *loved* blond hair. And lush, curvy bodies like hers. No bony, starving skeletons allowed. A big guy like him required a woman you could get a firm grip on. A *real* woman. Plenty of cushion for the—

You're such a pathetic loser, Six-Pack. Focus.

Very carefully, he lowered her to the ground on her back. Taking her wrist between his thumb and forefingers, he forced himself to concentrate on her pulse. Not on the hourglass flare of her hips in skintight low-rise jeans.

Shazaaam!

Or the killer breasts proudly swelling against the ribbed tank top.

Ka-pow!

Or the teensy little diamond belly button stud peeking from under the edge of her hitched-up shirt. He groaned low in his throat, his starved libido sending fervent signals of appreciation to his groin.

Kill me now.

God, this had been a long frigging shift. They hadn't even exchanged a hello and he was already thinking with his sex-starved anatomy. The lady had been injured, for cryin' out loud. His job was to provide aid, not ogle the poor girl while she died of smoke inhalation.

He retrieved an oxygen mask and stethoscope from the ambulance, knelt at her side again, and listened to her lungs. Not totally clear, but not bad.

Concluding that her vitals were much steadier than his own, he pressed the mask over her mouth and nose, anxiety forming a cold, hard knot in his gut. Why, he didn't understand. As a trained paramedic, he'd done this hundreds of times and knew when a victim was in danger of going south. This one wasn't.

But he watched her intently, studying for signs of revival. Long, tawny lashes rested against cheeks like porcelain, smudged with black here and there. Delicate matching eyebrows arched over her lids, accenting a high, smooth forehead. Guessing, he placed her age as several years younger than his own. Fresh and lovely even with a bit of soot on her face, but no kid by any stretch.

Tanner, who'd been scouting the perimeter of the

house, keeping track of everyone's position and the progress on subduing the blaze, jogged over.

"How is she?" the captain asked, pushing back his hat.

"She'll be okay. Ought to come around any second." He hoped. His jaw clenched.

"Any idea who she is?"

"Not a clue. Neighbor, Good Samaritan?" Bet your bippy he'd find out, though.

"Probably belongs to that car parked in the driveway across the street. Driver's door is standing open," Tanner observed.

Howard tore his gaze away from his blond goddess long enough to cast a sideways look at the little red Beamer. He'd never fit into that sardine can in a million years. Shaking off the weird thought, he looked up at Tanner.

"How's things going inside the house?"

"Eve and Tommy are working up to the second floor. Downstairs fire is out, but the damage is heavy. The battalion chief and the engine companies from Stations Three and Four are on the way. We're going to have to call in the arson division on this one, my friend." Sean's expression was grim.

The girl stirred, and he frowned, trying to divide his attention between her and Tanner. "Yeah? What's up?"

"Nobody's home, but the point of origin appears to be the center of the living room. The blaze trails up the stairs, nice and neat. We've got a fuckin' torch job."

"Aw, man. That sucks. Why—"

Whatever he'd been about to say was lost as one of the team staggered out the front door and down the front steps, ripping at the black face mask of his SCBA—self-contained breathing apparatus. *Tommy.* He didn't have to see Skyler's last name emblazoned on the back of his coat in reflective lettering to know.

Tommy was tall, broad shouldered; Eve was shorter and thinner.

Sean spun around. "Skyler! What the hell?"

Tommy freed the mask, shrugged off his Air-Pak, tossed both aside, and sank to his knees in the grass. Doubling over, he began to retch.

Sean took off. Abandoning his position at the corner of the house, Julian did the same.

An ominous chill curled through Howard. Skyler, literally on the ground? Nothing got that kid down. Ever. Torn, Howard glanced at the woman to find her blinking up at him. Relief blossomed, coupled with a new urgency.

"Ma'am, are you all right?"

She hesitated. Nodded.

He flashed a big smile, giving her his best reassuring bedside manner. "Excellent! This is oxygen, and it's gonna make you feel better real fast. Can you hold the mask for a minute, just like this?" He took one of her hands and guided it to her face. She nodded again, holding the mask in place. "Good girl. Don't move, okay? I'll be right back."

Leaving a victim's side was a big no-no. Went against his grain, too. But as he jogged toward the small group huddled on the lawn, he didn't have to be a psychic to know the situation was about to get a whole lot worse. Sean squatted beside Tommy, apparently waiting for the kid to collect himself enough to speak. Julian stood next to them, but Eve hadn't yet emerged from the house. Zack stayed beside the quint, manning the pump and gauges, his hands full at the moment.

Tommy's hat lay in the grass a few feet away. Blond hair was plastered to his skull, a few strands hanging into his face, dripping with sweat. His hands gripped his thighs and he raised pale blue eyes to Howard's, wide with horror.

"Lieutenant," Tommy whispered. His throat convulsed. "Upstairs . . . my God . . ."

Exchanging a quick, worried glance with Sean, Howard laid a hand on Tommy's shoulder. "Easy, kid. Breathe in and out. Slow." His presence seemed to have a calming effect on the young firefighter. After giving him a moment, Howard went on. "Now, first things first. Is Eve all right?"

"She's good. The fire's out. She told me to go, but I know I shouldn't have left her, sir. I'm sorry, but it's just . . ." He closed his eyes, trembling. "I-I've never s-seen anything like that before. Oh, Christ."

Yeah, the kid was in a buttload of trouble for leaving his partner.

"Remember, deep breaths. What did you see?"

"A b-body, in the master bedroom. It's h-handcuffed to the fucking bed."

2

Stunned silence. Howard recovered first.

"*It?* Not he or she?"

"Can't tell what it used to be. There's just a charred p-person with no hair, all split and bloated like a roasted pig—"

"Son of a bitch," Sean rasped, flinching. "I'll radio for the police." He shot to his feet and strode for the quint as the battalion chief and another engine rolled to a stop on the street.

Julian swore, glaring down at Tommy. Immediately, the younger man caught on.

"Shit." Tommy moaned, pushing to his feet. "I forgot about the captain's family. How could I be so stupid?"

"I don't know, dickwad." Julian's face twisted into a snarl. "How could you? I'm sure that'll make breaking the 'Two in, two out' rule go so much better for your ignorant ass."

"I'm sorry. I'll talk to him later." Tommy stared at his boots, the portrait of misery.

Howard stood. "Knock it off, Jules. Let's feed your week into the crapometer and see how you come out in the standings, huh?" Romeo shut his trap. Good. "Tommy, don't worry about upsetting Sean. The fact is, he's going to be blindsided by scenarios that remind him of how his family died. No way to avoid it in this job, and he knows that's nobody's fault, especially yours. Got it?"

With a shaking hand, Tommy pushed the damp hair out of his eyes. "Just the same, I want to apologize. I can't believe I lost it like that."

Jeez, I'm everybody's daddy. I'll never have kids, so God handed me these guys to make up for it. Not exactly an even trade. He might be younger than Sean by five years, but he felt ancient as a freaking fossil. Just once, couldn't everyone wipe their own asses?

"Fine, talk to him. But if he gets nasty, don't take it personal," Howard advised. "I'm his best friend and he'll barely open up to *me*."

Skyler's answer was lost on Howard as he glanced toward his mystery woman. Since another engine had arrived, Knight had left the quint and was talking to the girl, helping her sit up, his hand enfolding hers. Zack said something that made her tilt her chin up and grace Boy Wonder with a blinding smile. Zack returned it.

And he hadn't let go of her hand. Yet.

"Excuse me," Howard muttered, leaving Tommy and Jules the Pain staring after him.

He bore down on the cozy pair like a heat-seeking missile. His usual paragon-of-patience-and-brotherly-love mojo took a last gasp for air and croaked. Irrational, violent thoughts invaded his tired brain. Like picking up A-shift's resident genius and squeezing with his bare hands until his eyeballs popped out and went rolling down the driveway.

A year without sex—your palm doesn't count— topped by twenty-four hours without sleep will do wicked things to a guy.

At his approach, Zack looked up and grinned. "Hey, Six-Pack. Your patient is ready to run laps. I was just telling Miss McKenna—"

"I need you at the house to help supervise the clean up. Now."

Zack's smile withered at his curt tone, and he blinked behind his wired-rimmed glasses. "But that's not—"

"Your job. I know." He sighed, sorry to have snapped. Knight was a superior team member, highly respected, not to mention gifted with an IQ of 150. A man everyone expected would make captain one day. Zack and Miss McKenna were staring at him uncertainly.

"When I'm finished with the patient, I'll help you. The captain will see to the engine for you while he waits for the police."

Zack's dark brows furrowed. "Why? What's going on?"

"We've got a body inside, possible homicide. It's badly burned."

His eyes met Zack's startled blue ones, and they silently acknowledged the gravity of the effect that must be having on Sean.

"Ah, shit." The younger man shook his head. "I saw Tommy run out. I was on my way, but I had to stop and check on the patient first. Yeah, I'll take over the scene, make sure the fire is out and nothing else is touched. The captain doesn't need to go inside."

"Thanks, man. I owe you."

"Forget it."

With that, Zack rose and strode toward the smoldering house. *Doing my job because I had to see the girl.* An uncharacteristic breach of etiquette for a rules-oriented guy like himself. Howard tamped down a wave of guilt.

"Body?" the woman squeaked, finding her voice at last. "A *dead body*? In Joan and Greg's *house*?"

Aw, man. He was a clueless idiot for mentioning a victim in front of her.

He gazed into her heart-shaped face. Pretty, he decided, rather than a classic beauty. Not one of those Amazon hardbodies who hung out at his fitness club, sweating off what God blessed them with. Not Miss McKenna.

Her lovely face was as soft and rounded as the rest of her. Full, kissable lips. Like a ripe, juicy strawberry, begging to be plucked. Ooh, a man-eating bachelor killer. She stared back at him, waiting for an answer.

"I'm afraid so." He scrambled for an intelligent response. "You know the people who live here?"

She nodded, causing the cute hair thingie to bob. "Joan and Greg Hargrave. They're on a cruise with my parents, who live right across the street." She jabbed a thumb toward the mini mansion hunkered behind her car.

"I've been coming by to check on things. Bring in the mail, water the plants. When I pulled into my parent's drive, I got out, saw the fire through the windows, and called 911."

Talking must've irritated her parched throat. She paused and covered her mouth, coughing a couple of times. He leaned forward in concern, instinctively curling his fingers around hers.

"We've got some bottled water on the quint. Can I get you one, Miss McKenna?"

Swallowing, she sent him a shaky smile. "That would be nice."

Faster than he'd ever moved, he grabbed a bottle and returned to her side. Twisting off the top, he handed it over, watching as she sent him a crooked grin.

"Thanks, you're a doll."

He stared in fascination at the column of her throat as she tilted her head back and took a long draw of water. A doll? Him—a brute who stood six-six and topped two sixty on the scales?

Doll. A meaningless endearment. She probably used that phrase all the time, on everyone. But the way she said it, warm and breathless, as if she really *meant* it, made his insides turn funny flips. Stupid.

She lowered the bottle, recapped it, and wiped her mouth with the back of her hand. "Kat."

Cat? He looked around. "I'm sorry?"

"My name. Katherine with a K, but my friends call me Kat. Miss McKenna is what my students call me."

"Oh! Sure. Kat," he murmured, trying the name. Yeah, Kat. All soft and green-eyed, perfect to pet and make her purr. "It suits you. I'm Lieutenant Howard Paxton. Please, call me Howard."

Call me anything you want, while I've got you flat on your back, sinking my co—

"Not *Howie*?" Her cheek dimpled.

He snorted. "God, no. The last guy who called me that wound up with a busted lip."

Julian walked by, rolling up a hose. "Sure did. Asshole." He kept going, disappearing around the side of the quint.

"Hey, it was an accident! And eighty-six the language around the lady!" Howard called out. Jerk.

Kat giggled. "You always let your men talk to you like that, Howie?"

He arched a brow and frowned, secretly pleased she felt comfortable enough in his looming presence to nettle him in fun. "Hmm. A woman with a dangerous streak. Kind of like running into a burning house with a frigging water hose."

"Guilty as charged. I couldn't just stand there like a dork, for all the good I accomplished."

He laughed, unable to help himself. "Dork? I haven't heard that word since I was a kid. What grade do you teach?"

She bristled a bit. "First. And no smart-ass comments about how I don't look or act like a teacher, whatever that means. I get that a lot."

"I think it means you're not the stereotypical old, dried prune wearing an apple jumper and a sour expression because your life has passed you by," he pointed out. "I'd take it as a huge compliment."

"Holy cow. Let me guess, you described your first-grade teacher." An amused smile played on her lips.

"Yep. Mean old biddy, rest her black soul. She used to smack the backs of our hands with a ruler to make us pay attention."

"Well, when you put it like that . . ." Kat sighed. "I just get tired of being judged by my appearance. People take one look at me and assume I couldn't possibly hold a master's degree in education."

If anyone could relate to being judged on appearance, he could, but his experience in that area wasn't all negative. Particularly with the female persuasion. A typical bachelor point of view he suspected this lady wouldn't appreciate.

Switching back to a safe topic, he asked, "Why come by so late on a Saturday night? Or Sunday morning, I should say, since it's nearly two."

"I was out with friends tonight. I didn't get to come over earlier today, and the stop was on my way home." She shuddered. "After calling 911, I thought I heard a scream. Very creepy. Which is why I ran to the house, but when the sirens sounded in the distance, I thought I was mistaken."

"Any idea whose body is inside? Do the Hargraves have children, anyone who might've let themselves in for a rendezvous?"

"No. Their kids are grown and scattered. Greg always talks about how the house is much too big for the two of them with everyone gone, but Joan doesn't want to sell. She loves this place," Kat said sadly. "But who'd want to stay after someone was murdered in their home?"

Cold fingers brushed the back of Howard's neck for the second time this evening. Something evil had taken place here tonight, and Kat knew the family who owned the house. And if she'd been a minute or two earlier in arriving . . .

"Oh, Christ." He glanced around, searching beyond the flashing lights of the emergency vehicles.

"What?"

"Think. Did you see anyone on the way into the neighborhood, either walking or driving?"

"Just a man in a dark truck—wait a minute! You don't believe I passed the *killer*, do you?" She paled, pressing a trembling hand to her mouth.

"I don't know. I'm not a cop. It's possible, though, so I want you to tell them everything you can remember. And be extra cautious for a while. Be sure and leave when the cops finish questioning you. Don't stick around, and when you come back to check your parents' house, bring a friend along, okay?"

She nodded, eyes round. "All right."

He'd scared her. Hell, he'd scared himself. But better paranoid than dead.

"Speaking of cops, here they are. Guess I'd better go talk to them."

"Sure." He glanced to where a black-and-white had pulled up on the street, next to the curb. His heart squeezed at the thought of letting her go without knowing whether she'd be safe. "Are you feeling better? Should I transport you to the hospital, maybe have them take a good look at your lungs?"

"Oh, no. I'm peachy, really. Help me up?"

Pushing to his feet, he offered his hand, which she took with a smile. Her small palm completely vanished into his as he hauled her up. Staring into her pretty face, he searched for one excuse, no matter how lame, to see her again. Before he could form one, Kat stood on tiptoe, leaned into his chest, and planted a kiss on his cheek.

"Thanks for rescuing me, big guy." She reached for him, touched his face thoughtfully, as though weighing an important decision. "Bye, Howard."

She turned and started across the lawn, toward the potbellied policeman emerging from his patrol car. And like an idiot, he stared after her, speechless, the soldier below his belt primed for a twenty-one-gun salute. His skin tingled from her kiss and blood rushed in his ears. *Stop her!*

But she'd deep-fried his brain and run it through a blender. Or maybe he was hopelessly inept at communicating with women like Kat. *Nice* women with smarts *and* sex appeal. Right about now, he'd sell his soul for one ounce of Julian's suave charisma.

Suddenly, Kat turned to face him again. "Oh, and Howard?"

"Yes?"

"FYI—my number is listed."

With her parting shot, she sashayed off, hips swinging, leaving him with his mouth hanging open. Slowly, a big, sappy grin spread across his face. *He scores! Nothin' but net.*

Beside him, a soft, appreciative whistle floated in the air. "*Caliente!* A little more junk in the trunk than I usually go for, but so what? I'll bet blondie's never experienced the unequalled pleasure of a Latino lover with hot Italian blood running through his veins. The best of both worlds, eh?"

His chest tightened. "You could try, Jules. But then I'd have to squash you like the pesky gnat you are. Painfully."

"Touché," he laughed. "You know, maybe Howie's not such a dull boy after all."

He let the barb go. Sensations swept him that he'd

believed long dead. Waking his senses as though surfacing from a coma. For the first time in ages, he held out hope tomorrow wouldn't dawn as just another endless, lonely day. A thrill of excitement sang in his blood, knowing he'd see Kat again. Soon.

Beyond tomorrow, who knew?

In spite of his joy, the prickle on the back of his neck returned. Like the devil staring a man down, unseen in the shadows. A menacing presence pulling the strings, making them all dance to whatever wicked tune he'd chosen.

"Christ, I need some sleep," he muttered, rubbing his eyes.

Peaceful, uninterrupted shut-eye. Perhaps sweet dreams of his angel would keep the nightmares away, just once. *Please, God.*

The rosy glow from Kat's bold invite began to fade, common sense returning to claw his heart with vicious talons.

A man can't exist on wishes and dreams. Hurts too much when your heart is ripped out. He'd learned that lesson a lifetime ago, and learned well. Sometimes the most unbreakable bond on earth isn't enough to hold the one you love and depend on most.

But Kat's impulsive kiss had been warm and solid, not a dream. A soothing balm over those old, aching wounds.

Heaving a tired sigh, he trudged to join the rest of the team. A man who'd been awake for twenty-four hours had no business poking a stick into a badger hole. After he'd been unconscious a few hours, the world would right itself again.

And this ridiculous itch between his shoulder blades? History. He was thirty-six years old, for God's sake. There weren't any demons lurking in the shadows, waiting to devour him.

Just the flesh-and-blood kind, and they were dead and buried.

Look at the clueless assholes swarming, a bunch of ants on a kicked mound. Scurrying to salvage the ruins. Getting their very first taste of his power.

Frank smiled. So fucking simple, the truth literally staring them in the face. They would investigate, test, take samples, photograph, autopsy. And in the end, they'd find exactly what he'd intended. The truth lay not in the *what* or *how*, but the *why*. Step back from the details, boys, and see the big picture.

And they would, eventually. They'd search for the pattern, and he'd gladly oblige them. He had control of the game board, and they were his pieces to move at will. Pattern leads to motive. Then the stakes peak, and the game becomes a nerve-racking race to the finish line. Winner takes the prize.

Vengeance.

"I'll get there first, 'cause *I* chose the destination." He chuckled. "Yeah, you'll know my name, you piece of shit."

By game point, the others would, also. Reward was never without risk. He wanted—*needed*—them all to learn who had dragged the entire Sugarland Fire Department into the pit of hell, and why. He craved it like heroin, this mad desire to feel their shock and horror wash through him when they understood why the master of the game had fucked them up the ass. In more ways than one.

"But *you* have to find out before the others." Relishing the idea, he shifted in his hiding place. "I'm going to tighten the vise until you crack under the pressure. Until you beg for mercy and fall to your knees. And when you're beaten like the mongrel you are, I'll rip your heart out."

Narrowing his eyes, he watched from a comfortable

vantage point as his prey commanded the team. A man among men. He'd be a fool to underestimate the big son of a bitch, extremely powerful not only due to his size, but his presence. They hung on his every word, scurried like mice at a flick of his hand. One more reason to hate the *lieutenant*.

They don't know the truth.

It would be all too easy to obtain a high-powered rifle with a scope and simply take his sorry ass out. Fuck this bullshit.

Careful. Harness the rage. Play the game.

And add a new piece to the board—the woman.

Goddamn, the bitch had seen him. The question was, how well? No doubt, she'd connect the fire with a man driving a dark truck, turning off the deserted street as she'd been rounding the corner. Tell the police about a stranger who had no business in this sleepy, aging upper-crust community in the wee hours.

Now he'd have to ditch the truck. Drive to another county and trade it in at some obscure lot where nobody required a damned DNA sample to do business. Cash 'n' dash.

His jaw clenched in anger. Two days of casing the area, studying the residents' comings and goings, picking the perfect empty house, only to have the woman show unexpectedly.

He'd observed Sweet Cheeks picking up the mail and newspapers both of the previous afternoons, performing the menial tasks of a friend or relative dropping by to check on things while the owners were out of town. Ten minutes per house, in and out. The dumb bitch may as well have posted a sign in the yard shouting THESE PEOPLE ARE VACATIONING!

Choosing between the two residences for his plan had been simple. As with many older homes, the complacent owners had never gotten around to installing an alarm system. Surprise, boys and girls. Life sucks.

So easy, his plans carried off without a hitch . . . until the girl presented a challenging new twist to the fun.

Of course, he'd have to dispose of her, though perhaps not right away. The sparks flying between the beauty and her beast had nearly started another blaze. There was truly no accounting for a woman's taste in men, even if she was a slut.

Interesting and potentially useful, however. For a relationship to blossom between them would be a gift from heaven dropped into his lap. To use the lieutenant's lady as the final tool of his destruction, the ultimate payback. The supreme irony.

Steal the one you cherish most, the way you stole from me. By God, you will atone.

So he'd watch, wait. Should their attraction to each other bear no fruit, well . . . no harm, no foul. In that case, he'd keep to the original plan.

Before Howard Paxton drew his last breath, he would regret the day he'd been born.

About time the worthless bastard joined the club.

3

Usually Kat preferred to sleep naked. Here in the privacy of her apartment, in the darkness of her own bedroom, she could feel sexy. Feminine. Close her eyes, let the sheets caress her bare skin, and pretend. Sometimes she imagined the brush of cotton sheets were the palm of a man's hand, skimming, exploring. In her fantasy, this man detested supermodel-thin women. He adored her plump curves, worshipping every inch of her.

Tonight, nudity only left her feeling horribly exposed.

In spite of the pajamas she'd donned like armor against the bogeyman, she began to tremble. Delayed reaction.

She slid between the crisp, cool sheets with a grateful sigh, wiggling to make them a warm cocoon. Her safe haven, even if an illusion. A long, hot shower had washed off the sweat and stink of smoke, but had no positive effect whatsoever on the black cloud suddenly hanging over her head.

God, that poor person, whoever he or she was. How terrifying it must've been to burn to death—if the person wasn't murdered before the fire. How horrible to have a psycho loose in the city, probably proud of what he'd done!

Howard said she might be in danger, a tiny detail she'd neglected to mention to her anxious parents when they'd received her emergency message and phoned from the ship. The roly-poly cop with the personality of a brick had agreed. The lawman's brilliant suggestion? Get a big, kick-ass dog. Right. Robocop didn't have to pay the enormous pet deposit, take it for walks, or clean piss off the carpet when it got mad because you were gone too long.

Forget the dog. A big, kick-ass man, on the other hand . . .

Mmm. Howard wouldn't pee on the rug, either. Oh, the guy probably had several nasty and annoying habits. Most men did. What she wouldn't give to learn every single one of them.

"Lieutenant Howard Paxton," she said, trying it out.

Strong and solid, like the man himself. A big dude nobody in their right mind messed with. Yet reserved, almost shy, at least when he'd spoken with her. He'd been so solicitous, genuinely concerned. Best of all, he'd made her feel small and delicate. No mean feat for a woman "built like a brick shithouse," according to her last boyfriend, Rod the Sleaze.

Okay, Howard was a firefighter. A real-life hero. For sure, the guy treated everyone with that same gentle care. He was doing his job, that's all. Still . . .

What did he look like out of the heavy coat, without the hat shadowing his chiseled features? Damn, if only she could've seen his hair, the real color of his dark eyes.

Even so, true chemistry wasn't all about appearance, she reminded herself. She didn't need to drool over his fabulous bod to feel the wonderful hum shoot clear to her toes simply from being near him, talking to him.

No question. Howard possessed the mysterious *it*.

That elusive, magical male *something* that made a woman forget to breathe. Almost as if he'd recognized her on the most primitive level, the key in the lock. The encounter was unlike any she'd ever experienced.

And she'd blown it by acting like a stereotypical pushy blond bimbo, when nothing could be farther from the truth.

FYI . . . my number is listed.

"Jesus Christ on roller skates, Katherine Frances." Her face heated at the memory. "If he cared enough, he would've figured that out by himself."

So much for cosmic male-female mojo. The poor guy had probably run screaming for the hills, thankful to have escaped her razor-sharp talons. After he stuffed his tongue back in his head, of course. He was a *man*, as prone to their weaknesses as any other, if the stupefied expression on his handsome face was an indication.

Which left her alone and saddled with much bigger worries than when she woke up this morning. The major-league, hairy-monster-under-the-bed kind. Holy shit.

Her parents absolutely could *not* find out she might've seen the arsonist/murderer, and vice versa. Her sister, Grace, could handle it, but Daddy's heart couldn't take the stress. Thus the forced holiday from his law practice and what should've been a relaxing cruise with friends. Push comes to shove, she'd have to lie to their faces, and the idea made her cringe. She'd always been *such* a pathetic liar, especially to the three people she loved most in the world.

"A fine mess, Ollie." She burrowed deeper into the covers.

Dawn had crept through the blinds and across the carpet with pale, orange-gold fingers by the time her eyelids finally drooped in defeat. As she sank into Neverland, she envisioned a big, sexy man sweeping her effortlessly into his arms, without throwing a disc in his lower back.

She smiled into her pillow. In her scenario, the studly firefighter revived her using decadent, delicious methods that belonged between the covers of an erotic romance.

For the first time in months, fantasies weren't enough.

Her last thought before sleep took her was maybe—just maybe—she was ready to take another chance on reality.

He loved the garden at night.

No yelling. No whippings.

This was his magic forest, and the good witch protected him from the evil troll here. She sprinkled her dust all around, and nobody else could get in.

He liked to hide in the rows of plants. Especially the corn and tomato ones. They were the tallest, even if sorta scrawny. That was okay, 'cause he was scrawny, too.

But he'd grow big one day. Bigger than the tomato plants or corn stalks. Bigger than his crummy house!

And when he did, Daddy couldn't hit him ever again.

The dirt felt good between his toes. Soft and cool. He wriggled them deeper into the soil, wishing he could find an earthworm.

He fingered a silvery leaf, smiled at the curly vines and round veggies. Would there be lots and lots of juicy red tomatoes this year? He hoped so. Mommy used them in salsa and spaghetti sauce.

Shouting, angry voices, reached his ears.

Who was in his garden? The magic dust didn't work!

A muffled thump. A very bad swear word.

He stopped, peering down the long row of plants, heart pounding in his thin chest. The beam of a flashlight swept back and forth, searching. Instinctively, he stepped off the path, hiding himself among the leaves.

In the glow of the flashlight, he saw a pair of legs and—

His eyes rounded. Fear clogged his throat, preventing him from screaming.

He backed away. Tripped and went sprawling on his rear. Bolted to his feet and ran.

No! Get away!

No, no, no . . .

"Ahhh!"

Howard jerked awake, panting, staring at the ceiling of his bedroom. The storm raging in his brain slowly quieted as the terror of the dream receded.

"God," he rasped. "What the hell *is* that?" Hand shaking, he wiped a trickle of sweat off his brow and shook his head to clear the sticky tendrils of fear. Calm his thundering heart. Again.

Months of this weird nightly film reel attacking his sleep was getting to him. He had no freaking idea what the dream-turned-nightmare meant, beyond the hellish, scattered recollections of his childhood.

Okay, so the nightmare wasn't all fragmented nonsense, if he admitted the truth. The abuse had been real enough, as had his mother's garden. His haven. He vaguely remembered how, as a small boy, he'd loved the plants, the smell of fresh soil.

The garden was one of only two positive memories he had of his first home, the one he'd shared with his biological parents. The other was how much his mother had loved him—before she'd run off for parts unknown, leaving him to suffer at the hands of a violent man. But not for long. His father had been dead and buried for over thirty years. Thank God Bentley and Georgeanne Mitchell had swooped in to rescue a half-dead little boy from a hellish existence.

As for the recurring terror, he'd told no one about the onslaught. Bentley and Georgie would understand and want to help, but he'd held back from worrying them. He couldn't do that to Sean, either. The poor guy

had a real-life horror to survive. He didn't need to deal
with a best friend who just might be going crazy.

With a groan, Howard rolled onto his side and
peered at the digital clock on the nightstand. Two
thirty in the afternoon? What a shameful waste of a
nice Sunday. On the bright side, he'd managed nearly
six hours of blessed sleep before the rude awakening.

Untangling himself from the sheets, he pushed out
of bed and padded for the kitchen to switch on the cof-
feemaker. No matter the time of day, becoming con-
scious called for java. The juice of life, and his worst
vice. Yes, he worshipped the god of Starbucks. Too bad
he hadn't invested early.

The coffee brewing, he headed for the bathroom to
shave and shower. Twenty minutes later, he was
dressed in clean jeans and a black T-shirt, sipping his
brew at the kitchen table.

And eyeballing the phone on the counter. To call or
not to call? His stomach knotted. Jesus, he sucked at
the boy-meets-girl thing, and his track record with sus-
taining a long-term relationship blew. Call it a catch-22
brought about by his own choice of company. Most of
the women he'd dated in recent years wanted to sleep
with him, period. Minus the sleeping part. The ones
who started talking his and hers toothbrushes, he
broke things off with quick. And yeah, for a while he'd
let his happy cock do all the thinking. He was a man
with intense sexual desires, after all.

Eventually, however, the casual sex left him feeling
lonely and used. Yet the thought of being emotionally
vulnerable to a woman, depending on her for his happiness? The idea congealed a ball of cold, greasy nausea in his belly.

He'd abstained from women for about a year, trying
to figure out a solution to his problem. Julian, incredulous, had said he'd lost his effing mind. Why should a

confirmed bachelor fix what isn't broken? Maybe the guy was right about this one point.

He was stinking tired of his own company. Meeting Kat last night had been his breaking point. The girl had a quirky sense of humor, was educated, gorgeous, lush, and unless he'd missed his guess . . . *willing*. She'd all but invited him to take her on an adventure neither of them would forget. Just fantasizing about the various ways he'd deliver caused his shaft to harden and push against the zipper of his jeans. Why fight the attraction?

Crossing to the counter, he nearly tore the junk drawer off the track by yanking it open to grab the phone book. Quickly, he flipped it open to the M's. "McKenna-comma-Katherine. There!"

Punching in the number, he waited, assailed by a sudden case of nerves. He wasn't used to assuming the role of pursuer. What if he screwed up? What if he'd misread her signals or—

"Hello?" a soft, groggy voice greeted him.

Christ, she was still in bed. "Um, Kat?"

A hesitation. "Yes?"

"It's Howard Paxton. From last night."

"Oh!" A rustle. "Howard! Hey, what's up?"

He closed his eyes, barely stifling a groan. "I was wondering, that is, I thought maybe you'd like to—"

"Absolutely!"

His eyes popped open. "Ah . . ."

"I'm sorry," she laughed, now sounding merry and fully awake, and not the least bit apologetic. "I suppose I should wait and let you finish. What do you have in mind?"

Uh, I'd like you to go down on me until I come so hard I shrivel like plastic wrap?

He cleared his throat. "Well, I thought I could take you over to check on your parents' house, then maybe we could grab a bite to eat? Casual, nothing fancy."

"Sounds great. What time?" The smile in her voice practically lit his kitchen through the phone.

"I'll pick you up in half an hour."

"I'm still in bed!"

"No complaints here." He sighed.

"What?"

"Nothing. Half an hour. Jeans and a T-shirt are all you need for what I have in mind. No makeup, either."

"Ohh, you're an evil man, Lieutenant Paxton," she drawled. "Remember, when the swamp monster answers my door, you asked for it. I guess we'll find out right off the bat what you're made of, huh?"

Her teasing warmed him, inside and out. "Tough stuff, Miss McKenna. Bulletproof."

"We'll see, big guy. Need directions?"

"Sure." He fumbled for a sticky note and pen, scribbling the route to her apartment ten minutes away. "Got it."

"Thirty minutes, then. Bye, Howard."

Hanging up, he replaced the phone in the cradle, let out a whoop and punched his fist in the air. Who cared if he was acting like a lovestruck teenager? Talking to Kat for five minutes had worked a miracle.

Grinning, he realized he looked forward to spending the afternoon with her more than he ever had with any woman. *Down, boy.*

He snatched his denim jacket from the arm of the living room sofa and shrugged it on. On the way through the kitchen, he scooped up his key ring and headed out the door into the attached garage. His mammoth Ford F-250 and stout Harley motorcycle were parked side by side.

"Oh yeah, babe. Let's see what *you're* made of."

He swung onto the Harley and cranked the ignition. The machine roared to life as he hit the garage door opener, then pulled on his helmet. Whoops, the extra helmet.

Dismounting, he jogged to his workbench, retrieved the one he'd purchased for his last girl-dash-friend and hoped Kat wouldn't mind too much. How else did a guy happen to have a female-sized helmet lying around?

He strapped it onto the back, resumed his seat, and drove out of the garage. As he guided the bike carefully down the drive, he happened to glance to the right, toward his front door. A flutter of paper caught his eye and he slowed, raising the sun visor of his helmet.

A white, letter-sized envelope was stuck between the screen door and frame, about chest high. A note from one of his "brothers" at the station? Nah, they'd have called. Something about a letter in his door struck him as strange. Whoever put it there hadn't seen fit to simply ring the doorbell and talk to him in person? The fact didn't rest easy.

He paused. Almost got off the bike to fetch it.

No. For personal business or pleasure, anyone who mattered knew how to reach him. The envelope could wait. He had more important places to be.

A very special lady to impress.

Smiling, he lowered the visor, opened the throttle, and let the horses run. As he reached the end of the street, a glimpse in his rearview mirror gave him a start. For a second, he could've sworn he'd spotted a figure standing in the shade of the oak tree in his front yard.

At the stop sign, he braked and whipped his head around.

Arson, murder, sleep and sex deprivation, strange envelopes, and now hallucinations. There was no one under the damned tree, but . . .

The ominous foreboding returned.

Like he'd been strapped into a car with no brakes and pushed toward a cliff. His life, about to spiral out of control, a phantom calling the shots.

With one major difference. He was no longer the

starving, beaten little mouse he'd been as a kid. These days, any fool who wanted a piece of Howard Paxton would receive a proper attitude adjustment.

Trouble?

Bring it on.

Throwing back the covers, Kat leapt out of bed and dashed for the closet. Thirty minutes! Was Howard really so eager to see her again he couldn't wait for a girl to look halfway decent? Or maybe half an hour seemed an eternity to a man used to hitting the door in thirty seconds. Making split-second decisions that saved lives.

Pawing through her jeans, she decided the second explanation suited the lieutenant better. He didn't strike her as a rash person, but a steady rock. In complete control. A man who set his sights on a goal and followed through, no fuss. Wishful thinking? Maybe, but based on their brief, pleasant encounter last night, albeit under awful circumstances, she didn't think so.

As a teacher, she spent hours on end working with the varying personalities of students, parents, and staff. She liked to believe that over these first five years of her fledgling career, she'd become pretty good at reading people.

Every instinct told her that with Howard, what you see is what you get.

And so far, Kat liked what she saw.

Excitement rippled through her, settling as a quivering bubble in her tummy. Yeah, the man might end up being a toad, turn the nice fizzy feeling to acid indigestion, but so what? That was the risk anyone took when getting to know someone new, and something told her Howard was worth a Hail Mary.

Chewing her lip in indecision, she finally selected a pair of old, comfortable jeans. They were broken in, faded but not frayed, and hugged her full figure in gentle curves without looking painted on. Next, she jerked a green babydoll T-shirt off the hanger and held it up, debating. The color complemented her eyes, and the shirt, her favorite, sported the winged Aerosmith logo across the chest in dark print.

The clingy T-shirt emphasized her generous breasts, creating the impression that "the girls" might take flight, wings and all. Rod—what an unfortunate, ironic name—had hated the shirt. Or rather, the stares that somehow never found her face when she wore it.

The few painful months with Rod had been a real eye-opener. When they met, she hadn't had a lot of experience with men, save her own family. Still didn't. The men in her family cherished their women, adored them. Rod put on a good front, at first.

Then came the friendly "suggestions" concerning her appearance. *Your clothes are too tight, Katherine. Darling, you know I love you, but you just don't have the figure to carry off what you're wearing. Really, hip huggers and a belly button ring?*

She gave an inch, and he quickly graduated to criticism. His constant disapproval had put a chink in her armor. But he hadn't pierced it. Thanks to her folks and her sister, she was made of tougher stuff than that. Fed up, she'd given Flaccid Man the boot, and hadn't looked back.

With an impish smile, Kat carried the clothes into her bedroom. "The lieutenant prefers the natural look? Fine."

Whistling, Kat discarded her pajamas and dressed quickly, opting for comfy tennis shoes. In the tiny bathroom, she tamed her bed head, leaving it loose around her shoulders, then brushed her teeth. Finished, she peered into the mirror and grimaced.

Ugh. The natural girl look had limits, and the smoke-induced saddlebags perched on top of her cheekbones must go. Brandishing a tube of concealer like Excalibur, she dabbed and smudged the puffiness into submission. Sort of. The results were anything but magical, her appearance only slightly less scary. Cheating just a bit, she dusted her cheeks with a tiny amount of blush to avoid greeting the poor man looking as though she had the flu.

This done, Kat searched the medicine cabinet for eye drops. Her throat was a little sore and her bloodshot eyeballs felt like they'd been battered and fried, another gift from last night. But at least she was alive this morning to complain, unlike the person murdered in Joan and Greg's house.

Squeezing a couple of drops in each eye, she blinked away the grit, Howard's chilling words a mantra in her brain. A body, *badly burned.* Kat shivered, recalling how the fire spread from the center of the living room outward. Deliberately set. God, she'd missed the killer by a matter of moments. Who would do something so horrible, and why? She hoped the police caught the monster fast, but the sad fact was they might never find the answers.

With an effort, she pushed the horrid incident to the back of her mind and walked into the den, plopping on the sofa to wait for the lieutenant. Funny how the remaining fifteen minutes suddenly yawned ahead, an eternity. Flipping through the newest *People* magazine to admire George Clooney did nothing to calm her jitters or distract her from trying to picture Howard.

Were the man's shoulders really wide enough to block for the Tennessee Titans, or had the drama of last night only made her rescuer seem larger-than-life? A strong, capable leader. A gentleman.

"No guy is that perfect. Not even you, George." She sighed, tossing the magazine onto the coffee table.

In her limited experience, God had a way of evening things out with infinite humor. Howard probably had gingivitis. Bushy nostril hair, flatulence, a pencil penis graced by teensy acorns—

A low rumble interrupted her dire predictions, distant thunder growing louder. She cocked her head, placing the noise. A motorcycle. None of her buttoned-up neighbors drove one. The cyclist in question pulled in to park outside her door, and shut off the engine. Kat's heart did a funny leap as heavy boots scraped up her walk. Hesitated.

She was on her feet and moving toward the door even before the brisk knock. Squinting through the peephole, she saw nothing but an island of broad, muscular chest, leaving little doubt about who waited on the other side. Steeling herself against a second attack of nerves, she unlocked the door and stepped back. Swung it open.

And forgot to breathe.

Oh. My. Gawd.

Six and a half feet of gorgeous male perfection filled the entire entrance. A black T-shirt stretched over his buff pecs and taut abs, but the denim jacket hid too darned much from view. Her appreciative gaze slid down mile-long legs encased in soft jeans that hugged hard thighs and cupped the bulge of his sex like a glove.

Teensy wasn't a word she'd ever entertain in association with Howard Paxton again.

"Can I come in?"

Ohh, that deep voice, whiskey and tangled sheets on a hot summer evening. One more impression that had not been her imagination. Kat blinked up at her guest, who flashed a tentative smile. Embarrassed to be caught ogling the man's crotch, she stepped aside, trying for a light, friendly greeting.

She waved a hand. "Sure, come inside! Would you like something to drink? Water or soda? Or I've got beer—"

"I'm good, thanks. I had coffee before I came over."

"In the middle of the afternoon? I thought cops had the market cornered on that particular habit," she teased, shutting the door behind him.

Howard laughed good-naturedly, making her heart ping-pong between her lungs. A huge smile full of straight white teeth lit his ruggedly handsome face. A thin, white scar running from his left temple to his cheekbone and a nose that had been broken more than once saved him from being too perfect. Good thing, because the man had the biggest, most beautiful chocolate brown eyes she'd ever seen, framed by long, thick lashes any woman would kill for. Short, spiky sable hair stuck out in artful disarray all over his skull—the strands bleached blond on the tips.

Lordy, if he weren't a fireman, she'd think he'd just walked off the set of a testosterone-pumped Vin Diesel movie. Howard was, hands down, the most stunning man she'd ever laid eyes on.

"Not by a long shot. Most people don't realize we have to respond to many of the same calls as the police. Car accidents, disputes resulting in injuries, rescue situations. You name it, the list goes on forever. After arson and homicide took over the scene last night, we got three more calls. When I went off-shift at seven this morning, my butt was dragging."

Stand back, ladies. I'll be the judge of that!

Shaking her head, Kat forced her attention from the state of his butt back to the thread of their conversation. "Thus, the broken sleep and all-consuming need for go-juice."

"Yeah, the stuff is my worst vice."

She arched a brow in disbelief. Coffee, the worst vice of a man tailor-made for seven kinds of sin? Right. Before she could form a suitable response, however, she noticed he was holding an arm behind his back.

"What are you hiding there, Lieutenant? A weapon?"

"Naw, nothing so exciting. Just these." With a flourish, Howard brandished his surprise, holding it out for her.

A pretty spring bouquet bobbed in front of her nose, brimming with daisies, carnations, a couple of roses, and those vibrant, tiny purple flowers resembling baby's breath. The gift bore clear plastic wrap around the damp stems, and the sticker he'd forgotten to remove boasted seven dollars and ninety-nine cents—from the local Brookshire's grocery store.

Right then and there, Kat melted into a gooey puddle.

"Oh, Howard." Taking them, she inhaled the fragrant scent. "I love flowers. Thank you."

She hadn't realized he'd been watching for her reaction like an anxious little boy. His tense expression dissolved into a shy, pleased grin as he nodded.

"You're welcome. You deserve more than a few puny blossoms after what you went through," he said. "But they seemed appropriate. How are you feeling today?"

He'd actually been concerned about her well-being, wanted to brighten her day in some way. She scoured her brain for the last time someone besides her parents had done that, and came up empty. What a dear, lovely man!

There must be *something* wrong with him.

Shaking off the uncharitable notion, Kat stood on tiptoe and planted a kiss on his smooth cheek. Mmm, he smelled fantastic. Some sort of understated cologne reminiscent of cedar, fresh air—and 100 percent man. She longed to capture his sensual mouth with hers, nibble and explore, learn whether he tasted as good as he smelled.

Instead, she contented herself with the quick peck. For now. "Throat's a bit sore, but I'm fine. And flowers are always perfect for what ails a girl, big guy. Why don't I put these in water? Then we can leave." Turning, she headed into the adjoining kitchen, laid the bouquet on the counter, and fished under the sink for an old vase. "Where are we going, anyway?"

Howard followed, bracing a brawny shoulder against the arched entry to the kitchen. "If you still need to run by your parents' house, we can go there first. I don't want you dropping by alone." His jaw tightened.

"I'd planned to, but Daddy called back early this morning and said not to bother since it's Sunday and there's no mail. Plus, Joan and Greg caught an emergency flight from Puerto Rico when they docked, so they'll be back tonight and staying at my folks' house while they straighten out the mess at theirs. I don't believe that's Daddy's real reason for telling me not to drop by, though."

Grabbing a pair of utility scissors from the junk drawer, she sliced the plastic off the stems. "I didn't tell him I missed the killer by a hair, but I think he and Mom suspect. The old parental radar on full alert."

"Yeah, I hear you. Bentley and Georgie have always been superprotective of me. When I was a kid, I couldn't sneeze without Georgie rushing me to the clinic."

Puzzled, she threw him a questioning glance. An odd shadow passed across his face, a certain . . . sadness. "They're your parents?" Arranging the flowers in the vase, she pretended not to notice his sudden discomfort.

"My adoptive parents. I went to live with them when I was four years old. Bentley Mitchell is Sugarland's fire chief and my boss."

How strange to hear Howard refer to the people who raised him by their first names. There was a distance between him and his folks, yet she couldn't mistake his love and pride as he spoke of them. Didn't most young children grow to call their adoptive parents Mom and Dad, given time to recover from whatever trauma they'd been through? Kat was no expert, but this seemed to be true of her few students who were adopted.

"They must be wonderful people," she said carefully, filling the vase with water.

"The best." Blinking, he cleared his throat, then pasted on a cheerful smile. "Are you ready?"

"To go where?" Quickly, she discarded the plastic and dead leaves, and wiped her hands on a small towel.

"It's a surprise. Afraid of riding a motorcycle?"

"Ha! Remember, I teach six-year-olds. Takes a lot more than a piece of loud machinery to scare me, Lieutenant."

His lips turned up, mocha gaze warming with approval. "Woman after my own heart. I've got a helmet for you, so get a jacket and we're off."

Lifting the vase, she took it to the round oak dining table and placed the arrangement in the middle. Festive, she decided, just what the room needed. Next she snatched her blue windbreaker off the back of a dining chair and shrugged it on, then grabbed her purse and keys.

"Ready."

"You don't really need your purse where we're going."

Kat's brows rose. "You don't date much, do you, hotshot?"

Thumbs hitched in his pockets, he ducked his head briefly, then glanced back up with a sheepish grin. "No, ma'am."

Good answer, even if it was a bald-faced lie.

Deciding to take his word, she left the purse behind and brought only her spare apartment key. Outside, she locked the door and followed him to the hulking Harley, shoving the key into her front jeans pocket. He strapped on her helmet, making sure it fit snugly before donning his own. Climbing onto the bike, he gestured for her to get on behind him.

"Scoot close and hang on tight, arms around my waist."

Ohh yeah. Got it covered, sugar.

She climbed on and molded her front to his broad back, the insides of her thighs pressed to the outsides of his.

Never had Kat imagined riding double on a motorcycle would seem like such an intimate act. The heat of his powerful body seared her to the core, brought every female hormone in her system leaping to attention. She wrapped her arms around his middle, suddenly very glad to have a reason to touch him. Any reason.

He pointed down. "Put your feet up on those rests." When she was positioned, he called, "Here we go!"

Howard backed slowly out of the space, straightened, and started off. He wasn't going fast, but Kat couldn't stop the squeal, part fear, part exhilaration, from escaping. She felt the rumble of his laughter as she clung to him for dear life, and knew she was already in deep doo-doo. And not because of the ride.

She didn't know Howard Paxton at all, but sometimes a girl just *knew.* She was in real danger of losing her heart to a big, sexy teddy bear of a man.

An honest-to-God hero who'd saved her life.

A gentleman who'd brought flowers.

Who loved and respected his parents.

And had secrets haunting his beautiful brown eyes.

Holy craparoni, Katherine Frances. You're a goner.

4

The woman drove him stark raving mad with lust. If Kat knew what Howard wanted to do to her—and how many different ways he envisioned doing it—she'd probably jump off the bike and head for the hills.

Or maybe not.

The lady hadn't exactly thrown up any "keep off the grass" signs. Yet. In fact, everything about Kat—her warm welcome, the casual jeans and eye-popping shirt, the way she beamed over the flowers—suggested she was willing to see where things went between them. Positive signals.

Jesus, even in his own mind he sounded like a horny jerk. Just because a woman looked terrific and wanted to get better acquainted didn't mean he had the right to anticipate a quick roll in the sack. Georgie would smack him upside the head for thinking like that, whether he outweighed her by a hundred and fifty pounds or not. And rightfully so. She'd raised him to be respectful of ladies. . . . Even if she didn't approve of the type of women he'd been seeing before.

Turning left down Cheatham Dam Road, he decided to be himself with Kat, no pretense. Let things develop naturally, or not. He had nothing to lose that hadn't already been taken from him.

Closing the last couple of miles to their destination,

he relaxed and let himself enjoy the soft, warm woman pressed to his back. The balmy fall air whipping his clothes, the Tennessee hills and valleys rising and falling around them, exploding with red, orange, yellow, and brown. Majestic, ancient forests, much of the timber still untouched, the occasional homestead nestled right among the thick foliage. The people who lived and worked in Cheatham County were part of the land, not the conquerors of it. A man couldn't hope to tame something so wild and beautiful, and these folks understood that, just like their predecessors.

To feed their families, they labored in the tobacco fields, tended livestock, worked the barges that traveled the Cumberland River for endless weeks. Some held jobs in nearby Sugarland at small businesses like the barber shop, local feed store, or the new shopping center. A few had civic jobs at the police station or the fire department, like Howard and his buddies. Some made the twenty-mile drive to Nashville and back each day, earning their pay in the glittering high-rise buildings downtown, forced to abandon community tradition in the wake of a struggling economy.

Old and new, battling for supremacy. Whatever their profession, they toiled long and hard to make an honest dollar, and to raise a generation of children who believed in doing the same. Oh, this little patch of heaven on earth wasn't perfect.

But it was pretty darned close.

Which was why he wanted to share this afternoon with Kat. If she'd lived in Sugarland for long, she'd probably visited the park by the Cheatham Dam. Most people had, at one time or another. But not on a day like this. *And not with me.*

The trees opened to clear sky, the road ending at the Cumberland River straight ahead. This particular stretch had been a public park for as long as Howard could recall. To the right, a small beach area provided kids and adults a place to play in the sand and water. A half mile farther was the dam and the lock, which visitors were no longer allowed to walk on and marvel at up close, thanks to terrorist precautions.

To the left and slightly behind them was the parking lot at the base of a hill, near the head of several hiking trails. Beyond that, a grassy area next to the river boasted a few picnic tables, most of them occupied. Frowning, he steered the bike toward the parking area. Of course there'd be a gazillion other people enjoying a nice Sunday, complete with a horde of screeching children, a couple of big dogs, and some sort of family get-together taking up three tables.

As much as Howard adored kids and pooches, he'd hoped for a more intimate setting to woo his prospective lady love. He'd have to improvise. Bypassing the revelry, he steered the bike to the far end of the lot, near where the cultivation of the picnic area ended and native foliage took over. He stopped and shut off the engine.

Kat slid off the back and he felt the absence of her body heat immediately. He liked having her squashed against him, and wondered if she'd enjoyed their closeness half as much. Beside him, she unstrapped the helmet, pulled it off, and shook out her hair. A fall of shiny, white-blond silk belonging to an angel.

"That was fun!" she enthused.

Lifting off his own helmet, he ran a hand through his spiky hair. "Glad you thought so, 'cause we'll have to do it again when I take you home."

"Maybe we can take the long way back." Her green eyes danced with mischief as she nibbled her lower lip.

Climbing off the bike, Howard swept her a gallant bow. "This knight and his noble steed are ever at your service, milady." He felt more than a little ridiculous, but her merry giggle made acting like an idiot worthwhile.

"You're a romantic, milord?"

"Nope. History Channel buff." She slapped his arm

playfully and he laughed, securing their helmets to the rear of the bike. "What do you want to do first? We can go for a walk or—"

"Oh, Howard, look!"

Kat's expression melted and she pointed over his shoulder in the direction from which they'd come. Turning, he scanned the large group they'd passed. A baby girl dressed in jeans and a pink cotton turtleneck detached herself from the distracted grown-ups and made a beeline for one of the tables, little legs churning, wispy blond hair flying. She couldn't be more than two years old, in Howard's estimation, but determination made up for size.

Unguarded on top of the table sat a rectangular cake with white icing, perhaps for a birthday or anniversary. In seconds, the tot scrambled up to kneel on the bench, and with a squeal of glee, slapped her chubby hand smack into the middle of the dessert. Holding her hand up to view her accomplishment, the baby opened and closed it in fascination, squishing the sticky confection between her fingers a few times, then shoved them into her mouth.

"Isn't she adorable?" Kat breathed.

Arrested by the longing in Kat's eyes, his chuckle of amusement at the baby's antics died in his throat. Glancing to the little girl again, his lungs constricted painfully. A desperate ache that never quite went away, and returned sometimes without warning to rip at his heart.

There were more reasons than one for Howard to remain alone. Complicated, honest-to-God relationship killers tangled in the phantoms haunting his broken sleep. He'd never be able to make a nice, stable, family-oriented woman like Kat happy. How could he have forgotten?

Because you're praying for the impossible, Six-Pack. No smart woman will settle for what you have to offer.

A tall young lady with light brown hair finally noticed the miscreant, who was now holding out her tiny hand to a golden retriever eagerly licking the rest of the icing, and bolted for the table. "Oh, *Emily Jean!*"

"Yeah, she's a cutie," Howard said hoarsely, turning to the leather bags hanging behind the seat of his bike. He fumbled with the straps, his fingers clumsy. "You hungry? I brought some deli sandwiches and stuff."

So much for unveiling his surprise with finesse. Not that store-bought grub snatched on the fly qualified as a big deal. A player like Jules, on the other hand, would've made reservations for dinner at some trendy restaurant in Nashville. Wine, candlelight, witty conversation. A skilled seduction perfectly choreographed to a snazzy Latin beat—

"Is something wrong?"

Kat's hesitancy snapped him back to attention. Pretty green eyes studied him, concern dimming the merriment of seconds before. Because of him. A curious pang stabbed his gut. Whatever his failings, she deserved the glorious afternoon he'd led her to expect.

"Just a little off after last night," he lied, lifting a plastic grocery bag from the leather pouch. "Nothing a picnic with the prettiest girl in five counties won't cure. Shall we?"

The last part, at least, was the truth.

"Hmm, I think you need your eyesight checked," she said, humor restored. "But a picnic with the hottest guy in five counties sounds fabulous. Lead the way."

Hottest guy? Jesus. Heat flooded his face. Okay, he'd set himself up for that one. True, women generally found him pleasing enough, but to hear Kat baldly state her approval in return made him squirm.

And yet, coming from an angel, the compliment eased the terrible ache in his chest some, lighting places in his soul that had been cold and dark for . . . well, always.

Confusion warring with a hum of satisfaction vibrating to his toes, Howard took her hand and nodded toward a grassy spot down the riverbank, away from all the activity. "Let's try over there."

"Won't there be snakes?"

"Nah, we'll scare 'em off."

"What if they're sleeping? They're much harder to see in the fall with the grass turning brown and all the dead leaves on the ground."

Beside him, Kat shuddered. He shook his head, lips turning up. "A fearless teacher who has no problem running into a burning house with a garden hose, afraid of snakes. Go figure."

"I'm never going to hear the end of my stupidity, am I?"

"Not as long as you're around me." Which he hoped, in spite of the self-doubt serving a fat black eye to his confidence, would be a long while. "It's my job to protect people, from themselves more often than not. Promise me you won't do anything like that again." The sudden steel in his voice surprised them both.

"No argument here. I promise." As they walked, she shot him a searching look before steering the topic away from her ill-advised Good Samaritan act. "Anyway, I never said I was afraid of snakes. I just prefer not to commune with those particular beasties."

Howard made a sound of agreement and kept walking. Allowed himself to shrug off the heavy burden of his past, unwilling to let the monster in the shadows screw up his life. Not today. He cast his worries aside, focused on Kat, her small hand engulfed by his huge paw. All soft, fragrant woman, firm and round in the right places.

Especially her cute butt, shaped like an upside-down heart. Two tempting globes contoured by jeans he imagined sliding past curvy hips, down toned thighs. Would her ass cheeks be as pale and creamy as the rest of her skin? What would it feel like to cup them in his big hands, knead the flesh in his fingers as he knelt between her spread thighs, teased her slick entrance with the head of his throbbing—

"Hey, that looks like a good spot!" Kat pointed to a flat grassy area just ahead.

Howard's fantasy scattered to the wind and he suppressed a groan, willing his erection to cooperate, praying she didn't notice the divining rod pushing at his zipper. God, he was such a pathetic horn dog.

He cleared his throat. "Yep, this works. I just wish I'd thought to bring a blanket. For the food." Well, hell, it sounded even worse when he explained. "I'm not some kind of creep or anything, I just didn't know the picnic tables would be full and—"

"Relax, big guy. You're wound tighter than an eight-day clock," she said, patting his shoulder. "I don't make a habit of joyriding with pervs."

As they reached their destination, he set the grocery bag on the dried grass and faced her. Stroking his thumb over the back of her hand, he asked, "How do you know I'm not?"

Cocking her head, she peered up at him, considering the question seriously. "Because you're a lieutenant in the fire department." She said it with confidence, as though this fact settled the matter entirely.

Howard shook his head. "Doesn't mean I'm a nice guy."

"But you *are*. All the evidence supports my being perfectly safe and happy in your company."

"What evidence?" He waited, intrigued by her assessment of his character. He'd never met a woman so forthright. Honest.

"You rescued me after I'd inhaled too much smoke, made sure I was all right before we parted ways."

"Doing my job."

"You were very kind and gentle. Concerned."

Oh, jeez. Though a secret part of him arched like a

cat having his chin scratched, he continued to play devil's advocate. "Could've been an act."

"How long have you been a firefighter, Lieutenant?"

Lord, he loved when she called him that. The way she drew out the title, breathy and sexy as a caress.

"Sixteen years. I was assigned to Station Five right out of the fire academy, along with my best friend, Sean Tanner. When our captain retired three years ago, Sean got promoted to his position and I moved up from FAO—that's the guy who drives the big engine— to lieutenant."

"He got promoted over you, even though you two started together? You seem like a natural leader to me."

"So is Sean. He's five years older than me, did a stint in the Marines and survived Desert Storm before joining the fire department. Major points with the department for military service, and he deserves it."

Green feline eyes sparkling, Kat regarded him as though he'd revealed some monumental secret. "You love him."

The pronouncement startled him. Love? He snorted. "Sure. We send each other valentines and everything."

"Oh, don't be such a *guy*." She poked him playfully in the stomach with one finger. "Tell me, what would you do to save one of your men if he were in life-threatening trouble?"

"Anything," he said without hesitation.

"Even at the cost of your own life?"

"Absolutely."

"I rest my case."

Christ, she knew how to pump a man's ego. All he needed was a red cape and a capital S emblazoned on his chest. He chuckled in spite of himself. "All right, I give in. I'm not perv material. But I'm not perfect by a long shot."

By a wider margin than anyone knew, save his parents and Sean.

"Nobody is, but our faults won't make a difference to those who truly care for us." This time, it was her turn to flush. "Holy cow, that was *so* Pollyanna. Sorry."

He arched a brow. "For what? For believing trial brings out the best in people? Actually, you sound a lot like Georgie, and I respect her more than any lady I know."

Kat recognized the huge compliment in the comparison. "Thank you . . . but what do *you* believe?"

Whoa, getting deep here. Still, he gave an honest answer. "Georgie's an optimist. I'm a realist, like Bentley. I take my blows as they come, deal with them, move on. I think all of that 'Adversity makes you stronger' stuff is what people say to comfort themselves when the going gets rough. Friends and family can stand by you, lend support. But in the end, your inner core of strength pulls you through, period."

"Or not."

"Yeah," he agreed quietly, thinking of Sean. Of the man's shattered world that no amount of drugs or hand-holding could ever patch back together. "And sometimes, no matter how strong you thought you were, the damage takes you out of the game."

Kat laid a palm in the center of his chest, concern etched on her smooth features. "Are you referring to yourself, or someone else?"

Good question. A second ago, he could've sworn he was talking about Sean. God, it was hard to think with her standing so close, touching him, fingers scorching his skin through the fabric of his T-shirt. Lord help him, he needed to touch her, too.

"A friend, and too sad a story for a day like today. Kat?"

"Yes?"

"May I kiss you?"

Her eyes widened and she started to say something, but nothing emerged.

"Jesus, I'm a jerk. Forget I—"

Kat stepped into his body, reached up to curl one hand behind his neck. She tugged his head down and Howard went willingly, taking her mouth with a groan of pure bliss.

Her lips were plump and sweet, every bit as kissable as he'd imagined. Strawberries on the vine, waiting for him to savor, nibble. Not wanting to rush her, he started slowly and gently. Parted her Windbreaker, rested his palms at the curve of her waist, brushed his lips against hers, tempting. Maximizing the initial tingle, the anticipation. Drawing out the moment to make them crave more.

He worked his hands under the edge of her shirt, skimmed her ribs, wondering if she'd protest. Ready to back off if she did. She sighed instead, melted into him, and he increased the pressure. Swept his tongue past the seam of her lips, into her moist heat. Tasting, exploring as she did the same, tangling her tongue with his.

Oh, God, so good. So right. They were sealed together now from head to toe, Kat playing with the thick hair at his nape as they drank one another. Two people dying of thirst for too long.

So much soft woman pressed against his starving body. Full breasts and lush hips. Spreading his legs, he cupped her bottom with his big hands, pulled her in, seated her against his hard length as intimately as possible. At least part of his fantasy came true. Yeah, she was everything a woman should be. *Mine.*

His body ignited, his rigid shaft desperate to be inside Kat to the point of pain. To be whole, no longer fractured and alone in a base act of sex. To feel filled afterward, rather than empty. And something else he couldn't name, elusive and frightening. Enough to finally cause him to break the kiss and hold her close, breathing as though he'd run the training course in record time.

"Wow." She collapsed against his chest.

His laugh emerged as a wheeze. "My thoughts exactly, sweetheart. If I don't stop now, the good citizens of Cheatham County are going to see more of nature than they expected."

"Mmm. Now I know the truth. You're a very bad boy under that gentlemanly exterior, Lieutenant. I like. A lot."

His inner bad boy stood up and cheered. Along with his outer one. "Have mercy—you're killing me here. I still have to go home later to a cold, empty house. Wait." He frowned. "I wasn't hinting for you to come home with me. Not that I don't want to—I mean, it's obvious. . . ."

Nice move, idiot.

Putting him out of his misery, Kat dimpled, giving him a quick kiss before pulling away and gesturing to the sack. "Deli sandwiches, huh? I'm starved!"

Howard blinked in amazement. Any of the women he'd been with would've gotten all huffy and offended for one reason or another, accusing him of either not wanting her or of moving too fast. Lose-lose, whatever he said or did. Not his Kat. She seemed to understand exactly what he'd been trying to say. Even if he didn't.

"Me, too." Shrugging off his denim jacket, he knelt and spread the material on the ground. "Here you go, have a seat."

"Oh, no, I don't want to ruin your nice jacket."

"You won't. Sit," he ordered, stretching out next to her spot. For a second, she looked ready to protest, then sat.

"Okay, thanks." She shot a pointed look at his chest. "I thought coffee was your only vice. Smoker?"

"What?" Looking down at himself, he patted the tube-shaped bulge in the front pocket of his T-shirt and grinned at what she must've thought was a lighter. He plucked out a roll of candy. "Only if you can smoke Pez. Want one?"

"Ha! A grown man who still eats Pez candy can't tease me for using kid words like 'dork,'" she informed him smugly, peeling two off the roll he offered.

His lips twitched. "My other vice. I'm an addict; carry them everywhere I go." Tucking the candy back in his pocket, Howard grabbed the sack and dug inside, fishing out four six-inch subs, four small packages of potato chips, and two bottled waters. "Ham or turkey? I got two of each."

"Turkey's fine—good Lord! Who's going to eat all that food?"

He grinned at her. "Hey, I'm a growing boy. Gotta have fuel to deal with whatever life throws at me."

"And you work out a lot." Her eyes raked his body with appreciation. "How often?"

"Pretty much every night," he said, handing her a turkey sub. Then realized he'd blundered.

"At night?" Kat glanced at him, curious, as she peeled the plastic wrap from her sandwich. "Don't most people go to the gym in the morning or during the day?"

Setting Kat's chips and water bottle on the jacket next to her, he scrambled to come up with a plausible reason for his odd schedule . . . other than the whole whacked-out truth. "I work twenty-four hours on shift, forty-eight off. During the days I'm on, we're pretty busy, so it's easier to work out in the evenings when things are slower. At home, I have equipment in one of the spare bedrooms, so I can hit the mats whenever I want. Or I can go to my health club for a change of scenery. Easier just to stick with my routine, though."

Not exactly a lie. Still, it made him sound like sort of a fitness fanatic, one of those pretty boys who spent hours obsessing about staying buff, when nothing could be farther from the truth.

Problem was, the truth led right back down the dark and dangerous tunnel he'd been running from his entire life. And getting close to any one person meant sharing a nightmare not even he could fully understand—assuming he wanted to understand, which he didn't.

"Good for you. I tried an exercise plan, three days a week for about six months. Weights, jogging, the whole deal. Finally gave up the ghost." She opened her chips and took a bite of her sandwich.

"Yeah? How come?" Ravenous, he followed suit, glad to have dodged a bullet.

"Didn't make a difference," she said, chewing thoughtfully. "I can drop pounds, but I can't change my body shape. I can be dry and round or sweaty and round. I don't like to sweat, end of story."

Uh-oh. Discussing a woman's weight wasn't a bullet. More like a rocket launcher.

Aimed at a man's balls.

Shrugging, he said, "You don't have to sweat to stay in shape. Something simple as a daily walk will do, especially for you."

Arching a tawny brow, she eyed him in suspicion. "Yeah, why's that?"

"Because you already look great." Like the railroad spike in his jeans hadn't given away his opinion. "But walking is good for your cardiovascular health, not to mention lowering stress levels." God, he sounded like a pinhead.

"Good point. I propose we test the theory after we eat. Up for a hike later?" She took another bite.

"You bet."

They ate in companionable silence for a few minutes, soaking in the gorgeous afternoon. The lazy Cumberland was smooth as glass, not a barge in sight, though one could appear around the bend at any moment. A water bird piped along the bank, spindly legs dancing, long beak flashing in and out of the mud. Howard thought he'd never seen a day so fine, enjoyed a meal so tasty.

And he knew the woman at his side was the reason.

She gestured to his left cheekbone. "How'd you get the scar?"

"A ninety-three-year-old lady with a golf club didn't take too kindly to being made to leave her burning apartment with her kitty still inside." He gave her a sheepish grin.

Kat's eyes rounded. "Oh, my gosh! What happened?"

"Twelve stitches."

"No, to the cat!"

He rolled his eyes. "Rescued the darned thing."

"Good. So, you've lived in Sugarland since you were four?" Kat prompted, popping a chip into her mouth.

Howard tensed, wishing he hadn't mentioned being adopted. Playing *This Is Your Life*, at least with his own, had never been his bag. "Yeah." He braced himself, knowing what was next.

"And before that?"

"I lived in a run-down shack on the other side of Clarksville, or so I've been told."

"You don't remember?" Sympathy laced her soft voice.

"Not much."

Unless you counted the rotted boards of the front porch steps, the old mongrel that used to slink underneath to take refuge. The stench of beer and his father's unwashed body, the boiling anger permeating the rank air like a terminal sickness. His father's bellows of rage, his mother's screams. The sting of the razor strap across his thin back.

"My mother loved her garden more than anyplace else," he said instead, his throat gone tight. "She'd spend hours out in the sunshine, and I remember how beautiful she looked kneeling in the dirt, poking seeds into thumb-sized holes. She had long brown hair the same color as mine, but past her shoulders. And when she laughed . . . the whole world lit up."

"She sounds wonderful."

Oh, God. A bolt of old pain and anger sliced through his chest. "She was." *Before she left me to a monster.*

"What happened?"

His appetite vanished and he wrapped the uneaten half of his second sandwich in the plastic. "One day she left and didn't come back. I don't imagine anybody blamed her, from what little I remember about my father. He had a mean streak as long and wide as the Cumberland."

"Your father was abusive?"

"Yeah." The pity and disgust on Kat's sweet face was almost more than he could stand.

"And nobody blamed her for leaving?" she asked softly. "Not even the son who loved her so much?"

She worked with young children every day of the week, and he didn't have to tell her how emotionally devastating it had been for a boy to be discarded like an old shoe by the person he adored most. How much the knowledge hurt decades later, despite the healing magic of time.

He shrugged. "I was a kid. I got over it."

From her knowing expression, Kat didn't believe that any more than he did. Silence stretched between them, broken only by the laughter and whoops of the party downstream, as she waited for him to continue.

"Anyway, the night my mom left town, my father ditched me in the woods between here and Clarksville, then obliged everyone by crashing his truck into a tree and burning to death. Since I had no other family, I became a ward of the state until Bentley and Georgie rescued me."

After he'd recovered from the final, severe beating his father had dished out before dumping him like so much trash.

"Did anyone try to find your mother?"

"I'm sure the authorities did, otherwise the adoption couldn't have legally taken place. I believe the correct term is 'child abandonment.'"

Kat hesitated, looking uncertain whether to ask the next logical question. "Have *you* searched for her?"

"What for? If the lady wants to see me, she can find me. It's not like I've gone far." His answer came out harsher than he intended, and he cringed.

Patting his shoulder, she didn't appear to notice. "Oh, Howard. How horrible all of that must've been for you, especially that last night."

Taking her hand, he gave her a reassuring smile. "I don't actually remember that part." But recalling the nightmare, a niggling part of him wasn't sure.

"Thank God!" She squeezed his hand, green eyes luminous.

"Yeah. What I know is based on evidence the sheriff's department pieced together and eventually passed on to the Mitchells. From what Bentley told me years later, the cops were a constant presence at my old place. Nobody in the county was surprised about the blowout the night my mother left."

"This is none of my business and I won't take it personally if you don't want to answer, but . . . why is your last name different from your adoptive parents'?"

Howard looked away, wondering how she'd managed to locate and poke at every painful sore in his life in record time. Except for Sean, his brothers had never asked him outright, and he'd never offered to share. Then again, he'd never felt compelled to come clean on the subject before. With Kat, everything was different.

She made him want to be . . . more. He saw no reason he shouldn't open up for her, just a tiny bit.

"When Bentley and Georgie took me home, I was traumatized," he said quietly. "No matter how they loved and nurtured me, tried to heal my wounds, I remained withdrawn. I didn't speak for months, and when I finally started to respond, they thought it best not to push me too hard on the 'Call us Mommy and Daddy' thing. For a while, at least."

"Makes sense. You weren't a baby anymore, and you needed a period of adjustment."

"And I came around, eventually, after we traveled the mother of all rough roads together. But by the time we bonded, they were Bentley and Georgie to me, permanently. They decided to leave the decision to me whether or not I'd take the Mitchell name when I turned eighteen. Of course, as a teenager, I was full of myself, determined to be my own man. I went to court and legally dropped my last name, period. From Howard Paxton Whitlaw, Howard Paxton was reborn."

The first and last time he'd ever hurt Bentley. The terrible disappointment etched on the face of the man he respected and admired the most; he'd live with it until he drew his last breath.

"You regret your decision." The observation was spoken with complete understanding.

Howard swallowed hard. "Every day of my life."

"You could go back to court."

"Yeah, but it wouldn't change what I did to them. Wouldn't fix anything. I waited too long."

"Oh, I don't know. You might be surprised."

Down the river, from the direction of the large party, a woman's voice called out, searching for someone. Focused on Kat, Howard missed who the lady was yelling for.

"Optimist," he teased, hoping to lighten the mood.

She grinned back. "A perfect partner for a realist."

The woman called out again, louder. More strident.

Damn, why did there have to be so many people here today? Trying to tune out the racket, he did some nosing of his own. "Tell me, how does one of Sugarland's spoiled rich girls wind up teaching first grade and doing the bachelorette gig across town from the McKenna minimansion?"

"My family isn't rich." She laughed, not offended in the least. "Daddy has a successful law practice, which my older sister, Grace, joined as a partner last year, but he's worked like a dog for as long as I can remember. He—"

"Emily!" A woman's shrill scream shattered the beautiful afternoon. *"Emileeeeee! OhGodohGod!"*

Howard bolted to his feet, heart pounding. He knew the awful, keening sound of a mother's grief and terror. Was more intimately acquainted than most with the stab of fear driving straight through a man's sternum, knowing every second counted. Years of training kicked in as he scanned down river, toward the crowd.

Two men plunged into the river at a dead run, toward a small figure bobbing a few feet from shore.

Kat came to her feet beside him. "Howard? What is it?"

"The baby," he rasped. "Jesus Christ."

Adrenaline turbo-charged his legs as he took off, but his mind was sharp as a knife blade. Assess the situation, take the appropriate action. Nothing else mattered.

One of the men scooped a limp, wet bundle into his arms, screaming frantically for help.

Howard ran harder, praying sixteen years in the trenches was enough to save Emily Jean.

5

Kat took off after Howard and stumbled, unable to keep up with his long-legged stride. For such a big man, he covered ground like a deer, swift and with purpose.

That precious baby! Dear God, let her be okay.

But she wasn't. That fact became horribly clear as Kat skidded to a halt in the middle of pandemonium.

The tall brown-haired woman Kat presumed to be the mother was completely hysterical, grabbing at the baby in the man's arms, unintentionally creating more of a problem rather than helping. Howard took control of the situation, barking orders like a man used to having them followed.

"Lay her on the ground," he fired at the white-faced man holding Emily. To the second guy, the one who'd followed the first into the river, he gestured to indicate the mother and snapped, "Hold her, *now.*"

Without a word and barely a nod, both men jumped to do as instructed.

Howard glanced to Kat. "Make sure someone is calling 911."

Scanning the crowd to do as he asked, Kat felt a tap on her shoulder. She turned to see a teenager behind her, pointing to another young woman already making the call. Nodding, Kat returned her attention to the drama.

As he lowered Emily to the grass a few feet from the bank, the first man glanced at Howard, eyes wild. "Are you a doctor?"

"Paramedic. You the father?" Howard knelt, taking the baby's arm and checking for a pulse at the bend of her elbow. Next, he pushed up the baby's pink shirt, probing the upper abdomen with his fingertips.

"Yes." His voice cracked. "Please, she's so little—"

"I've got a pulse, so we're gonna get this water out of her lungs, then get some air in there," Howard said, the picture of calm authority. "What's your name?"

The man blinked. "Phil."

"Okay, Phil, I need you to keep a cool head in case I need an assist. You with me?"

Kat suspected he needed no such thing, but was trying to keep the man calm. Watching the lieutenant in action, she felt the kernel of respect planted last night grow by leaps and bounds.

"Sure." Phil swallowed hard.

"Good. Right now I need you to talk to Emily, Phil. Let her know you're here. That's real important, okay?"

While Phil crooned to his daughter and stroked her wet hair, Howard used the heel of his hand to push upward on her diaphragm, careful not to apply too much force. Water gushed from between her lips, but not the copious amount Kat would've thought. After several pushes, Howard supported the baby with one hand under her back, the other on her tummy. As he carefully turned the baby over, Kat was struck by how huge his hands were, how tiny the child. His hands spanned her entire torso, could easily crush the little girl with their incredible strength, but the lieutenant handled her as though she were a priceless treasure.

Kat could tell Howard was getting the rest of the water from the baby's lungs, pounding firmly on her back, but not hard enough to injure her. Only a thin trickle dribbled from the child's lips now, and she prayed hard for the child to breathe.

Howard laid Emily on her back once more, then covered her nose and mouth, giving her puffs of air. To her right, the mother's hysterical babbling became the low wail of an animal in agony. The awful sound raised gooseflesh on Kat's arms, prickled her neck. Even if everything turned out all right, the eerie howls of a woman's fear and grief would haunt her for a long time to come.

Oh, no, please—

Emily's thin chest heaved, she gasped ... and began to cry.

Kat's legs went rubbery. A collective burst of joy and relief exploded from the crowd, people exclaiming, crying, hugging one another. The man who'd been holding the mother let go, and the woman fell to her knees beside Howard, tears streaming down her face.

"Emily, oh, sweetheart, thank God. Thank God!"

At the sound of her mother's voice, the little girl held out her chubby arms and bawled louder, her cries interrupted by rattling coughs. The mom scooped up her daughter, holding her close, the two of them clinging to each other and making enough racket to rival a siren as Phil threw his arms around his girls.

It was a beautiful noise.

Forgotten for the moment, Howard lowered his head and closed his eyes, gripping his thighs so hard his knuckles were white. He sucked in a couple of deep breaths, then raised his head, his dark gaze connecting with Kat's. His face was lined with strain, the near-tragedy catching up with him.

As he pushed to his feet, Kat closed the distance between them. Without pausing, she walked straight into his waiting arms. He crushed her against the warm, solid wall of his chest, and she felt his heart galloping madly as he rested his chin on top of her head.

God, he was shaking, vibrating like he'd been plugged into a socket. This pillar of awesome strength had been as frightened for Emily as anyone here, but he'd pushed his fear deep to utilize his training and save a little girl.

"You were fantastic," she whispered, hugging him tight.

He didn't get the chance to reply. The father stood next to them, offering his hand. Shifting Kat to his left side and keeping his arm around her, he shook the man's hand.

"I don't know how to thank you," Phil croaked. "I mean, Jesus, there aren't any words."

Howard attempted a smile. "Just keep a sharper eye on that little imp of yours. And maybe bring her by the Sugarland Fire Department for a visit next time you guys are out that way. I work the A-shift at Station Five."

"We'll do that." Phil beamed, apparently glad to have a way to thank the man who saved his baby girl.

A fire truck and ambulance arrived three minutes later from nearby Ashland City, which was closer to this rural area than Sugarland. In minutes, the paramedics had conferred with Howard and Phil about the incident, examined the patient, then loaded mom and baby for a trip to the hospital. Emily would be just fine, but whether to have her checked out wasn't even a question.

The crowd began to disperse, but not before much hand shaking and back thumping for Howard, who took the attention in stride.

Or appeared to. Once the last of the bunch departed, Howard turned to face Kat, linking his fingers with hers. Before he spoke, he had to clear his throat. More than once.

"I could sure use that walk now," he said quietly.

Kat smiled, skimming his dear face with her free hand. "Sounds like what the doctor ordered. Under the circumstances, we can clean up our picnic stuff when we get back."

Tugging on her hand, Howard led them across the parking lot to the trailhead at the base of the bluff overlooking the Cumberland. The switchback zigzagged upward to their left, the path rocky and steep. Howard had to let go of her, so she followed behind, enjoying the great view of his tight ass swinging in the Wranglers. She supposed she ought to feel guilty in light of what had just happened, but darn it, he was so freakin' much *man*. Every muscled inch a treat for the female eye.

She frowned. How many pairs of female eyes had been treated to those gorgeous inches? The lieutenant claimed he didn't date much.

Yeah, right. And I'm Paris Hilton.

Beating down the icky green monster, she scolded herself to suck it up. A man like Howard hadn't spent the last couple of decades as a monk in Tibet, any more than she'd remained a lily-pure virgin awaiting her white knight. And wasn't that a lovely thought?

Okay, no mud-slinging regarding ex-significant or not-so-significant others. But, damn, she couldn't help but wonder how many women had lain in his arms, pressed against his big, naked body. How many had shivered in delight at the sensual slide of his bronzed skin against theirs, the hard length of him sinking deep, mastering his lovers as no man ever had, spiraling them into mindless oblivion.

Lordy, she must be one sick woman. The eroticism of those images had her panting and hot from more than the climb. The warm, tingling sensation between her legs begged to be stoked to a blaze only Howard could douse.

What did the past matter between two healthy, consenting adults? He'd made it abundantly clear he wanted her, and she knew for a fact firefighters must pass regular physicals to keep their jobs. Minimal risk, discounting the part about the possible mangled and bleeding heart at the end.

Howard wasn't even breathing hard as he reached a level clearing halfway to the top, the stinker. Her teasing complaint died on her lips as he walked to the edge of the scenic overlook and hooked his thumbs in his jeans, staring out over the river below. She went to stand beside him, taking a minute to catch her breath.

"Is it always this hard?" she inquired softly.

He didn't have to ask what she meant. "With anyone, but especially kids." His deep voice broke on the last word.

"You should be proud of yourself. Emily's going to be all right because of you."

"I'm relieved, don't get me wrong." He sighed. "It's the rush, you know? All the emotion we keep locked down to do whatever it takes. Then when the crisis is over, it's like . . ." He trailed off, searching for the right analogy.

"A dam breaking," she suggested.

He nodded. "Exactly. Fear, anxiety, relief, all that stuff jumbled together, trying to come out at once. And Christ, when we lose one, throw sadness into the mix. We grieve, not the same as the families because nothing could touch their feelings, but we have to work through the loss all the same."

"I've never thought about firefighters grieving. I mean, I see the fire trucks and ambulances going to calls, maybe to a wreck, and I think about the victims and their families, wonder what happened. I guess in the back of my mind, I always thought the emergency crew just shrugs their shoulders, chalks up another life lost, and walks away." The admission shamed her a little.

"You're talking about compartmentalization. Shoving the horror into a tiny box and burying it deep, never to be examined again. Cops get that rap most often, and there's a lot of truth to the stereotype because they work

alone. Whatever is thrown at them, they deal, alone."
His lips turned up in a ghost of a smile.

"With us, it's different. Believe it or not, we *talk*.
After a bad call, we've been known to stay up all night
rehashing the incident. Decompressing. Did we follow
every single procedure to the letter? Was there anything else we should've or could've done? We're a
team and we deal as a team so every single guy can do
his job next time without any doubt or fear to cloud
good judgment."

"That's remarkable." A surge of pride welled in her
chest. Just standing next to this incredible man made
her feel good, like she could conquer the world.
They'd just met, and yet somehow, she felt as though
she'd known him forever. They clicked.

"You're remarkable." He cupped her cheeks, mocha
brown eyes searching her face. "How did I find someone so beautiful *and* so easy to talk to? How did I get
so lucky?"

She had about two seconds to read the sincerity in
his gaze before his lips met hers. Brushing the sides of
her face with his thumbs, he kissed her gently, their
bodies not quite touching. Center-of-the-sun heat radiated off him, but he didn't press close like before. He
held back as his tongue invaded, danced with hers, exploring. Seducing, making her want.

Oh, God, yes. Oh yeah, she wanted. She wanted him
horizontal, his big, naked body wrapped around hers.
Ached to have him inside her, completing them both.
Judging from the impressive erection, he'd be long and
thick. Hot and hard. She had to *know*.

"Kat." Howard sank to his knees, pulling her down
with him. She went eagerly, taking her cues from him.
Excited and aroused, she wondered how far he'd go
and knew she'd let him, despite the danger of discov-
ery here in the open. Or perhaps, in part, because of
the thrill of it all.

He eased Kat onto her back in a patch of grass and stretched out beside her. Rolling, he angled himself over her, tunneled his fingers through her hair. He ate her mouth like a man born to kiss, a rumble of pure male satisfaction vibrating in his chest. She loved the delicious weight of him, the cords of muscle standing out in relief on his neck and arms as he held her. She reveled in his hard thigh thrown over hers, entwining their legs, his erection riding her hip.

"We fit," he murmured, face taut with desire.

"Yes, we do."

A hand crept under the edge of her T-shirt, skimmed her ribs. "May I touch you?"

"Please, yes!"

His eyes darkened as his palm slid upward, over the plane of her belly, higher still. His fingers brushed the swell of her breasts, a light caress. He lingered, tracing their shape, then rubbed a thumb over one nipple, causing it to peak under the sheer fabric of her bra. First one nipple, then the other. Teasing, rubbing, sending sparks zipping through her limbs. She went boneless at just that slight attention, a sigh of pleasure escaping her lips.

"I want to see you." Not a question this time. His voice had thickened, husky with arousal, low and seductive.

Kat's blood sang, pounded in her ears, between her thighs. At her nod, he pushed up the T-shirt. With an expert flick, he opened the front clasp of her bra and parted the silky cups. Cool air kissed her overheated skin, and the dusky rose nipples tightened to perfect cones.

"My God, you're beautiful." Touching her with reverence, he brushed one breast with gentle fingers. Kneading, weighing her flesh in his work-roughened palm.

Being exposed like this to him totally turned her on. So did his unguarded expression of awe no man could fake. She arched her back, craving his touch, saying without words she needed more, anything he was willing to give.

Groaning, he accepted, bending his head. "So pretty." A puff of his warm breath fanned across the sensitive point, followed by a flick of his tongue. "So sweet."

His mouth claimed her breast, tongue rasping the nipple. Teeth grazing, spiraling the sparks into flames. Every nerve ending leapt in delight as he sucked, paying homage to a feminine part of her Rod had always scorned as too much. Imperfect.

But not for Howard. Unhappy memories of what's-his-name poofed to dust as her lover's palm traveled to her tummy. Fingers circled the diamond stud. Toyed with the waistband of her jeans, dipping slightly inside. Asking permission, waiting. Reaching between them, she unbuttoned and unzipped, granting him access. On fire . . .

Capable fingers delved into her panties, swept through the curls at the apex of her thighs. Parted the slick, bare folds of her sex, already wet for him.

"Jesus," he gasped, pupils dilating. "You shave *there*."

Pleased by his lusty reaction, she gave a low, throaty laugh. "Personal preference. Less is more and all that. You like?"

"Pretty Katherine, you tie me in knots. Let me make you feel good."

She took that as an enthusiastic *yes*.

It didn't escape her notice that Howard was deriving satisfaction simply from pleasuring her. A man seeing to her needs above his own. And that was saying a helluva lot, considering the massive proof of his need resting against her side.

Two fingers slid between the lips of her sex, stroking, creating magic unfurling in her center to bloom outward. They thrust inside, then out. In and out. Spreading the dewy moisture, swirling the wet pearl of her clit. Taking time to spoil her as no man had before. Just a simple caress for her alone, only giving.

She moaned, clutching his broad back, her knees falling wide open. His fingers pumped her channel in a faster rhythm, mimicking the action of his absent cock. Showing her an inkling of what could be if she accepted all of him. Driving into her soaking wet sex, the motion and the wicked little sucking sounds setting her entire body ablaze.

"That's it, let yourself go. Come for me."

The erotic command, dripping with male dominance, hurled Kat over the edge and into space. She cried out, the orgasm washing though her with blinding intensity. Spasm after spasm shook her as her sex pulsed, far surpassing every secret fantasy she'd ever harbored about how great the right man could make her feel someday.

"Oh, Howard, yes, *yes!*"

Helpless, she gave herself over to him, undulating until he'd wrung every drop from her body. Until she lay spent, vision clearing, gazing up into his very smug face. At last, he slid his hand from her jeans.

"Well!" She smiled, floating in bliss. "So *that's* what an orgasm is supposed to be like!"

Howard blinked. "What?"

Heat crept up her neck, but she couldn't hold back the grin. "You heard me."

"You've never had an orgasm before? Be serious."

"I am, like a heart attack. I've, um, gotten as far as the warm, fuzzy feeling, but—" She made a face. "I guess I thought that's all I was capable of reaching. Until you."

His brows rose. "Wow, you must've dated some real jerks."

She gave him an arch look, body still humming. "One jerk in particular. I'm starting to realize how much of a shit Rod truly was."

He snorted. "Rod? Now that's what I call ironic, especially if he couldn't make his woman happy."

"Hmm. Speaking of making your lover happy." Reaching between them, she caressed the rock-hard erection pushing at his zipper. Lord, she couldn't wait to get her hands on him. "Your turn, big guy."

To her surprise, Howard took her wrist and gently removed her hand, bringing it to his lips. Regret shining in his eyes, he kissed her fingers. She realized, despite his arousal, he was letting her off the hook.

Uh-oh.

"Why not? Did I do something wrong?" Self-conscious, she sat up and began to straighten her clothing.

"No, angel. I have my reasons, the first being today was about you. I wanted us to get to know each other a bit, show you a good time."

"You've certainly succeeded! And the other reasons?" *God, please don't let him say it's not working for him. That he'll call sometime when we both know he won't and—*

"I believe we have the start of something special between us, Kat," he said softly. "I want us to get off on the right foot."

Relief and joy turned her muscles to jelly. Thank goodness they were still sitting. "Me, too." Unable to keep from touching him, she reached out to explore his rugged face. She traced the scar at his temple, the line of his strong jaw, the fullness of his sensual lips. "I know we just met, but I feel like I found a missing part of myself. Crazy, huh?"

Well, if any admission was going to send a man screaming for parts unknown, that ought to do the trick. Instead, Howard stayed put, his expression open. Points for the big guy.

"Not to me, because I feel the same way. But I won't lie to you about where my life is right now. I need to explain, then you should take some time to think about what I said before we go any further."

Oh, boy. Here comes the proverbial brick over the skull.

"Go ahead." She kept her expression neutral. *Just don't make me deduct points.*

Stretching his long legs out in front of him, he hesitated. Groped for the right words. "I'm not looking for a one-night stand, Kat."

"Good news, otherwise I'd have to send you home with a serious case of blue balls."

He had the grace to look embarrassed. "I'm not implying you would've settled for meaningless sex, either. If I'd believed that, we wouldn't be here. I'm not in my twenties anymore, and I'm done with feeling cheap and used."

He was so serious, she couldn't resist teasing him. "Gosh, isn't that usually the woman's line?"

"Very funny." He plucked at a blade of dead grass, staring at her thoughtfully. "Being alone sucks. Don't you ever get tired of waking up to the same four empty walls, day after day?"

"Sure, who doesn't? Somehow, though, I have trouble picturing you all by your lonesome."

Even as she spoke, she began to suspect Howard was referring to more than being without female companionship, whether he realized it or not. No, his loneliness ran much deeper, had a wider scope than most people's. Considering what he'd revealed about his childhood—and he'd likely left out the most horrific parts—a person didn't have to be a genius to figure why a great catch like Howard was still single.

Any good teacher could tell you an abused child will carry feelings of inadequacy and fear of abandonment into adulthood. In many cases, all his life. She could be wrong about this in regard to Howard, but she didn't think so. His next words seemed to confirm her suspicions.

"It's easy to remain alone when you aim low. No strings, easy sex. Then when she leaves, your heart doesn't take a beating in the process."

"And how well did that theory work for you?"

"Can't you guess?" By now, he was picking his patch of grass bald, studying the decimated spot as though it held a profound secret. "One day, I woke up next to a stranger and hated what my personal life had become. Instead of a stud, I felt like the world's biggest slut. I was miserable, and I wanted *more*. So I asked her to stay for breakfast."

"What did she say?"

"She said, 'I don't eat breakfast, Harry.'"

"Ouch."

He gave a humorless laugh. "Lesson learned, right? That was the last time I was with anybody, over a year ago."

"A year! Wow." She joined him in his therapeutic weed plucking, thrilled by his self-imposed abstinence and doing her best not to show it. "Tell me, what great wisdom did your year bring? What's changed?"

Scooting close, he ran a palm down her arm. "I met you."

A shiver of delight zinged along her spine, tempered by a healthy dose of caution and her own hard lessons. "Which means what, exactly?"

"Do you like bacon?" A small smile played about his sensual lips.

"And eggs." She arched a brow. "I also like waffles, French toast, and pancakes. Not all in one morning, of course."

"Good to know. Movies, dinner, long walks in the park?"

"Check, check, and check. Okay, what's the catch?"

The question seemed to surprise him, but he quickly recovered. "No catch. We muddle through this thing together, like regular people, pass or fail. Obviously, I have a huge learning curve with the long-term deal, and I have to admit the idea scares me a little. You might get tired of putting up with me, but I'm willing to try, for you." Leaning forward, he gave her a slow, sexy kiss. "What do you think?"

"Mmm. I'd say the idea has promise," she mused, warming inside.

His gaze darkened. "There are things you don't know about me. Things that might change your mind—"

"Relax, Howie." She patted his hand. "It's a little early for the buzz kill."

"But—"

"Are you wanted by the IRS or FBI?"

"Um, no."

"Being sued for child support by a former fling?"

He flinched. "Not even possible."

"Do you have warts on your ass or a penis the size of a number-two pencil?"

Howard's mouth began to curve upward in response to her teasing. "*Definitely* not."

"STDs?"

He laughed aloud, threw a wad of dead grass at her head. "Brat."

"Then the rest can wait. All in good time, right?"

Howard studied her for a long moment, sobering. "I suppose it can," he said, sounding relieved. He stood, offered his hand. "I guess we should go clean up our mess."

With a twinge of disappointment, she accepted his hand and pulled herself up. Stalling a bit, she shook the grass out of her hair and brushed off her jeans. Though they'd been gone quite a while, the hours had passed quickly. The sun was beginning to dip in the sky. A wonderful interlude, over much too soon.

She followed him down the path to their picnic site. He scooped up the sack with their leftovers, tossed the empty water bottles inside, and retrieved his denim jacket.

"Ready?" His expression was closed, unreadable.

"Sure." Not.

On the walk back to the Harley, Howard went quiet. He dumped the sack into a garbage can by the parking lot, but at least he took her hand in his.

What was going on in his head? The second thoughts of a serial bachelor? Or was he brooding about his secrets and how she might react once they got to know each other better?

Everyone has a past. Besides, the lieutenant had been nothing but thoughtful and kind. He'd brought her pleasure all afternoon, while denying himself the one thing she knew for a fact he wanted.

Howard Paxton was a *good* man.

Too good to be true.

They walked right past him. Never noticed death lounging at a table no more than twenty feet from the lieutenant's ride.

"Well, looky here." Frank grinned, lighting a smoke. "Caught up in paradise already."

Almost made him feel sorry for the big sonofabitch. He knew firsthand the hell a man's faithless whore could put him through.

Course, sympathy for the almighty Howard Paxton might come easier if the bastard weren't responsible for every goddamned thing going to shit. All his fault.

He'd pay. Watching him suffer as Frank fucked over his life was going to be a riot. Seeing the shock on his face when he figured out who and why, as satisfying as a pair of lips sucking his cock.

Watching the horror fade from the motherfucker's eyes as he died, orgasmic.

"Play the game, Frankie boy."

All things in good fuckin' time.

6

Kat.

Sweet Jesus Christ, she was good for him.

Too good.

Howard had never been so confused in his life. This was why he'd sworn off women. Better for his boring existence to roll along like an unfunny version of *Groundhog Day* than to set himself up for rip-your-guts-out pain somewhere down the line. Better to float in a cocoon of numbness than to have your balls clamped in a vise by a green-eyed kitten with brains and a body that set him on fire.

By God, he didn't understand the female mind, probably never would. She'd stopped him from confessing his darkest secrets. Maybe, deep down, she didn't want to know the truth. And what *was* the truth?

Easy. A woman like Kat would want forever, eventually. But Howard couldn't go there.

Emily Jean's cute, pudgy face, the sweet way she'd held her arms out to her mother, rose in his mind. Broke his heart. How was he supposed to say he wasn't *able* to give that precious gift to Kat, or to any woman, no matter how badly he might want to?

Second, what lady wanted to be jolted awake by her lover's night terrors? Worse, letting someone in on his problems meant sharing his vulnerabilities. Intimacy.

God, he'd nearly spilled his guts. How had she gotten past his defenses?

Because she'd been so damned easy to talk to. Today, he'd told her more about his past than he'd ever revealed to anyone, except Sean. The problem was, Kat deserved more than a head case she had to fix. Hell, he couldn't even address his parents as *Mom and Dad*, for God's sake.

Best to forget Kat before both of them got hurt.

He repeated this mantra during the ride back to her apartment. Lined up all the heady nights in her arms like tempting shots of whiskey he'd never touch.

One taste. Just one sip of her in his mouth, teasing his tongue, and he was a goner. Every bit as intoxicating and ten times as potent as alcohol must be to those who indulged.

Outside Kat's place, he shut off the engine. He couldn't tell her good-bye above the noise, and the manners Georgie had drilled into him as a boy wouldn't allow him to simply dump her and drive off.

He knew better than anyone how lousy it felt to be ditched.

Kat slid off the back, took off the helmet. Held it out. "Well, thanks. For today. I, um . . ." She bit her lower lip, as though sensing his withdrawal.

He wanted to bite it, too.

"I'll walk you to the door." He took the helmet from her, then removed his own.

"No, you don't have to." She dug in her front pocket, removed her key. "I'm sure you have a million things to do."

"Nothing that can't wait." Whatever the right answer was, that wasn't it. *Idiot.*

"All right." With a shrug, she turned and shuffled toward the door, leaving him to follow. Or not. Frowning, he left the helmets behind and hurried after her. In the wake of her retreat, his gallant intention to say "so long" disintegrated faster than a five-alarm blaze at a paper factory.

She stuck the key in the lock, hesitated. The bewilderment shadowing her heart-shaped face when she turned drove through his chest like a serrated knife. A gorgeous mouth like hers was made for laughter, kissing, any number of wicked things. But not drooping as though she'd lost her best friend.

"You're in full retreat mode." Her direct gaze pinned him like a butterfly to a corkboard. "Did I say or do something wrong?"

"God, no. Not a chance." He shook his head, gave her a rueful smile. "Whatever's going on with me are my problems, not yours. Sorry if I came across like Rod the Jerk."

She laughed then, a soft tinkle caressing his skin, skimming each vertebra along his back with silky fingers. "Oh, you'd never be in danger of walking in his polished loafers. The two of you couldn't be more polar opposites."

"A good thing?"

"Like you need to ask."

There you are. Ball is in your court, Six-Pack.

"Well, I should go." Saying it aloud made him miserably unhappy.

"Will I . . . see you again?" Her tone gave her away, even if her expression didn't. Breathy. Hopeful.

His for the asking.

"Tomorrow night? Dinner at my house?"

Kat's beautiful face lit, righting the world again. "Monday's a school night, but I'll manage."

Yesss! "I go on shift Tuesday morning myself, so we'll keep it reasonable. Why don't you come over around six thirty and we'll eat at seven."

"Sounds great. What should I bring?"

"Nothing but yourself, beautiful. One thing firefighters can do really well, among many, is cook." His chest puffed out and he couldn't keep the smug satisfaction off his face.

In spite of his unresolved issues, the real deal was within his reach. Kat was willing to take a chance. On *him*. Every last stupid thought of letting her go without a fight went belly-up.

And Howard Paxton was nothing if not a fighter.

"Directions?"

"I'll call you tonight," he said, brushing a tendril of hair from her face. Jesus, he couldn't keep his paws off her. Didn't want to try. He'd been an idiot to believe otherwise.

"Good. Gives me an excuse to talk to you before I go to sleep."

He nearly groaned at the image of her in bed, white-blond hair fanned across her pillow, pleased at the sound of his voice. "Baby, you don't need an excuse. Any hour, any way you want me, I'm yours."

Kat's amazing green eyes flashed with very real hunger an instant before his lips captured hers. Nice and easy. His tongue stroking the inside of her mouth just as he would someplace else on her curvy body, hot and wet.

His balls grew heavy, his beleaguered shaft throbbing once more. Aching. Tomorrow night had never seemed so far off. He had to stop now, before this wild, combustible spark ignited and left them both decimated.

Breaking the kiss, he pulled back, wondering whether he'd have to seek relief later. Alone. Because, by God, it was damned painful to stand this close and not scoop up Kat, carry her inside, and make love to her. All evening.

All night.

"Talk to you later." He fingered the stray, shiny lock of hair. Even windblown, wearing hardly a stitch of makeup, she looked cute as hell.

As he turned and headed down the sidewalk, he didn't think she planned to answer.

"You're a good man, Lieutenant."

Howard froze. Looked over his shoulder. Slowly, his lips curved upward. "Not *that* good, sweetheart."

"I wouldn't have you any other way." She punctuated her retort by giving him a once-over that sent his blood pressure into the stratosphere.

He was still chuckling to himself as she went inside and closed the door. After securing her helmet behind his seat, he climbed on the bike and revved it up. Took the roll of Pez out of his shirt pocket and popped a candy into his mouth. He pulled out of the parking lot onto the street, already thinking about his grocery list for dinner tomorrow.

Wondering if he should rent them a movie on a school night.

And almost missed what had to be the oldest Buick Regal on the planet.

The same car he'd seen hulking a few spaces from his Harley when he and Kat left the riverside park. The ancient vehicle with peeling puke green paint had to be the same one, didn't it? Christ knows there couldn't be two identical cars in the county so butt-ugly.

As he drove past where the car was parked next to the curb across the street, a dark-haired man inside ducked his head, cupping his hand to light a cigarette.

Howard went cold. All freaking over. Just like he had last night at the residence fire that ended in a gruesome death. As though some unknown entity not only walked across his grave, but stopped and spit on it, as well.

In his side mirror, he saw the Buick leave the curb and head in the opposite direction.

Shaking his head, he quelled the willies with an effort. People's worlds collided, often more than once. Nothing weird or threatening about coincidence.

Nothing whatsoever.

* * *

Howard was on his third series of reps at half past midnight when he remembered. The envelope, stuck in his front door. He'd forgotten all about it.

Carefully, he set the silver weight bar in the holder—yeah, Sean would be ticked to see his best friend lifting without a spotter again—and wiggled from underneath before sitting up on the padded bench.

Grabbing a nearby towel, he wiped the sweat off his face and bare chest. Tossing it at the chair in the corner, and missing, he stood and strode from the workout room and down the short hall into the living room, rolling his shoulders as he went.

He was getting too old for this crap, staying up half the night, working his ass off to make himself tired enough to sleep four or five hours. As a trained paramedic, he was all for drugs if they helped, but he'd been living with insomnia for so long, he didn't see the point. Maybe he was far too stubborn to let his demons win.

Or maybe, if he were honest, the horror of being trapped in his nightmares, unable to awaken, was sufficient threat to keep him from reaching for even the mildest sleep aid.

The white, letter-sized envelope fluttered to the porch when he opened the front door. As he bent to retrieve it, his name printed on the front in a plain computer font sent a chill racing through him that had nothing to do with the bite of the fall night air swirling in to steal his warmth. Not just his name, but his rank.

Lieutenant Howard Paxton.

Creepy. For a split second, he had the fleeting thought that he shouldn't have touched the thing, though he wasn't sure why. Shutting out the cold, he locked up and walked into the living room, studying both sides of the envelope. Ordinary. Blank. Except for the name, printed like that.

Lowering himself to the sofa, he tore open the seal. Peered inside.

And lifted out a single photograph.

For a moment he couldn't comprehend what he saw. Had trouble getting air into his lungs. Making sense out of the impossible. His brain misfired like a bad starter on a car before catching hold. Staring at the picture, he gasped.

"Jesus Christ Almighty."

A naked woman. Propped up and handcuffed to a bed, each wrist fastened to the headboard railing on either side of her. Her chin was tilted up, back arched, nipples thrust through long dark hair, knees bent with her heels planted into the mattress. Her legs were open wide for the camera, revealing a thick triangle at the apex of her thighs, the pink flesh of her gleaming sex.

"My God."

Who would take a perverted photograph like this, then leave it in his door? With his freaking *name* on it?

Julian? No. No damned way. Even Salvatore's warped idea of a joke didn't lean toward anything this disturbing. He shook his head. Not disturbing. Sick.

Something was off about this photo, besides the fact some perv left it as a present. Squinting at the woman's face, he wondered what bothered him, outside the obvious. What was missing? And then the realization smacked him in the head.

Arousal. Howard knew what a woman who was enjoying herself ought to look like, and the tight-lipped, hollow expression on this lady's beautiful face wasn't it. Her eyes were . . . empty. Resigned. She might've been a mannequin, or a stoned-out druggie posed for a BDSM magazine.

Or a woman who knew she was about to die.

A memory seized him. Skyler, stumbling from the smoldering house. Retching on the front lawn.

A b-body, in the master bedroom. It's h-handcuffed to the fucking bed.

Charred beyond recognition.

His hands began to shake. This wasn't happening. The person who died last night couldn't be the lady in this photo, because why in God's name would anyone deposit a lewd picture of the possible homicide victim on his porch?

He laid the awful image on the coffee table. Went straight to the phone, hit Skyler on speed dial. He had the whole team programmed in there, in case of emergency. This more than qualified.

Skyler answered on the third ring, fumbling with the receiver. "Yeah?" he croaked, voice raspy with sleep.

"It's me. Howard. Sorry to interrupt your shut-eye, kid. You awake?"

"Um . . . yeah. I mean yes, sir." More fumbling, and a huge sigh. "What can I do for you, Lieutenant?"

His grip on the phone tightened. "I need to ask you a couple of questions about last night. The fire and the body. You with me?"

"Got it." A loud yawn. "Whatcha need to know?"

"You dealing okay?"

A hesitation. "I'm good." The unspoken afterthought, *considering*, fell between them like a rock.

"Most guys go years before having to work a scene like that. Some get lucky and never do."

"I'm fine. Sir." More bite this time.

Relief washed over him. The kid would be all right. "Glad to hear it. Listen, I need you to tell me about the bedroom where you and Eve discovered the body. Start with describing the bed." Silence. "Tommy?"

"What for?"

"Humor me."

"The bed. Right. Ah, king-sized. Dark, maybe cherrywood. Massive, with stout posts. Paneled headboard with a fancy metal railing across the top. It had, I dunno, curly vines, leaves, and shit in the pattern."

Somehow, Howard's feet carried him over to the coffee table. He stood, turned to stone, staring down at the photo he wasn't going to touch again. "Were the victim's wrists fastened by the cuffs through the metal vines?"

"Yes," Tommy said slowly. Suspicious now. "How did you know that when you didn't go upstairs?"

"What about beside the bed? Was there a night-stand?" he asked hoarsely, as though he'd sucked in a gallon of smoke.

"Two. There was an ashtray on the right-hand nightstand as we were looking at the bed."

Staring at the ashtray in the photo, cigarette perched casually on the lip, Howard fought the sudden urge to throw up. "Cigarette?"

"The room was fully involved with flames, sir. With all due respect, we didn't have time to take inventory. What's this about?" Then, softly, "Am I in trouble?"

"No, it's nothing like that."

"What—"

"I'll explain when I see you Tuesday on shift." If the whole fire department hadn't gotten wind of this before then. Which they probably would. "Get some sleep, Skyler."

"Yes, sir," Tommy muttered, baffled and apparently unhappy about the lack of answers.

The next call went to the police. The bored dispatcher perked up considerably after Howard stated his situation. Claiming you might have evidence tied to a homicide tended to get peoples' juices flowing.

He waited for the cops, confused. Sick at heart. *Why, why, why?* drummed in his skull, pulsed at his temples. He prayed that the authorities had some leads by now, perhaps an idea why this atrocity was left at his door.

But when they arrived the police were rude and

sarcastic. The fact that they were addressing a lieutenant in the fire department meant zilch to these
pricks. Starsky and Hutch fired off the same fifty questions Howard had been asking himself for the last half
hour. They got nowhere and didn't like it.

"Whether or not this woman is the victim from our
fire last night, I don't know her, never met her,"
Howard reiterated. They'd refused the seats he'd offered, so he remained standing also, unwilling to allow
them to loom over him. He crossed his arms over his
chest, spine straight, feet spread, face hard, the exact
stance he employed when the team needed a good ass
chewing. He looked big, intimidating, and he knew it.
They didn't like that, either.

He didn't give a damn.

Officer Peters, the Starsky of the duo, flipped
through his notes. The pencil-nosed cop didn't notice
his interviewee curling a lip at his bad 1970s 'fro. "Let
me get this straight. You saw the envelope in your
front door this afternoon, but didn't stop to get it because you had a *date*."

The cop emphasized the last word as though he
doubted this was the truth. Howard ran his tongue
across his teeth, biting back a retort. "Correct. I didn't
think to retrieve it until about a half hour ago."

"After you ate dinner, called your girlfriend to
make plans for tomorrow night—or technically
tonight—and worked out."

Well, Kat wasn't his girlfriend. Yet. "Right." Better
to keep this simple.

Peters looked up, spearing Howard with shrewd,
beady little eyes. The guy likely never believed a word
he heard anymore. "Assuming this woman is our
homicide vic, why would someone, presumably the
killer, taunt you personally with her photo? You claim
not to have known or met her, and you didn't even go
inside to witness the murder scene. Your captain is

first in command, so if the taunt was directed at the fire department, why not address the envelope to Tanner? Better yet, why not just send it to Chief Mitchell?"

He didn't miss the deliberate use of the term "murder scene." He knew the arson and homicide divisions were already holding hands. Digging deep. And he'd just handed them a bomb. God knows what any of this meant and who'd get caught in the explosion.

"I'm sort of hoping you guys can answer those questions, Officer Peters. I'm not a detective. I've given you what I've got and told you what I know, which isn't squat."

Peters and his string-bean partner, Holden, exchanged a glance. The former flipped his notebook closed. "All right. I'd say we're spinning our wheels for now. The homicide detective in charge of the case will want to talk to you and your team. Probably tomorrow. You're off shift?"

Fantastic. "Until Tuesday morning at seven."

"Might want to keep yourself available." This from Holden, who seemed to feel the need to interject something important.

Jesus save them all if these two fools represented Sugarland's finest hope for truth and justice. "Gee, guess I'll have to cancel my one-way ticket to the Bahamas."

Both snapped their gazes to Howard. He smiled. They pursed their lips as though they'd bitten into a lemon.

Peters took the photo and envelope in a plastic bag as evidence and they left. Howard sagged against the door, his facade of in-control tough guy draining through his feet and into the floor. None of this made sense, and out of sheer self-preservation, he wasn't sure he wanted it to.

Mental snapshots from the past twenty-four hours launched an assault.

The fire, and the eerie prickle on the back of his neck.

A lone figure, standing under the tree in his front yard.

An old green Buick. At the park.

Near Kat's apartment. *Oh, God.*

A man inside the car, ducking his face.

Lighting a cigarette.

The awful photo. A woman's dead eyes.

A cigarette on the nightstand.

On trembling legs, Howard checked every door. Made sure the house was locked tight. In his bedroom, he removed his tennis shoes and socks, pulled off the T-shirt he'd put on before the police arrived. Stripped off his loose nylon workout shorts.

The hot shower didn't do much to relieve the cold in his bones. He couldn't get warm. No matter how long he stood under the steamy spray, he couldn't wash away a growing horror. The kind that seeped in almost without notice. Like a venomous snake, slithering toward a man's ankles in the dark. Masked until its deadly strike.

He wasn't a stupid man. For whatever reason, someone had him scoped on their radar, and the bastard wanted him to know. Message sent and received.

Had a killer been watching him with Kat? Why? In order to taunt him before he captured and burned her to death like he'd done to the other woman?

"My God." He shut off the water and stumbled from the shower, grabbing a towel from the rack on the wall and wrapping it around his hips.

Hurrying for the kitchen and the phone book, he dribbled a wet trail across his house but didn't care. He'd write Kat's number on a sticky note this time, and memorize it. Item in hand, he jogged back to the bedroom.

Spying the phone on the nightstand, he sat heavily

on the bed and snatched the handset. Punched in her number. Waited, heart racing.

"Um, hello?"

She's all right. He sagged, resting his elbows on his knees, dropping his chin. "It's Howard. Sorry to wake you, sweetheart."

"Howard?" Kat repeated sleepily. "What time is it?"

"Going on two in the morning. I just needed to hear your voice." How lame was that? But he couldn't blurt out the real reason for his call. He might be completely off base, jumping at shadows. He'd scare her for nothing and she'd believe her new guy was a head case.

Maybe she'd be right.

"Aren't you sweet?" she said, low and husky. "You, however, don't have to be at work by seven thirty to deal with a class full of miniature hellions all day."

"Call in sick. Spend the day with me." An inspired idea. He longed to hold her. Let her soothe away the nightmares with her hands, her luscious body. Take her up on the offer he'd bypassed during their interlude. Jeez, did he sound as desperate as he felt?

"Whispered the devil into her ear." A pause, then she sighed with regret. "I can't, though. Even if I had plans in order, we have two teachers on my team who'll be out for all-day training. If I ditch, that leaves the other two to handle three substitutes."

Disappointment speared his chest, although he admired her work ethic. He rarely called in, either, unless he really was ill. "Hey, no problem."

"Rain check on the skip day?"

"Absolutely."

"I'm looking forward to dinner, Howard." Her voice softened, almost shy.

"Same here. Say, forget six thirty. Come over as soon as you can." Lord, this lady was fast becoming a fever in his blood. He heard the smile in her answer.

"I'd love that. School's out at three thirty. If I sneak

right out and go home to change, I can be at your house by four thirty. Does that work?"

Oh yeah. "You bet. I'll count the hours."

"Me, too. Night, Howard."

"Good night, beautiful."

Placing the phone in the cradle, he shivered. Little water droplets clung to his freezing skin. Well, one place on his body wasn't cold anymore. His renegade cock rose between his splayed thighs, poking at the towel around his waist. Just the sound of her voice aroused him to the point of agony. Blue balls? Forget it. Try a nice shade of eggplant.

He dried off quickly. Leaving his hair damp, he sprawled on the bed, hands clasped behind his head, forgoing the boxers he usually wore. Scowling at the ceiling, he wondered whether Kat alone had him in a vise, or if his neglected libido would respond this violently to *any* woman after a year of celibacy.

Anyone might do to ease his pent-up sexual energy. The notion didn't quite ring true, but he needed to find out almost as much as he craved release. And there was only one way to test his theory without anybody getting hurt.

Spreading his legs, he lay with his arms resting at his sides. Let himself sink into the mattress. Closed his eyes. Breathed deep, exhaled, crawling into the memory.

The redhead. The last lady "friend" he'd brought home, the one who didn't eat breakfast. Not food, anyway. They'd met at his fitness club. She was supermodel, drop-dead gorgeous. He was lonely. He took her for a ride on the Harley, bought her the helmet. They'd wound up here, in his bed, for two days. He'd used her—and willingly allowed her to use him—in wicked ways guaranteed to make even Jules gape in shock.

He'd always been an intensely sexual man. He might lead a pretty safe, vanilla lifestyle in most aspects. But never, ever in the bedroom. Here, all bets were off. He needed touch, sensation, like a man must have air to breathe. Skin on skin. He loved taking a woman hard and fast, or slow and gentle. He loved letting her take him, too. Any way she wanted.

Lady's choice.

And so she had. Janine—or Janice?—had straddled his hips, coppery bush tickling his belly. She leaned over him, small breasts and long red hair grazing his chest, and whispered in his ear. He must keep his arms by his sides, she'd ordered. Must not touch himself, or her. He'd remain compliant to her wishes, or their game was over.

She kissed his neck, throat, chest. Licked a trail down his belly. Kneeling between his spread thighs, she cupped his sac in skilled fingers, hefting the twin weights with a purr of feminine approval. Squeezing.

Heat pooling in his groin, Howard groaned at the recollection of Janine's mouth surrounding his shaft. A warm, wet glove sheathing him to the base, sucking hard. Lost, he'd raised his hips off the bed. Encouraged the slender hand working between his ass cheeks, the moist finger massaging his entrance. Delving inside. A dark, decadent indulgence for them both, one only a woman was allowed to give. The tigress in her exulted in this delicious power over him.

In spite of his innate dominance, the male in him loved giving over that power to her.

The phantom redhead sucked, licked, penetrated him. Any man's wild fantasy come true. Still, vague dissatisfaction mired him in the here and now. He couldn't get beyond the pleasurable ache in his tormented erection, couldn't totally lose himself as he'd done before. She'd meant nothing to him and vice versa, and he suddenly knew, without a single doubt, if she were in his bed this second he'd have to send her home.

No, any woman would *not* do.

He freed his mind to roam where it desired. The

hair cascading over his lap became flaxen silk, the cat eyes gazing at him from between his legs green as cut emeralds. Her plump breasts bounced in rhythm to her ministrations on his cock, his ass.

"Kat." He moaned, his body heating like a torch. God, yes, to have Kat working him, doing those things to his body, he'd promise anything. Whatever she wanted. However she wished. He'd gladly be hers, only hers, now. Next week, next year. Always.

Come boiled in his balls, shot from the base of his spine.

"Ahhhh, God! Yes!"

He erupted like Mount St. Helens, came with more violence than ever before. On and on, thick rivulets of semen jetting over his flat belly. When the last of the tremors subsided, he lay panting, blinking in amazement as his room came into focus. If this was how he exploded from simply imagining Kat's hands and mouth on him, he could hardly wait for fantasy to meet reality.

Christ, he hadn't even once touched himself.

Nope, no other lady for him.

Whistling, he pushed aside ominous thoughts of arson and murder. Notes and stalkers. Tomorrow, the terrible sense of approaching doom would begin to fade. None of that had anything to do with him or Kat. A crackpot, most likely. An isolated incident.

"Katherine McKenna," he said aloud. Liked how her name sounded on his lips. "You're *mine,* angel."

The grin stayed fixed on his face as he showered again, pulled on his favorite boxers, and slid between the crisp sheets. Sleep descended fast for a change, deep and content.

For a while.

Until a monster pursued a terrified little boy through his mother's garden.

And caught him.

7

Homicide Detective Shane Ford turned out to be a pretty cool guy, despite Howard's initial dread of the meeting. A tall, lean man in his mid-thirties with over-long sable hair, keen intelligence in his gray eyes, and an easy smile, Ford dispelled most of Howard's tension over talking with the cops.

Unlike Peters and Holden, the detective was courteous, taking him patiently through the night of the fire and the events leading up to this morning, including Kat's involvement and their first date. Though Howard's concerns seemed ridiculous in the light of day, he told Ford about the fleeting glimpse of what he believed was someone in his front yard, and the reappearing ugly green Buick.

Ford, to his credit, treated his disclosures seriously in light of the awful photograph. Seated in Howard's living room in a leather chair, the detective tapped a ballpoint pen on his knee, studying his notes with a slight frown.

"I assume you have reason to believe the woman in the photo is the victim from the fire," Howard said, taking advantage of the lapse. "Or you wouldn't be here."

Ford looked up, nodded. "I do. The room in the picture appears to be identical to the Hargraves' bedroom. Besides, the woman in question matches the description of a woman reported missing yesterday by her husband. Dental records should settle the ID today, one way or the other."

"Jesus."

"Yeah."

God, he wished Tommy and Eve hadn't seen the charred remains. Still, better anyone other than Sean, who hadn't returned his phone call this morning. "Why bother to burn her? The killer obviously didn't care about concealing her identity."

"Punishment, retribution, or for a sick thrill. Any number of twisted reasons." The detective spread his hands. "Why'd the bastard throw the murder in your face? Maybe he picked you at random, but we don't know enough to speculate at this point."

"The head game with me could've been an afterthought. I could've been anyone. He might move on and forget about me." Sounded good, but Howard wasn't certain he believed the claim even as he tossed it out.

Ford's lips thinned. "We'll know soon enough. A sociopath isn't going to stop killing. He'll either raise the stakes, or move to another hunting ground and we'll never hear from him again."

Both of those options sucked. His burgeoning hope that the killer would simply disappear deflated. If the psycho left town, it might take years, if ever, for him to be caught. In the meantime, the bastard would kill as before, in another county or state. Howard's creepy problem resolved. . . . At the expense of countless victims and any leads the cops might've gained.

Recalling the mystery woman's hollow resignation staring at him from the photo, guilt assailed him for his selfishness. He'd never backed off from trouble like a lily-livered little pissant, and he wasn't going to start now. If some sick puppy insisted on bringing this filth to his door, he'd find out who and why. When he did, the perv had better pray the cops got to him first.

Ford stood, concluding his visit. "I won't keep you. I need to get in touch with Miss McKenna about the fire and the pickup truck she saw leaving the area."

"She already told all that to the cop who showed up." He hated the thought of Kat being put through the drill again.

"The officer gave me his notes." The detective gave Howard a speculative look. "But I prefer getting her observations in person. Once the drama passes, people often recall details they hadn't before and don't even realize are important. Since Miss McKenna was gone by the time I arrived on the scene, and I couldn't reach her yesterday, I need to talk with her as soon as possible."

Made sense. He didn't have to be thrilled about it, though. The idea of the spotlight being put on her as the only possible witness to murder scared the hell out of him.

"Detective . . . do you think she might be in any sort of danger from this sicko?"

"Wouldn't hurt for her to be careful for a while. Does she need to know about the photo? Tough call, but from a cop's viewpoint, the fewer details shared about a case early on, the better. Unless it becomes necessary, of course."

Yeah, that's what worried him. Keeping the creep's little present from her put him in a bad position, considering. Put her at a disadvantage, too.

Ford shook his hand, promising to be in touch, and left.

Howard paced the living room, wrestling with his conscience. Agonizing over what to do about Kat. Despite his reluctance to create lasting ties, she'd already gotten under his skin. He'd almost convinced himself he might have something positive to offer her, and now this. Despite his hopes, the truth wasn't easier to dismiss in the light of day.

A crazed murderer was playing games with his life.

A killer who might've been watching Kat. Good God, what was he going to do? Leave her protection to the police? Entrust her safety to bozos like Starsky and Hutch?

Not frigging likely.

"But the sick bastard won't get to her through *me*." Anger churned his gut. Let him try.

In the kitchen, Howard poured one more cup of coffee and glanced at the clock on the wall. Not quite nine thirty. He had time to run errands, come home and straighten the house, and get cleaned up for dinner with Kat. If he hauled butt.

Polishing off his coffee, he set the mug in the sink, then tried calling Sean. On the fourth ring, he winced as the answering machine picked up. Again.

Hi, you've reached Sean, Blair, Bobby, and Mia, each voice piped through the phone in merry greeting. Ghosts standing sad watch over Sean's empty house. *Leave your message at the beep.*

"Hey, bro. It's me again. Pick up the phone or I'm gonna come over there and kick in your door. Dammit, I mean it, Sean!" Nothing. He pinched the bridge of his nose in frustration. "I'll be there in twenty. If you get this message, call my cell."

Hanging up, an electric thrill of fear jolted him into action. Grabbing his wallet and the keys to his truck, he hurried out the door.

Please, God, let him hang on one more day. Don't let me find him dead.

A prayer he'd repeated several times a week for months. Something had to give. Sean had reached the crossroads and remained mired there, immobilized. His best friend would either survive the loss of his family, or he wouldn't.

A tall enough order for any man whose loved ones had been wiped out in one tragic twist of fate. Add the fact that Sean had been working overtime with the B-shift team instead of attending his son's varsity football game, had responded to a call leading him straight to the burning, mangled husk of a familiar car . . .

"You know they're not going to be okay when they don't cry," Clay, B-shift's FAO, remarked sadly to Howard after the funeral.

To this day, Sean had never cried. Not once.

He knew because they'd discussed it. Or rather, Howard beat his head against the wall while his friend shut down. Closed him and everyone else out. Sean wanted him to give up so he'd be free to drown.

Not gonna happen.

In minutes, he turned down the long gravel drive leading to Tanner's place. The sprawling log home came into view, a rustic jewel set against the beautiful, multicolored carpet of a Tennessee holler. Thirty acres of heaven Sean and Blair shaped into the perfect place to raise their children, now a hellish prison without bars.

His friend's Tahoe was parked next to the house. He pulled in behind it and shut off the engine. Stomach clenching in dread, he mounted the porch steps and pounded on the front door with his fist.

"Sean! Open the door!" Silence. He pounded again. *"Sean!"*

Dread morphed to panic. The frame splintered on the third kick, banging open like a gunshot. He ran through the living room, down the hall toward the back of the house. Halted in the doorway to Sean's bedroom, letting his eyes adjust to the gloom.

The odor hit him first. The sickly sweet stench of old vomit and despair. Gagging, he clamped a hand over his mouth and searched the room. The shades were drawn to block out the light, but he made out the tall form on the bed. Too still.

"Sean?" He moved closer, flipped on the bedside lamp. "Oh, my God."

Capsules littered the floor in front of the nightstand, along with the container and an empty fifth of Jack. Bending, he snatched the small bottle and read the label. Sleeping pills. *Sweet Jesus, no.*

Howard placed the medicine bottle on the nightstand. Heart in his throat, he sat next to Sean. Dressed in sweatpants and a plain white T-shirt, his friend was on his stomach, face turned away, covers tangled around his legs. Terrified, Howard laid a hand on his shoulder. Felt the slight rise and fall of even breathing.

Not dead. He could've wept with relief, but they weren't out of the woods yet. Shaking his friend, he said gruffly, "Wake up, buddy. Come on."

A muffled groan met his efforts. After several failed attempts to wake Sean, he hauled the man up by his shirt and rolled him over. Took one wrist, checked his pulse. Slow, but strong.

Sean stirred, moaned, lost in his private hell. "Nooo, don't go . . . Daddy's sorry . . ."

Howard closed his eyes briefly, heart twisting. Reaching out, he patted his friend's cheek. "Sean, it's me. Wake up."

The man's face was cadaver gray, a day's growth of whiskers shadowing his cheeks. At least he hadn't thrown up in bed, thank God, so the smell must be drifting from the bathroom. Surfacing from the depths of one nightmare into another, he blinked at Howard in confusion.

Sean's voice was the rasp of a rusty can. "What the fuck?"

"That's what I'd like to know, buddy."

"Howard?" He sounded unsure whether he might be dreaming.

"In the flesh."

"How'd—" He swallowed, turning an interesting shade of split pea soup. "How'd you get in here?"

"Let myself in."

"You don't . . . have a key."

"You don't have a front door."

Green eyes closed. "Shit."

He fell silent for a moment. Best to let his friend's brain cells start firing again before he gave him the third degree. He could almost see the wheels turning as Sean processed what he'd done to himself.

"When did you start bingeing?" Howard asked quietly.

Apparently uncomfortable having this conversation while flat on his back, Sean sat up. Slow. Eased himself to rest against the headboard. "What's today?"

"What day do you think it is?" He struggled to keep his temper under control. Anger borne of fear for the man he loved like a brother.

If possible, Sean's face sickened even more. "I . . . I don't know," he whispered, hanging his head in shame. "Did I miss the Tuesday shift?"

Cruel as it seemed, he allowed his friend to stew over the question before answering. Let the possibility loom thick and heavy in the air between them. "No. It's only Monday."

Sean blew out a breath, but said nothing.

Howard lifted the pill bottle from the nightstand with a shaking hand. "You wash some of these down with the Jack?"

Shuttered eyes met his. "I'm still here, aren't I?"

Howard's temper erupted. His hand shot out, grabbing the front of Sean's shirt. He yanked his friend close, got in his face. "Don't shut me down again! Not *me*!" he shouted, shaking him hard. "How many did you take? Answer me!"

Startled, Sean grabbed at the steely arm holding him fast. "Stop, goddammit!"

"Tell me!" Howard roared.

"Almost the whole bottle!" Tanner shouted back. Panting, he hesitated as the truth reverberated from the walls. Fell into the silence like a dead, stinking corpse. He went limp as Howard took him by the shoulders.

"I downed a handful," Sean said hoarsely, looking away in misery. "I don't remember much, but I changed my mind. Went to the bathroom and . . . took care of it."

God almighty. "Y-you tried to kill yourself." He knew his friend had been heading down this slope. They both knew. But to be faced with the truth of how far Sean had fallen was devastating. He felt blown apart.

"I didn't go through with it, Six-Pack."

"I would've found you. Don't you realize that?" His voice broke. He couldn't help it.

"I'm sorry." Sean's face was etched with sorrow. "Forgive me."

"You couldn't save them, old friend. No one could. Forgive *yourself.*" Tears threatened, and dammit, holding them back took all of his willpower. *I would've found my best friend dead.*

"I don't know how." Tanner shook his head, face crumpling. "The witnesses said Mia d-died screaming for D-Daddy to put out the f-fire. They couldn't get her out, Howard. I was too late. Too fucking late . . ."

He'd heard this before. But never from Sean's lips.

Unthinkable. Horrific. The killing thrust driven into a man's heart, stilling it forever.

He pulled Sean into his arms. Didn't care how the embrace might've looked to someone else, someone whose life had never taken a side trip through hell.

Neither spoke. Howard simply held the man who

was his brother in every respect save blood. Wished to God he could will a healthy dose of his strength into his lost friend. Were it possible, he'd siphon the life force out of his body, gladly give the last drop to Sean, just to see him smile again.

Howard pulled back first. "Get showered while I put on a pot of coffee."

Sean nodded and pushed from the bed, swaying unsteadily on his feet.

"Can you make it?"

"I think so." Sean didn't sound too sure.

"Good. 'Cause I draw the line at getting naked to hold you up in the shower, dude. I mean, we ain't even dating." There. Not quite a smile from his friend, but at least a relaxing of the white lines around his mouth.

Leaving Sean to his privacy for a few minutes, he busied himself putting on the coffee. This done, he returned to the bedroom, picked the remaining sleeping pills off the carpet, flushed them, and threw away the bottle.

Ten minutes later, Sean wobbled into the kitchen, brown hair damp, dressed in clean navy sweats and a Sugarland Fire Department T-shirt. He lowered himself to a chair across from Howard at the breakfast nook table, eyes downcast. Clearly shamed.

Howard fetched Tanner a mug of black coffee and pushed it to him, saying nothing. Waiting him out. What could he say to Sean that he hadn't a hundred times already?

Promise me you won't try that again, he wanted to yell. But he was too afraid of the answer. So they drank in silence, Sean sipping his coffee as though suspicious the stuff might not stay down. Finally, his friend lifted his gaze. Met his silent inquiry squarely.

"What will you do with this?" Sean's hand tightened on his mug. "Are you going to report me?"

Ah, here we are. The million-dollar question to

which there was no good answer. Get the higher-ups involved—and yeah, this would place Bentley in an awkward position—and a situation like this had the potential to take on a life of its own.

Howard set down his mug. Braced his elbows on the table, fisted his hands together. "How do *you* think I should handle this?"

"I can't ask you to cover for me. You should make a report." He sat like stone, expression grim, as though bracing himself for a blow.

"How do you *want* me to handle it?"

Misery darkened his eyes. "Give me another chance. A little more time. *Please.*"

"So I can rush out here and find you dead tomorrow? Next week?" Sean jerked as though he'd punched him in the gut, but neither of them could afford to be less than honest.

"God, no. That won't happen now. I swear—"

"You want to handle this without the department's interference, you gotta shape up. Take the Zoloft every day and throw out the booze," he ordered Sean in a tone that brooked no argument.

He sighed, gaze dropping to his hands. "Done."

"Get outside on your days off, mess around this beautiful place of yours. Mow your own damned front acreage so that poor old fart next door doesn't have to come over and do it. What is he, like, eighty-five?"

Sean flushed with embarrassment. "I get it. Shit."

He leaned forward. "Do you? Because I can't leave here without your promise to start making a real effort. My heart can't take another scare like when I busted in here, thinking you were dead."

"I'll try, but—"

Frustrated, he slapped the table so hard their coffee sloshed. "Your word, Sean."

"All right. I give you my word I'll do all of those things you mentioned. I'll do my best, I promise." He pinned Howard with a look of determination. "And there won't be a repeat of last night."

He meant every word, but they both knew the score. "You'll have more bad days, some as bad as yesterday or worse. And when you do, you'll call me, understand?"

"Yeah. And Six-Pack . . . thanks."

"That's what I'm here for, buddy." Digging in his front shirt pocket, he offered his roll of Pez.

Taking a handful, his friend popped a couple into his mouth, gratitude flickering across his face. Crunching the candy, he cocked his head thoughtfully. "So, what's up with you?"

"Not much. Why?"

"You're lying."

"What? How do you know?"

"You're scratching your chest. You always do that when you're lying your ass off."

Howard stopped scratching and scowled. "Do not."

"Do, too." Sean's lips quirked. "Come on, throw me a bone. Give me something to think about besides myself for a change."

He hesitated. Telling his friend about the creepy photo and the guy in the Buick would mean telling him about Kat as well. On the other hand, if he didn't spill, Sean would eventually find out from one of the guys. And he'd be hurt at being left out of the loop.

"I've started seeing someone."

Sean's brows lifted. "Since when?"

"Yesterday. Her name's Kat McKenna."

"The cute blond from the fire Saturday night?"

"One and the same."

Sean whistled in admiration. "Damn, boy, you work fast."

"I'm making dinner for her at my place tonight." He shrugged, downplaying the intensity of his combustible feelings for the woman for Sean's benefit. "Keeping things casual, seeing how it goes."

"Well, good luck. One of us deserves to be happy." Sean smiled, not quite covering the shadows lurking behind his expression.

He wasn't going there. His friend wasn't ready to hear that he deserved to be happy again, too. "There's more. When I got home from seeing Kat last night, I found a nasty-gram stuck in my front door."

"What kind? Jealous ex-lover?"

"Nope. Deranged killer."

That got Sean's undivided attention. "What the hell?"

When he finished explaining, Sean was gaping like a landed trout. "Basically, Detective Ford doesn't have a clue why the killer would leave me the victim's photo, and neither do I."

"Holy fuck. They're going to provide protection, right?"

"Based on what? Kat and I haven't actually been threatened."

"What? If leaving you a picture of a woman taken before he killed her isn't a threat, I don't know what is!"

"You and me both." He met Sean's worried gaze. "Hey, this might be a sick prank. Or a fluke. Maybe it's not the same lady at all. I'm not gonna bust my nuts unless it happens again."

"Have you told Kat?"

"No, and I'm not planning to just yet. No need to freak her out if it's nothing."

Sean didn't look convinced. Hell, he wasn't, either. At least his buddy got what he wanted. He had something else to think about now, in spades.

Howard stood. "You gonna be okay after I leave?"

"I'll be fine."

Sean sounded stronger, steadier than he had in

months. Howard wasn't certain whether leaving him was safe, but to hover too much risked undermining his miniscule progress.

"All right," he said. "See you on shift in the morning."

Sean walked him to the front door, grimacing when he saw the damage. "Jeez, you ripped a solid oak door right out of the frame."

"I'll call someone to come fix it this afternoon."

"No. This is my fault. Besides, now I've got something productive to do." He flashed a rare sincere smile that died just as quickly. "Thanks for keeping my screwup in the family."

Howard pulled him into a bear hug, slapped his back. "You bet, my friend. I'm here, anytime you need me."

Only time would tell whether he'd made the right decision.

If he hadn't, he'd never forgive himself.

8

Kat's Monday was par for the course. Run, run, with not one second to spare. Too much to accomplish and not enough hours to get the tasks completed. With a parent conference scheduled during her normal planning time, lunch was her only break all day.

Or would've been, if Detective Shane Ford hadn't dropped by and used every one of her precious twenty-five minutes to ask questions about what she'd witnessed Saturday night. The cop was charming and polite, and the conversation pretty painless. She didn't have much to reveal, although he seemed pleased by her description of the dark truck.

All told, an exhausting start to a new week. But she couldn't complain. In fact, the closer the big hand crept toward three thirty, the more her spirits lifted. Soon she'd see her big, sexy firefighter again.

At home, she freshened up, shedding her sedate khaki pants and rust-colored sweater. Quickly, she ran the razor over her legs and underarms. Not that she *planned* on allowing the sexiest man in the state to have his wicked way with her. Rule number one in the Girl Code: *hairless legs and pits at all times, ladies. You never know when you might land in the hospital.*

Or be swept into the strong arms of a six-foot-six hunk of smoldering, sexy man.

Refreshed after a brief shower, she toweled off, slipped on a matching silk bra and bikini panties of emerald green, and padded to the closet. Selecting a pair of black pants, black leather ankle boots, and a green blouse, she dressed and reapplied her small amount of makeup in record time. Last, she swept her hair into a twist and secured the mass with a large gold clip.

Turning around, she eyed herself critically in the mirror. Too dressy for eating in, but she wanted to look good for the lieutenant. She wasn't used to pleasing anyone except herself with her appearance these days, and she hoped Howard would be pleased.

So what if he wasn't? She wouldn't compare herself to her older sister, like Rod had been fond of doing. She was happy in her own skin. Unlike Grace, Kat was short, curvy, and stacked. Nothing would ever change that fact. Yesterday, Howard certainly hadn't seemed to mind.

Flushing, she thought of their interlude on the scenic overlook. Good God, she'd nearly made love with the man in broad daylight! Anyone could've stumbled upon them doing the horizontal bop, and the naughty idea sent a shiver of forbidden delight to her toes.

"Girl, you've got it bad."

On the drive to Howard's, her nerves jumped in anticipation of having the yummy man all to herself. No park filled with people, barking dogs, and kids to rescue. Just the two of them. Food for thought that had her body tingling all over, excitement building like steam in a pressure cooker.

She turned onto his street, pleasantly surprised by his neighborhood. The homes were older, small, but well maintained. Neat lawns boasted trim shrubs, and flowers burst everywhere to contrast with the fall colors.

Howard's home was red brick, with pansies edging

the sidewalk and encircling the large oak in his yard. She pulled her Beamer into the drive in front of his garage and shut off the engine, staring. The mental image of a behemoth of a man on his knees, holding the delicate stems and roots in his huge hands, planting them in the soil with loving care, did something strange and wonderful to her insides.

She rang the doorbell and waited on the porch, seized by the weird notion that her life was about to change forever. The powerful feeling was almost enough to make her turn and run—then she heard heavy steps approaching.

Howard opened the door, smiling broadly. "Hey, come in!" He stepped aside to let her in, raking her with an appreciative gaze. "You look beautiful."

"Thank you." She eyed him from his spiky two-toned hair to his bare feet. He'd dressed nicely in tan Dockers and a crisp navy and beige–striped button-down shirt, open at his tanned throat. The shirt stretched across his massive chest and the pants hugged muscled thighs to mouth-watering perfection. "So do you, handsome."

Delicious enough to eat with a spoon.

Shying away from the compliment, he waved a hand in the general direction of the living room. "Set your purse down anywhere. I'll show you around—not that there's much to see."

"You've got to be kidding. Your place is super, and a lot bigger than my dinky apartment." She walked over to place her purse on the coffee table. Right next to a wooden bowl full of Pez. Dozens of rolls of them. She smiled.

He shrugged. "It's home."

But she saw how he straightened, the light of pride glowing in his soulful chocolate eyes. This modest little house was his haven, and he wanted to impress her.

He succeeded. Oh, it wasn't a decorator's showplace or anything close. But the house was tidy, attractive, and the masculine touches in leather and earth shades were all Howard. His overwhelming presence, his spicy scent with a hint of musk, permeated every nook and cranny, tantalizing her nose. Raising her feminine awareness of him.

Walking over to the brick fireplace, Kat ran a finger down the edge of a framed portrait sitting in the center of the mantel, surrounded by various smaller photos. An attractive older couple beamed from the portrait. The large man was fit and handsome, with salt-and-pepper hair, contrasting with the pretty, petite brunette at his side.

"Your parents?"

"Yes, that's Bentley and Georgie." The warmth in his voice was unmistakable.

"They make a fabulous-looking couple."

"They're fabulous people."

She peered at the chief. "You resemble Bentley. Big frame, square jaw, brown eyes."

"We get that a lot. Most folks don't realize I was adopted."

Lips curving up, she studied the smaller snapshots. One was a group photo of six firefighters lined up in front of an engine, five of them men, and one lovely woman with lightly bronzed skin. Black or Hispanic, Kat couldn't tell. Her dark hair was pulled back from an angular face with striking features, complementing a slender runner's build. Kat marveled at any woman being able to pass the grueling physical tests required to become a firefighter. Tests geared toward men. How did the woman compete in a male-oriented environment?

The team smiled for the camera, arms draped over each other's shoulders, the lieutenant towering above the others. If mutual love and respect could be made tangible without words, this picture told the tale of the team's closeness.

"My brothers," he said simply.

Kat tapped on the photo. "And sister."

Howard cocked his head. "Maybe I thought that way in the beginning, when Eve was new. But now I can't say I think about her any differently from the guys. Although she has her own quarters with her own bunk for propriety's sake, Marshall's just one of us." Howard's easy manner suggested there wasn't anything between him and Eve, and never had been.

Interesting. And a bit of a relief, though, under pain of torture she wouldn't admit to the brief flash of jealousy.

"The rest?"

He pointed at the picture, starting from the left. "Next to Eve is Tommy Skyler, and you've met Zack, who took over as the FAO when I made lieutenant. The Hispanic dude is Julian Salvatore, our resident pain in the ass. The tall, brown-haired guy on the other end is my best friend, Sean Tanner."

Howard's voice hitched on Sean's name. Kat glanced at him, catching the look of pure grief, such profound sadness it took her breath away. His melancholy statement from the day before came rushing in.

Sometimes, no matter how strong you thought you were, the damage takes you out of the game.

"The ex-Marine." She put an arm around his waist, hugging him. "Taking a wild guess here, but is Sean the friend with the sad story you referred to?"

With a heavy sigh, he put an arm around her shoulders, tucking her close. "Yeah. His family was killed in a car accident several months ago. His son, a senior in high school, was driving them home from his football game instead of riding back with his team on the bus, and ran into the back of a stalled eighteen-wheeler.

The car burned to a shell with Sean's son, wife, and six-year-old daughter inside."

"My God," she gasped, horrified. "Was Sean hurt?"

"He wasn't with them. He had to work overtime with B-shift that night." Howard dropped his chin to the top of her head. "His engine company was called to the scene, and that's how he found out."

"Oh, Howard." She squeezed him hard. "Sweet merciful God. And Sean hasn't gotten over it. How could anyone?"

"Especially when he found out his little girl was alive after the crash and burned to death before they could get there," Howard said hoarsely. "Mia was screaming for her daddy. Several witnesses tried to get to her, but she was pinned."

Speech deserted her. Tears filled her eyes, though she didn't know Sean Tanner. Mia had been the age of her own precious students, and she could well imagine a father's horror, rage, and grief.

Howard didn't have to tell her the man wasn't doing well. That he'd probably never be the same, if he survived at all.

After a few moments, Howard straightened and kissed her forehead. "Would you like to see the rest?"

Grateful to put aside the awful topic, and feeling somewhat guilty about the ease of escaping someone else's hell, she nodded. "I'd love to."

Three bedrooms, the living and dining areas, were filled with sturdy oak furniture suitable for a big man. Including the mammoth king-sized, four-poster bed in the master bedroom at the end of the hallway.

"This is my room."

Kat's stomach did a funny flip at the image of his body sprawled on cool, crisp sheets. Naked.

Awareness sparked between them, stretching the sexual tension as taut as a bowstring.

"Yeah. Anyway . . ." Clearing his throat, Howard

hurried back down the hallway the way they'd come, continuing the tour. One bedroom had been converted to his workout area, and bristled with equipment she couldn't name and had no clue how to use.

She'd seen gyms that weren't decked out this well, and couldn't help the stab of unease knifing her breast. Howard was physically the most beautiful man she'd ever seen, and she wasn't naive enough to think he hadn't had dozens of women. Gorgeous, leggy women who'd complete the other half of a striking couple.

Inwardly, she scolded herself to knock it off. Howard had made it clear he wanted to be with her, and no one else. So far, he hadn't done anything to deserve her doubt.

"Wow, this is something. Cool setup."

"But not your thing, as I recall," he said.

Giving him a narrow-eyed look, she saw he wasn't making fun and schooled herself to relax. "Nope, sorry. I never had the burning desire to be perfect, just appreciated for who I am."

His lips quirked. "You think I'm vain?"

"I didn't say that. I only meant I've accepted what I can't change about myself."

Digesting this, he nodded thoughtfully. "Just like I've accepted what I can."

"Meaning?"

"Meaning I'll never be scrawny and beaten again," he said quietly, hands fisting at his sides. "For me, being capable of defending yourself is not about vanity, Kat. We have so little control over our destinies, maybe none in reality. But I can be ready for whatever comes."

Moved, Kat touched his arm. Her heart ached for the boy huddled inside the grown man, determined never to be vulnerable again. "Nobody's going to hurt you the way your father did, Howard."

The shadows in his brown eyes eased, though she

wondered at the odd expression that flickered across his face. Taking her hand, he kissed her fingers. "Want to see the deck?"

Subject closed. She took the hint. "Sure."

He pulled her through the living room, opened the French doors, and stepped out onto a wide, impressive redwood deck meeting the jewel-green backyard dotted with huge trees. She sucked in an appreciative breath.

"This is fabulous!"

He smiled. "Thanks. Bentley and I built the deck together." He pointed to a barbecue grill to the right, along with a table covered by a large umbrella and flanked by several chairs. "I've got plenty of space for friends to hang out."

She glanced to the left edge of the deck at a hexagonal-shaped structure. "And a hot tub, too. Lucky duck."

"All the comforts a man could want." Hesitating, he leveled her with a heat-filled gaze. "Well, almost all."

He melted her with a look. Nothing more. Before he stepped close, took her face in his hands, she was already burning up from the raw sexuality blazing in his eyes. If she ever got his clothes off, felt the slide of his naked skin against hers, she'd probably incinerate.

"Kat," he whispered, voice like sandpaper. Cupping her cheeks, he slanted his mouth over hers. Angled himself to press against her full length. His erection rose hard against her belly, insistent with need.

Kat moaned, twining her fingers in his hair, stroking his tongue with her own. Suckling, loving his spicy taste. Her nipples tightened, grazing his chest, and she arched into him, seeking his warmth. She wanted—*needed*—him inside her, enveloping and protecting her. Wanted to drown in his essence, his flavor. To savor and explore.

Howard broke the kiss but remained wrapped around her, arousal hot and unyielding even through his trousers. His desperate expression mirrored her own as he spoke for them both. "I want you."

"I—I want you too, Lieutenant." She smiled to cover her jitters. She'd never been good at the "sex siren" thing.

Unlike his former lovers.

Stop it, Katherine Frances.

His eyes darkened, muscles tightening as his erection jerked, burrowed into her stomach. One highly aroused man, ready to take what was his. But his touch was gentle as one finger trailed her cheek, traced her lips.

"I can wait until you're ready. As long as it takes. I don't want anyone else, and I'm not going anywhere."

Solid and steady. A gentleman who meant every word.

Joy burst in her heart. "And if I'm ready now? Life is much too short," she mused, thinking of Sean's terrible loss.

Howard laid his forehead against hers, a tremble shuddering through him. "Then say yes, baby. I need to hear you say it."

"Yes." She brushed his lips in a slow kiss. "Yes, *yes*."

A slow grin lit his face.

Grabbing Kat by the hand, Howard pulled her inside, barely pausing to shut and lock the French doors. They got as far as the living room before he swooped in for another scorching kiss, palms skimming up her sides. His thumbs rubbed her nipples through the sheer blouse, electrifying every nerve ending.

His shaking fingers fumbled with the tiny buttons on her blouse, endearingly clumsy. Freeing the last one, he pushed the material from her shoulders and flicked the front clasp of her bra. Parted the cups and stared in awe.

"So perfect." Gently, he stroked the swell of her breasts with his fingers. "Let me taste you."

It wasn't a request. Kneeling, he nuzzled the swell between the mounds of flesh, licking the delicate skin. She touched his spiky hair, marveling that the man was so tall, the top of his head was even with her chest. Looking up at her, he ran the tip of his tongue in circles, first around one areola, then the other. Making her anticipate the moment he'd capture his prize. Compelling his lover to *watch* what he did, the intimacy as important as the act. His seduction was the most erotic thing she'd ever seen, yet she knew this was only a sneak preview of his prowess.

Howard grazed one taut nipple with his teeth, nipping, sucking, never breaking eye contact. As he pleasured her nipples, a hand slid upward along the inside of her leg to her thigh. Between her legs.

"God, you're already so hot." He stroked her mound through the fabric. "These have to go, too."

In a couple of smooth moves, he unbuttoned and unzipped her slacks, grabbed the waist and slid them off her hips, panties and all. Still kneeling at her feet, he helped her off with her boots and socks, and tossed her clothing out of the way.

Now she stood completely exposed before him, her vulnerability further amplified by his position. She could hide nothing from him, nor would he allow it. Afternoon sunlight streamed through the windows to catch at the desire in his eyes. Arousal radiated off him in waves, no less than her own.

"Spread your legs for me," he rumbled, low and dangerous.

Trembling, she complied. Waited.

Two fingers rubbed her slick folds, and she gasped, steadying herself by gripping a brawny shoulder. He spread the moisture along her slit, paying special attention to the little nub. Flicking, sending whorls of delight shooting to her limbs. As he did this, he dipped his tongue into her navel. Sampled.

"Oh, Howard!"

"That's it, sweetheart. Christ, that little diamond stud drives me nuts." His palms slid up the outsides of her thighs, then around to cup her buttocks. He pulled her in so close, she felt his warm breath fanning across her sex. "Open for me."

She shifted to a wider stance, closed her eyes. His tongue dipped between her wet lips, penetrating her entrance slowly. In, out. Mimicking the motion of his absent cock, spearing her very core.

Her fingers dug into his shoulders. "Oh . . . oh, yes . . ."

"Good," he whispered. "So sweet, pretty, and pink."

Under his expert ministrations, she *felt* pretty. Adored. Freed. For the first time.

He laved her folds, tongued her clit to the point of torture. Little tremors began in her womb; spread outward with the delicious edge of heat.

Howard paused, swirled her wet clit with his thumb. "Look at me."

She complied, and her body went hot all over. His feral expression blazed into her soul, telegraphing his knowledge. He knew what she craved. Deserved. And he wasn't stopping until she received it.

He gave her sex a long, slow lick, a man enjoying a creamy dessert, eyes still fixed on hers. Slid two fingers into her channel, stroking. His mouth joined in the love play, suckling as he drove her higher with his touch. Oh, Lord, she couldn't take much more.

"Mine," he said quietly. A man in complete control.

"Y-yes." She was going to come undone. Any second. "Howard, m-make love to me."

"That's what I'm doing, baby."

More torture, fingers and lips. Feasting on her sex,

devouring her will. Demanding her submission. His power washed over and through her, cleansing, making her new. Never any connection like this with a man. Immediate, unbreakable. All her life, she'd waited for him. She'd known him not days, but forever.

"Howard," she panted. "I need you inside me."

"Not yet. Come for me, sweetheart. Let go."

No resisting. He made sure of that, working her sheath in pounding rhythm, drawing on the plump pebble of flesh until she writhed. Mindless. Dug into his shoulders so hard she'd leave bruises. She gave herself up to him. Let go.

"Oh, God, yes, *yes!*"

She cried out as her orgasm exploded with blinding force. Her vaginal muscles spasmed around his fingers, and he milked her, on and on. Relentless. He growled with pleasure, eating his fill, drinking every drop.

When the waves subsided, he stood, wiped his mouth. She wobbled slightly and he bent, scooping her against his chest. Limp as a noodle, she draped her arms around his neck, wondering what he planned next.

The wait was brief.

"I'm not finished with you, not by a long shot," he murmured, lowering his head for a kiss.

Good, she started to say. *Because I'm not through with you, either.* But his mouth plundered hers, their combined flavors rich and exotic on her tongue. Arousing her all over again.

Howard carried her to his bedroom, placed her with tender care atop the covers. Standing beside the bed, he unbuttoned and removed his shirt. Let it drop to the floor.

Oh, my! The body of a god should never be clothed. A god with broad shoulders and a deep, smooth muscular chest. Biceps she couldn't span if she possessed three hands, ripped abs that looked liked he'd swallowed six miniature paint rollers.

She licked her lips. "Quite a six-pack you're sporting there, Lieutenant."

"That's what the guys nicknamed me years ago. Six-Pack."

"Mmm. Go figure." Yum. Howard reached for his fly, but Kat leaned toward him, swatting away his hand. "Let me."

His lips quirked, dark gaze burning. "Anything my lady says."

"Anything?" She unzipped his fly slowly, slid her fingers into the waistband of his boxers. Teasing.

He tensed. "Oh yeah."

Grinning, she pulled the pants and underwear down, off his hips. His erection sprang free, proud and eager. Lord in heaven, Howard was enormous! Eight inches or so of rock-hard, blue-veined delight nested in a smattering of brown curls between his big thighs. His testicles hung large and heavy, even drawn tight in excitement.

Scooting closer, she wrapped her fingers around his penis. Stroked him with a light touch, exploring. Allowing herself to become accustomed to his shape and size, to this special intimacy. No great hardship. His skin was silky and supple as a baby's, yet scorching as desert sands. She tightened her grip, squeezed harder as she pumped.

"Jesus, you're killing me," he rasped, hips jerking forward.

"What a way to die, hmm?"

A drop of pre-cum seeped from the plum-shaped head. Bending, she licked the bead away, kissed the tip. He groaned, reached for the gold clasp at her nape, freed her hair from the twist. Tossing the clip, he buried his hands in her tresses, urged her closer.

A newfound sense of feminine power buoyed her confidence. Not once had she ever used her mouth on a man *there*, though she'd been curious and willing. Caressed, sure. But what's-his-name didn't enjoy fellatio, and had refused that sort of connection with her. The truth hit with remarkable clarity.

Howard was 100 percent sensual *man*, not a boy.

Kat tasted the purple head, swirling it with her tongue. She licked the underside of his shaft to the base, enjoying the pungent musk of his sex, the taste of him. Encouraged by his groan, she laved his balls, kneading them with her fingers. Kissed and suckled him there, entranced by the idea of such a huge man being reduced to a puddle under her care. The pads of his fingers dug into her scalp as she rolled one testicle, then the other, in her mouth. Greedy, unable to get enough of him.

More. Kat licked his penis once more from base to tip, then took him in her mouth. Began to work his cock in deep, fucking him with her lips and tongue as she pumped the base in her hand.

"Ahh, shit!"

Kat blinked. She'd never heard Howard curse before. But she supposed she'd given this paragon of gentlemanly behavior good reason to slip. On the inside, she whooped with glee.

She went down on him with no more mercy than he'd shown her a few minutes before. Sucked and stroked him until his eyes nearly rolled back in his head as he pulled away, breathing hard.

"Stop, baby, or I'm gonna go before I get inside you."

"Your point?" Smug, she watched him shed his shoes and socks, kick away the rest of his clothes. In a hurry.

He arched a dark brow. "I'm about to make it."

9

Howard opened the drawer of the nightstand and fished out a foil packet. Ripping it open, he sheathed his erection with quick efficiency, then climbed onto the bed with her.

"Lie on your back, sweetheart."

Kat scooted to the middle to give him room. Grasping her knees, he spread her legs and positioned himself between her thighs. Rubbing her clit with his thumb, he nestled the head of his cock into her folds, nudged inside an inch or two. Then an inch or two more. Stretching her, letting her adjust to his immense size.

"How does that feel?" He gazed down at her, obvious concern taking precedence over desire.

"Ohh, Howard . . ."

His brow furrowed. "I can stop. Just say the word and—"

"Don't you dare! Make love to me."

Relief swamped his face, along with sheer lust. Despite the agony backing out would cause him, he'd given her two chances to do so. Nothing would stop him now.

Kneeling, he raised her legs, draping them over his brawny shoulders. Placed her totally at his mercy. Cupping his palms under her ass, he lifted her backside clear off the bed. Parted her sex and impaled her. One delicious, maddening inch at a time. He was so big, her channel burned as he filled her deeper, deeper. Until he was seated to the balls, completing a part of her she'd never known was empty.

Until Howard.

"How's this?"

She gripped his thighs. "Good . . . so damned fantastic . . ."

He began to move in slow strokes. "And this?"

"Oh, God, don't stop. Faster, please! I need—"

"Tell me, sweet Katherine." He increased the strength of his strokes. Just enough to make her want more.

The muscles of his chest and arms bunched and rippled as he pleasured her. Beautiful. This man, his length shiny and slick from their loving as he pumped in and out. She couldn't form the words, so he did.

"You need me to fuck you hard, don't you?"

A ripple of shock cut through the languid haze, firing her blood. Igniting the heat between her legs all over again. This raw, blatantly sexual side of him topped every secret fantasy she'd held dear.

"Yes," she whimpered. "Howard, *please*."

Without another word, he slammed home with a powerful thrust. Remained still for a few seconds, sweat rolling down one cheek, then thrust again. And again. Increasing in tempo. Harder, faster, until his hips pistoned his shaft into her depths like a jackhammer. Flesh slapping flesh, decadent music to the rhythm of their bodies spiraling higher.

The flame began to burn out of control, and she gripped his arms as he drove her into the mattress. Anchoring herself to withstand the storm ravaging her from the inside out. "Oh, oh, *oh*! I'm gonna—I have to—"

Wave after wave broke, crashed over her, and she

cried out, spasming around him. Howard's hoarse yell registered from somewhere far away as he threw his head back and sank to his balls in one final thrust. His big frame shuddered on and on, every muscle straining over her. A pagan god, taking and giving, as well.

The fierce storm gradually subsided to a gentle throb of pleasure. Kat floated, gazing at her lover in awe. Sweat gleamed on his chest and his lungs heaved like a bellows. His funky hair spiked in every direction, and liquid brown eyes bored into hers, sated. A man well satisfied.

Carefully, he withdrew, lowered her to the bed, and moved from between her thighs. She felt his loss immediately, and a small sound of distress escaped before she could squelch it. Leaning over, he kissed her cheek.

"Don't worry, I'll be back."

He disappeared into the bathroom but returned in seconds, the condom discarded. Stretching out beside Kat, he gathered her into his arms and pulled her half on top of him, resting her head on his chest.

"That was incredible." Basking in happiness, she kissed a pert male nipple. "*You're* incredible, Lieutenant. Nobody's ever given me an out-of-body experience before."

"Hey, you stole my lines," he complained.

But his chest puffed out under her cheek, and she smiled. "You don't need any smooth lines with me, hotshot. Sadly enough, all you have to do is give me *the look*, and I'll come running."

His arms tightened around her, and one hand skimmed her back in lazy caress. "Doesn't sound so bad to me."

"I'll endure."

"Smarty-pants."

"I'm not wearing any."

He cupped her bottom. "Let's keep it that way for a while longer, shall we?"

"If you insist." She snuggled into his heat, wrapping an arm around his torso, content not to move for the next year or so. "Howard?"

"Mmm?"

"I've never heard you curse before."

He chuckled. "Sorry. When making love with a beautiful woman, all bets are off."

Oh! Grr. She was *not* thinking about his other lady *friends* and what they'd enjoyed with her Howard. Speculating about his sex life before was one thing, but now the image made her want to choke someone. So she changed the subject to something she'd been curious about.

"What's up with the bleached hair?"

"You don't like it?"

Propping her chin on his breastbone, she peered at the top of his head. "It's a cool look, totally works for you. Yeah, I like it. I just have trouble seeing a six-foot-six, two-hundred-and-sixty-pound giant sitting in a beauty parlor chair with foil tubes all over his head."

He gave her a sheepish grin. "Surrounded by giggling women, too. A humbling experience I'll never forget, trust me."

"So why'd you do it?"

"I lost a bet."

She snickered. "With who, José Eber?"

"With five classes of first-graders."

Ugh. She could sympathize. "Even worse. How, pray tell, did this wager come about?"

"You know how the different stations and shifts take turns going out to the schools to teach fire safety to the little ones? Well, Station Five's turn rolled around, and A-shift went to the elementary school closest to us to do our thing. In short, I bet the little tyrants they wouldn't all get their homework turned in by the next day."

"And if they did, you'd bleach your hair!" Kat laughed in delight. "What was their homework?"

"Drawing a map showing where their families would meet in case of fire, and at least two escape routes from their homes. I went back the next day to check with their teachers, and every last one of them had completed the assignment. Never make a bet with a kid."

He didn't fool her. She heard the contentment, the love of children in his voice. As if there weren't enough to adore about Howard, this sealed the deal. He'd bleached his hair to make a group of kids happy.

A mountain of a gentle man who risked his life on a daily basis, could cook, was an excellent lover, and loved his family *and* kids. What more could a girl want?

The one word that wasn't part of her hunky firefighter's vocabulary.

Yet.

Howard always believed he'd die an old man before he thought watching a woman chop salad in his kitchen was sexy. Somehow, two people sharing vegetables after a roll in bed had always seemed way too . . . domestic. After hot, sweaty sex, cuddling and cooking hadn't made the agenda. With his angel, though, the normalcy was strangely comforting.

Kat didn't seem to want to leave anytime soon. In fact, she appeared right at home in his life. At his side. Wearing one of his old T-shirts that hung to her knees, blond hair mussed. Shaking his head in amazement, Howard retrieved a rectangular Pyrex dish from the fridge and peeked under the foil.

Kat glanced up from her cucumber. "Whatcha cookin'?"

"Chicken lasagna rolls." He peeled back the corner of the foil to reveal several orange-sized lasagna noodle pinwheels rolled with sautéed chicken and cheeses, topped with white wine cream sauce. He studied her reaction. Wanting to impress someone, the tight knot of anxiety, was a weird new feeling.

Kat sniffed in appreciation. "Ohh, looks yummy. I'm hungry."

In the wake of her enthusiasm, the knot loosened. "I tried the recipe on the team last week. It was a hit, except with Zack, who hates pasta. Of course, a horde of ravenous firefighters will eat almost anything. The menu is usually carb city, but we burn the energy fast."

"Goody for you." She stuck her tongue out at him.

Laughing, he planted a quick kiss on her nose. "You're cute when you get sassy."

"Oh, right." She rolled her eyes, a slight blush staining her cheeks as she gathered the cucumbers and dumped them into the bowl with the lettuce. The diced tomato she dumped into a separate bowl to garnish her salad. "Can't believe you don't like tomatoes on your salad. That's just wrong, my friend."

He shivered. "I don't eat tomatoes in any form, if I can avoid them."

"Thus the white sauce instead of marinara."

"Yep, afraid so."

"Weirdo."

"That's me," he agreed. "Funny, I vaguely remember liking them when I was a kid. My mother's homemade spaghetti sauce—"

His hand froze over the dish. A strange chill enveloped his body, as though he'd stepped into a walk-in freezer. His head swam and he felt a little sick.

"Howard?" Kat touched his arm. "Are you all right?"

Starting, he blinked at her. Kat's sweet face was scrunched into a concerned frown. He took a deep breath and exhaled slowly, glad that the nausea and chills were already receding.

He gave her a kiss on the forehead. "I'm fine."

"Are you sure? You looked ready to fall over." She ran a finger down his cheek, clearly not convinced.

"Whatever came over me, it's gone. Promise." He smiled to reassure her. In fact, the sensation had fled so fast he might've imagined it.

"Okay. But if you start to feel bad again, let me know."

"Yes, ma'am."

The oven beeped, indicating the temperature was ready. Grinning to himself, the incident forgotten, Howard squished the foil down again, then slid the dish into the oven to heat. *Lovemaking, dinner, and meaningful conversation with a cutie who's wearing my clothes. I could get used to this.*

"Thirty minutes. Want some wine while we wait?" he asked.

"After the day I had at work, that sounds fantastic."

He retrieved a bottle from the fridge, held it out for her inspection. "Will this do? It looked nice, all pink and whatever. I don't know squat about the stuff."

"I love white Zinfandel! You're a lifesaver, buddy."

Kat put the salad on the table while he fished a cheap corkscrew from the depths of his kitchen junk drawer. Curious, she eyed him, and he waited for the inevitable question.

"I take it you don't drink much wine."

He shook his head, began to twist the corkscrew through the wax seal. "I don't drink alcohol, period. Tried it once, didn't like the taste or feeling fuzzy. Doesn't bother me one bit if my friends partake, so enjoy."

"Hoping to get me drunk and have your evil way with me again, Lieutenant?" Lowering her tawny lashes, she sent him a sultry look.

"Doesn't say much for my manly skills if I need to get you soused to achieve that." The cork came out with a soft pop. "Hope you don't mind drinking from a juice glass."

"An IV would do."

"Yeah? I could fix you up." Opening the cupboard, he retrieved a glass and filled it with wine. "Fortunately, that won't be necessary. Here you are."

She took a sip and sighed with pleasure. "Mmm, heavenly. Thanks."

"For you, no problem."

The phone chirped from the corner of the bar separating the kitchen and dining room, interrupting their nice interlude. He frowned, hoping it wasn't the station needing a man to sub on shift. Or worse, Sean, off the wagon and off his rocker. A glance at the caller ID didn't do much to relieve his mind.

"Excuse me for a minute." Leaving Kat to enjoy her wine, he answered. "Paxton."

"Ford here," the detective said, sounding grim. "Got a confirmation on the victim through dental records. Does the name Sherri Pearce mean anything to you?"

Howard searched his brain, came up empty. "Nothing, sorry. Never heard of her."

"Think back. Maybe you met her through a call. Traffic accident, medical emergency, treed cat."

Rolling his eyes at the bad joke, he walked into the living room and lowered his voice so Kat wouldn't overhear. "I saw her picture. I'd think knowing how she was murdered would've jarred my memory real quick."

"Damn. Good point." The detective sighed, the deep sort of tired that cut to the bone. "Was worth a shot. Anything else unusual happen since my visit?"

"It's been quiet. Maybe he's lost interest."

"Maybe." Ford didn't sound convinced. "Keep an eye out. Call me directly if he fucks with you again."

"That's all? We just wait?"

"*You* wait, and watch. I investigate. I'm not leaving you out of the loop, you got my word. The sick bastard used your station's sector for his deed. The photo left specifically for you indicates he carefully chose his location to bring in your team."

Cold blew through Howard like ice. "You think he'll continue his spree in my neck of the woods? Endanger my men?" The thought was enough to make him want to break the perv's neck with his bare hands.

"I believe his game has very specific rules, with a desired end result. Not random," Ford replied. "Are you the center of the game? No way to tell yet. Could be he'll choose another station to taunt with his kill next time, perhaps in another city. But I don't doubt he'll enact the scenario again."

"Sweet Jesus."

"Hang in there, Lieutenant. I'll be in touch."

"Wait—" Glancing toward the kitchen, he saw Kat busying herself with gathering plates and forks, humming. Still, he kept his voice quiet. "Did you say anything about the photo and my involvement in the case to Kat?"

"No, and I wouldn't unless it were absolutely necessary. We're also holding back those two details from the media—the picture and your involvement—as our ace. I do want to run Pearce's name by Miss McKenna, though, just to be sure the two women aren't connected."

"I don't think they will be. The killer used the Hargraves' house, not the McKennas'. Besides, Kat wasn't even supposed to be in her parents' neighborhood at that hour." His protective instincts surged to the fore with a vengeance. He wanted her out of this, *now*.

"Kat's here. Why don't you go ahead and ask her." *And then leave her the hell alone.*

"Sure." Ford did not sound surprised by this news.

Howard covered the mouthpiece and carried the phone to the kitchen. "Kat? Detective Ford has a question for you."

"Oh . . . okay." With a puzzled frown, she took the receiver and mustered a pleasant greeting.

Howard pretended to be absorbed in checking their dinner in the oven, while hanging on every word. No, she wasn't acquainted with Sherri Pearce. Yes, she was positive. His knees went weak with relief. Now Ford could put Kat at the bottom of his priority list.

Kat hung up and replaced the phone in its cradle, rubbing her arms. "Poor woman. How awful. Did you know her?"

"No, thank God."

"Why is the detective still questioning you?" she asked, cocking her head. "Is that normal procedure? I mean, your station responded to the fire, but it's not like you'd know anything about the murder."

"Well, this one was particularly grotesque, and it happened on my watch. I guess he's covering his butt." Christ, he hated lying to Kat. He ought to tell her the truth, but he didn't want a pall cast over their evening. Before she left tonight, he'd have to come clean for her safety. He couldn't be around to protect her twenty-four/seven. He hoped she'd forgive his deception and still want to hang around.

He thought about that—the sticking-around part— through dinner. Went fifteen rounds with his conscience. A wonderful woman like Kat deserved a guy who could give her stability. Kids. *Love.* The first, he had covered. But the other two?

She had no idea how much he wished he possessed the ability to give those things. One was impossible, the other improbable.

You're a fighter, he reminded himself. *And she's the best thing that's ever happened to you.*

"Gosh, that was delicious." Kat leaned back in her chair, patting her stomach with a groan. "I'm not used to eating a big meal during the week."

He smiled. "Glad you liked it. Don't you cook?"

"For myself? Why bother? Eating alone is no fun."

"True."

"But my mom is a great cook," she went on. "We do the family deal at my parents' on Sundays once or twice a month. My sister drives in from Nashville since it's not far, and she's got no good excuse to bail. Sometimes she brings a guy friend, but mostly it's just us four."

Do you ever bring a "guy friend"? he almost asked. And stopped himself. He was not going there. Didn't want to know.

"We don't get together as often," he said instead. "When we do, it's usually a big blowout. Like this Saturday." The idea hit as soon as the words left his lips. Why hadn't he thought of this before? Kat tilted her head, an inquisitive expression on her face. He was starting to dig when she looked at him that way. Or any way, really.

"What's going on this Saturday?"

"It's Bentley's birthday. The big six-five. We're gonna grill burgers and dogs out back," he said, jabbing his thumb in the direction of his deck. "A lot of people coming, mostly firefighters and their families. Some of Bentley's cronies and guys from several stations, including ours. You're officially invited, if you're brave enough to take us on."

Her eyes rounded. "Wow, sounds like quite a crowd. Grace and I had plans for lunch and shopping Saturday. I don't know . . ."

"Bring Grace along. We're harmless, I promise. Well, most of us." He grimaced, thinking of Julian. "I'll run interference for you ladies, so no worries. I want you here, and I know everyone would love to meet you. They're a terrific group of people. Say you'll think about it."

"Well . . ." She chewed her lower lip, looking tempted. "Oh, what the heck. How much trouble can we get into at a sixty-five-year-old man's birthday party? I'll ask Grace. If she's game, we'll come. Work for you?"

"Oh yeah. That works just fine."

Inviting a lady into the sacred fold. A first for him. He'd never hear the end of the curious questions, the third degree from the guys.

He must be losing his mind.

If so, he sort of looked forward to the trip.

Second Avenue. A little too business-class for Frank's liking, full of suits and tourists. The bars along this street weren't quite right for his purposes. Too eclectic for his personal taste—not his crowd, the fucking yuppie fat cats—except for the Wild Horse Saloon, which was a big, two-level country-and-western dance bar. Crowded even on a Monday night, the place might've shown promise—except for the bouncers checking ID at the door.

Someone might remember. Not good.

Walking on, he bunched his shoulders against the crisp October night. At the corner, he hung a right on Broadway, heading away from the river toward the old part of downtown he knew better. Much more suitable for his mission.

The area hadn't changed much. Storefronts showed age and wear, a combination of dirty brick and peeling paint. Tired, but still standing, like the middle-aged cowboy leaning against a building in the darkness, strumming a six-string and singing for tips. Praying for a break that would never come his way.

What a goddamned waste of air, Frank thought. *Go home, asshole.*

Picking up his stride, he passed a gift shop, a Western-wear store, and a music store with tons of guitars and shit. The "World Famous" Tootsies Orchid Lounge was just a few doors ahead, and he considered the benefits of hunting there.

Tootsies was split-level, small, always packed to the brim with tourists and locals. Some a bit rough around the edges. If a man didn't find a woman looking to get laid in Tootsies, she couldn't be found. The major drawback was the live music being played on each level, the establishment frequented by talent scouts, agents, country music industry professionals.

Everyone went into Tootsies looking to get noticed, which meant they'd pay real close attention to new faces in the joint. Hoping to spot their elusive big break. Too bad he didn't dare use the same bar where he'd picked up the other bitch. Too risky.

On impulse, he pushed into a joint two doors down from Tootsies. Busy, but not so crowded a guy couldn't breathe. No band on the small stage tonight, which meant he could listen to conversation unhampered, make a connection. Bait tomorrow night's hook, reel in the big fish.

Sink a certain sorry bastard a little deeper into his personal hell before filleting him like a gaping trout.

He took a seat at a scarred wooden table along the wall, half hidden by shadows, yet close enough to the bar to make eye contact with a dark-haired slut trolling for company.

Patient, he stayed put. Let her feel him, build her curiosity. Halfway into his second beer, she approached him. They always did.

Silky brunette tresses fell past the shoulders of her crop top, framing full breasts ripe for tasting. Her oval face was attractive enough, though her dark eyes glinted with a jaded attitude. She'd seen a little too much, lived a little too hard.

Her shapely figure suited her medium height, even with a few extra pounds clinging to her hips. But he eyed the skintight low-rise jeans in silent disgust. A tart pushing the backside of thirty had no business dressing like a teenager when she no longer had the body to carry off the look. It never fucking ceased to amaze him that a broad would believe the little fat roll hanging over the waistband was something to admire.

"Waiting for someone?" she asked, the question a mere formality.

She studied him from the top of his head to his long legs stretched out and crossed at the ankles. Frank knew she liked what she saw. An older man, still taut in all the right places, silver threaded through his short black hair. Good-looking, with strong, arresting features.

Or so Sherri Pearce told him, before he gagged her, doused her with gasoline, and lit her up like a blowtorch.

His new target's mouth curved into a knowing smile even before his answer.

"Not anymore, sugar."

No, you stupid bitch. Not anymore.

10

Howard rolled his shoulders and neck, trying to work out the kinks as he and Julian loaded a seventy-six-year-old man with a possibly fractured hip into the ambulance. As MVA's went, the accident could've been worse. A whole lot worse.

Tell that to the hysterical teenaged girl standing by the curb, wailing, "My parents are gonna kill me!" while staring in disbelief at the mangled front end of her Explorer. A patient traffic officer spoke to her in soothing tones, attempting to calm her enough to get the information he needed for his report.

No, Howard thought. Her parents were going to take her in their arms and thank God that the elderly man who'd run the red light hadn't killed their little girl. Or at least they should.

With a wrecker on the way and he and Jules ready to transport their patient to the hospital, the team's job at the scene was almost done. The officer would see to the shaken girl until her parents arrived to fetch her and the SUV, which didn't look pretty, but could be driven.

During the ride to the hospital, he noticed how Julian spoke calmly to the old gentleman. Concerned, polite, and respectful. Professional yet caring. No trace of the bad-boy jerk. Jeez, the guy was a puzzle.

At the hospital, they left the man in good hands.

With a quick wave good-bye at the ER doc, Salvatore strode out to where Howard waited beside the ambulance.

"Why can't you be that nice to everyone?" Howard grumbled as they climbed into the vehicle.

Salvatore buckled his seat belt, expression guarded as he glanced at his lieutenant. "You got a problem with me, Six-Pack?"

"Depends. What hour of the day is it?"

The other man's brows snapped together in a scowl. "*Cristo*, what crawled up your butt and died? You still sore about my hassle with Knight? Shit, all I did was stick one of Eve's maxi pads on the quint's steering wheel, and he went fucking nuclear."

"You drew a smiley face on the extra-absorbent dry weave," Howard deadpanned. "With Zack's *name* on it. And did you forget the tampons you tied together and hung from the rearview mirror like fuzzy dice?"

Immediately, he felt bad about picking on Jules. Since the altercation with Zack over the stupid engine prank, the guy had been on his best behavior around the team. "Best behavior" being relative for Salvatore. And although Knight had been good and pissed, the harmless joke *was* pretty inspired.

"He's over it." Julian shrugged. "So, what's eating you?"

"You got about an hour?"

At his resigned tone, Julian's dark gaze switched to wary concern. "I got as long as you need."

"Nah, forget it." Why the hell had he opened the door? Jules was about the last person he wanted to spill his guts to. He pulled into the flow of afternoon traffic, heading toward the station, hoping his companion would drop the subject.

"Seriously, man. I may be a wiseass, but I can keep a secret. Ask *mi hermano*."

"Your brother hangs out with drug dealers."

Julian rolled his eyes. "Tonio's a narc. I'm the one who got the warm, fuzzy personality."

"God help us all."

"But—"

"Forget it."

Salvatore hesitated, then lifted one shoulder in a careless shrug. Pushed a strand of straight, jet-black hair out of his eyes. "Whatever."

Just before Julian averted his face to stare out the window, Howard caught a flicker of emotion in his dark eyes, quickly covered by a mask of indifference. Hurt? Disappointment?

Aw, hell.

There were a load of things going on that he *could* discuss with Salvatore, some of which didn't bear repeating. He'd already told Sean about the photo of the murdered woman, and the fewer people who knew about it, the better. And the nightmares? Forget it. Nobody had a clue about those, not even Sean.

But there was one area Jules excelled at, hands down.

"How do you do it?" Howard mused aloud.

Julian glanced at him, curious. "Do what?"

"Keep all your women satisfied."

A slow grin spread across the man's face. "If you need pointers in bed, *amigo*, that's more help than even I'm willing to give."

"Not like that, idiot," said Howard, waving a hand. "I mean, you see several ladies at any one time. How do you manage to keep things casual, but send them off happy, too?"

"Ah." Julian nodded sagely. "The best of sex and companionship, without the cement shoes of matrimony. Friends with benefits."

"Exactly!" What red-blooded guy wouldn't love that arrangement?

"It's not as simple as it sounds. You know about me and Carmelita, right?"

Howard stopped at a traffic light and took the opportunity to study Julian's face. He'd never seen the guy so serious. "Not really. I've heard you mention her, that's all."

Julian fell silent a moment, as though considering the best way to explain. "Carmelita and I are . . . close. Lovers. My family and hers are lifelong friends. Everyone thought we'd marry someday, but we like our gig the way it is. We *need* our freedom, so we both see other people."

The light turned green, and Howard stepped on the gas, amazed by what he was hearing. And yeah, intrigued. "And this works for her?"

"Yes. But our situation is unique, Six-Pack. We've known each other our whole lives. We're friends, and we love one another in our own way. We talk about everything, except the forbidden territory of other lovers."

He barked a short laugh. "I'll bet. Christ, you're something else."

Grinning, Julian waggled his brows. "I've heard that before, and in prettier company."

Howard shook his head, smiling in spite of himself. Jules really wasn't so bad. Sometimes. Full of crap, but not so bad.

He tried to imagine Kat going for an arrangement like Julian had with Carmelita, and the picture wouldn't gel. Not only that, but quite suddenly, just thinking of Kat with another man in her bed, letting him pleasure her as he'd done yesterday afternoon and half the night . . .

The smile died on his face. The thought made him physically ill. Made him sick to his stomach, made him want to hit something.

By God, Salvatore's open relationship policy was definitely *out*.

"What's with the quiz about my love life, anyway?"

The question jerked him out of black thoughts of slowly torturing a man caught attempting to poach on sacred territory. "No reason in particular."

"You seeing somebody?"

"Sort of. Maybe." At Julian's arch look, he gave. "Okay, yeah. I'm hoping to see her a lot."

"Cool. Who is she?"

Howard sighed. What reason did he have to keep her a secret? Everyone would meet her and Grace at Bentley's party on Saturday. "Kat McKenna, the blonde from the fire."

The blonde he had yet to level with about the photo, in spite of his best intentions. God.

"I knew it!" Julian chortled, slapping his leg. "Hot damn, it's about time! Howie scores!"

"Kat's not a *score*," he replied evenly, choosing to ignore the annoying nickname. A deaf man could've read the dire warning in his tone.

Julian held up a hand. "Whoa, chill. I didn't mean any disrespect to your lady. It's just that, holy shit, Knight gets more action than you, and he's a freaking virgin."

"He is *not*," Howard scoffed, glad for the diversion.

"Man, I'm serious. You didn't know?"

"Zack's what, twenty-six? No way."

"Yep. I overheard him talking to Eve on shift not long ago. Not that I was listening on purpose—"

"Why would he tell Eve something so personal? Maybe you took the conversation out of context."

"Jesus, where have you *been*? Under a rock?" Julian tilted his dark head back against the seat and closed his eyes. "Those two are tight, like best buds. And I know what I heard."

Whether Zack was a virgin or not, it wasn't any of their business. Though that would sure go a long way toward explaining the man's hostile reaction to Julian's prank. "I don't feel right talking about Zack like this."

"Hey, I thought you knew or I wouldn't have opened my big mouth. Shouldn't have, anyway, so consider the subject dropped." After a brief pause, he said, "So, do I get an introduction to your hot *chica* on Saturday?"

"A brief one," he enunciated deliberately. "Real brief."

Julian's lips curved up. "Message received."

"Good, 'cause here's another one. Kat is bringing her sister, Grace."

"Yeah?" Julian lifted his head at that bit of news, blinking at Howard in undisguised interest. He smiled. "She as pretty as your lady?"

Howard's hands gripped the steering wheel, tight. God, what a disaster it would've been to unleash a player like Jules on Kat's family. He was damned glad he'd brought this up in time to head off catastrophe.

"Got no clue, but it doesn't matter to *you*," he said firmly, lest the guy have any doubt where they stood. "Grace is a lawyer. A classy woman from a nice, normal family. Kat adores her, and anything that upsets my lady would be very unpleasant and unfortunate for the person doing the upsetting. We clear?"

Julian's smile froze on his face. There it was again, the flash of deep hurt, then his expression turned hard. Brittle. His eyes glittered like onyx, cold and unfathomable.

"More than clear, Lieutenant."

Well, son of a bitch. Salvatore was insulted, which hadn't been his intent. All the same, he wasn't about to stand aside and let the man work his mojo on Kat's sister. Not if he could prevent it. That whole scene hit way too close to home, in more ways than one.

"Hey, Jules, man, I didn't mean it like that. I just don't want to see Kat's sister get hurt. I invited her, so I'd feel responsible."

Julian turned his face away, gazing out the window. "Yeah, sure."

They rode the rest of the way to the station in tense silence. Howard let his thoughts drift to Kat and wondered how her day at work had gone. He checked his watch. Almost three thirty. He'd give her a while to get home, then call her.

He wanted to hear her voice, her laughter. He missed her already, wished she'd stayed longer last night. The second time he'd fucked her, after dinner, had been even hotter and faster than the first.

Next time, he'd slow things down, give her a reason to stay until dawn. Make love to her slow and easy.

It's not fucking, not with Kat, he realized. *Hard and fast or slow and deep, with her, it's making love.*

His balls tightened, and his cock began to ache. He needed her, and shift change was too damned far off. He hadn't planned on seeing her again so soon, perhaps not until the party on Saturday, and yet . . .

He was already getting in too deep with the curvy, green-eyed blonde who knocked his socks off. Twisted his heart in knots.

This thing between them was progressing at warp speed. He ought to back off a little. Tell her about the photo of the murdered woman. Be honest, share all the ugly truths about himself and what he'd never be able to give her.

But he couldn't.

Soon, he told himself. When the moment was right, he'd tell her everything. When he did, she'd run far away from him.

And he'd be alone.

Again.

Kat barely got through the door, slung her heavy bookbag onto the sofa, and kicked her shoes off her throbbing feet when the phone rang. Checking the caller ID, she grinned and snatched the receiver from its cradle.

"Hello!"

"Miss me?" Howard's voice rumbled in her ear, deep and seductive.

She flushed, warming all over. "Come over and find out."

"Damn, you know how to bring a guy to his knees," he complained, following the gripe with a low, husky laugh.

"You looked pretty fine in that position, as I recall," she crooned, carrying the phone into her bedroom. He groaned, and she giggled. Cradling the handset under her ear, she unzipped her pants and slid them down. "How's your shift been so far?"

"Busy. We've had two medical emergencies in the home, a kid who touched a downed power line while walking to school, and an MVA."

"MVA?"

"Oh, sorry—stands for 'motor vehicle accident.' An old man ran a red light, and a teenager hit him. He's banged up, but he'll make it. The girl walked away without a scratch. The ten-year-old boy who touched the power line might not be so lucky. We had to restart his heart."

"Oh, my God." She halted in the attempt to shrug off her blouse and sat on the bed. This was a typical day's work for Howard? How did he deal with the pressure? He'd said the team talked over the rough stuff, but was that always good enough? Kids, he'd told her, were always the hardest.

"I wish you were here." For a completely different reason than before.

"Me, too," he said softly.

She wanted to hold him, offer him comfort. Unfortunately, the in-person variety would have to wait. "I'm so sorry."

"It was a freak accident. I feel bad for his parents."

"Of course. Will you be able to learn his condition?"

"I know one of the ER docs pretty well. He'll find out for me."

He sounded so glum, her heart went out to him—and the boy's family. "You don't think he'll survive, do you?"

"I hope I'm wrong." His tone said he probably wasn't. On Howard's end of the line came another man's voice, muffled. Howard covered the receiver and replied low enough so Kat couldn't hear, then came back on. "I have to go. I'm hogging the office and Tanner needs in here."

"No problem. I'm glad you called."

"And dumped my day on you? Right." Before she could protest, he jumped in again. "Listen, I don't want to end our chat on a downer. Can I take you to dinner and a movie tomorrow night? I promise not to keep you out too late."

Cheered by the lovely idea, she smiled. "Sounds terrific."

"Great, um . . . I'll call you tomorrow?"

"I'm looking forward to it."

"Bye, Kat."

"Bye," she said, and hung up.

Katherine Frances, you're dead, stinky meat.

She only hoped the lieutenant didn't guess how far gone she really was.

Howard made one more phone call before relinquishing the office to Sean. He waited for an ER nurse to fetch his doctor acquaintance, tapping a pencil on the desk, every muscle in his body coiled as if to ward off a blow. Why did he do this to himself? Because the myth that the good outweighed the bad might actually, for once, prove true?

Didn't matter. Where a kid was involved, he had to *know*.

"Lieutenant," the doc said, his tone somber.

Howard didn't have to ask. The pencil snapped in his fingers as he closed his eyes. The conversation was brief and one-sided. He listened, thanked the doctor, hung up, and buried his face in his hands.

"Six-Pack?"

Lifting his head, Howard stared at Sean. He hadn't heard his friend enter the office. "Steven Carter is brain-dead."

Tanner leaned against the closed door, breath leaving his lungs in a rush. "God*dammit*. Skyler's going to take this hard."

Howard nodded, grim. At twenty-three, Tommy Skyler had been with them less than a year, had only recently graduated from EMT to full paramedic status. The kid was smart, well liked. The good-looking, all-American son every parent wished for and every guy envied, just a little.

But not too much, because Tommy was such a sunny, free spirit. His irresistible, natural charm made people smile, drew them like bears to a honeypot. Hell, he even got along with Salvatore—no small feat. Skyler's youth and innocence, his optimism, were assets to the team.

That innocence was about to take its second serious hit in one week. First, discovering the charred murder victim, and now this.

"We should bring him in here for the news before making the announcement to the others," Howard said. "Losing your first patient is tough enough, but a *child*? Jesus Christ."

"Bad luck. Could've been any of us." Tanner raked a hand through his brown hair, visibly struggling to contain the backlash of emotion caused by the kid's death. Nobody knew that particular tragedy better than he did. "I'll find him."

Zack happened to be walking by when Sean opened the door. At the captain's terse inquiry about Skyler's whereabouts, Zack's laser-blue gaze flicked from Sean to Howard. Took in their solemn expressions and read the situation in an instant.

"Oh, man. He's mopping the men's bathroom," Zack said, blinking behind his wire-rimmed glasses. "I'll send him this way. You want me to stay?"

Tanner clapped Knight on the shoulder. "Not this time, but thanks."

"No problem."

Knight went in search of Skyler. In moments, the youngest team member knocked and pushed open the office door. Ducking his blond head in greeting, he stepped inside, straightened his lean, six-foot frame, and flashed them a tentative smile that carved dimples in his cheeks.

"Hey, Cap, Six-Pack. What's doing?" Pale blue eyes searched their faces. The truth plunked into the silence between him and his superiors. All color drained from his face as he straightened, fists clenched. "The boy died."

His hoarse voice was heavy with guilt. Howard stood and rounded the desk, stopping a couple of feet from Skyler. "There was absolutely nothing you—or any of us—could've done differently," Howard emphasized, crossing his arms over his chest. "The child was dead for at least three minutes before we arrived, and we worked on him another seven before his heart restarted. Few beat sorry odds like that, Tommy."

Skyler shook his head, throat working, eyes glassy and bright. "I should've—"

"Done what?" the captain demanded. "Go through the procedures in your head and tell us what you could've done that you didn't."

"I—I . . ." He trailed off, expression miserable, chest heaving.

But Skyler was working it through, Howard knew. Every emotion warred on his face. The kid's brows furrowed as he stared at a framed picture on the wall, reliving, assessing his actions. Accepting the inevitable conclusion.

Finally, he nodded. "I know you're both right, it's just . . . God, this hurts."

"You got a raw fucking deal to try and defibrillate your first patient on a freak call like this one," Tanner said, unyielding as granite. The voice of reason. "Nobody could've saved the boy, period."

Howard glanced at Sean, wishing the man knew how to follow his own advice regarding those who can't be saved. But now wasn't the time to worry about Tanner's near-tragic binge. He seemed to be holding up, making an effort like he'd promised.

Howard turned his attention back to the younger man. "We won't lie to you, Tommy. Losing a kid will stay with you forever, and coming to terms isn't easy. You've got us, though, and the department counselor when you need to talk."

"A shrink?" Skyler muttered. "I don't think so."

Not surprising. Most guys didn't care to spill their guts to a stranger. Especially one tied to administration and that had at least some power over whether a firefighter was declared fit for duty.

"We're here for you, whatever you need," Howard said, and Sean seconded.

Tommy's mouth trembled, but he held himself together. "Thanks."

Howard pulled Skyler into a brief, manly hug, slapping him on the back. Sean opted for shaking his hand, keeping a bit of distance. Such was the captain's way. Few outsiders would guess the straightforward, sometimes harsh man housed a huge heart buried under the facade of a hard-ass. A huge, broken heart.

Tommy left, and Eve stuck her head in, lowering her voice. "Is he okay?"

Sean's narrow gaze snapped to hers. "Tommy's not made of glass. The quicker you stop babying him, the better off he'll be."

Uh-oh. Eve Marshall wasn't the type to take crap from anybody, even the captain. Howard opened his mouth, but before he could interject, she stepped inside, hands fisted on her slim hips. Her eyes widened in mock surprise, and the smile on her face was feral.

"My goodness, someone is PMSing today! If you need a tampon, I've got one in my purse."

Howard stifled a grin. The woman was a bundle of dynamite, for sure.

She snapped her fingers. "I would offer you a maxi pad, but Julian filched my last one—"

Sean's face darkened with anger. "Goddammit, Eve! Don't you have something productive to do?"

Cocking her head, she pretended to consider it. "Hmm. Nope."

Snarling something unintelligible, but undoubtedly profane, Tanner stalked from the office. The second the captain cleared the doorway, Eve whirled to stare after him, false bravado withering to dust. Helpless longing flared in her eyes for a split second before she slammed an iron wall over the emotion and stiffened her spine.

"Asshole," she spat, and strode from the room.

"Whoa." Howard sighed. So that's the way it was for Eve. Looked like he *had* been under a rock. He wondered if Sean had a freaking clue, but doubted it. Jesus H., what a bomb waiting to explode. For the whole team.

The shift couldn't get much worse, he thought idly.

He was dead wrong.

11

Three loud tones over the call system shattered Howard's hard-won, albeit fitful, sleep. His nightmarish flight through his mother's garden dissipated like a wisp of smoke, leaving him disoriented and struggling to determine reality.

Confusion lasted only a second or two. Working on autopilot honed by years on the job, he'd nearly finished bunking out in his gear by the time the computerized voice plunged him headlong into another nightmare.

A residence fire. In their sector. Again.

What were the odds? Slim to none.

On the heels of that thought, a second realization slammed him wide awake. *Thank God it's not Kat's address. Thank you, sweet Jesus.*

His blood chilled. His churning brain barely registered Julian's vicious curse as they jogged out of their dorm-style room. The team poured into the bay with no sound save the pounding of booted feet, the opening and slamming of truck doors, the whir of the big garage doors sliding upward.

"Another house fire? This is freaking unreal." Julian rubbed the sleep from his eyes.

You have no idea.

God almighty. If this was another murder orchestrated

by his mysterious tormentor, he'd have to come clean with the guys and the chief. Tonight. With Kat, too, as soon as possible. In his defense, only two days had passed since he received the terrible photo, and he'd hoped no one would have reason to know and worry over it.

But he'd waited too damned long. His silence could've cost Kat her life. The knowledge sickened him.

Shaking his head, he forced thoughts of brutal murder and the aftermath from his mind. He had a job to do. Firefighters who let emotions or personal problems distract them at a scene risked going home in a body bag. And, Jesus, he had too many good things on his horizon to allow some sicko to take him out.

All the same, his focus didn't stop the strange prickle creeping up the back of his neck. Like before, an eerie sense that someone had just danced across his grave.

As he followed Zack into the night, he clamped down hard on the fear unfurling in his chest. This went beyond his scope of reality. He couldn't battle an enemy he didn't understand.

Worse, by the time he shoved the puzzle pieces together, the why could be revealed far too late.

Frank rolled underneath the big door to the bay just before it shut. A close shave. Shit, his timing had nearly been off. He'd used his stolen cell phone to call in the fire himself and had to haul ass in order to get inside the station, even with the house he'd used located only two miles away.

The house. He almost laughed, thinking how gullible the two sluts were to believe the pads belonged to him. Sure, it would've be easier just to use their places, but Sherri Pearce hadn't lived near Sugarland, much less within Station Five's sector. Lorna Miller had a clueless hubby at home. No good.

Didn't matter. Casing an empty house as a backup plan was child's play. All he'd had to do was break in beforehand, then pretend to unlock the door when he and the bitch arrived—this time in Lorna's car. He'd driven the Maxima from the fire and left it parked a mile or so away from the station for his latest move.

After he finished here, he'd drive the vehicle back to the downtown area, ditch it, and fetch his own piece of crap, the whole thing a done deal before the limp-dick cops figured out what the fuck was going on, or nailed the whore's identity.

He stood and listened intently as the sirens faded into the distance. With the team focused on rushing to their destination, he doubted anyone could've spotted him, even without the cover of darkness working to his advantage.

They'd be gone for a while, longer than normal, considering the hellacious mess they'd discover. He had plenty of time to leave the lieutenant a little gift. Not that he wanted to hang around any longer than necessary.

The bastard's bunk was the perfect target. More personal to have your space violated. Sinister. Finding the right one presented the real problem. He'd search quickly and if all else failed, he'd leave his surprise in the station's office.

Stepping through the door separating the bay from the hallway leading to the inner sanctum, he glanced back at the lettering on the window and smirked in dark amusement. EVERYBODY GOES HOME.

"Not always, boys." And definitely not after Paxton's beloved team got a load of what he planned for the next go-round. A thrill of anticipation bolted down his spine. To annihilate the lieutenant's comrades was to deliver a crippling blow to the big sonofabitch.

Wait for it. Savor the moment.

Then cut Paxton off at the knees.

Until then, he had a task to perform. Keeping his head low and away from the windows, he tugged his pistol from the waistband of his jeans and made a cautious sweep through the living quarters and kitchen area. No one was supposed to be left behind on a call, but you never knew. Anyone remaining here would discover this was the unluckiest fucking day of his life—right before Frank's bullet plowed between his eyes.

The front rooms, however, were empty. A single lamp had been left on in the living area, and in the kitchen, a dim bulb over the stove cut the gloom. The whole building felt deserted, but he kept the pistol at the ready, tightening his grip on the bag in his other hand.

Another hallway off the kitchen led to the office, which housed a desk, computer, phone, and a charger stand for two walkie-talkies, one missing. The usual crap.

Farther down the corridor, lights in four rooms had been switched on. These would be the bunks in use on this shift, he guessed. Hit the lights, dress in a hurry. Made sense, and made his mission easier.

The room closest to the office he figured was the captain's. Simple reasoning, with inspection yielding no solid proof, except that one bed hadn't been slept in. Whoever was staying in this room didn't share, which seemed consistent with the highest rank. A small framed photo beside the bed showed a brown-haired man, a gorgeous broad, and two equally good-looking brats. Not the lieutenant's digs, then.

The next room held two occupants—but which two? Damn, the space was tidy to the point of sterility. On each small bedside table were three framed photos, an assortment of different families, lovers, a couple of dogs. Yeah, he should've realized each of the three shifts shared the bunks, so they didn't have room for a lot of personal memorabilia.

His eyes found a shelf above one bed, a football trophy perched there. Moving closer, he read aloud. "Thomas Skyler, Varsity MVP, Broadmore High School." Dated five years ago. This was one of Paxton's team. He'd seen the name in reflective lettering on the guy's coat when he'd stumbled from the burning house and puked his guts out. He laughed. "Fuckin' rookie."

The other bed was anyone's guess, the photos revealing no clues. Frank moved on, aware of the minutes slipping by. He needed to get this done, get the hell out of here. A sense of urgency tensed his shoulders, stealing some of the fun from snooping. That pissed him off.

The third room wasn't quite as bare. One table boasted a pic of a hot Mexican babe, among others. This one might belong to the man named Salvatore. And the other—

Pay dirt. Staring Frank in the face was a photo of Fire Chief Mitchell and his scrawny bird of a wife. His gun hand clenched hard around the pistol's handle. His head swam with sudden, consuming rage. A volcanic maelstrom of hate so deep and explosive, he thought he might die from the sheer force of it. A blinding hurricane that *must* have a more satisfying outlet than his pathetic efforts so far.

Concentrate, dammit. They'll return soon.

Tucking the gun in the waistband of his jeans, he emptied two small items from the bag onto the lieutenant's bed. Shook his head to clear the shrieking storm. There. Another move on the game board, perfectly executed. He only wished he could hang around to see high-and-mighty Paxton's face when he discovered his present.

Tried for the most unforgivable sin.

Sentenced to suffer in prolonged agony, desperately seeking the truth.

And finally, to whisper my name with his last bloody, goddamned breath.

The interior of the small white A-frame house was well on its way to becoming fully involved with flames by the time they rolled to a stop out front. Howard grimaced. Anyone still inside had to be rescued *now*. The place was about to go up like a tinderbox.

As he, Julian, and Tommy slapped the masks over their faces and turned on their Air-Paks, he worked to maintain his calm focus. A routine call, nothing more. Get in, search for survivors, get out fast.

At a glance, Howard noted Zack already at his post beside the engine, connecting the hose, manning the pump, and pulling gauges. Readying the small hand-held thermal imaging camera that used heat to "see" in a dark, smoked-filled structure, Howard raced for the front door. Julian and Tommy were on his heels, carrying the hose.

Sean, Zack, and Eve would remain outside as this shift's RIC—or rapid intervention crew—readied to form a rescue if their teammates inside got into a tight spot. Sean barked into his radio to the battalion chief, indicating that his men were executing a primary search of the premises. Once again, the engine companies from stations Three and Four were en route.

One fact became readily apparent. No hysterical family had come running to greet them, screaming for their belongings or another family member to be saved. Which meant the people were trapped inside, or they weren't home.

And if the residents weren't here, there was a very

real chance the team had just inherited a repeat of last Saturday night. *No, don't think that. Not yet.*

On the porch, he and Julian positioned themselves on either side of the door. At Howard's nod they slammed booted feet into the area around the lock. Once. Twice. The flimsy mechanism gave on the third blow. Immediately, the men leapt aside as a wall of searing heat and flame exploded from the opening.

"Shit!" Julian gestured with a gloved hand, yelling to be heard over the noise. "Let's try around back!"

The three of them jogged to the entrance on the back porch, unhampered by a fence or a snarling dog. Howard had a bad feeling that was about all they had going their way.

Flames dancing in a corner window to their right illuminated the yard and the porch where they stood. He'd lay money that was a bedroom, and if so, he dreaded knowing what awaited them. Like he had a choice.

Julian and Tommy dispatched the lock with ease, kicked in the door. Smoke billowed outward, black and thick, but no flames issued forth to bar the way. Howard stepped inside holding the thermal camera, leading them into hell.

A boiling furnace of heat seemed to melt his skin right through his protective clothing. Orange fire licked along the walls and ceiling of the living room and down a hallway to their right, like an angry dragon's fiery breath. A beast, roaring its challenge, daring them to meet her wrath and escape unscathed.

Forging through the murk, they made a quick sweep of the kitchen and living area. Finding no one, they moved down the hallway single file, Julian in the lead. In succession, they checked the first bedroom they came to, then the next.

Howard searched with the camera around the beds and underneath, inside the tiny closets. Anywhere a frightened person might've taken refuge, especially a child. Nothing. He peered through the murk at his partners, shook his head.

"Empty!" The crackling inferno was almost too loud for communication, the heat nearly unbearable.

"Let's hurry, man." Julian went on toward the last bedroom, where the blaze appeared to be concentrated.

Howard searched a shotgun bathroom off the hallway, moving straight toward the shower curtain, and flinging it back. His relief to find no one there was fleeting.

"Lieutenant!"

Julian's hoarse shout brought him at a run. In the three years he'd known Salvatore, he'd never heard that note of horror in the man's voice. The awful sound electrified every nerve ending, and he swallowed the bitter tang of fear, intent on getting to his comrade.

He skidded to a halt just inside the doorway to the main bedroom, where Julian and Tommy were desperately spraying the bed, dousing a wall of flames.

And on the burning bed were the remains of a person, handcuffed to a post. Charred to a crisp.

"Motherfucker." Tommy groaned, averting his gaze. "Not again."

For two heartbeats, he allowed himself to process the terrible reality of what he saw. The metal links of the cuff that had bound this poor soul to a gruesome death. The blackened flesh, split and peeling away from prone limbs and the grinning skull.

Sweet merciful God. He needed to vomit. Instead, he grabbed Julian's arm, dragging him backward. "Fire's out! There's nothing else we can do!"

Julian whirled, dark eyes wild. Hesitating only a second, he and Tommy stumbled after Howard, who glanced behind him to make sure his partners were keeping up. When they made the living room, the blaze in the entry was out, the exit clear, courtesy of the other companies who'd arrived.

Outside, Julian stripped off his mask and was bent over heaving, hands on his knees, obviously battling the urge to be violently sick. The discarded hose lay at his booted feet. Nearby, Tommy appeared shaken but okay. Then again, he'd gotten a load of this the last round. Next to him, a grim-faced Sean barked into his handheld, requesting the police.

Howard yanked off his own mask and gulped in a few deep breaths to steady himself. Meeting Sean's gaze, he wheezed, "Have them contact Detective Shane Ford." Howard braced himself.

"Julian said there was a body. *Another goddamned body*. You're telling me this is related to—"

"Yes."

Sean's mouth tightened. "You have to tell the team what's going on, Howard. Tonight." He let out a ragged breath, scanning the fire, which was pretty much out. "Every call is a risk, but this is different. Out of our league. Fuck."

Julian, who'd managed to collect himself, straightened, his attention bouncing between both men. "Tell us what?"

"Later," Howard said. "When we hand off this mess to the cops and get back to the station. We'll meet in the TV room."

"A meeting? In the middle of the frigging night?" Julian snorted. "Must be some shit, *amigo*."

Howard's voice was as hollow as he felt. "Yeah, my friend. It's some bad shit."

Two hours later, Howard paced the station's television room as his friends trudged in, filthy and exhausted. A headache built at his temples, borne of anger and bone weariness. He hated that the others were being dragged into this insanity. He'd love to meet whomever was responsible, tear his head from his neck, and ask questions later.

"Dude, what can't wait until after we get some shut-eye?" Tommy grouched, swiping an arm across his dirt- and sweat-streaked face. "Or at least a shower?"

A rumble of agreement echoed through the room as the rest plopped in various states of undress onto the sofa and chairs. All except the normally quiet Zack, who surprised them by snapping, "Shut up, assholes. Can't you see the lieutenant is serious?"

Everyone shut up, whether out of sheer surprise at the uncharacteristic thread of steel in Zack's tone or out of dawning realization that something heavy was taking place, Howard couldn't guess. Either way, he was grateful, and shot Knight a look of approval before beginning.

"This won't take long, but it's an issue that's affecting the whole group." Issue. What an understatement. He hesitated, chewing on the right words. "I have a problem involving the two arson murders, if that's technically what they are, and it's putting you all at risk."

"Six-Pack, what's wrong?" Eve asked softly, dark brows furrowed in concern.

"Seems that for whatever twisted reason, the killer has decided it would be fun to include me in his sick game. He left an obscene photo of the first victim on my front porch, taken before she was murdered." A round of colorful curses greeted this news. "The police confirmed the woman's identity."

Eve clapped a hand over her mouth, eyes wide. Julian leapt to his feet and let fly a string of Spanish expletives that needed no translation. Tommy said "dude" about twelve times, and Sean, who'd already known, still clenched his fists like he wanted to hit something. Or someone. Only Zack appeared to keep his cool, his laser-blue gaze studying Howard calmly.

"I'm glad you told us, Lieutenant," he said. "But no matter who sets the fires or why, it's our job to put them out. Period. This isn't your fault."

In his head, Howard knew he had no control over the killer's actions, but it hadn't stopped him from feeling somehow responsible. Zack's vocal support, quickly echoed by the rest of the group, lifted some of the burden off his shoulders.

Eve folded her arms over her chest. "You don't have any idea who this pervert is or what his grudge is against you?"

Grudge. The word freeze-dried him inside. Not once had he entertained the notion that this was some kind of revenge directed at him personally. Who hated him with enough passion to drag him into this nightmare? He had Bentley and Georgie, a few good friends, and led a mostly solitary life. Well, before Kat.

"This came straight out of left field. Total *Twilight Zone* material. I've got zilch." He sighed. "If anyone wants to swap shifts with the B or C team until this goes away, I'll understand."

"Bullshit."

"Fuck that."

A chorus of loud protests ensued, peppered with colorful descriptions of the ass-whooping the perpetrator would receive if any of them got their hands on him.

Grateful, Howard ended the meeting with a wave of his hand. "Thanks, guys. Now go get showered and try to catch a couple hours' sleep before shift change."

Eve stepped forward and gave him a brief, sisterly hug. "You need anything, big guy, you let me know."

"I appreciate that, Evie."

"Same here," Zack said, squeezing his shoulder. "Whatever I can do."

One by one they drifted out, much to his relief. He disliked the spotlight, and hated being the object of sympathy. He'd always been the team's pillar of strength. The one they counted on to be their rock.

Right now, *he* couldn't count on himself.

Dragging his tired carcass to the bunk was a huge effort. In their small room, Salvatore had removed his boots and stripped off his outer layer of protective clothing.

"*Cristo*, I smell," he grunted, peeling off the navy polo. He stretched, flexing the lean, bronzed muscles that made women lose their morals. A gold cross rested against his chest, seeming out of place on such an irreverent guy. "Mind if I go first?"

"Naw, go ahead." He turned toward his bed. And stopped cold. "Jules?"

"Hmm?"

"Is this yours?"

"What?" Clutching a clean pair of boxers, Julian glanced toward the lieutenant's bed. "Oh, the cell phone? I thought it was yours, man."

Howard stared at the black, rectangular flip phone, jaw clenching. Fear rose to choke him, lethal as the smoke from the fire. The tiny object lying next to the cell phone quadrupled his alarm. "You thought the ring was mine, too?"

"Say *what*?" Julian strode over to peer down at the diamond ring resting atop the spread. "How in the hell did that get there?"

Salvatore's confusion was genuine. Any hope that this might be one of the man's stupid pranks fizzled. Instead of attempting an answer he didn't have, he bent, reaching for the phone.

"Wait!" Julian grabbed his arm. "I don't think you ought to touch it. That detective might want to see this. Look, that could be blood." He pointed to the miniscule prongs holding a solitaire diamond.

Julian was right. A dark reddish substance could be seen in the crevices. He swallowed hard. "I need to open the phone. The damned thing wasn't left here for no reason."

"Use the edge of the sheet," his bunkmate suggested.

"Good idea."

Right. Like either of them had a freaking clue. Using the sheet, he pried up the earpiece. The screen saver blinked on, and the bottom dropped out of his stomach.

"Oh, God, no." He dropped the hideous thing, backpedaling into Salvatore.

"*Madre de Dios,*" Julian whispered, crossing himself. "I'll get the captain."

"Tell him to call Detective Ford, and get the cops here pronto."

The other man bolted from the room, leaving him alone with victim number two.

Mouth open in a silent scream, eyes bulging in horror. Bound to the bed, helpless as the dragon's flame ignited her creamy skin and long, dark hair.

12

Kat rolled onto one elbow, peered at the digital clock through bleary eyes, and groaned. Thirty minutes until rise and shine. Reality was creeping in with the brightening of the sky outside her window. All too soon, she'd have to leave her warm, comfy nest and get ready for another day with the rug rats.

Flopping back onto the pillows, she smiled to herself. She was supposed to have been born a rich, bored heiress. Obviously, there'd been an error at the soul factory, and she'd become a poor teacher instead.

On the other hand, she'd met Howard. Maybe her divine guide knew what was best for her after all.

A knock from the direction of the living room startled her, and she sat upright, one hand splayed across her chest. Under her palm, her heart beat a mad tattoo. Had the noise been someone rapping on her door, or was it an intruder?

She slid out of bed, grabbing her terry cloth robe from the foot. She tied the belt around her waist and knelt, fingers closing around the handle of the Louisville Slugger on the floor. Not as efficient as a gun, and using it required getting way too close to an attacker, but at least a bat couldn't accidentally go off and kill an innocent person.

As she stood and moved out into the short hallway,

four soft knocks sounded. Someone was at her door, trying not to wake the neighbors in the process of rousing her. If she'd been fast asleep, she might not have been awakened by the quiet noise. The idea gave her the creeps.

Kat tiptoed to the door and squinted through the peephole. A flood of relief whooshed the air from her lungs. Even in the hazy, dim predawn light, the huge shadow standing outside could only belong to one man. She simply didn't know anyone else so darned big.

"Who is it?" she called, just to be certain.

"Kat, it's me, Howard."

Convinced, she unlocked the door and let him in, then closed and locked it behind him. He walked past her and stood in the center of the room in the darkness, hands in his jacket pockets.

"Jeez, you scared the ever-lovin' hell out of me," she scolded, without too much heat. Marching past him, she propped the bat against the back of the sofa and switched on a floor lamp beside it. "What on earth are you doing here at six in the mor—"

She turned to face him, and the words strangled in her throat. Howard was dressed in his regulation blue pants and polo shirt, brown jacket open. Why had he left his shift an hour early to come here, and why did he look so down?

His gaze was trained on the floor as though the carpet held life's answers. His funky hair was even messier than usual, and he smelled of smoke. A black smudge streaked from his jaw down his neck, but his face and hands were basically clean. Like he'd washed but missed a spot or two.

Slowly, he raised his head. Misery swam in his chocolate brown eyes. The devastation on his handsome face squeezed her heart. Lines of exhaustion bracketed his sexy mouth, and the weight of the world seemed to rest on his broad shoulders.

"Good Lord, what's wrong? Howard?"

"Kat, I . . . I need you," he whispered.

"Oh, honey." She reached him in three steps, burrowed into his warmth, his strong arms around her. He pulled her so close, they might've been one person. Surrounded her, held her tight, his face buried in her hair. She wrapped her arms around his waist, thinking how strange it was for this mountain of a man to need comfort, and how wonderful that he'd sought her and nobody else.

Cheek pressed against the hard wall of his chest, she listened to the frantic thud of his heart. His pain was a tangible thing, a deep ocean, drowning him in furious, relentless swells. She held him, trying to be his anchor, not knowing what else to do. What to say.

"The boy," she said in sudden realization. "The one who touched the power line. He died, didn't he?"

His big body shuddered. "God. Yes, he did."

"Oh, Howard." She gave him an extra hard squeeze. "I'm so sorry."

"Me, too. But that's not why I'm here."

Kat's concern for him grew by leaps and bounds. By his admission, nothing in his job was more difficult than the loss of a child. She pulled back to see him better, cupping his face in her hands.

"Then what has you so upset? Sweetie, talk to me."

"Later." His lashes lowered, his dark gaze fixing on her mouth. He kissed her gently, his tongue sweeping past her lips to play with hers. To brush behind her teeth, seeking, tasting. He broke the kiss. "Later."

"But—"

"I need you, Katherine," he said, his voice thick. "I need to be inside you, making love to you. I *have* to. Please don't turn me away."

The soft plea, raw with honesty, shattered something inside her. No one had ever needed her so much. No man had ever gazed at her as though she were the air in his lungs, as though she had the power to crush him with a word. This man—*her* man—was hurting. Badly.

And he came to me.

Clasping his hand, she led him to her bedroom. He stood watching as she peeled off her robe, tossed it to the floor. The woman in her relished the barely audible intake of breath, the tensing of his body. The predatory glitter of his eyes in the darkness as he stripped off his jacket and shirt.

She positioned herself on the bed, enjoying the view as he made short work of the rest of his clothing. Naked, he approached, crawled onto the bed, straddled her hips. He rose above her, muscled thighs trapping hers, big, work-roughened hands cupping her full breasts. She studied the curve of his jaw, his neck, his smooth, luscious chest. She loved the indentation at the hollow of his throat, the tufts of hair under his arms, the line from his navel to the base of his penis that ended in a soft nest.

Ooh, yes. Best of all, she loved how his long, thick erection rested atop her belly, his sac nestled against her sex. His body language vibrated male dominance. Possessiveness. And Lord help her, she longed to be possessed.

"You're so beautiful," he murmured.

"You make me *feel* beautiful." Capturing a tiny bead of pre-cum on the tip of one finger, she swirled the moisture around the head of his cock. "Nobody's ever made me feel so great before. Just you."

He groaned, rolling her nipples between his fingers. Plumping them to attention, sending little sparks of delight shooting to her sex. She felt herself grow wet and shifted, squirming a bit.

Scooting back to gain access, he skimmed a palm

down her tummy. His fingers brushed her tawny curls, found the dewy folds. Deftly, he parted the lips to her opening. Dipped one finger into her heat, then out. In and out. Spreading the wetness all over her slick flesh.

"You're so hot for me, aren't you, baby?"

She arched into his touch. "Yes, oh, God, please . . ."

"Please what?"

"Make love to me," she begged.

Parting her thighs, he rose over her. Guided the head of his cock to her sex, parted her opening. Stretched her as he slid inside. Deeper, deeper than she'd believed possible. He sank to his balls with a moan, filling her completely. Bracing his arms on either side of her head, he took her mouth in a slow, passionate kiss. Sucked her tongue as he began to shaft her in smooth strokes.

The earthy scent of him filled her senses as he stuffed her with his cock. Smoke, sweat, and the salt of his skin. So physically superior, yet vulnerable. All man.

All hers.

Howard broke the kiss, tilted his head back and closed his eyes as he made love to her. She'd never seen anything so erotic, so sexy as this man lost in passion.

"God, yes, *Howard*."

The fire at her core, licking at her entire body, leapt higher. Burned hotter. Wrapping her legs around his waist, she clutched his shoulders, urging him faster. Deeper.

Gathering her close, he increased the tempo of his thrusts, sliding his cock out almost to the head, then driving home again. Each plunge brushed his penis along her clit with sizzling friction, driving her to a near frenzy.

His muscles flexed and bunched under her fingertips. His sheer power wrapped around her body, sweeping her closer to the precipice, yet protecting her. Promising to catch her when she flew apart.

His hips pistoned into her now, his balls slapping against her rear. The decadent sucking noises of sex, their pungent scent, the potency of the man loving her, flipped the switch. Drove her over the edge, decimated her scant control.

Kat cried out as her vaginal muscles began to spasm, clenching his cock. Three more thrusts, and he joined her with a shout, burying himself to the hilt. Spilling into her as she clung to him and milked his shaft, on and on.

Breathing hard, Howard held her tight, cock jerking for several long moments as he rode out his release. They were both drenched in sweat, but she'd never felt more wonderful in her life. She couldn't fathom how she'd survived all these years without this man's incredible lovemaking. Not only did she love his vibrant sexuality, but his warmth and companionship. The way he cared about others, even if he tried to keep his emotions hidden.

I love him.

The knowledge flattened her like roadkill twitching on the highway. How could she have fallen for Howard already?

But a woman's heart knows what it knows. Lord help her, she didn't have a clue what to do next.

One thing for sure, letting on to him definitely wasn't on the agenda. Not for a while, until she knew how he felt.

He slipped out of her and rolled to his back, pulling her with him. She used his shoulder for a pillow and splayed a hand on his chest, stroking the supple bronzed skin.

"Now that you've had your comfort sex, is this the part where you spill about what's eating you?"

The hand smoothing her back stilled. "You gave me comfort, true. But our loving was more than that."

The words cloaked her in light. "I agree."

"But I do owe you an apology."

Rising, she peered at him. "What for?"

His expression was unreadable. "For barging into your home like a nutcase, and pouncing on you like a rabid horn dog, for starters."

"Well, I sorta enjoyed the horn dog part," she teased.

"I made love to you without a condom, baby. I'm sorry."

He sounded so pissed at himself. Her lips curved up. "I was there, remember? I think at least half the responsibility is mine. Besides, we're both healthy people and I'm on the pill—although accidents do happen."

He looked away, mouth thinning. "Not much chance of that."

"Why not?" Next to her, he stiffened. "Howard?"

"I use a condom only for disease protection. I can't have children," he said quietly.

Stunned, at a loss, she stared at him. Howard was one of the most virile men she'd ever laid eyes on, and he couldn't have kids? A memory seized her, of Howard gazing at little Emily Jean's antics in the park. A look of stark longing etched on his face. An innocuous moment pulled into sharp focus.

There are things you don't know about me. Things that might change your mind.

"Bet you weren't expecting to hear that." His slight smile was lopsided and sad.

"God, sweetie," she breathed. "I—I don't know what to say. I'm so sorry."

He shrugged, but didn't quite succeed in hiding his regret behind false indifference. "It's a fact about me, like my eye color. No big deal."

Oh, she didn't believe that nonsense for a second. "So you were born unable to father children?"

"No. That's not what I meant."

His tone said *subject closed.* Curious, she pushed a tad more. "Then what happened?"

He sighed, perhaps wishing he hadn't brought it up. "Remember I told you my father dumped me in the woods before he took off and crashed his truck?" She nodded, her silence urging him to continue. "Before the bastard left me, he beat me nearly to death."

Kat pressed her fingers over her mouth in shock. Howard's father had attempted to murder his own son. How could anyone do something so horrible to a little boy?

"It's ancient history, Kat," Howard said, tipping her chin up with one finger. "I beat the odds and survived. Because I was so sick with a prolonged raging fever, my sperm didn't. End of story."

Not by a long shot. She was beginning to realize there was much more to Howard Paxton than she'd ever believed. A part of him that he kept buried in the grave of his past, never to be resurrected. He'd made it clear he was finished discussing his ghosts, but there were many more where this revelation had come from. She was certain.

Howard didn't want to reopen his wounds for anyone, even her. And if he forever withheld a vital part of himself, refused to talk with her about important matters, putting her off with hot sex—glorious as it was—as an invisible barrier, the distance would slowly wear on them both. Even now, he was avoiding discussing the reason he was there.

The first sign of real trouble in paradise.

Letting him off the hook for the time being, she brought the conversation back to the present. "Do you want children eventually? There are other options."

He raised a dark brow. "Do you?"

"I asked first."

"Someday," he hedged. "There's always adoption."

She tried an encouraging smile. "You bet. Hey, you didn't turn out so bad, right?"

Her teasing coaxed a small smile from him. "I don't know. Ask Bentley and Georgie on Saturday."

"I will." She poked a finger in his chest. "Now, are you going to keep running me in circles, or tell me what brought you to my door, looking like a car crash victim?"

If he noticed she hadn't answered his question about kids, he didn't let on. She wasn't avoiding the issue, but she sensed that if she allowed him to turn the subject off himself, wringing the truth from him would prove even more difficult.

"When do you have to be at work?"

Sitting up, she glanced at the clock. Damn. "In an hour, and I still have to get showered and dressed. Why don't I call in, tell them I'll be a little late? They can get someone to cover my class."

"No, don't do that." Slipping from the bed, he stood and raked a hand through his spiky hair. Frustration etched lines around his mouth. "Why don't you get cleaned up? Then I'll drive you to work. We can talk on the way."

Thus allowing Howard to distance himself from whatever was upsetting him. If he had to pay attention to the road, he could retreat, so to speak. But unless she wanted to wait and wonder all day, what else could she do?

"All right. Want to wash my back?" She began to crawl out of bed, pausing to shake her bottom and waggle her brows.

Which earned her a swift smack on one butt cheek.

Kat squealed. "Oow! Hey!" Scrambling from the bed, she stood rubbing her bottom, scowling at his

shit-eating grin. "I'll get you for that, Lieutenant.
When you don't see it coming."

"Don't threaten me with a good time, sweetheart,"
he drawled. "Unless you can deliver."

"Oh, you!" Biting her lip to keep from laughing, she
turned and headed into her bathroom. Only when the
water had heated in the shower and she stepped in did
she realize he wasn't going to join her.

And that he'd managed to use his charm to temporarily distract her from his continued withdrawal.

The knowledge put a damper on her spirits, so she
countered the self-defeating doubt with the facts. One,
when the chips were down, her big, strong man beat a
path to *her* door. Launched himself into *her* arms. Two,
they were still getting to know one another, and men
historically required more time than women to "come
around," as her mother was fond of saying. She just
had to be patient.

Twenty-five minutes later, dressed in black pants
and a blue sweater, hair pulled up and clipped in a
simple twist, Kat gave her appearance a final, critical
eye in the mirror. Not bad, considering how fast she'd
put herself together. She wanted to make sure Howard
had time to explain what was going on before her du-
ties interrupted.

She found him in the living room, dressed once
more in his smoky work clothes, wearing a trench in
the carpet. Every female hormone in her body sighed
in appreciation of him, so tall and breathtaking, commanding with his mere presence. She had to remind
herself that he was keeping secrets. And wouldn't
share, if something drastic didn't force his hand.

"I have a few minutes," she said. He turned to face
her, and she gestured to the sofa, injecting steel into
her voice. "Sit, and lay it on me. We're not leaving here
until you do."

Resigned, Howard lowered himself to the cushions

with a weary sigh, elbows on his knees. She went to sit beside him, waiting with growing alarm. Whatever she'd imagined was wrong, nothing could match the electric shock his next words sent singing through her body.

"I've been targeted by the murderer who torched Sherri Pearce."

She gaped at him, trying to assimilate this information into something that made sense. "Wh-what? Targeted, how?"

Hands clasped between his spread knees, he looked at her, brown gaze filled with misery. Guilt. "He's left photos of the victims specifically for me to find. No note, no other clues."

"Wait. Victims, plural?" She stared at him, feeling as though she'd stepped off a ledge into empty air.

"Yeah. We got another call last night. A woman, bound to a bed and set on fire, but we didn't know until we entered the house. When we got back . . . " He paused, swallowed hard, eyes darkening in memory. "The bastard had somehow gotten inside the station, found my bunk. He left the woman's cell phone on my bed, and when I flipped it open . . . oh, God."

Howard's shoulders slumped, and he buried his face in his hands. Kat laid a palm on his broad back. "Tell me."

"He'd used a picture of her as the screen saver." His voice was almost inaudible. "She was screaming . . . burning."

Horrified for the poor woman, for Howard, Kat slipped her arm around his waist. Rather than peppering him with questions, she waited, hoping he'd open up. Get the grief and anger he must be feeling off his chest.

"Why is he doing this?" Howard agonized, lifting his head. "Is he killing them because of me, as punishment for something I've done wrong? I'd never be able to live with that."

No, he wouldn't. The knowledge terrified her. "You don't know what's in his sick mind, Howard. No more than you can control his actions."

He barked a bitter laugh, his eyes flashing with barely suppressed rage. "And he's loving the hell out of it, too. Saving lives is more than my job, it's my passion, my legacy from Bentley. And for some reason, the monster is getting his kicks by rubbing my nose in failure. No, he's *reveling* in torturing me."

Therein lies the truth. Kat shivered, unable to suppress the notion that Howard hit closer to the mark than he realized. "What about the first picture? Did he leave it on your bunk with the second one?"

Howard shifted, glancing at her uneasily. "No. I found it stuck in my front door in an envelope, late Sunday night."

Frowning, she began to follow the thread to its natural conclusion. And didn't like what she found one bit. "Monday night, you didn't say a word, even after the call from Detective Ford." Thinking back, she stiffened, removing her arm from around him. "I asked you why he phoned, and you lied to me."

After they'd had hot, pulse-pounding sex.

After she'd opened herself to him in a way she'd never done with any man.

"I didn't want you involved unless—"

"I'm the only witness to murder, and I'm seeing the man he's jacking with." Angry, she pushed off the sofa. "What part of my *involvement* didn't you get?"

"I didn't want to scare you unnecessarily."

She glared at him, incredulous. Damn it, she felt bad about what he was going through, but he had to understand the seriousness of his mistake. "Well, I guess that makes it all right, then. Because God knows I'd much rather be dead than afraid and prepared."

Howard closed his eyes, hung his head. "Jesus."

Stepping away from where he was seated, she turned from him and crossed her arms over her chest to hide the tremor in her hands. To conceal the blooming fear, squeezing her throat with cold, bony fingers.

What if the killer had come after her last night instead?

What if that plan was still on his hideous agenda?

She heard the rustle of his clothing as he stood and moved to stand behind her. Big hands caressed her shoulders, and his warm breath fanned against her ear.

"I'm sorry," he entreated softly. "Forgive me."

His quiet, heartfelt plea melted her, though she remained firm against giving in just yet. He'd made the wrong decision for the right reasons, but the fact was he'd lied. Flat out. To her face.

"I can forgive a lot of things, but lying isn't usually one of them. Especially if the fib can get my ass toasted like a marshmallow." She turned in his arms, and the deep hurt in his eyes speared her heart. Reaching up, she cupped one shadowed cheek. "Promise me it won't happen again, Lieutenant."

"God, yes." Wrapping his arms around her, he crushed her to his chest. "I promise. I'd never do anything to put you in danger, you know that. Baby, I'll protect you with my life."

She burrowed into the solid wall of his body, hugging him close. Accepting. "Then I forgive you, but I'm sure it won't come to anything so dire. The police will catch him."

"I'm sure they will." He sounded as convinced as she was, which wasn't much. Letting go, he pulled back and tipped her chin up with one finger, giving her a slow kiss. "I'd better get you to work before you get a tardy."

She heaved a shaky sigh, glad to put the unhappiness aside, even temporarily. "Students get tardies. Teachers just get annoyed e-mails from the principal."

"Which all of you promptly delete and ignore."

"Because that's what you guys do when the brass gets their boxers in a bunch?"

He grinned. "I'll never tell. Might get back to Bentley."

Sending him a wan smile, she retrieved her purse and bookbag from the end of the sofa. Deep down, she was still upset with Howard for keeping the truth from her, and anger sat in her stomach like a brick. She'd never been able to stand a man who could lie without batting an eyelash, and the man she'd fallen for had done it easily.

With good reason.

She wished she had time to talk to Grace, but her sister was probably already headed to court. She could use a dose of her sibling's wisdom and serenity right about now.

"I'm not totally back in your good graces, am I?"

Damn. She could hardly fault the man for being less than honest, then follow suit. "No, but I'm working on it."

"Ouch." Wincing, he shoved his hands in his jacket pockets, looking very much like a boy who'd lost his best friend. A two-hundred-sixty-pound boy with linebacker shoulders. "Let me make it up to you."

She cocked her head. "I'm listening."

"Dinner out, like we'd planned," he said, a hopeful look on his handsome face. "My place afterwards. Bring a bag, and your appetite for bacon and eggs."

"Hmm. Presumptuous."

"Begging mercy."

"I highly doubt you've ever begged for anyone's mercy in your life, Lieutenant."

"Don't be so sure." Closing the short distance between them, he took one of her hands in his. "Please come over tonight, Kat. Stay with me."

Lord, what a tempting offer. Her resistance was taking a beating under his gentle assault. "I'll think about it."

"I'll pick you up at work around four."

"I can drive myself, you know. I'm not helpless."

"Absolutely not. Until this maniac is caught, I'm not letting you out of my sight more than necessary. You're safer with me."

"Howard—"

"Forget it."

Oh! Stubborn man! "Fine. We have a staff meeting this afternoon. Better make it four thirty." *Way to stick to your guns, girlfriend.*

Triumph flickered in his eyes, and his lips curved into a sensual smile. "It's a date."

"Didn't say I'd stay."

With that, she hiked up her bookbag and marched out. His amused chuckle floated in her wake, ringing in her ears. They both knew she'd dissolve into a gooey puddle at his first touch. Angry or not, her resistance would incinerate as his rough palms slid over her skin. As his length slipped between her thighs, impaled her throbbing sex.

She already wanted him again. Anywhere, any way she could have him. And she would, tonight.

Until then, she had only to survive the longest frigging day on record.

And somehow, try to dispel the feeling that they'd merely placed a Band-Aid over a festering wound in their blossoming relationship.

To shake the awful suspicion that Howard's body might be hers, but his secrets would always be his to keep.

13

"If you're gonna screw up, might as well do it royally," Howard muttered, dragging his sorry carcass into his bedroom.

Kat had been upset at his delay in telling her about his tie to the killer, but she'd been angry and hurt by his outright lie regarding Detective Ford's call. A fine woman like her would tolerate that sort of mistake only once, and causing her pain lanced him like an ice pick in the chest.

Problem was, he'd never learned to play show-and-tell with the bad stuff—and had no idea how to share the load after thirty-six years of keeping the crap locked in a tamper-proof box.

Trailing clothes across the floor, he lurched for the sanctuary of his bed. Wearing only his boxers, he flopped onto the soft mattress with a bone-weary groan. The shower could wait. At the moment, he couldn't move if the heavenly trumpets sounded, announcing the judgment.

Judgment.

The word chased him into exhausted sleep, conjuring the lurking demons. Manifesting them into the monster flying through the moonlit night. *Crashing through prickly brush and skeletal trees behind him as he ran for his life. Gaining ground with every stride. He hardly registered the limbs scratching his skinny arms and legs, tearing his favorite pajamas.*

He wasn't fast like his superheroes. Couldn't fly into the air and away from here for good. Or turn and face the bad man, zap him with his superpowers, and make Mommy happy again.

His heart filled his mouth, nearly strangling his terror-stricken screams.

"No! Mommy! Mooommeeee!"

"Goddammit, come back here, you worthless little shit!"

He ran harder. Knew what would happen if he obeyed. Daddy would hit him, not with the razor strap, but with the big stick in his hand. Hit and curse him, hit and hit and hit until he was bloody and still. Stiff and sticky like Andy Roger's dog after Daddy caught him sniffing around in the front yard. Like—

A cruel yank at the back of his collar jerked him clear off his feet. Screaming, he kicked and fought with everything he had, out of sheer instinct. A sixth sense his now-adult brain recognized as the knowledge that he had nothing left to lose.

That he was about to die.

He scratched and bit the arm holding him, sinking his tiny teeth in deep. Daddy's enraged bellow gave him only a second's satisfaction before he was slammed bodily to the forest floor.

Sucking in a breath, he started to let go another scream, but a hard kick to his stomach stole his chance. The blow lifted him off the ground, waves of sickening pain blowing to dust what precious little defense he had.

He'd never pretend to be a superhero again. Daddy was making sure of that. In Howard's small, sad world, the bad man always won.

He never saw the next kick coming, aimed at his privates. Curling into a tight ball, he made himself as small as possible. Vomited onto the ground, hurting so badly. Praying for the monster to go away.

More blows, the steel-toed boot connecting with brutal force. Hammering his frail body all over.

Daddy's hands grasped the front of his pajama shirt in an iron hold, shaking him like a rag doll. "I'm finally rid of you," the monster sneered, features twisted with hate. Soulless eyes gleamed in the darkness and he fully comprehended what no young boy should.

With deadly precision, the monster rammed his head into the ground. Again and again. The night exploded into a million stars, and hot liquid bubbled to his throat, choking him. He couldn't cry, couldn't move. He began to float, his brain and battered body disconnecting from the terror. A mercy.

"Die, you mangy bastard," the monster gloated, releasing his helpless prey, getting to his feet.

And drawing back his boot for the killing blow.

Howard jolted awake with a strangled shout on his lips. Blood pounded in his ears, thrumming in ruthless tempo to the headache knifing his skull. For one horrifying moment he glanced around wildly, half expecting to find himself trapped in the nightmarish past. His broken and dying shell clinging to life. Abandoned and forgotten.

But the tentacles of long ago gave way to the present light of day seeping through the vertical blinds. To blessed reality. He'd survived, though not completely unscathed.

This crap had to be a suppressed memory. The details were becoming too clearly defined, the curtain lifting a little more each time. The nightmare wasn't just a by-product of the abuse, as he'd hoped.

No, his flight of terror had been real. He was almost certain.

And even more certain that out of sheer, gut-level self-preservation, he didn't want the scenario to become any clearer.

Some doors were better left sealed forever.

* * *

Kat watched Howard sleep, thinking love ought to be simple, and rarely was. Not even in fairy tales.

After picking her up from school in his enormous truck—to the delight and rampant curiosity of her friends and coworkers—Howard had been polite and solicitous all afternoon. Over a pleasant dinner at Don Poncho's, they'd made *nice* conversation about *nice*, safe topics until she'd wanted to scream at him to get real. To talk to her the way he'd done at the park, reveal more about himself.

Following dinner, there hadn't been any talking at all. Forgoing the movie, he'd driven them to his house, carried her to his bedroom, and made love to her with fierce urgency, as though she might disappear any minute. Then again from behind, slow and deep, savoring every inch of their bodies joined as one.

A gentle half smile curved her mouth. The sexy devil had managed to distract her yet again. For hours. Even now, at three in the morning, she couldn't sleep for the sheer thrill of simply looking at him.

Howard was sprawled on his stomach, his face toward her, hugging his pillow, one arm draped over the pillow behind his head, the other arm buried underneath it. The position caused the ropy muscles in his biceps and broad back to bunch admirably. Her gaze traveled down his spine to the indention at the small of his back, which she found oddly endearing, to his bare, sculpted buttocks. Then on to his long legs, entangled in the sheets.

Warming inside, she let her gaze roam to his face, so vulnerable in sleep, his hair untamed, poking in every direction. Long, dark lashes curled against his stubbled cheek. His lips were slightly parted as he breathed in and out, his back rising and falling.

She'd never had the chance to observe Howard this way before, and the man made a darned fetching sight. Especially when he had no clue he was being studied.

A quiet sound issued from his throat, very much like a whimper, and Kat frowned. His arms tightened around the pillow, and his breathing grew shallow. Frantic.

"Noo," he moaned, big body jerking as though receiving a blow. "No, please . . . don't . . ."

"Howard?" She laid a hand on his back, and he flinched like she'd struck him. "Sweetie, wake up."

"I'll be good," he whispered, ducking his head. "Daddy, stop."

She tried again, shaking his shoulder hard. "Honey, it's Kat. Wake up!"

His lashes fluttered open and he stared at her, suspended between worlds. Even in the darkness she saw his eyes were moist, fathomless with untold pain. He blinked, awareness of his surroundings returning, though the haunted shadow in his expression remained.

"Kat?"

Nodding, she stroked his hair, combing her fingers through the soft strands at his temple. "It's me. You were having a nightmare."

Heaving a deep sigh, he sat up and ran a shaking hand down his face. "God. I'm sorry, baby."

Sitting up to see him better, she touched his arm in a gesture of comfort. "I was already awake, and even if I wasn't, there's no need to apologize." She hesitated, then tried nudging him toward opening up. "Tell me about it?"

A nudge he apparently had no wish to act upon now any more than he had earlier, judging from the grim set of his mouth. "No. It's ancient history, not important anymore."

"How often do you have these nightmares?" She guessed that this wasn't a rare thing. He'd dismissed the disturbing episode much too easily. His shrug confirmed her suspicions. "Obviously something is bothering you if this happens a lot. You should talk to someone. Who knows? It might help."

Turning to her, he lowered his lips to hers. "You do help me, pretty Katherine. Just by being here with me, just by being you."

Not fair, dammit! The man was incorrigible. Insatiable. "Wait—"

Instantly, he had her flat on her back, his hard length pressed against her thigh. Determined not to let him get his way this time, she tore her mouth from his and pushed at his chest. Which was a bit like trying to move a bus.

"No, Howard! Get off me."

Stiffening, he stared at her like he'd been slapped. "What?"

"You heard me. Rev down that turbo-charged libido and give me a break before you wear me out."

"Oh. Sorry." His disappointment was palpable as he unwrapped himself from her and scooted to lay on his side, facing her.

"I mean, three times in one day," she teased, attempting to soften what he obviously saw as a rejection.

"I was saving up for the right woman," he protested, a little sulkily.

"Me, too, for the right man." She smiled at him in the darkness, touched his face.

"Am I? The right man?"

She felt the weight of his stare, heard the longing behind the casual question. "I can't imagine wanting anyone else, Lieutenant," she said honestly. That didn't exactly give him a direct answer, but it was the best he'd get for now. Until she was sure about his feelings and her place in his life.

Until Howard was comfortable sharing his deepest

thoughts and emotions without using sex as an evasive maneuver.

Rolling to his back, he opened his arms. "Hold you?"

Without hesitation, she snuggled into his warmth. Into the circle of his strong arms, protecting her from all the bad stuff life might throw in her direction.

But who would protect Howard?

A chill whispered over her bare skin and she burrowed closer, trying to dispel the notion that she and Howard were rushing toward disaster. A train wreck of cataclysmic proportions.

Who was operating the controls? She and Howard, or a ruthless killer bent on ruining her lover's life? And why was she certain the three of them were impossibly entwined?

Nothing made sense, and she was too sleepy to think about terrible visions of impending doom. Nothing bad was going to happen to either of them, from any source.

Their relationship would strengthen, continue to grow.

And the police would catch the murderer.

She had to believe that, because the alternative was too awful to consider.

Howard pressed ten pounds of seasoned ground beef into hamburger patties and laid them on two huge silver trays, one by one. Sure, he could've done those frozen ready-to-cook kind from the store, especially for a large crowd. But they tasted like cardboard hockey pucks, and only the best would do for Bentley's birthday.

And for Kat. Yeah, he admitted he wanted to impress her. He wanted her to love Bentley, Georgie, and his friends. It was important to him that she enjoy herself. Grace, too. He was glad Kat's sister was tagging

along. Kat bringing Grace seemed significant somehow, though he didn't dig too deeply into why.

Patting out the last burger, he glanced at the kitchen
wall clock. Kat and Grace would arrive in an hour, a
little after everyone else. He'd asked Kat to come over
before the other guests, but Grace had a last-minute
problem to deal with regarding a client, right in the
middle of their planned shopping excursion, and Kat
insisted on waiting to accompany her. Defense lawyers
never rested, he supposed.

After washing his hands, he studied the place with
a critical eye. Spotless. He'd worked his ass off to make
today perfect, and his modest house gleamed.

Outside, the cool, sunny fall day couldn't be more
gorgeous. Extra chairs were arranged on the deck and
lawn. The umbrella had been raised over the picnic
table, the grill cleaned and ready. Two metal washtubs
of beer, wine, and soda were iced down in one corner
of the deck.

Some of the guys, like Jules and Clayton Montana
from B-shift, would bring hard liquor. Though he personally didn't touch any of the stuff, alcohol was fine
as long as everyone drank responsibly. If not, they'd
get their keys taken and find themselves settled in his
guest room or on the sofa.

He hoped that wouldn't be necessary. Three or
more bodies would make a definite crowd. Last night,
on his thankfully quiet Friday shift, he'd missed Kat to
the point that their forced separation made him nuts.
Two nights of her in his bed, making love at leisure, already had him spoiled.

Damn, he wanted more—and not just more sex.

More of Katherine McKenna.

And didn't *that* scare the hell out of a confirmed
bachelor?

He tore open a package of tortilla chips and
dumped them into a plastic bowl without really pay-

ing attention. Instead, he saw Kat's white smile lighting her from the inside out, her vibrant optimism and
simple joy of living bathing him like rays of the sun.
Loosening a tight, hard knot inside his chest. Making
him wonder if it was truly possible to place total trust
in another person, to risk devastating your soul for the
abstract promise of love and forever.

The scene shifted, and he pictured her on her hands
and knees, round bottom thrust upward, legs spread
wide. Plump curves and willing flesh, the gleaming,
juicy peach of her folds his for the taking. Wet and hot,
inviting him inside. Her blond head thrown back with
a cry as he plunged his cock into her moist sex—

The insistent peal of the doorbell shattered the orgasmic memory. Muttering an oath, he frowned at his
erection. His loose khaki cargo shorts and blue polo
worn untucked helped to cover his dilemma, just
barely.

By the time he reached the front door, he had the situation semi-subdued. Finding his parents waiting on
the threshold deflated the problem altogether.

"Sweetheart, you look wonderful!" Georgie cried,
stepping inside. Reaching up, she cupped his face in
both small hands and pulled him in for a loud smooch
on the mouth, followed by a rather bone-crunching
embrace for such a tiny lady. "Where have you been,
son?"

Lord, he loved this woman. The petite brunette
gave and gave, with very little thought for herself,
never asking more than that he stop by once in a while
for pie and coffee.

Emotion squeezed his throat, and Howard had to
clear it before he could respond. "I've been busy, gorgeous. The chief's a slave driver, but then you know
better than I do," he said, releasing her. "Jeez, you're
lookin' fine. You'd better not be dieting again, 'cause
you don't need to lose the weight."

"Oh, pooh!" Georgie smoothed her crisp beige slacks, her eyes twinkling. "Don't change the subject. You get two days off at a stretch and can't even make time for a bowl of my peach cobbler anymore. Who is she?"

Sharp as a tack, and direct. That was Georgie.

"Now, honey, don't harass the boy about his love life the second we walk in," Bentley admonished good-naturedly, albeit with the familiar bark to his tone that made grown men cower. Grown men, maybe, but not his feisty little wife.

"Oh, fiddlesticks!" Balling one fist, a scowling Georgie punched her husband in the arm, which had the effect of a fly swatting a bull. "How am I supposed to know what's going on with our boy when he keeps his lips sealed tighter than Ernestine Judd wears her support hose?"

Bentley rolled his eyes. "There's an image we need before we eat." He turned to Howard, sticking out a big hand. "You shouldn't have gone to all this trouble."

He clasped Bentley's hand and found himself pulled into a hard embrace, the older man's other arm coming around his shoulders. Returning the hug, he slapped Bentley on the back. "No trouble at all," he said gruffly. "Happy birthday, big guy."

Happy birthday, *Dad*. The sudden, overwhelming urge to call Bentley "Dad" almost bowled him over. Why couldn't he say what he really felt to the man who'd given him everything? What was so difficult about that?

But the moment was lost as Bentley withdrew and straightened, blinking away the suspicious moisture in his eyes. "Balloons?" he snorted, waving a hand at the festive latex and the streamers hanging from the doorways and ceiling fans. "I'm too damned old for balloons."

Georgie grinned. "Relax, Ben, dear. At least they're not black."

"Huh. You got a beer around here, or did you spend it all on ice cream and Pin the Tail on the Donkey?"

Howard laughed, not fooled by the grumpy facade. "For you, I've got plenty of brewskis. Out on the deck."

Georgie led the way, marching into the kitchen, enthusing over how much preparation he'd done for the party. Her voice drifted ahead of them, and Howard started after her, only to find himself stopped by Bentley's firm grip on his arm. Surprised, he turned to see the older man's face serious, and more than a little upset. An unseen fist punched a hole in his stomach. He didn't have to ask why.

"You had to know I'd be informed about the arson murders from the start. A horrible crime like that doesn't go unnoticed, especially a repeat offense in one particular sector."

He nodded, the hole widening. "Yes, sir."

"Then tell me, son, why the blazing hell I had to find out about this limp-dick bastard threatening you from a homicide detective? From a *stranger*?"

He stared at Bentley, at a loss. The man was furious. And hurt. "Because I haven't actually been threatened—"

"Don't piss up my leg, boy," he hissed, glancing toward the kitchen, where his wife was praising the crab dip. "You should've come to me from the start. I should've been the first person to know that you were being targeted by a deranged killer."

"I'm sorry, sir." Heaving a deep breath, he steeled himself. "I breached protocol by keeping it from you. I'll be in your office first thing tomorrow—"

"This has nothing to do with protocol, goddammit! You're my *son*." He clamped one big palm on Howard's shoulder and squeezed, fingers biting into his skin through his shirt. "You and Georgie are the only family I've got, don't you get it, kid? Losing either of you . . ." Bentley choked, visibly struggling to control his emotions.

Oh, God. This was precisely the scene he'd hoped to avoid, though he was stupid to believe he could have. Seeing solid, iron-willed Bentley Mitchell so undone came as a shock to his system. Lines of stress creased his forehead and bracketed his mouth, making the still-handsome man appear ten years older. He'd have been worried no matter who spilled the beans or when, but Howard felt responsible.

"I never meant to keep this from you," he murmured. "I hoped the first photo was a sick joke. And when he left the second one Tuesday night . . . Jesus. I was going to tell you and Georgie. I didn't want to ruin your birthday, that's all." Scant defense, but a truthful one.

"Christ almighty, you're as thickheaded as I am." Dropping his hands, he studied his son, his expression a mixture of exasperation and pride. "I don't give a shit about my birthday; I care about you. Don't leave me out of the loop again."

"I'm getting a lot of that." All told, he'd gotten off pretty easy with Bentley. "Georgie doesn't know?"

"No, but I'll tell her after tonight. Dammit, she's been looking forward to the party all week, mostly missing you."

"She'll be ticked at both of us."

"Naw, just at me." The older man shook his head, a rueful smile touching his lips. "She worships the ground you walk on."

"What on earth are you two whispering about out there?"

Georgie's accusing demand from the kitchen made them jump guiltily. Her husband recovered first.

"Stuff going on at work, petunia," he soothed. "I'll catch you up later."

"Humph! Today is your day to relax, O Great Chief, so put office politics on the back burner, grab your beer, and sit on the deck with me. The weather's beautiful!"

"Coming," he called. Turning to Howard, he raised his brows, pinning the younger man with his best Do Not Fuck with Me look. "We'll finish discussing this later."

Oh, goody. "Yes, sir."

Saved by the doorbell. Bentley ambled into the kitchen and out of sight while Howard answered the door, glad for the brief respite. The chief could smell a lie at a thousand paces, and he'd actually tried to keep the situation under wraps. Idiot.

The morose cloud hanging over his head vanished as Eve, Zack, and Tommy blew inside, wrestling a large wrapped gift. Safety in numbers. Security in friends. The trio was laughing at some wisecrack Skyler had apparently made, because Eve was smacking their youngest teammate on his flat belly.

"You sexist piglet!" She was nearly doubled over with laughter. "A grade-A pig in training, barely out of diapers!"

Leering, Skyler performed a perfect, rude Michael Jackson grab on his crotch. "Hey, I got your piglet hanging, baby. Try this on for size and we'll get your obvious confusion cleared right up for you, sweet thang."

"Ha! When I'm into pimple-faced teenagers, I'll let you know, *baby*." Spinning to greet her host, she clapped Howard on the shoulder. "House looks super, Six-Pack. Thanks for having us."

Behind her back, Tommy splayed a hand on his chest and mouthed *love me*. Oh, boy. Just what the team needed. A twenty-three-year-old walking gland with the hots for Evie, even though Howard knew the kid's lust was unrequited.

Because *she* had it bad for *Sean*.

The recipe for a full-scale disaster.

"My pleasure, Evie. Beer's out back, and so's my folks," he said, a note of collective warning in his tone.

Zack grinned. "Code for 'We have to behave ourselves around Georgie.' Bummer."

Howard grinned back. The idea of Zack Knight raising any kind of hell struck him as funny. "Poor lady's got her hands full enough with the chief, don't you think?"

"Damned straight," Zack agreed, shrugging off his jacket. "Where do you want to put the present?"

"I'll take it outside on the deck with mine. Toss everyone's jackets in my spare bedroom, would you?" Hoisting the heavy box, he grunted. "Christ, what's in here?"

"That new set of golf clubs you said the chief has been eyeballing," Eve said, handing Knight her purse and jacket. "All three shifts chipped in a few bucks."

Their thoughtfulness and generosity touched him. "That's really great of you guys. Man, he's going to love these."

"What'd you get him?" Tommy asked, as he and Eve followed Howard through the kitchen.

"Nope, it's a secret. You gotta wait."

Tommy snatched a chip, crunched down. "Must be sweet."

"It is, trust me." To the tune of a healthy dent in his savings, but the expression on Bentley's face would make the extravagance worthwhile.

Outside, Howard settled their present next to his while the Chief took a swig from his longneck and grumbled about everyone ignoring his no-gifts rule. Of course, he was full of shit, so they ignored the grumbling, as well.

"What's a birthday without the bling, right, Einstein?" Tommy saluted Zack with his beer bottle and threw an arm around his shoulder as their friend joined them from inside.

Howard noted how Knight's cheerful smile seemed to freeze on his face. What was that about? The reference to his near-genius brain—which Knight worked overtime to downplay at all costs—or to birthdays?

Zack's response sounded forced. "Right you are. Somebody hand me a Diet Coke, will you? I'm pulling double D's for my buddies here."

Meaning he was the designated driver of the trio. Good, dependable Zack. Someone ought to keep a clear head, but it seemed Zack always got stuck playing chauffeur, errand boy, confidant. Yet he'd never lost his smile.

Until recently. Knight looked . . . tired. Disheartened. Could be his imagination, this weird impression that the light in the younger man's blue eyes had been extinguished when nobody was looking. That the man standing there with a stiff set to his shoulders and hollows grooving his cheeks wasn't the quiet, gentle, happy soul they'd taken for granted.

Some of the chief's cronies from administration arrived along with their wives, interrupting his concern, though he silently vowed to make time to talk to Zack at the first opportunity.

The party became lively as more guests arrived, most of them old friends from the teams at the two stations where Bentley had served as a firefighter in the trenches. The rest were guys from Station Five who'd become personally acquainted with their boss through Howard. A couple of the knuckleheads simply never passed on a chance to drink for free.

Things were running smoothly, everyone laughing and having a ball, snacking on chips, dip, and shrimp cocktail. Not a single hitch—until he spied Sean weaving through the guests, accepting surprised but happy greetings. Shaking hands, eyes glassy and too bright, laughter a bit too loud.

Tanner hadn't attended a social function since the death of his family. Truthfully, no one had expected him to show at this one. God himself only knew what chemical fortification the man had used to endure his first public appearance in almost a year, but despite his promise to Howard, he was definitely drunk or high. For Sean's sake, Howard prayed nobody noticed, especially the chief. What in hell was the fool thinking? He wasn't, simple as that. Hard to think with a bloody, gaping hole where your heart used to be.

With a sigh of resignation, he went to light the grill, keeping a wary eye on Sean. A man losing it in private was one thing, but for the boys to see their captain totally wasted was way into goat-fuck territory. He couldn't let that go down.

Julian arrived with his usual annoying flair, grinning like a cat with telltale feathers on his muzzle. "Hey, *amigos*! Where are all the lonely, single *mamacitas* hiding?"

Amazing. The guy kept Carmelita in the wings and still possessed the stamina to cruise the ladies.

"Far from you and your STDs, scumbag," rumbled John Valentine from B-shift.

The two commenced to bullshitting with each other, drawing snickers from the knot of guys surrounding them. All in good fun. Val seemed to like Salvatore okay, another zinger in a day full of surprises. *Would you looky there. Jules finally made a buddy.* Wonders never ceased. Now, if only the little turd would make an effort with his own team.

Finished lighting the grill, he heard Clay exclaim, "Holy shit, who are the babes?"

Even before Howard looked up, he knew which cuties had drawn the appreciative gaze of every hot-blooded male in the vicinity. Kat and a woman he assumed to be her sister were hovering on the deck, glancing around uncertainly, exchanging warm hellos with an army of curious strangers. Kat added a small gift bag to the growing number of presents on the table, and pride swelled in his chest. She didn't even know Bentley, but that hadn't stopped her from honoring him.

Kat's sister topped her in height by several inches. Tall and willowy, she held herself with regal poise. Her stance spoke of a woman used to being the center of attention, completely comfortable in her own skin. But there was nothing abrasive about her demeanor. Quite the contrary. Her large eyes were tilted up slightly at the corners, her wide, brilliant smile honest and inclusive of everyone around them. Straight, white-blond hair tumbled unbound down the back of her blouse nearly to the waist of her neat chocolate brown slacks.

Grace. What a perfect name for such a beautiful, ethereal woman. Oh, her sleek, stunning corporate looks couldn't hold a candle to Kat's voluptuous curves and pretty, fresh-faced innocence, but she'd certainly snagged her share of admirers.

As he strode to greet the ladies, he couldn't help but notice the poleaxed expression on Julian's face as he gazed across the yard at Kat's sister. Drink suspended halfway to his lips, Salvatore stared at her as though he'd never seen a true lady in his life, nor one so gorgeous. Probably never had.

Stick your hand in that tigress's cage and see what you get, lover boy. Looked as though his warning to Jules to stay clear of Grace poofed to mist within two seconds of her arrival. Salvatore's tough luck. The idea of Jules meeting his match and limping away with a few bleeding arteries for his efforts brightened Howard's day considerably.

Reaching the only woman he had eyes for, he

wrapped Kat in a huge hug, holding her for a few seconds longer than necessary. Then, just in case any of these horny bozos hadn't received the message, he tipped her chin up and lowered his head. Captured her mouth and gave her the most sensuous kiss he dared in mixed company.

"Dang, Six-Pack," one of the guys joked. "At least wait until everyone goes home before you round third base."

Hoots and catcalls ensued. Belatedly, he recalled Bentley and Georgie lounging nearby and broke the kiss, cheeks flaming. Lord, the woman made him lose all common sense.

Kat cleared her throat and gave an embarrassed giggle. "Well. I missed you too, Lieutenant." Waving a hand at her companion, she struggled to regain her composure. "Um, this is my sister, Grace McKenna. Grace, this is my . . . this is Howard Paxton."

Ah. Dating rule number two: Before exposure to family and friends, figure out what the heck you're supposed to call one another. Right behind number one, practice safe sex.

Grace intervened like a pro, smoothing over the uncomfortable moment. "It's so nice to meet you, Lieutenant Paxton." She smiled, holding out her hand. "Kat has told me so much about you. I'm sure your ears have been positively scorching."

"Howard, please." He took her hand, intending to give her a light squeeze, but she surprised him by gripping him in a handshake as firm and strong as any man's.

She nodded. "Howard, thank you for inviting me."

What a great combination for some lucky guy. Regal and beautiful, yet straightforward and confident. On the spot, he decided he liked Grace. "My pleasure. These guys can be a rowdy bunch, but they're basically harmless. Enjoy yourself."

"Oh, I intend to," she assured him, violet eyes sparkling. "It's been a horrid week in court, and I'm due for some fun."

"Can I get you something? Beer or wine?"

"A glass of Chardonnay would be fantastic. I see there's a bottle already open—"

"I'll get it," a low, masculine voice interrupted from nowhere. "White it is, *querida*. Shall we?"

Julian. He should've known the oversexed dog would make for the beauty like a heat-seeking missile. Grace and Kat exchanged pointed glances, and Grace shrugged, offering her new admirer a serene half smile.

"Lead the way."

The pair wandered off, and Kat frowned after them in worry. "I remember that guy from the fire at Joan and Greg's. Will she be all right with him?"

Howard chuckled. "Julian? With anyone else's sister, I'd have to say not a chance. But I have a feeling Grace is fully capable of carving out his liver with one manicured fingernail."

"True." Dismissing the matter for the moment, she heaved a shaky breath and scanned the crowd. "So, are you going to introduce me to your folks?"

If his heart got any bigger, he'd burst. "You bet, sweetheart. This way."

Introducing the girl to his parents. Not long ago, he'd have run far and fast at the suggestion. Screaming and covering his balls. Too intimate, too personal.

Sort of like chopping veggies in his kitchen. And spooning after sex.

With Kat at his side, he couldn't think of anything that pleased him more.

He was *so* toasted.

14

Kat shook in her sandals every step of the way to where Howard's parents sat enjoying the afternoon and their guests. Holy craparoni. Besides Howard, Bentley Mitchell was one of the biggest men she'd ever laid eyes on.

There was a much more imposing aura about the older man than she saw in Howard. A hard-as-nails presence. Maybe because he was chief, and that sort of experience meant his shit-o-meter had a sensitive dial.

As Bentley rose to greet her, she was struck anew by how closely Howard resembled him in build and facial structure. Even his short, dark brown hair liberally threaded with silver might've been Howard's match when the chief was younger.

Howard's parents waited for their son to introduce the new girl, expressions filled with welcome, and no little curiosity. The idea of being an insect under a microscope made her squirm. Out of instinct, she pressed into her lover's side, seeking the sanctuary of his big, warm body.

"Relax, you'll be fine," he whispered in her ear. Placing an arm around her, he squeezed her shoulder in reassurance. "Guys, I'd like you to meet a very special lady. This is Kat McKenna. Kat, these are my folks, Bentley and Georgie Mitchell."

A very special lady. Yeah, she liked the way he'd said that, so poised and confident, in his deep, sexy voice. Beat the heck out of her stumbling intro to Grace.

Bentley took her hand in both of his, pumped it in a firm grip. "When my boy keeps a secret, it's a damned good one," he said gruffly. "Are you going to make an honest man out of the rascal?"

"Bentley!" The tiniest woman Kat had ever seen pushed her towering husband aside and pulled her into a quick, enthusiastic embrace. Drawing back, she shook her head, humor and exasperation etched on her adorable face. "Ignore him, dear. Working with mostly men for forty years and being the boss for the last twenty-five has left him with the manners of a goat."

Howard's dad grimaced. Smothering a nervous laugh, she scrambled with an appropriate response. "I, um, it's great to meet you both. Howard speaks very highly of you two."

What an inane thing to say. But it was true, and pleased his parents to no end, if Georgie's blush and Bentley's puffed-out chest were any indication.

"Oh, and happy birthday, sir," she added.

"Thank you, young lady. Not a bad turnout for a rude old goat." He shot his little wife a pointed glare.

Which the older woman ignored. "Won't you sit down? Tell us about yourself. You have us at a disadvantage, you know."

Howard placed a couple of lawn chairs next to his parents and gestured for her to sit by Georgie. He took the seat on her other side as she answered. "Well, there isn't much to tell. Howard and I met when my parents' neighbors' house burned the other night and his team answered."

"Oh, heavens," Georgie whispered in a conspiratorial tone. "What an awful thing about that woman who burned inside. You weren't injured, I hope?"

Oh, shoot. Belatedly, she regretted bringing up the

fire. She had no idea whether Howard had discussed his predicament with his parents. "No, no, I'm fine. Anyway, we've been, ah, seeing each other when our work schedules permit. I'm a first-grade teacher here in Sugarland."

That revelation prompted a round of positive commentary from the Mitchells on how important it was to pay teachers more to draw in the good ones and keep the experienced staff. For several minutes, they questioned her with avid curiosity about her job, how difficult it was sometimes, and how rewarding. Relaxing, she warmed to the topic she knew best.

The subject of teaching segued into her own parents and sister, all of whom she adored—even if she hadn't chosen to follow their father into his high-powered law firm like Grace had done. But she kept her dad's disappointment out of the picture. After rattling on for a while, she noticed Howard had taken her hand. She glanced sideways to find him smiling, brown eyes shining with unmistakable pride. His emotion, naked for all to see, left her lightheaded. And happy. Happier than she'd ever been.

This man would *never* be disappointed in her for being true to her own path. She knew that in the fiber of her being.

Deftly, she turned the conversation's focus to Howard's parents, encouraging them to tell how they'd met and later adopted their son. Their love for Howard radiated from their faces, threaded through every word as they spoke of a frightened, abused little boy who'd come into his own and completed their lives.

Howard shifted in his chair, his expression growing uncomfortable, either from the gushing praise or the reminder of his awful past. Damn, she hadn't meant to upset him. His parents went on, not seeming to notice that he'd paled under his tanned skin, looking faintly sick.

One of his friends picked up on his tension, though. The cute guy with the short black hair and gorgeous laser-blue eyes hiding behind his wire-rimmed glasses. A very sweet man, he'd assisted her at the fire. What was his name? Zack.

"Hey, buddy." Zack smiled, striding over to their group, holding a can of Diet Coke. "You gonna hog your pretty lady all afternoon or introduce the rest of us?"

"I don't know if I trust you dogs with my woman," Howard said, standing. "But I need to throw the burgers on the grill."

Zack dimpled. "We'll take good care of her. Really."

"You'd better." He arched a brow. "I'd hate to have to find a place to hide your body."

Good Lord. Kat choked with embarrassment, sliding a glance at Georgie. The older woman grinned at their antics and waved a hand to shoo her off.

"Go on, meet some other young people. Some of Bentley's friends brought along their grown kids and their respective dates, too. You don't need to keep us company. Us old fogies will stick together for now."

Kat gave the Mitchells a quick wave as the lieutenant and Zack steered her toward a group of their friends. As they neared, she tried to quell the flutter of nerves attacking once more. Sweet Lord, she'd never seen so many scrumptious, hard-bodied men in one place.

"Kat, these guys are some of the crew from my station," Howard said. "You've already met Zack. From left to right, the tough guy there is our transplanted Texan, John Valentine. Val to us. He works B-shift."

Thumbs hooked in his jeans, Val nodded. "Nice to meetcha."

"Next to him is Tommy Skyler, our newbie on A-shift, relatively speaking."

Whoa. The blond kid looked so much like the Brad Pitt of a decade ago, it was crazy. A true stunner, almost too beautiful.

"Hello," she said, including the huge, bald Val, as well.

"Next is Eve Marshall—she's on my shift, as well—and that's Clayton Montana, B-shift's FAO and resident cowboy with a death wish. Clay rides bulls professionally on his off weekends."

The lean, sandy-haired cowboy in question cocked an eyebrow. "Wanna see my scars?"

Howard clamped a hand down on Clay's shoulder, hard enough to make the other man wince. "No, she doesn't. Why don't you make your worthless hide useful and help me with the burgers?" Bending, he gave Kat a kiss and whispered, "I'll be right back."

Her heart thumped triple time. "Go ahead; I'm in good hands."

As he practically dragged Clay across the yard, Tommy whistled between his teeth. "Man, the lieutenant's, like, a *goner*. He totally just marked his territory."

"Kat's a woman, not a fire hydrant for some jerk to pee on, you idiot." Eve fisted her hands on her slim hips. "No wonder you don't have a girlfriend, Skyler."

He smirked. "Hey, I've got plenty of girlfriends. More than Salvatore."

Zack shot their buddy a droll stare. "No, you and Jules have an increased risk for contracting something contagious and inflammatory that requires antibiotics."

"Whatever, dude. At least my date isn't attached to my wrist." Dismissing Knight, he saluted Kat with his beer. "Great to meetcha. Gotta go talk to some people."

Val wandered off with Tommy, and Kat frowned after them, puzzling over his exchange with Zack. Harmless jabs between friends? Or had that been a flash of pain she'd seen on Zack's face?

"Boys." Eve shrugged. Soft, curly dark brown hair streaked with reddish-blond caught in a light breeze to tickle her pert nose, and she tucked the wayward strand behind one ear. "Can't live with 'em, can't shoot 'em."

Zack paused in taking a swig of his soda. "I'm a guy, and you don't want to shoot me."

"You're not a guy, you're my best friend."

"Well, gee," he sighed. "I think I'll just go find a corner and lick my raw, bleeding wounds. Later."

After Zack moved out of earshot, Kat leaned toward Eve, watching the man's fine, tight backside disappear into the crowd. Not as fine as Howard's, but she wasn't dead by a long shot. "Zack's too cute."

Eve gazed after him as though she'd never considered his desirability before. "Yeah, I suppose so. But he's even more beautiful on the inside, you know. A lot like Howard." Lips curving upward, she let the opening dangle. Odd pale blue eyes, striking in contrast to her lovely coffee-with-cream complexion, regarded Kat steadily.

"I guess that's my cue, huh?" She smiled, and Eve returned it in full. Something passed between them, the beginnings of a bond, perhaps? She liked Eve and wanted to make a good impression, not only on her, but on all of them. "Yes, Howard is gorgeous inside and out. I've never met anyone like him."

"The lieutenant is special to us, and one of the most respected men in the department besides. He's got that strong, silent mojo going on, but inside he's a teddy bear." Eve's voice lowered as she studied Kat from under long lashes. "I've never known a man with a bigger heart, and I'd hate to see his get broken."

"You don't have to worry about that where I'm concerned. If anything, he'll break mine first." *Because we're great in bed, but he doesn't talk to me.* But she didn't know Eve well enough to vent about personal matters. At lunch, though, Grace had given her some sage advice—don't push him too hard. Let it ride and see what happens.

"Hmm. Don't know about that, girlfriend. He seems pretty far gone to me."

"From your lips . . ." They laughed together, and Eve entertained her with several stories about calls the team had responded to in recent months, some hilarious, others downright scary. Why hadn't Howard shared any of this? The question nagged at the back of her mind like a sore tooth. Maybe he didn't think it was important. . . . Or maybe she wasn't important enough to tell.

Okay, this party was turning out to be a little more of an eye-opener than she'd bargained for.

"Damn, who drank all the Bud Light?" Scowling, Clay fished around in one of the coolers.

Howard stuck his head out from behind the open lid of the grill. "There's more in the fridge inside. Ice down a few, would you?" Busy with the burgers, he disappeared again.

Mounting the deck steps, Kat waved a hand at Clay. "I'll get them." The least she could do was be useful. Besides, the cowboy's attention had already been snagged by a couple of attractive—and presumably unattached—young ladies.

"Thanks, darlin'. 'Scuse me, duty calls." Like a hound on the scent, he made a beeline for the women.

Shaking her head, Kat grinned and went inside. Apparently, Clay had the attention span of a gnat. And gonads of steel, to hit on his superiors' daughters.

Opening the packed fridge, Kat found the large carton of beer wedged upright between two shelves and sandwiched between sodas, dips, and cold salads. Grasping the edge of the cardboard, she tugged, trying to work the box out. Darned thing was stuck.

"Here, let me help you with that."

Startled, Kat straightened and spun, bumping her head on the door of the fridge. "Ow!"

"Are you all right? I didn't mean to scare you."

Blinking at the attractive older man who'd done just that, she painted on a smile and suppressed a sudden jangle of nerves. "No, I'm fine."

In truth, the man was invading her personal space. Big time. She was effectively pinned inside the open fridge, no room to maneuver. And at the moment, everyone else was outside.

The man gave her a crooked smile. "The beer?"

"Oh! Of course." Good grief, he was only waiting for her to move out of the way so he could help. Feeling silly, she let him by, watching as he tugged the carton out with ease and placed it on the counter.

"Thanks."

"No problem." Expression welcoming, he stuck out a hand. "Duane Moore."

"Kat McKenna. A friend of Bentley's, I presume?" She shook his offered hand quickly, then backed up a couple of steps to put more space between them. Some people really didn't have a clue about maintaining a polite distance.

The man's lips turned up, his eyes flashing in amusement. "You could say that. Mitchell and I go way back."

Nothing unusual about that. Most of the guys here could say the same. "Do you work for the fire department or—"

The sliding glass door to the deck opened, and Clay stuck his head in. "Hey, darlin'! We're thirsty out here!" A round of feminine giggles floated from the deck. Clay was making a halfhearted attempt to disentangle himself from one of the beauties.

Kat shot Mr. Moore an apologetic smile. "That's my cue." Hefting the carton of beer, she headed for the revelry once more, addressing the man over her shoulder. "Anyway, how do you know Bentley? Do you two work together?"

Silence. Stepping over the threshold onto the deck, she turned with a frown.

Duane Moore was gone.

"What's the matter?" Clay took the beer from her grasp.

"Did you see the man I was just talking to?"

Clay glanced past her to the empty kitchen. "Didn't really notice him. Why?"

"I was just speaking with him and now he's gone!"

The cowboy shrugged. "Probably went to the men's room. Or maybe he had to leave."

"But . . . yeah, you're right." Shaking off the creeps, she sighed, dismissing Duane Moore altogether. "Since you've got the beer, I'm going to see if Howard needs help with the burgers."

"Got it covered, sugar." With a wink, he rejoined his new lady friends.

As the afternoon wore into evening, she had a great time. Well, except for an awkward introduction to Captain Sean Tanner, whose whiskey breath could be declared a lethal weapon. She didn't miss how Eve's attention strayed to Tanner the entire evening, not that he noticed. Now, there was a heartache waiting to happen. Run far away, Eve.

The burgers were juicy, Howard was attentive, his friends and his dad's older acquaintances a lot of fun. At some point, she realized Grace had been absent for a while, and after scanning the yard, spotted her with Julian Salvatore. They were standing together in a pool of shadows on the far side of the deck, beyond the glow of the tiki torches. The station's resident bad boy was putting on the moves with feral intensity, and getting nowhere fast.

Grace merely stood sipping her wine, one slender hip cocked in casual repose, listening to whatever crap he was spewing. Her body language had erected a barrier the poor man couldn't hope to scale with the tallest firehouse ladder. Kat smirked. Drop-dead, mouth-watering edible or not, Julian wasn't the first handsome slut puppy to get the royal smackdown. Wouldn't be the last, either. She almost felt sorry for him.

Later, she and Howard got a kick out of watching Bentley grumble about how he'd specifically said for everyone not to bring presents, then tear into them like a child at Christmas. He made a point to say something nice about each one, even Kat's modest gift card to Home Depot. A safe bet, since most guys she knew loved to pound on stuff.

A set of golf clubs given to him by Station Five were a hit, and she could tell how much their thoughtfulness meant to him. But what nearly toppled him was the envelope he opened last.

"From me," Howard said, studying intently for his reaction.

Bentley tore into the simple white envelope, removed what appeared to be some folded paperwork. He grew still and quiet, swallowing hard. "Georgie, look . . ." He held up the papers and two tickets.

"Oh, Howard." Georgie's hand went over her mouth. "An Alaskan cruise! Seven days? Oh, honey . . ."

The crowd exclaimed over that one. Howard just lifted a shoulder, trying to act nonchalant. "I wanted to get a gift you guys could enjoy together. I figured you've been talking about this cruise for years, so why not? Oh, and I booked you for July, so Bentley's got several months to square things at the office."

Georgie flew into his arms, and Bentley managed to hug his son, as well, in the excitement. One of those all-time great moments that left the guests a bit teary-eyed, Kat included. How many guys would do that for their parents? God, what a man.

After cake, the party began to disperse. Zack took Sean's keys and informed his woozy captain he was getting a lift home. The man didn't argue, thank goodness. Grace walked over to the deck where Kat stood, Julian still attached to her side like a burr.

"Need a lift?" Kat eyed her sister, the real question hanging in the air between them. *Are you taking this gigolo home?*

Grace smiled, looking flushed. "No, Julian has offered to drive me." Pulling Kat into a hug, she whispered in her ear. "Don't worry, he's just dropping me off."

They parted, and Kat sent Julian an icy smile. "Call me tonight when you're locked in, sis."

She laughed. "It's already late, and I'm sure the big guy won't appreciate the interruption. I'll call you tomorrow."

Julian tried a charming grin. "Relax, your sister is safe with me. I have no desire for you to give the lieutenant a reason to kick my ass."

Well, hell, what could she say to that? Her sister and Julian were both adults. Didn't mean she had to like it, though.

After all the guests departed, Howard helped his folks load the presents in their car and saw them off with promises to Georgie to come by next week for pie—and to bring Kat. Warm fuzzies all around.

Lord, she was pooped, so Howard must be exhausted. He'd really gone all out to show everyone a super evening. In the backyard, she was bent over tossing a few stray plates and napkins into a black garbage bag when a hand cupped one butt cheek, fingers skimming the curve between her legs.

Howard's voice rumbled low. Heavy with arousal. "Leave that. I'll take care of all this tomorrow."

The bag slipped from her grasp and she straightened, clean-up duty forgotten. Closing her eyes, she melted into him. "I thought you must be tired. . . ."

"Not too tired for this." He nuzzled her neck, fingers straying underneath her shirt to caress her ribs. "Never for this."

He pulled her flush with his body, his erection riding the small of her back through his loose shorts. Those wonderful roaming hands had her shirt yanked over her head and discarded in an instant. Found the clasp of her bra, freed her. Exposed her in a way she'd never been before. The chill night air licked her nipples like a ghostly tongue, hardening them to taut points.

"I want you out here, just like this." His tone brooked no argument, laced with pure male dominance.

He squeezed her breasts, pinched her puckered nipples sharply enough to wrench a gasp from her lips. Pain and pleasure streaked to her sex, awakening the sweet tingle and throb of her clit. "We can't. Someone might see!"

His laugh was quiet, dangerous. A man not to be denied. "What if they do?"

Oh, God! The idea of someone spying on them blew her mind. Made the place between her legs burn even more. "B-but it's getting chilly."

"I'll warm you."

Yeah, she was already about to combust! "Howard—"

"Shh. I'm going to fuck you, pretty baby. Right here under the stars, hard, fast, and deep, like you've never been fucked before."

A shiver racked her from head to toe. She was his, and there had never really been a question that she would let him do exactly as he wanted with her.

Taking her hand, he led her onto the deck to the hot tub. Removing the padded cover, he pushed a button on the controls and set the jets on low before turning back to her. "Take off the rest."

She slipped off her sandals, enjoying the feel of the

smooth boards under her feet. Next she undid her capris, sliding them over her hips along with her lacy panties, hyperaware of his glittering gaze. Of being naked and vulnerable to his wishes, and loving the wickedness of what he had in store.

The patio light had been turned off, only three tiki torches left burning, and she realized he must've dimmed the lighting before pouncing on her. The low glow the torches cast over the deck only served to make the setting more intimate, the lust in his dark gaze more dangerous.

"Hmm. Let's see about warming you up." One corner of his delicious mouth kicked up. "Now get in the hot tub. Kneel on the seat over there, facing away from me, and brace your arms on the edge."

Trembling with excitement, she did as told. Ahh, the hot water felt lovely on her chilled skin. She sighed in sheer bliss, enjoying the bubbles tickling her toes.

"Good, now spread those legs for me so I can see my prize. Wider, lean over a bit more . . . yeah, just like that, sweetheart. Jesus, I could come just looking at you."

Oh, sweet heaven. She was totally exposed, a banquet for his feast. A rustle of clothing sounded from behind her as he undressed and joined her in the tub with a splash. Then his hands slid over her hips. One slipped down her rear, between her thighs. Skillful fingers rubbed the folds of her sex, swirling the dewy wetness. Readying her.

"Know what I plan on doing to you, baby? Say you're mine."

"I'm yours," she breathed. "However you need me."

"Anything I want?"

"Anything, Howard." She was going to die from the anticipation.

He lifted her rear higher, spreading her even wider. Breath fanning her eager flesh.

And he ended the wait for them both, claiming her with his mouth.

Kat's complete surrender bolted through Howard like a million-volt shock. Making love vanilla style was wonderful, but his tastes had always leaned toward the wicked. Darker and more wild. He'd made it clear to her that he'd never been a monk when it came to sex, but she was an innocent, her prick of a former lover not withstanding. A novice.

Having her spread naked before him, ready and willing to give him total control over her luscious body, to let him fuck her right out in the open . . . Jesus Christ. Yeah, so he was a bit of an exhibitionist. Sue him. Janine had turned him on to the thrill of naughty sex in risky places that scorching night they met at his health club, and he'd loved the exhilaration of it. Ever since he'd sampled Kat's sweetness at the park, watched her climax under his touch, he'd dreamed of this.

Settling himself lower in the steamy water and bracing his feet, he nudged her thighs farther apart. Little droplets winked on her creamy skin like diamonds. Her juicy slit gleamed, dripping for him before the show even got started. Her rich, womanly scent teased his nostrils, spiked his arousal. His cock demanded to be buried inside her, but not yet. Oh, no, he had other plans for her first.

Lightly, he nibbled her tender folds. Nipped and gave the sensitive skin just a hint of tongue. Making her want as much as he wanted. Her whimpers were precious music to his ears, and he rewarded her with long, slow licks. Back and forth along her slit, her spicy flavor bursting on his tongue. She arched her back with a moan, opened wider.

"So pretty," he said, parting her with two fingers. His tongue slid between the soft lips, as far into her sheath as he could reach. Plunging in and out, he tongue-fucked her with relentless strokes. God, he loved the taste of a woman—this woman—craved the way she wriggled on his face, creaming as he ate her.

Kat's groans of pleasure had his cock aching to take her. Soon. Fastening his mouth to her clit, he suckled her mindless. Lapped the tiny nub until she was gone, swept away to the place where she didn't care what he did to her as long as he didn't stop. He knew from the scent of her musk, the surrender of her body, shaking. *His.*

"You're mine, sweetheart. I'm going to take you somewhere you've never dreamed."

"Yes, now!"

Need spiking to almost unbearable levels, he rose from the water to stand and better position himself behind her. Spreading her butt cheeks, he prepared to deliver on his promise. Using the lube coating his fingers, he rimmed her tight little hole. Without giving her time to emerge from the spell, he began to work his middle finger inside, past the resistant ring of muscle.

"Howard," she cried, tensing. "I've never . . . I can't—"

"You can," he said softly. "You *will.*"

And, by God, she did. He worked her gently and she began to open for him, a flower too long without water. Hot, dying for sustenance no other man had ever given her. He pumped, adding a second finger. Stretching, preparing the tight channel.

"Oh, oh . . . more!" She leaned into his touch, head thrown back, damp white-blond hair tumbling over her shoulders. So damned sexy, ripe for him.

She was ready, and he couldn't wait another second. Removing his fingers, he rubbed his wet cock along her sex, coating it with her juices. Satisfied that he'd done all he could to prepare her, he nudged the flared head to her forbidden entrance, barely able to speak.

"Relax your muscles, let yourself go."

As he began to push inside, she cried out again, but not in pain. Her cry was one of sheer, unbridled ecstasy, and it shot straight to his aching balls. To his heart. Not all women could take a man this way, especially one his size.

But Kat's curvy body was made for loving, any way he desired. Slow and tender, hard and naughty. She filled his hands, pillowed his throbbing length with softness. Never had he seen a more erotic sight than his shiny rod parting her willing flesh *there*. Sinking deeper, deeper as she writhed beneath him, taking . . . all of him.

Sweat trickled down the side of his face. Sweet mother, no woman had ever taken the entire length of his cock up her delicious backside. She rippled around him, sheathed him so snug, they were one. Gritting his teeth, he gripped her waist and began to thrust. Slow at first, so as not to hurt her. Praying for this to last.

"Oh, God, Howard, *yes*."

His control started to unravel. "Like me fucking you this way, baby?"

"Yes, yes! Harder, faster, damn you!"

That flipped the switch. French-fried his brain, freed the animal from his cage. He increased his tempo until he was pounding into her, waves of water splashing onto the deck. Relentless, taking his fill. As hard and deep as possible, giving them what they both desired. Stoking the fires to a wild inferno.

"I'm gonna come! Howard, I can't stop—"

Her spasms hurled him over the edge and into space. His release shattered all previous notions of what a fantastic, mind-blowing orgasm should be. Rocked to the core, he exploded, jetting into her on and on. Came until he lay draped over her back, lungs heaving, both of them drenched.

Sweeping her hair aside, he kissed the nape of her neck. "Are you all right?"

"My God, I think I died." A languorous sigh escaped. "If I'd known how great it feels to be a bad girl, I'd have done that a long time ago."

"So I've led you down the path to wickedness?"

"Very much so, hotshot."

"Good," he replied, smug. "I'm just getting warmed up."

"Hmm. Do I get to have my way with you next time?"

With a sigh of regret, he slipped out of her and hunkered down in the water. "I need a little time to recover, my lusty lady."

Straightening, she turned and smiled at him, trailing a hand through the frothy bubbles. Resplendent in all her naked glory. "How long, old man?"

His brows shot up. "I've got your old man right here, sugar. As soon as he gets a shower, he'll be glad to demonstrate his stamina again."

"Deal. A shower, then you're mine to do anything I wish. Fair play and all that."

Wading to him, Kat wrapped her arms around his neck, breasts bobbing against his chest. She pulled his head down for a kiss, delving that sweet little tongue inside, tasting their mingled flavors.

Jesus. His shaft perked, already at half-mast again at the mere idea. He couldn't wait to find out what being at her mercy entailed. Breaking the kiss, he skimmed a finger down her cheek. "Go ahead and heat the shower. I'll get our clothes and lock up for the night."

Throwing a sultry grin over her shoulder, she climbed out of the hot tub and flounced inside, trailing puddles in her wake. Lost in a pleasant postcoital haze, he followed suit and began picking up their discarded clothing. Somewhere down the street, a car started. An innocuous, everyday noise, nothing to worry over.

And yet a chill crept into his bone marrow.

He'd been certain that with tonight's festivities, his tormentor wouldn't dare come within twenty miles of his house. That he'd move on, wait for a better opportunity to sneak around unnoticed.

Howard cursed his own stupidity. What better opportunity than the one he'd just given the bastard? He'd allowed lust to blind him to the danger of being in the open, unprotected and unaware. Hadn't even considered that their voyeur might've been a ruthless killer instead of a scandalized neighbor.

Yanking on his shorts over his wet body, he laid the rest of the clothing on a chair and went inside to fetch the flashlight. Hurrying outside again, he walked the perimeter of his fence, scanned the hedges and peat mulch lining his landscaping. No broken bushes, no footprints that he could see.

He wasn't reassured.

Grabbing their clothes, he secured the house for the night and joined Kat in the shower.

For now, he wanted to lose himself in her arms and pretend there were no murders, no killer after his head. No nightmares stealing his sleep.

Just a soft woman to warm his bed and heart, without digging too deep into his soul.

He prayed that wasn't too much to ask.

15

Stepping into the hot spray, Kat felt her cheeks heat. She couldn't believe she'd let Howard make love to her *that* way. No, she'd practically begged for it. She'd never felt so wicked—or more wonderfully alive.

As the object of her scorching memories joined her, she eyed him in appreciation. Big and naked was how she loved him best. Naked and wet? Even better.

"Wash your back?" His small, sexy smile said cleanliness wasn't his first priority.

"Hmm. I don't know if I trust you in that position anymore."

"Too late, baby. You've created a fiend." Turning her gently, he spanned her waist with his hands and pressed his front to her back. His half-erect penis rode the cleft of her butt cheeks, reviving fast.

Kat leaned against him and closed her eyes, loving the sensation of their slick bodies together under the steamy spray. He nuzzled her neck, then rested his chin on top of her head and simply held her close for a moment.

She savored every second. Howard's sensuality was burned into his DNA, but she treasured this softer, affectionate side of him, too.

He released her and grabbed a bottle of men's shower gel from the ledge. Flipping open the cap, he squirted a generous amount into his palm and replaced the bottle on the shelf.

"You want me to smell like a man, Lieutenant?" Arching a brow, she glanced over her shoulder.

He shot her a playful grin. "I want you to smell like *me*."

Reaching around her, he soaped her breasts and tummy in lazy strokes. Her skin warmed, her nipples begging for more. But he worked down her back, to her rear. Worked the suds with care, washing away most of the evidence of his attentions.

"Sore?" he asked, concern edging his voice.

"Some."

"I'm sorry."

"Don't be. I loved it."

He brightened. "Really?"

"Couldn't you tell? I'm sure the neighbors had no doubts."

His soft laugh tingled her nerve endings. His hand strayed lower, soaping between her legs. She sucked in a sharp breath, thinking the whole shower thing was almost more intimate than lovemaking.

Then again, maybe this shared closeness *was* a form of making love.

His fingers skimmed her sex, then lingered to play with her sensitive clit. Every cell in her body was hyperaware of his expert touch. Begging for more. Unfurling, opening to let him have his way. Again.

Wait a second.

"No, you don't," she gasped, turning to face him.

"Aww, baby—"

Wrapping her fingers around his thick erection, she cut off his complaint. "You're not in charge this time. It's my turn, buddy."

He blinked, one corner of his kissable mouth kicking up. "Yes, ma'am. Whatever you say."

She squeezed his shaft. "I say you're my love slave.

Back up, then raise your arms over your head and grab the neck of the shower nozzle."

Dark eyes glittering, he complied, every muscle tense.

"Good. You're chained and at my mercy. Now spread your legs."

He did, and she knelt in front of him. Tasted the wet tip of him with her tongue. His fierce oath spurred her on, and she took him in her mouth.

She licked and suckled, taking as much of his length as she could manage. Droplets of water rolled down his torso and she licked those, too, relishing how the beads slicked his skin like a seal's. The rest of him she pumped with her fingers, her other hand playing with his heavy balls, drawn tight in arousal.

"Jesus . . . Christ!"

His head thumped against the tile and satisfaction purred in her breast. Having so much power over a dominant man like Howard was a heady feeling.

The lieutenant was going to lose control . . . and she'd savor the ride.

Relentless, she sucked and manipulated, worked his cock until his helpless moans of passion echoed off the walls.

Howard couldn't withstand the passionate assault. With a hoarse cry, he stiffened and his hips began to buck. Release followed swiftly, shaking Kat with its intensity.

Viscous jets of come pumped down her throat. Her plan of seduction hadn't included what to do now . . . so she swallowed. Drank all he had to give, marveling at his salty flavor and his total surrender.

When the last of his spasms subsided, Kat released him and stood, letting the warm spray rinse her face and the rest of the soap.

Howard lowered his arms, expelling a harsh breath. "Christ, lady, what you do to me."

"Worn out *now*, old man?"

He barked a short laugh and pulled her close, eyes heavy lidded. A man well sated. "Mercy. I give."

"Ha! I finally got the best of you. I think—"

"What the hell?"

Howard's eyes widened and his lips parted in surprise. "Look."

Kat followed his gaze and felt the blood drain from her face. "Oh, shit."

On the foggy glass shower door, a chilling missive had been written in some sort of clear, greasy substance.

TWO DOWN, MORE TO DIE . . . GREAT PARTY, ASSHOLE.

Detective Ford and two crime lab techs went over every square inch of Howard's home as he watched, boiling with impotent rage.

Once again, the murdering fucker had waltzed into Howard's space undetected and practically did a tap dance on his goddamned head.

"In *my house*. Right among all my friends."

Sitting on the edge of the sofa in nothing but the shorts he'd worn earlier, he clenched his fists on his knees, aware of Kat's worried gaze. He hated feeling so violated. Hated that he had no control over this unseen enemy or the situation.

That he'd failed to protect Kat.

Well, that was something he could—and would—rectify.

"I'm giving you my spare key and the alarm code," he announced. "Bring over plenty of clothes, because you're staying here with me. Indefinitely."

Kat stiffened, green eyes narrowing. "It occurs to me that this might not be the safest place for me."

He winced, the dart striking his pride dead on. "It will be. He won't get past me again."

"Bully for you, but I have my own place, Howard."

Her lips thinned and her chin thrust forward stubbornly.

"This is *not* negotiable."

"Oh, *really*?" With a humorless laugh, she pushed to her feet, prepared to do battle. "There's a good reason I don't live with my daddy. I don't take orders from you, hotshot."

Damn, she looked beautiful even when she was pissed. All that pale blond hair wild around her face, tumbling to the shoulders of her shirt. Braless bosom heaving in outrage. Large, expressive eyes snapping with fury.

Any other time he'd appreciate her spunk.

"On this, you do."

"I *so* don't fucking think so! You can just—"

"Excuse me." Ford cleared his throat, glancing between the combatants. "Sorry to interrupt, but we're done here."

Relieved by the detective's timing, Howard said, "And?"

"Nothing except the message on the glass, which appears to have been written in clear lip balm."

"Prints?"

"We lifted a couple of good ones off the shower-door handle, but count on them being one of yours," Ford said, indicating them both. Kat flushed as he went on. "I don't think our guy was stupid enough to leave prints. And with the number of guests you had here today, dusting the whole house would be an exercise in futility."

"Dammit." Howard rubbed his eyes, beyond tired and frustrated.

"Neither of you recall anyone suspicious? Out of place?"

Kat looked at Ford thoughtfully. "Nobody except the nice man who helped me tug the beer out of the fridge."

Dropping his hand, Howard stood, alarm prickling the back of his neck. "What man?"

She shrugged. "Just some older guy with dark, graying hair. Attractive. Said he's a friend of Bentley's." Frowning, she shook her head. "No, wait. When I asked if he was a friend who worked with your dad, he claimed they go way back."

"Not necessarily the same as friends," Ford said.

"I thought that was odd, but not as strange as the fact that he vanished after we spoke in the kitchen. I never saw him again."

The detective removed a pen and small notepad from his pocket and began to write. "Did he give you his name?"

"Moore. Darryl? No . . . Duane. Duane Moore."

Howard went cold. To the bone.

"Paxton?" Ford prompted.

"I don't know anyone by that name and I'm pretty sure Bentley didn't invite extra guests without telling me."

In fact, he was positive. "Rage" was too insignificant a word to encompass the emotion rolling through him.

The son of a bitch had gotten Kat alone just to show he could.

God have mercy on the bastard if he made that mistake twice.

The two weeks since Bentley's party had been wonderful—as long as Kat followed Howard's directives. He continued to shuttle her to and from work on his days off, insisted that she stay at his house. He protested when she went home to her empty apartment while he was on shift, arguing that it wasn't safe for her to be there alone. As though somehow the mere threat of his presence would warn off a killer.

As though Kat didn't have a brain in her head and couldn't possibly take care of herself.

Yeah, the big picture was idyllic. Who wouldn't want a handsome giant of a man taking care of her every need?

The real problem? He never *asked*.

Howard was used to issuing orders and having everyone around him jump to carry them out. Kat didn't take orders well at all, especially when they took over her life. No matter his good intentions and worry for her safety, the friction between them on the issue had congealed into a hard knot of stress.

To top that off, for all his wonderful qualities, Howard was a serial bachelor. Private in his thoughts, if not in regard to his space. Unused to explaining himself or having a meaningful conversation that didn't lead swiftly away from the topic of their future.

Their roadblocks might've been easier to handle if she didn't suspect the root of his emotional distance was much more serious than it appeared. He was afraid to open himself to hurt and betrayal.

Howard was afraid to love.

Worse, he simply didn't seem to realize he was trying to fit her into his existing lifestyle, rather than discovering a new, mutually satisfying one. Together. Depending on his mood, she felt like a temporary lover or a scolded child, not a true partner. A classic, easy-to-identify downer—not so easy to fix.

"Are we having fun yet?" Scowling, she dug in Howard's fridge for the stuff she'd bought at the store to make hoagie sandwiches. Tossing the deli ham and other ingredients onto the counter, she couldn't help but overhear Howard's side of the phone call from Detective Ford.

"I'm telling you, I've never seen the thing before," he said, sounding puzzled. "I'm positive. Why did her parents wait so long to clue you in?"

What on earth was he talking about? She sliced the hoagie rolls with a bread knife as Howard listened to Ford's answer, then went on.

"Beats me. Motives are your specialty, not mine." Pause. "Yeah, except for the standard calls, almost eerie. Why do you think that is?"

Listening intently, she spread mustard over the rolls and began to layer the sandwiches with ham, lettuce, cheese, and tomato.

"Ah. Makes sense. Well, we can always pray he gets tired of playing and moves on, huh?" Pause. "Sure. I'm back on shift Tuesday. If anything new happens, you'll be the first—correction, make that second or third—to know."

And that's what she was so damned afraid of, she couldn't breathe. What was the killer waiting for? A convenient target? An opportunity to strike after he'd stretched Howard's nerves to the breaking point? What?

And of all men, why *Howard*?

The awful questions bounced around in her frightened brain, demanding answers that remained elusive. Placing the hoagies on paper plates, she garnished them with potato chips and carried the plates to the dining table. And suddenly, indoors seemed far too stifling to enjoy a simple meal. Maybe eating on the deck would cheer them both.

"Do you want to eat in here or—" She broke off at the sight of her big guy sitting on the sofa with his head in his hands. "Oh, honey. What did Ford say?"

"Not much."

The ensuing tense silence was like a drawbridge being raised on an impenetrable castle made of twenty-foot thick stone walls.

Lunch forgotten, she approached him cautiously. "Sounded pretty significant to me."

"Nothing wrong with your hearing, I see." Scrubbing his face, he looked at her, brown gaze flat.

O-kay. Bristling, she crossed her arms over her breasts. "I couldn't help but hear, Lieutenant. This isn't a very big house, and you don't exactly have a soft voice." Cocking one hip, she studied his miserable expression, his grim mouth set in an unyielding line. No, she wasn't going to get sidetracked by tender emotions again.

"Furthermore, I'm involved up to my neck, as evidenced by your he-man-protects-woman routine. For over two weeks, I've barely seen the inside of my apartment!"

"Funny, I haven't heard any complaints until now. Especially when we make human fruit salad—"

"I'm not complaining about the sex, you jackass. I want to know what's going on with you, and not just with Ford's case. I need you to talk to me."

"Oh, boy. Here we go."

No kidding. *Looks like we're heading for our first meltdown, folks.* And she didn't know how to avert it, other than giving in and letting him crawl back into his shell. Which she wasn't about to do. Her stomach started to hurt.

"I'm spinning my wheels here, Howard. I get the feeling I'm about a day shy of my Flavor of the Month pass expiring."

He gaped at her in disbelief. "That's so not true. I enjoy having you here, and I don't want you to go anywhere."

Enjoy? Well, wasn't that frickin' nice. "You can get the same loyalty out of a golden retriever, buddy." She snapped her fingers. "But no sex. Unless you're one sick puppy, no pun intended."

Howard rose from the sofa. "Are you *trying* to pick a fight?"

Oh, he was getting good and pissed. And six-and-a-half-feet of solid, angry man was enough to make her take a step backward before she could check herself. "No. I want you to tell me about your nightmares. You don't sleep much, and when you do . . ." Spreading her hands, she struggled to make him understand. "Do you honestly think I wouldn't try to help? To be there for you when you need me?"

A muscle in his jaw clenched. "You can't help. Not with this."

"Dammit, Howard! It's fine for you to order me around for my own good, but you can't meet me halfway?"

"It's not the same thing."

Blowing out a deep breath, she studied her tennis shoes. Counted to ten. She'd have to find another way to crack this nut, but it wasn't going to happen now. "Why don't you at least tell me about Ford's call while we eat? You *did* promise not to leave me out of the loop."

Eying her warily, he nodded. "All right. Like I said, not much to tell." He trailed her to the table. "Sandwiches look great."

"Thanks. Go on." Taking a bite of her hoagie, she waited.

"Ford says the killer has gone quiet since the party because he's probably having trouble finding another good target in Station Five's sector. He either doesn't know he could carry out his deed in a nearby sector and we'd still have to respond, or he does and just wants to be sure I arrive first."

"That's what I thought, too. He's got a pretty limited area to work with, but he'll wait because he's getting off by putting you and the guys through hell."

"And doing a slam-bang job." He sighed, picking at his potato chips. "I'm not sure I mentioned this before, but when the killer left Lorna Miller's cell phone on my bunk, there was a lady's ring with it."

Her stomach pitched even more, and her sandwich didn't want to go down. "No, you didn't say anything about a ring. What kind?"

"An engagement or wedding ring with a solitaire diamond setting. Not too fancy. There was dried blood on it."

"But the jewelry didn't belong to either of the victims," she surmised, putting together his conversation with Ford.

"Right."

"That's . . . weird."

"Yeah. Tell me."

"What about the dried blood?" Ick. What a topic to discuss over food. Now that she had him talking, however, she wasn't going to let her chance slip.

"Wasn't theirs, either. Wrong type."

"A previous victim, then," she mused. "One we don't know about. But what does this mean to you?"

"That's the million-dollar question, isn't it? Ford thinks the ring is significant." Howard shrugged, gazing at his plate, stiff posture and lines bracketing his mouth giving evidence to his distress and exhaustion.

"What do you believe?"

He barked a humorless laugh. "That a one-way ticket to Tahiti sounds great."

Again, the wall, posted with signs shouting NO TRESPASSING. The subtle rebuff hurt, and she had to work hard not to let her disappointment show. "Why didn't Miller's parents realize sooner that the ring wasn't hers?"

"They didn't have it; Homicide did. The cell phone was Miller's, so the police had no reason to think the ring wasn't. Yesterday morning, Ford released the items to her parents and they said they've never seen it before. So Ford showed it around to the friends and family of both victims. Nothing."

"It was left for you. Are you sure you've never seen

it?" He shook his head no, and she took another bite of her sandwich, chewing on both the food and the mystery. Howard didn't seem inclined to do either. "You're not eating."

"Sorry." Contrite, he took a huge bite. He'd barely started chowing down when his eyes rounded and he gagged. Clapping a hand over his mouth, he shot to his feet so fast his chair toppled backward.

"Howard, what—"

But he was already bolting toward his bedroom. The door at the end of the hallway slammed, making her flinch. Alarmed, she sat staring at his abandoned food, unsure what had just happened. Was the meat bad?

Picking up his hoagie, she lifted the bread and sniffed. Smelled fresh, but she pinched off a bit of ham to be certain, and tasted. No, the food was fine. Then why . . .

"Oh, no."

Tomato. She'd put tomatoes on his sandwich!

Crap, he'd told her tomatoes made him sick. In her defense, he'd said that weeks ago, and she hadn't thought of it since.

An apology on her lips, Kat hurried to his bedroom door. No greeting met her knock, and she debated whether to go back to the table and wait or enter uninvited.

No, she couldn't just leave him without knowing whether he was all right. Lord, what if he was allergic or something? Turning the knob, she pushed open the door and peered inside. He wasn't in the room, but she noticed the bathroom door was closed. As she crept closer, she heard the distinct sound of retching.

Feeling terrible, she hovered, torn between going to his aid and giving him privacy. Just then, the awful noises ceased. She waited, anxious to tell him how sorry she was that her forgetfulness made him ill.

One full minute passed, then two, but Howard didn't emerge. Steeling herself, she rapped softly on the door. "Howard? Can I come in?"

Faint, muffled sounds reached her ears. Telltale noises she'd heard in the dead of night as he lay in the grip of his nightmares, but never in broad daylight. Not like this.

Slowly, she pushed open the door. . . . And her heart sank into her stomach.

Howard sat on the tile floor with his back against the porcelain tub, arms wrapped tight around his middle. Eyes screwed shut, he was gasping in harsh, sobbing breaths. His knees were drawn up, head bent as though to ward off invisible blows.

"Oh, God!" Rushing to his side, she knelt and cupped his smooth cheek. His skin was cool, clammy. "Honey, I'm so sorry! I totally forgot about the tomatoes! Are you having a reaction of some kind? Do you need a doctor?"

"No." He jerked from her touch.

All right. Perhaps he simply didn't like her seeing him sick. She laid a hand on his shoulder instead. "What can I get you? Some water?" Sure. Like water was going to fix whatever was wrong. But she had to do *something*.

"Don't," he pleaded in a broken voice, hugging his belly tighter. Drawing his body inward. "Please . . . I won't tell. . . ."

Kat froze. Realization leached the blood from her face, shot novocaine through her veins. Howard wasn't speaking to her at all, but to someone else entirely. God, he didn't even know she was here!

He was ensnared in terror, begging an unseen tormentor for mercy. Was this post-traumatic stress syndrome? If so, what had triggered the episode?

A slice of freaking *tomato*?

"Shhh, sweetie," she soothed, stroking his bicep. "It's me, Kat. Come back to me, big guy."

He groaned something unintelligible, but didn't withdraw farther. Encouraged, she continued to whisper comforting phrases as the tension gradually seeped from his muscles. His breathing slowed to normal and he shuddered, lifting his head.

"Kat?" He turned his head and gazed into her face, his pupils huge. "What . . . what are you doing in here?"

"Making sure you're all right," she said carefully. "How do you feel?"

"Queasy." Glancing around the bathroom, he appeared confused. "What happened?"

"You don't remember?"

His voice emerged as a croak. "Not really. I ate some tomato and I got sick. Ran back here. Must've passed out for a minute."

Sweet Lord, he really didn't know! "Howard, you didn't lose consciousness."

"I must have. I woke up—"

"Honey, you weren't out." She hesitated, wondering how to break this to him when she didn't know the right term to use. "You were having some sort of . . . flashback. You were afraid, pleading with someone and saying you wouldn't tell."

Howard stared at her. Swallowed hard. "That's ridiculous."

"I'm just relating what I saw. You were terrified, and I think the tomato triggered this—this episode somehow. Hear me out," she said when he started to interrupt.

"You have nightmares every time you fall into a deep sleep. I don't know how this ties in with what just happened, or whether it does. Maybe this is all due to the stress you're under with this maniac hounding you. But, sweetie, I think you ought to consider seeing someone. A good counselor—"

"I'm not crazy." He punctuated each word as though ripped from his throat with barbed wire. His face paled and his eyes darkened with raw emotion.

Pure, unmitigated fear.

"Of course not! I'd never believe that, and you know it. You've got to work through this, and if you can't trust me, you should give counseling a try."

"I'm not afraid, and I'm not having some stranger messing around in my head," he hissed, pushing to his feet. "And for the record, I *do* trust you."

Rising, she studied his growing fury with sinking dread. "No, you don't," she said quietly. "Otherwise, you'd share the important stuff with me."

"What in blazing hell are you talking about?" he demanded, sweeping an arm to indicate the entire house. "I've shared my home, my bed, my whole life with you. Everything! What do you want from me?"

Your heart.

"I only want you to let me in," she whispered instead. "Let me help you, like real partners do for each other."

"What, you want me to open a vein so you can watch me bleed?" He gave a nasty laugh. "Not gonna happen."

His words were a slap in the face. Stung, she struggled to speak past the burn in her throat. "How can you say that? This isn't about me, it's about *us.*" Getting angry herself, she threw her hands up. "This is pointless. Apparently, you don't *enjoy* having me around enough to take our relationship past the superficial stage of playing bedroom bingo."

Jerking backward, he bumped the bathroom counter, anger morphing to shock. Hurt. "Superficial? You think making love to you means nothing to me?"

"I'm beginning to think so," she retorted. God help

her, the lie had erupted before she could stop it. He wasn't the only one hurt.

"Just remember those were *your* words, not mine." The spark in his beautiful chocolate brown eyes died. Snuffed, like the flame of a candle. His expression went Arctic, chilling her to the bone. "I guess I was right not to spill my guts so you could stomp all over them."

Ohh, she'd played right into his hand. He'd orchestrated this scenario, maybe subconsciously, but still. He was running scared for some reason, and he didn't want to accept the unconditional love she'd willingly give. Not now, not ever.

"Seems we're at an impasse, Lieutenant." Turning, she strode into his bedroom, grabbed her overnight bag, and began to stuff discarded clothes inside with her toiletries. "I'll call my sister to come get me."

"No," he said from behind her. "I'll drive you home."

A heated protest formed, but she decided against refusing. Howard could have her home in ten minutes, versus the hour it would take Grace to drop whatever she was doing on her one day off and drive here from her condo in Nashville. While she and Howard sat in horrid silence, trying not to look at one another.

A no-brainer. "Fine."

Fifteen agonizing minutes later, Kat tossed her bag onto her sofa and listened to Howard's truck drive away.

He wasn't coming back. In spite of Grace's advice, she'd pushed too hard, asked for what he wasn't ready to give and perhaps never would be.

And she'd lost him.

She tried to stop the storm. Didn't want to feel as though her broken heart had been scooped from the ragged hole in her chest. But the deep, hitching breaths became sobs as overwhelming loss flattened her.

Kat sank to the sofa, buried her face in her hands, and wept.

God help him, he'd longed to tell Kat. To hold on to her as he recounted the night he fled his mother's garden in terror, and was almost murdered by his own father. How he'd cried for months afterward, inconsolable in his grief at being abandoned by the one person in the whole world he loved and trusted.

Or at least that's the way his nightmares recalled the events as they became more defined. More than thirty years later, it was hard to know what was real and what might be the fevered embellishments of a little boy's tormented mind.

And there was something else, a truth Kat might've hit upon had she pushed a tad harder.

Deep down, something in his psyche was stopping him from fitting all the pieces of that horrendous night into place. His own brain was at war with what his subconscious knew and what he'd keep hidden at all costs. A secret that would tear him in two. Finish him once and for all.

If he allowed the veil to lift and let the evil inside, he'd be destroyed.

Instead, he'd given in to fear and shoved Kat and her gentle understanding away.

And lost her forever.

The crushing pain in his chest, the absence of her sweet curves spooned into his body and her white-blond hair tickling his nose, wouldn't allow him to find oblivion. Tossing, he rolled to peer at the digital clock, disappointed to discover it was only one thirty in the morning. Wednesday, the third morning following their breakup.

Another endless day of regrets and the ache that would never cease. Even the station, which had always been a haven, had become a prison where the guys watched him like hawks. All day yesterday, they'd tiptoed around him like he'd contracted a fatal disease. After Jules had ragged him about not getting any and he'd ripped the man's head off, of course.

With Kat gone, what did he have to look forward to? Coming home after shift change to an empty house, colder and lonelier than ever before because he'd let the best thing in his life slip through his fingers.

Somehow, he had to bear the loss. Kat deserved better than being mired in his hellish situation, much better than his whacked idea of a relationship. *She deserves better than me.*

Didn't she?

Giving up all hope of sleep, he sat on the side of the bed and considered his options. Working out usually helped, but the walls were closing in. Kat's scent lingered in his sheets, her laughter haunted the air. If he didn't get out, he'd suffocate.

Decision made, he pulled on a pair of loose workout shorts, a T-shirt, and tennis shoes. He stuffed a change of clothes in his gym bag, grabbed his wallet and keys from the dresser, and was out the door in less than two minutes, heading for Hardbodies by Simon in downtown Sugarland, on the main square. Open twenty-four hours, and bound to be practically deserted this time of night. Perfect.

Half an hour later, he was well into his routine, praying the brutal workout would clear his mind as the short drive had failed to do. Arms, thighs, chest. Every muscle God gave him, he punished with weights, then set the treadmill to a brisk jog and started his usual five miles.

The pounding of his shoes lulled him into the boring rhythm, and he wished he'd remembered his MP3 player and headphones. Classic rock always made the clock tick faster.

Across the room, a burly police officer he'd seen

around the gym a few times huffed and puffed on a stationary bike, the spare tire at his middle jiggling with his efforts. He'd nodded in greeting as Howard walked in, not one for small talk. Suited Howard just fine.

At the three-mile marker, the cop left, and Howard found himself alone ... until a familiar, tall redhead sauntered into the room five minutes later.

Janine.

No big deal. Since their tryst a year ago, they'd crossed paths. Couldn't be helped, since they shared the same gym and she sometimes stopped by after her evening shift as a dispatcher. No reason to switch to another place, or expect Janine to do the same. They were adults.

She walked over to a set of free weights and began to work on toning her arms. Though she didn't acknowledge his presence, he knew Janine—or, more accurately, women like her—well enough to know she was aware of his gaze.

Reveling in the attention, like a feline being stroked.

Because he wasn't dead, he allowed himself to look. Her black sports bra hugged small, pert breasts and left her flat stomach exposed. Matching Spandex shorts were painted onto slim hips and thighs, making her appear even slimmer than normal. Coppery tresses, her crowning glory, tumbled in wild disarray about her shoulders and down her back. He'd never seen her hair bound.

Her wrists bound to his bedposts, but not her hair to her head. No doubt, she was a striking woman, any man's wet dream. These days, however, he found her stick figure less appealing than lush curves, plump breasts, and ass cheeks filling his hands to overflowing. He had a certain green-eyed angel to thank for that.

He shook himself. Kat wasn't his, never had been. He'd driven her away, and she'd never have him back.

As though sensing his tension, Janine glanced his way and graced him with a slight smile. Sly, knowing. But she didn't approach, praise Jesus.

Finished, he decided to call it quits. Cross his fingers and go home, hoping he'd exhausted body and mind enough to get some shut-eye. He turned off the treadmill, grabbed his hand towel from the rail and dismounted, wiping his face.

In the locker room, he stepped into the shower with a sigh, relishing the play of the steaming water over his tired muscles. He could've gone home to shower, but he hated cooling sweat and sticky, smelly clothing on his skin. Got plenty of that at work. He soaped his hair, his entire body, then rinsed, lingering a bit longer.

Finally, he shut off the spray and stood for a moment, the pain suddenly bashing him in waves. His past. The fires, the awful murders. Losing Kat. Going home alone.

He couldn't do this.

"Forget where your clothes are, honey?"

16

Startled, Howard turned, thinking he should've expected this. On some level, maybe he had. "Janine, what are you doing in here? The guy at the front desk—"

"Is half-asleep in his chair." She smiled, strolling into the stall. She stopped in front of him, placed a hand on his dripping chest. Skimmed a nipple, which puckered under her touch. "My, you look upset, Harry. Ready to . . . explode."

"*Howard,*" he said, gently brushing her hand aside, pretending not to get the double entendre. No use bothering to hide his nakedness from her when she'd seen and tasted all.

The roaming hand drifted downward, over his abdomen. "Ohh, what do we have here?"

Shit. He didn't want her, but his other head didn't know the difference. His groin stirred, the shaft thickening under skillful fingers kneading the damp flesh, cupping his balls. He stepped backward, away from temptation, bumping his head on the shower nozzle.

"No offense, but this won't work. I'm seeing someone else."

Another lie she saw right through. "Hmm. Which is why you're blowing off steam at the gym in the wee hours, exercising like you're trying to make yourself drop. Why you're still here instead of lying in bed between Mrs. Right's thighs, and getting harder than a rock in my hand."

"Janine," he began. She crowded his space, backed him against the stall. His options were to physically set her away from him—which might bruise her unintentionally—or make her see reason. He hesitated a second too long in deciding, and she went for the kill.

"Get real, honey. She's not here and I am," Janine purred, squeezing his sack again. Encircling his rigid shaft to stroke slowly, leaning forward to whisper to him. "I understand how it is, believe me. She ripped out your guts, didn't she?"

After I ripped out hers. He remained silent, but she read the answer all the same.

"Poor baby." The expression on her beautiful face was more hungry than sympathetic. "Let Janine make it all better."

"I don't think so."

Yet despair and lust were a deadly combination. He'd lost Kat, could never have her or any woman permanently. His life was just too much of a mess, and he'd been burned more than once by believing he might have forever. So what did this matter?

Howard groaned as the redhead kissed his bare throat. Allowed himself to imagine her tongue trailing down his wet chest to his stomach. Beyond.

One corner of her mouth kicked up as her eyes met his, sultry. Triumphant. Bringing him crashing back to reality.

"No." His body shuddered its protest and he moved aside, grasping her arms to carefully remove himself from her erotic manipulations. "I'm sorry, but I can't."

She stood, still caressing between his trembling legs. "One part of you says yes." She pressed her willing softness against his erection. Chipping at his defenses. "What do you have to lose that you haven't already?"

All too true. Kat said his lovemaking was superficial. *Her* words. Hadn't believed in them enough to give him time.

Had hurt him desperately.

His broken heart recoiled from what he was considering even as his arousal demanded release. She was right. He'd lost the lady who truly mattered, and he hadn't managed to halt the agony splitting his chest in two. "Not here."

"Your place. I'll follow you."

He yanked on his change of clothes while she watched in feral appreciation. Shut down his mind to everything except the course he'd set for tonight. He'd take Janine home, screw her until they were both senseless, until an angel from heaven no longer haunted his dreams. His lonely life would return to normal.

He deserved no better.

Hefting his gym bag, he strode from Hardbodies, Janine on his heels, heart a dead weight in his chest.

With every step, he felt more like he was going to his funeral than to a hot night burning up the sheets.

Steeped in misery, Howard barely registered the two other cars in the parking lot. One belonged to the kid at the front desk. The other?

He couldn't find it in himself to care.

What the hell was he doing?

"Christ, I'm an idiot."

By the time he'd driven halfway home, he knew he'd never go through with this. Sleeping with Janine was so not the answer to his problems. God, he'd like to think he'd learned a thing or two in the last year.

And if there were any hope of working things out with Kat . . .

Yeah, like that was going to happen.

Even so, he had to set Janine straight as soon as he got home. And somehow bank the fire in his shorts that wasn't particular about the method of relief.

Howard had a feeling both would be easier said than done.

"You're crazy, Katherine Frances. Completely certifiable."

Wringing her hands against the chill, she scrunched in the driver's seat of her Beamer and continued to grumble under her breath, more anxious than she cared to admit about where in the ever-loving hell Howard could be at two forty-five in the morning.

If he wanted to stay out until dawn, drinking with his buddies on his nights off, it really was no longer any of her business. But she'd wrestled in vain with sleep, miserable and alone, until she couldn't stand it another second. She'd needed so badly to talk to him. Set things right somehow.

And the jerk wasn't home.

Driven by a sixth sense she didn't understand, she backed out of his drive and parked across the street two houses down, like some sleezeball amateur private eye. Now what? Like she was going to sit here when she had to go to work in a few hours, while *he* got to snooze the day away?

Forget it.

Her hand reached for the keys in the ignition, ready to make tracks—and there came his truck. Unmistakable, the behemoth rumbled up the street toward her, slowing at his driveway to turn in.

Kat ducked, feeling stupid. Why hide when she'd waited to see him? Because she didn't want him to *know* she'd been waiting on his sorry ass, dammit. Counting to three, she sat upright.

Just in time to see a small sports car pull in behind

him. Dark, sleek, and snazzy. The driver's door opened, and a statuesque woman emerged, long curling hair tinted dark red under the glow of the lights from inside his garage.

Insides turned to water, numb with disbelief, she gaped in shock as the oh-so-perfect object of male lust, dressed in tight Spandex workout clothes, strolled into the garage and met Howard as he stepped from the truck. He closed his door and leaned against it as Red melted into him, palms on his chest, and proceeded to suck the oxygen from his lungs.

Kat's, too. "Oh . . . Oh, my God."

Red pushed her hands under his T-shirt, stroking as they kissed for what seemed forever, but was in reality only a few seconds. Then she broke the liplock and one hand slipped south to wriggle past the elastic waistband of his shorts. Howard grabbed her wrist, murmuring what appeared to be a short-lived protest, but she wasn't deterred. He tilted his head back and closed his eyes, resting his hands on her boyish hips.

Fixated on Howard touching Red, his palms sliding up her bare torso to cup the teensy breasts encased in the sports bra, Kat clenched her teeth, pulse pounding a drumbeat in her ears. She braced herself for the gut-wrenching hurt. The pain of betrayal. Instead, she was surprised and gratified to experience a slow burn of seething anger.

Pushing the shorts past his hips, Red freed his cock. His thick, erect cock, arching between the two lovers, ready and willing to give her whatever she desired. The burn in Kat's blood became a rolling boil.

Once, Howard had told her about a danger in firefighting called a flashover. When the temperature in the upper level of a burning building reached 1,800 degrees Fahrenheit, every single item in sight would simultaneously ignite. If a firefighter wasn't within a few feet of an exit when the flashover happened, he was a dead man.

Yeah, that was a pretty accurate description for the force that shot Kat into hyperspace when the woman's slender fingers squeezed his balls. Began to stroke his erection.

Whoosh.

Brain disengaged, Kill-the-Slut function activated.

She was out of the car and stalking up the driveway before she was aware her feet had hit pavement. Zeroed in on the grappling couple, she barely registered Howard dropping his hands, shaking his head, and moving out of her grasp, as yet unaware of his own personal flashover about to fry him in his tennis shoes.

"Janine, *no*. Wait—"

"Get off him, bitch," Kat snarled, doing a great impression of a demonic voice from the underworld. *Good God, was that me?*

The pair sprang apart as though they'd been electrocuted, Howard yanking up his shorts and gaping at Kat, speechless. All of his brains being between his legs, of course.

Janine—*fantastic, now she has a name*—was the first to recover, curving her lips into a sneer. "Haven't you heard? Three's a crowd, honey. Harry and I don't do ménages."

Red gloated.

Harry looked sick.

Kat willed herself not to commit murder and stepped close, invading the other woman's space. To her immense satisfaction, Red retreated a step, a flash of uncertainty chasing across her face. The woman wasn't secure in her position with Howard at all, had probably been waiting with baited breath to catch him vulnerable. Not that he'd resisted too damned hard.

"Really? Do you do child support?" she shot back before she could think twice about the fabrication.

"That makes it a quartet, right? Kinda disturbing when you think about it." Red frowned, trying to assimilate, obviously not the brightest bulb in the box. Oh, but the poleaxed expression on Howard's handsome, bloodless face was priceless.

His jaw dropped. "Kat—"

"You," she ground out, shaking a finger at his nose. "Shut. Up."

His mouth snapped closed.

"Oh," Red said, glancing from Kat to Howard. The light dawned. "Oh, wow. A kid? You got your friend here knocked up, and then you turn your back on her and dip your wick in the first partner who happened along?"

Howard's eyes widened, crimson staining his cheeks. "No, dammit, that's not true."

Red made a face. "I'm so out of here. I don't need this sort of drama, even for a great lay. I divorced one two-timing prick already, and he'll be paying child support to two different girlfriends until he drops dead of a heart attack." She snorted at Kat. "Good luck, sugar."

Problem number one solved. Too bad the haze of rage flared anew, seeking its true target. As Miss Do Me departed, Kat scanned the garage, searching for a weapon. Before she considered the wisdom of her actions, she grabbed a fishing pole leaning against the wall and brandished the thing like a samurai warrior.

Howard lifted his hands in surrender, palms out. "Katherine, this isn't the way it looks."

Flashover.

"Bastard!" Raising the rod and reel like an executioner preparing to lop off his head, she let him have it. With a yelp, he unsuccessfully tried to block the tip of the pole whacking his head and shoulders.

"Hey!"

Yeah, this was better than therapy. Much better. A

wild euphoria seized her and she proceeded to adjust his attitude, punctuating her point with each stinging blow.

"You—"

"Ow!"

"Sonofa—"

"Ow!"

"BITCH!"

"I wasn't—"

"Worthless, sorry asshole! I was so fucking miserable I had to come see you! *Make up* with you. How dumb was that?"

"Kat, stop—"

"Your sheets weren't even cold yet, and what do I find? Your hands all over each other, you primed and ready to nail her—"

"Shit! I said stop," he yelled, ducking under the pole and rushing her. Snatching the weapon, he hurled it into a corner, where it clattered and broke. He grabbed her arm and shoved her against the side of his truck, chest heaving in helpless anger. "If you'd been paying attention, you'd have realized I was about to refuse her. I was going to send her home, Kat."

"Oh, right," she laughed, shaking with adrenaline. With unspent tears.

"It's the truth," he insisted, pressing himself into her. "Right before you went postal, I pulled back. Yes, I was aroused, but I didn't want Janine. I wanted you."

"Please, don't degrade us both by playing that song." To her horror, her voice broke and her vision blurred.

He gripped her arms so hard, his fingers dug into her flesh. Tomorrow, she'd have bruises. But that paled in comparison to the scorching heat of his big body fitted to hers. His erection burrowing into her stomach. Arousal that, a short while ago, had been for another woman.

Despite her best efforts, a tear slid down her cheek. The nice, cozy blanket of rage dissipated, leaving only sorrow.

Howard cursed. "Sounds like a load of bull, but it's true. I swear to you I never wanted her, no matter how it appeared. I couldn't sleep, so I got up and went to Hardbodies to work out. She surprised me in the shower—"

"I do *not* want to hear this."

"I was hurting. About you, about everything going on in my life. I was weak, and I'm so sorry you had to see what you did. But as God is my witness, I didn't— I couldn't . . ." His eyes begged forgiveness as he raked a hand through his spiky hair. "Even if you hadn't shown up, I was going to send her home."

Gently, he wiped her tears. But they kept coming. The image of them touching one another, of Howard fully erect, knowing he'd gone so far as to bring Janine here . . . oh, God. Her chest burned and ached, the pain so bad she wanted to die.

"Please. He traced her jaw with his thumb. "Please forgive me."

"It's not a question of forgiving you. The way we left things, we weren't seeing each other." She took a deep breath. "But I don't know if I can forget, Howard. Ever."

"Don't say that," he whispered, touching his forehead to hers. "Give me another chance. My soul is empty without you. Without you in my arms, nothing else matters."

Pretty words. The right words. But the wound was still bloody and raw. A sob caught in her throat. "I don't know if I can. I need to think, and so do you. Maybe you're just not cut out to give your whole heart to one person."

She pushed on his chest, twisted out of his arms. Backing toward the entrance to the garage, she took in the defeated slump of his broad shoulders. Shadows were smudged under his dark eyes, devastation etched on his face.

"Don't go."

Tears welled in his eyes, and she couldn't take this anymore. Had to get out of here before she hurled herself into his embrace and let him have his way again.

In the beginning, he'd warned her, hadn't he?

It's easy to remain alone when you aim low. No strings, easy sex. Then when she leaves, your heart doesn't take a beating in the process.

I have a huge learning curve with the long-term deal. . . . The idea scares me a little.

She should've listened.

"I'm sorry. Good-bye, Howard."

"Kat." Her name was a hoarse plea.

Spinning, she hurried toward her car, half expecting him to follow and stop her. Afraid he would.

Terrified he wouldn't.

As she reached her car, she saw him still standing beside the truck as if carved from stone. Watching helplessly as she left him, perhaps for good. Lungs aching with harsh sobs, she started the ignition and peeled from the curb. She couldn't handle his pain and confusion.

Not when she couldn't deal with her own.

"Hot damn, dinner and a show." Frank chuckled, biting into a cold, greasy burger he'd picked up at the twenty-four-hour joint off the square.

With his free hand, he hefted the binoculars from the passenger's seat of his new ride and watched with amusement as the stacked blonde marched up the driveway toward Lieutenant Dumb-ass and the skinny redhead who looked like a praying mantis in comparison. The pair were playing Here's the Salami as the furious blonde descended on them—much to their surprise and Frank's delight.

"Busted, asshole."

The blonde, Kat, as he recalled, flew at them like an angel of wrath, and whatever she said had the redhead making tracks, fast. Then Kat proceeded to snatch a nearby rod and reel and get *all* up in his shit.

Frank hooted in laughter, almost choking on his burger. Whoa, you had to love spunk in a woman. *He'd* never put up with that shit from his bitch, but still. She was giving Paxton ten kinds of hell, so that made it fine by him.

Attention diverted by Paxton's fleeing would-be fuck de jour, Frank narrowed his eyes as she backed out of the drive and began to pull away. Laying his burger and the binoculars on the seat, he put the wheezing van in gear and followed the redhead, disappointed to have to abandon his post just when the action was getting good.

The payoff, however, was going to be worth the small sacrifice. Time to put in motion the plan that had been simmering ever since Paxton departed the gym with a new slut in tow and a hard-on visible from forty yards.

Time to drive the lieutenant's lesson home using much more personal methods. The end was near.

Two moves remaining on the game board.

Frank's dry spell was officially over.

Halloween. The second-worst frickin' day of the year for calls, right behind New Year's Eve. Wouldn't you know, it was A-shift's turn to work the Day of Ghouls this year. All day long, the team had responded to calls, almost every one of them for teens skipping school and pulling stupid stunts resulting in minor injuries or property damage. Who wanted to sit and stagnate in class on a balmy Friday when you could be out destroying stuff?

This evening, the calls had skyrocketed, including the old burning sack of dog crap trick on an elderly man's front porch, which caught the modest wooden structure on fire. At least they got the blaze doused quickly, and nobody was hurt.

Unlike the unfortunate kid who'd gone with his friends to the cemetery, yanking over tombstones, and got cold-cocked by a falling six-foot marble Virgin Mary. His brains would be scrambled for a week. Some might call that divine justice.

On top of all this, Howard was coming down with something. He lay flat on his back in his bunk, one arm thrown over his eyes, thinking it might be too much to hope for that every juvenile delinquent in Sugarland suddenly got tired of wreaking havoc and went home.

The burning ache in his chest had grown steadily worse in the two days since The Incident. Food turned to ash in his mouth, cramped his belly, so he'd stopped eating. On downtime, between calls and after chores, the guys and Eve joked around as usual, played cards, whatever. But he couldn't seem to focus on anything they said. His mind was wrapped in fog, his body weighed down by bricks.

Naturally, they'd all gotten concerned, tried to get him to talk. Even Sean came out of his own funk for a change, worried about his best friend and not bothering to hide it. Problem was, Howard had nothing to say.

At least he wasn't having nightmares, because you had to sleep to have them.

"Six-Pack? You awake?"

Stifling a sigh, he lowered his arm and blinked in the darkness. As his eyes adjusted, he made out Zack standing in the dim light from the hallway, shuffling his feet. Nervous.

"For you, sure thing. What's doing?"

"I, um, need to ask you a question. In private, before Julian comes in." The younger man walked in, hands in his pockets. He spoke quietly, voice strained. "It's important."

His own ailments put aside for now, Howard sat up and switched on the bedside lamp, gestured for Zack to sit. The man was drawn tight as a bowstring, laser-blue eyes grim as he took a spot on the other end of the bunk. In a flash of memory, Howard recalled this same vibe from his friend the day of Bentley's birthday party, and the mental note he made to speak to Zack. He'd never followed through, and now he felt bad. He waited, giving the guy time to say his piece.

"I need a couple of days off," Zack said, clasping his hands in front of him, elbows on his knees.

Howard shrugged. "That's it? We can swing it."

"Next week."

"Hmm. Tricky, but not impossible." He eyed his friend, speculating. "I assume you've run this by Sean."

The younger man's mouth flattened. "With all due respect, the captain isn't exactly receptive to anything I say or do lately. No, I haven't."

Oh, boy. "What, you're afraid to talk to Sean? Since when?"

"If I'm scared of anyone, I guarantee you it's not him." The sidelong, icy stare Zack leveled at Howard chilled him to the bone. "I've got some stuff to take care of. Personal. For this once, I'd like to avoid taking his shit."

What the hell was going on? "What kind of shit?"

"Man, if you haven't noticed, I'm not saying jack. You two are tight and I'm *so* not going there. I can deal a while longer and pray he gets it together, because the only other option would tear our team apart."

Howard blinked at him. "A formal grievance? Things are that bad between you?"

"And then some." Zack raked a hand through his short black hair, yanked off his wire-rimmed glasses, and rubbed his eyes. He appeared as tired as Howard felt.

"Look, I just need two days off next week. I rarely ask, but that won't mean squat to the captain. I'm not asking you to grant me the time off over his head, just to smooth the way after I talk to him. Help me make sure this happens, because I *have* to be somewhere else. I've got no choice."

"Sounds dire, my friend."

"God." He hung his head, glasses dangling from one hand. After a long silence, he murmured, "I've sold my house."

"Why?" He frowned. "After you worked your ass off to get the loan? You've only been there a year."

"Again, no choice. And I can't talk about this yet."

Judging by Zack's defensive stance, there wasn't anything Howard could say right now to budge him. "All right, whatever you need. Whenever you're ready to talk—"

"I know." Some of the tension drained from his friend's shoulders. "Thanks, Six-Pack."

Zack left as quietly as he'd come in. No sooner had Howard settled himself on his bunk again when his cell phone vibrated on the nightstand. Irritated, he considered letting it go, but he held out slim hope the caller might be Kat. Very slim, based on how badly he'd hurt her when she'd showed at his place.

He'd never forgive himself.

He grabbed the phone, flipped it open. "Paxton."

"I have an old friend of yours here, Lieutenant," a low voice hissed. "She's gonna burn for you one last time, but not in the way you'd like."

"Who is this?" Sitting up, he swung his legs to the floor. The caller laughed, and his blood ran cold.

"Wouldn't you love to know, boy. Here, bitch," he barked at someone on the other end. "Tell our fine, brave hero you need to be rescued."

A woman's scream nearly arrested his heart. "He's going to kill me! Oh, God, don't let him kill me! What are you doing? Nooo . . ." Her voice faded, the phone snatched away.

Oh, God, no. "Kat!" he yelled. "Where is she, you sonofabitch?"

"No blondes on the menu tonight, only redheads. Lucky for sweet Katherine. Isn't that right, slut?" In the background, the woman's bloodcurdling screams intensified.

A redhead. *Janine.*

He stood, swaying on his feet, and lurched for the door. "Where is she? Tell me!"

"Oh, that's right. She means less than nothing to you, so you wouldn't remember." After rattling off an address, he taunted, "Better hurry, Lieutenant. The clock is ticking."

The line went dead. Howard ran, shouting orders. Tommy and Eve emerged from their bunks, sleepy and confused.

"What's going on?" Tommy yawned. "I didn't hear an alarm."

"There wasn't one." Howard skidded to a halt. Briefly, he gasped out what was happening. "Get everyone rounded up and bunked out in their gear. Tell Sean to have dispatch radio a full alarm and notify the police! We need to roll—now!"

They raced toward a disaster he couldn't have conjured, even in his nightmares. As he hurried out the door to the bay, his palm landed on the black-and-white letters.

EVERYBODY GOES HOME.

But not always.

17

Janine might still be alive.

Howard's brain numbed itself to the probability of her murder. Desperately, he clung to the hope that they might reach her in time. Even though he knew in his gut it wasn't true.

Don't think. Just do your job.

Because if he allowed himself to think, he'd have to face his role in leading a killer straight to Janine's doorstep. That her death was ultimately his fault.

That the victim could've been Kat.

He and Julian leapt from the ambulance, donning their SCBA units, turning on the air. Sean, Eve, and Tommy poured out of the engine, shrugging on their tanks, letting the masks hang around their necks. Zack took his post beside the quint to connect the hoses and man the pump.

"Engine 171 initiating primary search. Three going in," Tanner barked into his handset to the battalion chief and everyone else listening on the airwaves. Two more engine companies from nearby stations were en route.

"Be fucking careful," Eve ordered, expression fierce. As the RIC crew this shift, she and Sean would remain outside in case Howard, Julian, or Tommy got into trouble.

Howard unhooked the handheld thermal imaging

camera from his shoulder strap as Julian took the nozzle of the hose, Tommy behind. "You guys ready for this?"

"I'm good," Salvatore said, and Skyler nodded.

A gloved hand landed on Howard's arm, restraining him. Sean shook his head, the brim of his hat shadowing his eyes and nose. "I'll go with them. You stay and coordinate, wait for the battalion chief and the others."

"Uh-uh. No way."

"This sick animal wants you to go inside, Howard. I don't like this. Something's wrong."

"No time for this." He clapped his best friend on the shoulder. "Be back in a few."

He and Jules kicked in the front door as sirens from the assisting engine companies wailed in the night, approaching. Using the camera, he stood slightly behind Salvatore in the lead and helped guide the three of them through the dark. They had no problem negotiating the hallway leading to the bedrooms, following the lure of angry, writhing flames to the last room on the end.

They stepped inside, into hell. The bed was a torch, flames licking the ceiling. But the room wasn't yet fully involved, the window glass intact, which meant the killer had set the fire less than two and a half minutes ago. The bastard had waited until he heard them coming.

Then he'd murdered her.

In the center a figure was sprawled, handcuffed to the posts. A person unrecognizable as his former lover, jaw frozen open in a scream, burning.

Dead. *She's dead and it's my fault. Jesus, God . . .*

Shut it out. Do your job.

Pulling back the nozzle, Tommy at his back, Julian easily controlled the immense water pressure that would otherwise turn the hose into a wild, living thing. Turning the stream on the blaze, he doused the bed, the draperies, the ceiling. Tamed the beast into submission. Nothing more they could do for a woman who hadn't deserved this fate.

The guilt threatened to buckle Howard's knees.

"I guess we're done," Julian said, raising his voice. "I don't envy the crime tech—what the *fuck*?"

"What is it?" Turning, Howard blinked, peering through the mask and thick smoke to see what Julian was staring at on the wall behind them.

When his vision cleared, he gaped at the message illuminated by Tommy's flashlight. The red fluorescent letters ran as though written in blood: BOOM.

In spite of the stifling, superheated air in the room, his body went cold.

The clock is ticking.

Fear kicked his heart into overdrive. "Get out!" he shouted at his partners. "Go, go!"

His men didn't need to be told twice. Dropping their section of hose, they bolted from the room, likely assuming Howard was on their heels.

And he would've been, except, holy shit . . .

"Cap, get everyone away from the house! Tanner!" Nothing but crackling static. He paused, keyed the microphone on his left shoulder strap again. Damned radio wasn't working.

He ran to the window and without a thought, doubled his gloved fist and smashed it though the glass three times, ignoring the pain slicing into his hand and arm. Bending, he yelled through the jagged hole at his startled team and others who'd arrived to take up positions.

"Get away from the house and take cover! Do it *now*!"

No time to explain. He had to trust they'd do as he'd ordered. Had to get the hell out of here. Not daring to look again at the charred body on the bed, he ran as fast he was able in his cumbersome gear. He cleared the door and sped down the hallway.

Probably the killer's idea of another sick joke, like

the note in the shower. Make them scramble like rats, laugh from somewhere nearby when his quarry realized nothing was going to—

The deafening explosion hit his back with the force of a runaway 747. The blast lifted him off his feet and hurled him through black space shot with flame that reached with deadly arms to consume him. His flight ended abruptly as he crashed into something hard, jarring his right shoulder. He bounced and fell, slammed onto a sharp table corner that caught his ribs in a glancing blow, before finally landing on his side in a shower of glass and debris.

Immediately, he tried to roll to his hands and knees, only to double over in agony and slump prone on the floor. His right arm wouldn't work; dislocated shoulder. His head swam and the pain in his side stabbed like a serrated blade. He couldn't see or hear a damned thing, either, except inky blackness and a loud roaring in his ears. Couldn't move to reach the button on his PASS device to sound the alarm for help. Heaving a deep breath, he tried calling out.

But nothing emerged except a hoarse wheeze, his effort rewarded by a fit of coughing. Dull horror seeped into his brain. God help him, his mask had been ripped from his face. On his back, the Air-Pak hung to one side, useless weight. His throat and lungs burned, filled with smoke.

Since he'd been motionless for too long, the PASS device on his coat began to emit a shrill wail even the dead could hear, alerting his team to his location.

Stay calm. Breathe. But it was no use. His limbs were encased in cement, his lungs heavy and full. He was suffocating.

Dying.

"Howard!"

Funny, the pain was lessening. Just flowing out like

blood from a wound. He'd heard death was surprisingly easy, and guessed it must be true.

"Lieutenant, where are you?"

Except for leaving Kat. Sadness washed over him, regret thicker than the smoke snuffing out his life. He wished he'd had time to make things right between them. Earn one more chance with the lady who meant everything to him.

I don't know if I can forget, Howard. Ever.

Tell her . . .

"Howard? Oh, God," someone cried. "He's over here!"

Sean?

Boots crunched through the mess toward him. Ripe curses cut the gloom. The pressure of the tank was removed from his back. Hands turned him over, slow and gentle, onto something hard. A backboard. Then he was being lifted, the sensation of flying as he was carried outside. Into the cool night air caressing his scorched face.

Air he still couldn't draw into his lungs.

More sirens. Dozens of them. Too late.

He felt himself being lowered. His coat was shoved open, his shirt torn in two. A mask placed over his face, fingers pressed into the hollow of his throat, checking for a pulse.

"Not working! Get him intubated, dammit!"

"Come on, old friend, stay with us."

With every last ounce of willpower, he tried to obey. And lost.

"Sweet Jesus, he's not breathing! Six-Pack, don't . . ."

His friends' insistent shouts faded into nothingness.

Kat blinked awake, not quite sure what had jerked her from a bout of fitful tossing. A noise? She listened, not hearing anything except the low hum of the ceiling fan overhead.

Lord, it was hot in here tonight, even naked. How weird. Normally, she enjoyed bundling in the covers.

Or she had until a few days ago, snuggling into Howard's big, warm body. Self-pity and loneliness knifed her breast. Was he lonely, too? Maybe he'd taken up with the lithe, toned Janine after all, and was well on his way to forgetting all about the few weeks they'd spent together.

A distant cry gave her goose bumps, and she sat upright in bed, trying to place the sound. The wail grew louder and she recognized the cacophony of sirens, the low, repeated honking of engine horns miles away. Lots of emergency vehicles, heading for some terrible tragedy. Was Howard among them? She shivered, skin crawling. She hated that awful din, always had. It meant someone's life had been shattered, perhaps lost.

As the sound faded once more, she settled in bed again, no longer hot. In fact, she was chilled to the bone.

Sleep didn't come easily, but she managed to drift off after a while, thankful it was Saturday and she could sleep late. Or so she thought, until persistent rapping filtered into her drugged brain. She groaned. Whoever had decided to hammer early on a Saturday morning was so dead.

Rap, rap, rap. Pause. *Rap, rap, rap, rap.*

Louder. Not hammering . . . someone knocking on her door.

Could it be? "Oh, my gosh!"

Howard had shown up after shift change before, when he was upset and needing her. Who else could it be? Maybe he wanted to plead his case. Talk, work things out. Damn her traitorous heart, she wanted that, too. Was it too soon to cave after what he did?

Okay, *almost* did. The memory still hurt like hell, though.

Stumbling out of bed, she slipped on a big T-shirt, finger-combed her hair into submission, then padded for the door. She didn't have a clue what she'd say to him. How hard of a line to take.

"I'm coming." Peering through the peephole, she frowned in puzzlement, then unlocked and opened the door. Blinking, she stared right into Eve Marshall's face. Her sooty, grime-covered face, streaked with sweat. Howard's teammate wore navy regulation pants and a SFD polo, which were nearly as dirty as her skin. The visit was so out of context, she was at a loss.

"Eve! What a—a surprise! How did you know where I lived?"

"Phone book," she said simply, voice tired. Strained. "Can I come in?"

"Oh! Of course." Stepping aside, she let the other woman pass. "Is this . . . about Howard?"

"Yeah." Eve swiped a hand down her face. "Kat—"

"Wait. You're here to run interference, right? Tell me he's miserable, he can't live without me, blah, blah." She snorted a bitter laugh. "Well, you tell lover boy he can bite the bullet and face me like a man."

"Kat."

"Not that I'm interested in anything he has to say, you know. He can just burn in—"

"Kat." Eve's mouth trembled, her voice shook.

Kat's hand went over her mouth. She knew that look of pity, the one always accompanied by *I'm so sorry* and *Is there anything I can do?* Truth be told, she'd known the second she saw Eve standing at her door. The ground shifted under her feet.

"What's happened to him? Eve?"

"There's been an explosion. Three of our guys were injured, but Howard was caught directly in the blast."

All those sirens, piercing the darkness. *An explosion.*

"H-he's dead." God, no, please.

"No, but he's hurt pretty badly. By the time Sean and Tommy got him out of the rubble, he'd inhaled too much smoke and wasn't breathing." Eve sniffed, a tear leaking from the corner of one eye. "Damn doctor won't tell us shit."

To see this tough, no-nonsense woman cry spoke volumes about how bad Howard's injuries were. He'd almost died, and wasn't out of the woods yet. Kat had never been more terrified in all her life.

"I have to go to him," she whispered.

"Get dressed and I'll drive you."

"Okay." On impulse, she stepped forward and wrapped the other woman in a hug. "Thank you for coming."

After a brief hesitation, Eve returned the hug, patting her back awkwardly. "You deserved better than a phone call. Six-Pack loves you, even if he hasn't said so." Pulling back, she offered Kat a watery smile. "I've known the man for years and I've never seen him so down and out. You've brought the big guy to his knees, girlfriend."

"Right. He's so *in love*, I busted him about to drill another woman three days after we broke up."

"Oh, ouch." Eve grimaced. "What did he have to say?"

"That he'd changed his mind and was going to send her home. Under the circumstances, what else *would* he say?"

"He was telling you the truth," Eve replied. "Howard is the most honest man I know. If he'd intended to go through with having sex, he'd have admitted it to your face. Even though it would've broken your heart, he would've told you, because he never hides behind lies."

"Okay," Kat said slowly. "Given how well I've come to know Howard, I believe you. But he was going to have sex with someone else, before his conscience interfered. Can't you understand how hard that is to just blow off?"

"Better than you know. I suppose the question now is whether you believe his love is worth fighting for."

Those words and the recollection of Howard begging her not to go haunted her as she headed for the bedroom. If he didn't survive, would he die thinking she hadn't loved him enough to work past their crisis? To be patient and support him, help him slay his inner demons, despite his resistance?

No! He'd make it, and she wouldn't leave him alone and hurting one moment longer than necessary. In five minutes, Kat was dressed in jeans, tennis shoes, and a long-sleeved cotton shirt.

On the way to the hospital, she began to assimilate what Eve told her about the blast. And what she hadn't. An awful suspicion formed. "Was the explosion intentional?"

The other woman's slender hands tightened on the steering wheel. "Yes. According to the cops, a homemade device had been placed in the victim's bedroom."

"Bedroom? This was another killing courtesy of the bastard tormenting Howard?"

"That's right," Eve spat, her anger at the unknown monster obvious. "He called Howard on his cell phone this time, put the woman on the line. Six-Pack had to listen to her scream for help, knowing there wasn't a fucking thing he could do."

"My God! Who was she?" Knowing the helpless anger he must've felt, she ached for him.

"No clue. He'll have lots of questions to answer when he wakes up."

When, not if. That mantra kept her sane the rest of the drive. As Eve pulled into the parking lot, she remembered others had been injured. "Who else was hurt? Are they all right?"

"Lord." Eve blew out a breath, tucking a curly strand of dark hair behind her ear. "Sean and the battalion chief were thrown to the ground, but they're both too mean to get hurt. Especially Sean. Zack was blown backward into the side of the quint. Ended up with the wind knocked out of him, some scrapes and bruises. Julian took more of the brunt. He came hauling ass out the front door after Tommy, just as the house blew. Caught a board in the back of the head. Hit so hard his hat cracked."

"Is he okay?" She liked Julian, even if he had put the moves on her sister. She wondered how Grace would take the news.

"Knocked him cold. He sustained a nasty concussion and they're talking about keeping him overnight. He'll recover, thank God." Eve parked, shut off the ignition.

"Good, I'm glad. What about you and the others?"

"Tommy said Julian saw a message spray painted on the wall, and Howard yelled at them to get out. Howard punched out the bedroom window and yelled to take cover, so the rest of us were able to get clear before the house blew."

And now Howard might die because of his sacrifice.

In the ER waiting area, they found the rest of the team.

"Go home, Knight," Sean was saying. "We'll let you know how they're doing, I promise."

"No can do, Cap."

"You almost broke your back, goddammit! We need you healthy."

"I'm fine." Zack turned and noticed the women. Eve gave him a fierce hug, which drew a frown from Sean. Clearing his throat, Zack deftly changed the subject. "Kat, it's good to see you again, though I wish it weren't like this."

"Me, too," she choked out. "Has anyone heard news about Howard?"

"Doctor finally showed a few minutes ago," Sean said, raking a hand through his dark brown hair. "He's been upped from critical to guarded, but stable. They're treating him for smoke inhalation, which is definitely the worst of his injuries. His lungs are in rough shape, but he doesn't think there's permanent damage."

Kat's knees went weak. "Oh, thank the Lord."

"And all His angels. We almost lost him." Sean blew out a breath. "His other wounds are minor in comparison. A shallow six-inch cut starting on his right hand and running up his arm from smashing out the bedroom window. No stitches, due to his gloves and coat."

"Man, if he hadn't done that, Eve might've been fried," Tommy said. "She was standing, like, *right next* to the house." A round of agreement for the lieutenant's bravery ensued.

When the murmurs calmed, Sean continued. "He's also got a mild concussion, a dislocated shoulder, a cracked rib, and bruising all along his right side. After a week or two of rest, he'll be good as new. All told, he got damned lucky."

Yes, he had. They all had. If Howard still wanted a second chance, she was ready to try for them both. He needed her, and she planned to make sure he rested and was well taken care of.

"How's Julian?" Eve asked Sean.

"Awake and sweet-talking the nurses." Sean finally cracked a small smile, and the effect softened his harsh features. Made him appear almost handsome. "I think he's already made a date."

The group laughed halfheartedly, keeping their voices low. Relief for their two fallen brothers was palpable, but no one felt like celebrating just yet.

Kat fidgeted, glancing around. She'd been so upset she hadn't noticed several small groups of hovering men, some police officers, some in regulation navy pants and shirts. The ones in uniform were B-shift, she guessed, hanging out here to wait for news about Howard and Jules, or for a call, whichever came first.

She didn't see Detective Ford, and wondered if he'd already been here. If so, he'd be back to talk with Howard about the latest killing—which had escalated into an attempt on many innocent lives.

Suddenly anxious, she laid a hand on Sean's arm. "Can I see him?"

"Soon. Bentley and Georgie are taking turns sitting with him until he wakes up." Sean covered her hand with his, striking green eyes warm and understanding. "Don't go far, though. I know he's going to ask for you the second he's able."

Hours passed as cops took information for reports, then drifted out. Detective Ford came and went, promising to stop by again to speak with Howard. The B-shift team got a call and had to leave, and hadn't been able to make it back. An assortment of people trooped in and out, some Kat had met at Bentley's party, all there to support the family.

Strange, but nobody had arrived to claim Julian. Didn't he have family or at least a concerned lady friend?

All the while, she sat in a corner of the waiting area next to Eve and Zack, seizing this new connection of their friendship like a lifeline. She felt so out of place. Unnecessary. These people had known and loved Howard for years; she only a few weeks.

What if he didn't want to see her? What right did she have to stay? Maybe she should call Grace for a ride home.

"Kat? Thank heavens you're here!" Hurrying across the waiting area, Georgie launched herself at Kat with no little enthusiasm and wrapped her in a hug. "How are you, dear? If I'd known you were waiting, I'd have fetched you sooner."

For such a tiny woman, she had an embrace of steel and a will to match. Her son had almost been killed and she was asking after Kat's well-being? "I'm fine. How are you and Bentley?"

Releasing her, Georgie offered a wan smile. "Could be worse. We have our son, and at the moment that's all we can ask for. Well, that and a certain lunatic's head on a rusty spike."

Kat had to fight down a smile. The situation wasn't anywhere near funny, but Georgie was an amazing, wonderful person. Kat hoped she'd get to know her much better.

"I agree. The police are going to catch this monster, and when they do, he'll never get out of prison."

"Right you are. In the meantime, my son needs you," she declared. "He's been saying your name for the past ten minutes, but his father and I can't seem to rouse him. They've moved him to a private room. Would you mind terribly if we took a break while you sat with him?"

Yes, finally! She squeezed Georgie's hands. "I'd love to. Actually, I've been anxious to see for myself he's going to be okay."

"He will now," the older woman said, a twinkle in her eye.

Suppressing a wave of guilt for jumping ahead of Howard's buddies waiting to see him, she followed Georgie's directions up to Howard's room and knocked softly.

"Come in." Bentley rose to greet her, relief etched on his face. After giving her a bear hug, he said, "Thanks for the backup. Georgie and I wanted to be here when he awoke, but we've got to take a break. My wife needs to eat something before she falls over."

"No worries," she said, nodding. "You guys go ahead. I'm sure he'll be fine."

"Yeah. Anyway, I doubt it's my mug he wants to see." He gave her a piercing look from under his lashes that mirrored Howard's to a T. "We'll be back."

"Take your time."

The moment of truth. Chest tight with anxiety, she let her gaze drift toward the big man in the bed. Even flat on his back and unconscious, he filled the entire space with his presence. His broad shoulders were almost the width of the mattress, and his legs were bent so his feet wouldn't hang off the end.

She moved to his left side and studied him, unable to hold off the rush of tears any longer. A clear oxygen mask covered his nose and mouth, the little elastic strap digging into a livid bruise on his right cheekbone. His right arm was in a sling, the cut covered with gauze, the skin that was visible purple, as well. She could only imagine how battered the rest of his right side looked.

"Oh, honey," she whispered, taking a seat in the vacated chair. Reaching out, she rested her arm on his pillow and stroked his spiky hair. He must be in such pain, inside and out. "Why did he do this to you?"

She kept forking her fingers slowly through his hair. She had to touch him, and this was the only place she was relatively certain wouldn't cause more pain. His wheezing breaths sounded awful, each one gripping his chest in a vise.

Howard turned his head toward her as though seeking her touch, movement flickering behind his eyelids.

"Sweetie, can you hear me? Come on, open those peepers for me."

His thick lashes fluttered, swept upward. He blinked at her, eyes dazed, no hint of recognition for her or his surroundings. At least not right off.

"Hey." She smiled, wiping at the wetness on her cheeks. Careful of his IV, she took his hand. "You're in the hospital. Do you remember what happened?"

He blinked again, making an obvious effort to process what she was saying. The blank stare gave way to confusion, and his brow furrowed. His scratchy voice emerged as barely a whisper. "Kat?"

He sounded terrible, like he'd gargled with sandpaper. "Shh, don't try to talk. Just nod or squeeze my hand. Do you remember the fire last night? The explosion?"

For about five seconds he frowned, studying their clasped hands, wrestling to make sense of the incomprehensible. Then his gaze snapped to hers and sheer horror flooded his face. "The . . . others . . ."

"Your team is fine," she reassured him. "Julian has a concussion, but they've already let him go home with overnight supervision." She thought of the knockout Hispanic chick who'd finally showed to collect Salvatore. Supervision. Right.

She sincerely hoped Grace had better sense than to get involved with a player.

Howard closed his eyes, exhaling a rattling sigh. But the second he opened them again, lines of distress were etched on his face. "She's . . . dead."

"The victim? I know, sweetie," she said quietly, trying to lend him her strength. "Eve told me how that bastard called you at the station, and I'm so sorry. You couldn't have saved her, honey. He wasn't going to let you."

He swallowed, throat working as he struggled to speak. "My fault."

"No, it most certainly is not. You have no way of predicting what random woman he's going to target next. He—"

"Not random. *Janine.*"

Kat stared at him, struck dumb by *her* name falling between them like a boulder. And by his expression, rife with anguish and guilt. "Are you saying . . ."

"He murdered Janine." He turned his face away in shame. "She's dead. . . . Because of me."

18

There was only one reason Howard could figure why he ought to be grateful he hadn't died, and she was sitting at his side. Holding his hand. Lending him quiet support, love shining in her beautiful green cat eyes.

Devotion he didn't deserve.

The pain, however, he owned. In spades. Pain sinking deep into his bones, far beyond the physical, though his body hurt plenty. His throat was raw, his lungs so heavy they felt filled with lead. Just turning his head made him dizzy, and forget trying to move. Muscles he hadn't known he possessed screamed in protest at the slightest twitch. Those were just for starters, yet none of his ailments mattered.

Because he was alive, and an innocent woman wasn't.

He may as well have murdered his former lover

"You can't blame yourself for her death," Kat insisted. "She could've been anyone."

Ignoring her protest, he pulled down the irritating oxygen mask, letting it dangle around his neck. "She could've been . . . *you*."

He was shaking apart inside. Coming unhinged. Thanking God the killer hadn't chosen Kat, knowing he'd likely burn in hell for favoring one human life over another. For feeling such overwhelming relief that he'd awakened to see Kat's sweet face hovering over him in concern. That the bastard hadn't cruelly ripped this woman from his side.

The woman I love.

God help us both, I love her.

Gently, she cupped the left side of his face, stroked a thumb over his whiskered cheek. "Hush, I said don't try to talk. I'm here and I'm fine, Lieutenant. And I'm not going anywhere unless you want me to."

Jesus, how he wished he could believe that. Trust a woman, and she'd rip your heart out. Love her—or anyone—too much, and she'd leave. Sooner or later.

So he'd opt for later, because he wasn't a strong enough man to do what was best for Kat and watch her walk out the door a second time. Out of his life and away from the danger stalking him.

One vital issue, however, remained unsettled between them. "I wasn't going to sleep . . . with Janine. I knew it was wrong. . . . Changed my mind. If you don't . . . believe me . . . nothing I say will ever matter." He swallowed hard. The burning in his chest and throat wasn't just from the smoke. "If I've lost your trust . . . we've got nothing to build on."

Worked both ways, and the irony of asking for what he had trouble giving wasn't lost on him.

The wounded look in her eyes was quickly replaced by determination. She squared her shoulders, pinning him like a butterfly with her knowing gaze. "I saw you start to pull away from her before I interrupted, and even if I hadn't seen, I believe you're telling the truth. But you did let her follow you home with every intention of having sex."

"Yes." He'd been running scared, but there was no sense in trying to justify his actions.

"Well, I wanted honesty, didn't I?" Her sad smile tore his heart into a million bloody pieces.

He reached for her hand again. "Baby, I'm so sorry I hurt you. Never again . . . I promise."

"People hurt each other, Howard," she said, linking her fingers with his. "It's not realistic to think we could go our whole lives, everything all sunshine and roses, never having to really work at our relationship. For my part, I love you enough to stick it out."

"I—what?" He stared at her serene face as she studied his reaction, beautiful green eyes peeking from under tawny lashes. A woman at peace, now that she'd said the words aloud. He had to hear it again, to be sure. "What did you say?"

"I love you, Howard Paxton." Her full, sexy lips curved upward. "I've known since the day you saved that baby at the river. How far and fast are you gonna run now? Oh, wait. You're not running anywhere at the moment," she teased.

His mind spun. Hadn't he just admitted to himself that he loved her? Hearing her put it out there . . . wow. "Kat, I—I . . ."

How could three little words make him feel like a king and scare the crap out of him at the same time?

He knew how. Making her understand meant giving her what she needed and deserved—all of him. His whole heart. His trust.

"You don't have to say the words." She faltered, looking uncertain. "If you want me to go—"

"No," he rasped, his voice shot. "I was miserable without you. I *need* you. I've been a loner my whole life, baby. I've never had to share with anyone else, but . . . I'm learning. With you, I want it all. Please don't . . . leave me again."

"Hmm, pretty persuasive." She gave him a small smile. "All right, I'll stay." Leaning over, she pressed a kiss to his lips. Soft and sweet.

Her full breasts grazed his chest through the pink cotton long-sleeved T-shirt she wore. His groin stirred and he groaned at the temptation he couldn't indulge. She pulled back and he angled his head, catching a nice glimpse of the way her round, squeezable butt filled out those faded jeans.

She settled in her chair, and he forced his mind from lusty ideas and his burgeoning, unsatisfied erection.

She'd given him another chance, whether he deserved it or not. Thank God. "I want to tell you about my nightmares. About my past, anything you want . . ." His voice faded. He struggled to finish the sentence, but no dice.

"Oh, now look what you've done," she admonished, without any real heat. She raked her fingers through his hair, massaging his scalp. "You can tell me everything when we get you home, okay?"

He nodded. Home. With Kat. Jesus, her fingers felt fantastic. His eyelids grew heavy. So tired.

Wait a second. His eyes popped open wide as a troubling idea occurred to him. He obviously wasn't getting out of here for another day or two. Who'd protect Kat?

"Sweetie, what's wrong now?"

Somehow he pushed the words past his scorched throat. "Where . . . you . . . staying?"

"Don't worry, I'm parking right here until the nurses make me go home, then I'm sleeping at my parents'. Grace offered to let me stay at her condo, but Nashville is twenty minutes away and I didn't want to be that far from you. Besides, with Joan and Greg there while their house is being repaired, I'll have a houseful of people to protect me."

"Police . . ."

"Detective Ford mentioned having a unit patrol your place and my parents'. He'll be by later, when you're feeling better. Sleep, honey." Gently, she replaced the oxygen mask.

Wheezing a sigh, he gave up the fight. He had Kat back, making the world almost perfect.

And it would be, as soon as he sent a murdering lunatic to hell.

Kat stirred a pot of chicken tortilla soup on Howard's stove, thinking firemen made sucky patients. Especially when they started to feel better and wanted to push themselves too soon. No matter how many times she tucked him snug on the sofa with stern orders to rest, he ended up following her around the house as though afraid she'd disappear.

Beat the hell out of the shape he'd been in when she'd brought him home from the hospital on Tuesday. As annoying as having a permanent shadow could be, she'd take Howard's constant looming presence over that depressed silence any day. Just when she'd started to get seriously concerned about his lack of appetite, he'd begun to rally.

Now, a week later, he still hadn't spoken much, but his brown eyes had lost their dull glaze and he'd been watching her with unmistakable heat. A big, hungry lion waiting to pounce the second his body cooperated.

"Mmm, something smells good."

Case in point, the devil leaning on his good shoulder against the entry to the kitchen. Even with one arm in a sling, shirtless, and covered with multicolored bruises, wearing nothing but gray sweatpants slung low on his hips, he looked scrumptious enough to make a nun reconsider her vows. She held aloft a spoonful of spicy, fragrant soup. "Want to taste?"

"You bet."

Pushing off the wall, he crossed the short distance separating them and spun her to face him. She squeaked, dropping her wooden spoon into the pot, and found herself backed into the counter. Pressed flush against six and a half feet of aroused male.

Invaded. What a perfect word for his tongue sweeping into her mouth, his left hand skimming low to untie her drawstring pants, push them past her hips. His fingers brushed the curls between her thighs, found the bud of her clit to rub in lazy circles.

"That's it, my angel. Open for me."

A surge of moisture dampened her sex, his probing fingers. Pure pleasure melted her limbs.

"You're the only woman for me, always. Let me in, sweet Katherine."

She wrapped her arms around his neck. "I'm all yours."

"Hold on to me," he growled, wrapping his good arm around her waist. He lifted her to sit on the counter and tugged her pants down her legs.

"You're going to aggravate your injuries!" The surface felt cold under her bare bottom, and she wriggled.

Shoving his sweatpants low on his thighs, he parted her knees and stood between them. His sex jutted toward her opening, thick and hard. Ready to take what belonged to him. "Scoot all the way to the edge. Good girl. Now wrap those gorgeous legs around my waist and hang on."

God, she loved this dominant sexual side of him. She'd love to turn the tables on him again sometime and have him begging for mercy—in the shower or out. Right now, he was unstoppable. *Oh yeah.*

In the next instant, he was inside her, buried deep. He held her as close as possible with his right arm in the sling between them. Wholly connected.

"Feel this," he murmured. "Feel me. Only yours, baby."

"Yes." She twined her fingers in his hair. "Mine."

Her soft claim was met with a groan. Tightening his hold, he began to thrust with long, sure strokes. Increasing in tempo until he pistoned into her hard and fast. Sweeping her higher, higher, a category five hurricane blasting her senses. Devastating her from the inside out in the most delicious way. Primal. Raw.

The pressure built in her womb, the flames licking her sex spreading to her limbs. She felt her body go molten, and the quiver began. Her orgasm, driven to the precipice of detonation. No holding back.

Her orgasm shattered and she heard her cry of joy from far away as she clung to his shoulders. Her channel pulsed around his cock, so good. So right.

"Yes, angel . . . oh, God!"

With a hoarse shout he joined her, lunging as deeply as possible, spilling into her. His shaft jerking, pumping for several long moments as they floated gently to earth.

"Wow." She gave a shaky laugh. "You were fantastic."

"We're fantastic together," he corrected, kissing her nose. "Though you might get tired of me jumping your bones in unusual places."

"Not a chance. Jump to your heart's content, until you run out of places."

Howard cocked his head, one corner of his sexy mouth kicking up. "That's gonna take a long, long time. Forever, in fact. Just to give you fair warning."

Forever.

With you, I want it all.

Not exactly the word "love"—but pretty darned close. Huge strides for a loner like Howard.

In the meantime, she needed to learn what made him tick.

Slipping out of her, he hitched up his sweats and sniffed toward the simmering pot of soup. "Dang, I'm starved."

Laughing, she swatted him lightly on his good arm. "Men! Food and sex. And here I was, wondering what made you tick."

Blinking, he gazed back, the picture of innocence. "Is there more?"

"Humph! No more nookie for you, buddy."

He flashed her a smug grin, slid a hand up the inside of her bare thigh as she shuddered in anticipation. "Really?"

Okay, so he spent the next hour making a big liar out of her, sating a different sort of hunger. But oh, what an hour.

Her lusty fireman gave the term *dining table* whole new meaning.

No fruit salad required.

Later, she and Howard lounged on his deck, enjoying the sunny Saturday afternoon and each other's company. There was a bite in the air, not cold enough to drive them inside, but enough to hint at Thanksgiving a mere three weeks off.

Howard had overdone it and worn himself out, his movements stiff after their mini marathon. After their late lunch, he'd lowered himself gingerly into the padded lounge chair with a grateful moan, and hadn't said much since. He looked tired and drawn. Pensive.

"I'm sorry Bentley placed you on indefinite leave," she said. The chief had delivered that bit of unpleasant news this morning in person.

"He had no choice. My presence has put everyone else in jeopardy." His words were matter-of-fact, but his tone conveyed how much he hated it. He fell quiet again.

Kat didn't push. She'd made that mistake before, and it wasn't one she planned to repeat. All good things come to those who wait.

Which was why she looked at him in surprise when he finally said, "I'd like to tell you what I remember about my past . . . and the nightmares."

As badly as she wanted to know, her reply surprised

her even more. "Honey, you don't have to. I was self-
ish to pressure you when you weren't ready."

"No, you were right. I do need to talk to somebody
I trust, and that person is you, angel." He reached for
her hand. She took it, and his broad palm swallowed
hers.

At last. He'd reached out. "If you're sure . . ."

"I am." Studying her from under his thick lashes, he
began, his voice soft. "Did you ever see that creepy
movie *Final Destination*?"

"The one where a group of teens escape death, and
it tracks them down one by one? Good for a cheap
thrill on movie night, but way farfetched."

"Is it?" He looked out over the yard, his gaze faraway. Lost in the past he'd never wanted to remember.
"What if we're all set on a certain path, one that can't
ever be changed? Maybe it's true you can run, but you
can't hide from your fate."

"I don't believe in superstition and neither do you."
She frowned, not liking where he was going with this.

He shrugged. "Doesn't sound quite as stupid to me
now as it would have a few months ago. Anyway, I
meant it more as a metaphor."

A disturbing one, but she refrained from interject-
ing her opinion. As he collected his thoughts, the only
sounds were the brown leaves rattling in the trees,
caught by the breeze before floating to the ground, and
an occasional bird.

"When Bentley decided I was old enough to handle
the answers to my questions, he told me I was one of
the worst child abuse cases in Tennessee history," he
said, point-blank.

"Based on what you'd told me about your father
beating and dumping you in the woods, I'm not surprised." Sickened on Howard's behalf, but not surprised. A sudden, horrible thought occurred to her, and
she gasped. "And I hit you with the fishing pole!

Howard, I'm so sorry! I swear, I've never done anything like that in my life. I didn't mean to remind you of—"

"You didn't," he reassured her with a rueful grin. "Not even close. Your swing is kinda puny, sweetheart. Besides, I was too embarrassed about the whole situation to make the connection. I sort of had that one coming."

Looking back, there was no excuse for what she'd done, even as pissed as she'd been. Her loss of control shook her anew, especially given his history. But if he was willing to put it behind them, so would she—with a vow she'd never lay a hand in anger on him or anyone else again.

Dismissing her concern over the incident, he continued. "Anyway, I have a few clear memories of my father's rages, but most of what I recall has a dreamlike quality, as though it happened to someone else. Or my mind embellished the terror he put me and my mother through, made up its own script to fill in the blanks."

"You were very young, so that's not an unreasonable assumption. What do you remember for sure?"

"My mom screaming while my father held me down and forced me to drink some sort of cleaner from under the kitchen sink. How the stuff burned and I vomited for hours, and he beat me for making a mess. Another time, he chained me naked outside next to our dog's house because he said the dog minded better than I did. He left me there all night, and I got pneumonia."

She stared at him, speechless, unable to fathom such sadistic cruelty or that young Howard lived in spite of this treatment.

"He never called me by my name, just Rat. He'd laugh when he caught me rummaging in the pantry or fridge for scraps. Just like an ugly little rat, he'd say. One of his favorite games was to withhold food for so many days I could hardly stand."

"Where was your mother during all of this?" She couldn't imagine standing by while anyone beat her child. Then again, she'd grown up safe and well loved.

"Probably planning her escape." Bitterness crept into his voice. "Oh, on the few occasions she stood between me and him, he'd beat her unconscious. Then, his rampage would be worse than ever and he'd think of new ways to torture me—or her by proxy, I suppose. He was a master at inflicting suffering. Satan incarnate. And he hated me with a passion I'll never understand."

Neither would she. What father wouldn't be proud to claim a handsome, sweet little boy? To watch him grow into a fine man? Thank God Bentley and Georgie had come along to mend his shattered life.

Her eyes went to the thin scar on his cheekbone. In her gut, she knew before she asked. "You didn't get that injury from a ninety-three-year-old lady, did you?"

"No, I got it courtesy of my father's boot." He sighed, one corner of his mouth kicking up. "We really did save her cat, though."

Dear, sweet heaven.

"How long have you been having the nightmares?"

"Several months. I didn't want to admit this aloud, but . . . I think they're repressed memories, Kat," he said quietly.

"Of when your father almost killed you?"

He nodded. "At first it was easier to pretend they were meaningless, just dreams. I mean, I'd gone my whole life without being able to recall many details of the night I became an orphan. I didn't *want* to remember, still don't. If the curtain lifts, I'm afraid there's going to be something horrific on the other side."

"If they are actual memories, I think you'd better be prepared for the worst. They'll surface eventually. Are they always the same?"

"Mostly. It's always the same two scenes. They had lots of gaps in the beginning, but the holes have filled in piece by piece. Remember I told you about my mom's garden? I used to follow her through the rows, begging to help plant seeds. She let me, too. Those are my happiest memories."

She squeezed his hand in encouragement. "I'm glad you have them."

"Me, too." He sighed, letting go of her hand to sit on the side of the lounger, facing her. "In the beginning of the nightmare, I'm in her garden. I liked to hide in there, pretending it was my magical, moonlit forest and the evil troll couldn't hurt me. Then I hear arguing. A thumping noise. I see . . . something. I don't know what, but it terrifies me and I run."

"What you saw is the key. An atrocity the fragile mind of an abused little boy couldn't handle. And now it needs to get free."

She had her own idea of what he might've seen, and it didn't bear thinking, much less mentioning. Not with her total lack of experience in the effects of psychological trauma. Plus, the authorities had closed this case long ago, so what did she know?

"I'd just as soon it didn't." He clasped his hands between his spread knees. "Next, I'm running fast as I can, and my father is crashing through the woods behind me. I have to get away, or he'll kill me. I know this, just like I know it's him even though I can't see his face in the dream."

"Does he catch you?"

"Catches me, kicks me, beats me with his fists. Hauls me up by my pajama shirt and snarls that he's finally rid of me. 'Die, you mangy bastard.' His exact words."

Tears pricked her eyes. "I don't know what to say."

She rose and went to sit next to him, snuggled into his left side and linked her arms around his middle, laid her head on his shoulder. He tucked her close and they stayed locked together for a few minutes, neither one speaking. Kat tried to absorb what it would be like to carry the burden of such staggering pain for more than thirty years. The huge effort his brain had undertaken to keep those secrets buried forever.

How they might rise from the dead to destroy Howard.

He trembled in her arms, this mountain of a man with an even bigger heart. He needed her so much, wasn't pushing her away any longer. Had opened all of himself to her.

She couldn't love him more than at this moment.

"Why now?" she mused aloud. "The nightmares start plaguing you, and now a killer is tormenting you. It's almost like your dreams were some sort of omen. Can these events be a big coincidence?"

He kissed the top of her head. "I don't know. My mother hit the road, my father was confirmed dead by the county sheriff, who was always coming out to the house. I don't think we had any friends. Nobody's left from back then to even make a connection."

"Except Bentley."

He pulled back and looked down at her, startled. "What are you saying? You believe Bentley has something to do with the murders?"

"No, not at all! What I mean is, at the party Georgie said Bentley has been in the Sugarland Fire Department for some forty years, right?"

"Right," he said slowly. "So?"

"So he was right here in Sugarland before you were born, before he met and married Georgie. Years later, he and Georgie adopted you. He's the one and only tie to your past. Has he ever told you *exactly* how you came to his and Georgie's attention as a boy needing a home?"

"No." Howard's dark brows drew together as he considered the question. "Not really. Just that they didn't have kids of their own and when they found out about me, they went through legal channels to be able to bring me home."

"Why you? I know you were a sweet, beautiful little boy," she said gently, "but most couples prefer infants, not older children with deep trauma who need special attention. Statistically, it should've taken months or years to place you with a permanent, loving family. This was especially true thirty years ago. People just weren't as accepting of children with special needs as they are now."

Howard stared at her, processing this. "Do you think Bentley knew my parents somehow?" He shook his head. "No, he would have said something to me."

"Maybe he knew *of* them, had heard talk in the community. Sugarland and the surrounding communities were a lot smaller nearly forty years ago. People tended to know one another's business even if they didn't know each other personally. I'm sure there would've been gossip at least, especially with the sheriff's department constantly getting called out there."

"Maybe. But I still don't know why Bentley wouldn't have told me if that were true. What difference does it make if he knew about my home situation? And how the hell could any of that possibly relate to what's going on now?"

She wasn't sure, but there might be one way to find out. A method he wasn't going to like one bit.

"The old house where you grew up . . . is it still standing?"

"I-I don't know." He faltered, eyes shadowed. "The place was a dump. No better than a shack, really. I've never driven out there to take a look. Why?"

"Sweetie, maybe your past has squat to do with the monster who's making your life miserable, but I think there's something we might try to at least put the nightmares to rest." She heaved a deep breath. Cupped his cheek.

"I think you need to go back to where it all began."

19

"I can't believe I let you talk me into this. Why don't we do this next weekend?" Howard sounded like a pouty little kid.

Kat, sitting on the edge of his bed in those snug jeans cupping her marvelous ass just so, was bent over tightening the laces on her hiking boots. Thanks to the V in her cotton shirt, he had a fantastic view of "the gals," plump and swaying to and fro, begging for his hands and mouth.

"Because if we wait, you'll come up with five more excuses not to go by then." She straightened, cutting short his ogling. "There's no reason to be afraid. Bentley said it's just an old, overgrown ruin. The place probably won't even resemble what you remember."

"I'm sure he's right." *So let's forget the whole thing.* No point in denying he was already shaking in his boots. He'd never had the slightest inclination to visit, had avoided the dark, tree-lined county road leading to his childhood home every time he drove to Clarksville. He'd pass it by, feeling an odd, horrible pull, knowing he couldn't go there or something truly evil would befall him. Like a hapless hero from a Stephen King novel, he'd disappear down the road and into the waiting arms of death, never to be seen or

heard from again. Or a fate worse than death, tormenting him for eternity, making him wish for oblivion.

Kat stood, shrugging on her jacket. "I'll drive your
truck. You'll be more comfortable than in my Beamer."
Taking in his expression, she put her arms around his
neck, biting her lip. "You look like you're going to be
sick. Listen, forget what I said. We don't have to do
this, honey."

Great. Now if he took the out, he'd look like a
wimp. "I can handle it. How hard can it be to stomp
around in the weeds and look at a rotted pile of
boards?" His attempt at a smile came out lopsided.

"Only if you're sure."

"I am. Let's go."

She gave him a soft kiss on the lips and they were
on their way. He eased into the passenger's seat with a
grunt of pain, studying Kat from the corner of his eye,
thinking how strange to have a woman drive his truck.
The huge vehicle dwarfed her, and he was surprised
she could see over the steering wheel. She looked so
darned cute with her white-blond ponytail bouncing,
wrestling the mammoth hulk of machinery, he felt
proud she belonged to him.

He'd also love to bend her over the tailgate, show
her all the creative new functions of four-wheel drive
machinery.

As they neared their destination, any ideas of a se-
cluded country rendezvous vanished like smoke. His
hands shook, his stomach churned. The temperature
outside was in the high fifties, yet his body was as cold
as the dead of winter.

At his direction, Kat turned onto the county road.
With every passing foot of the last two miles, it became
harder to breathe. Like suffocating after the explosion,
except slower and more excruciating.

"Pretty isolated," Kat observed. "Only a couple of

old farmhouses around for miles. Bet it's creepy out here at night."

"Actually, night was my favorite time. My father would pass out drunk, and I was free to roam without fear of his wrath, for a little while."

She cut a quick glance at him, and her voice was edged with sympathy. "Your magical forest."

"Yeah." For all the protection it gave him. He pointed at a weed-choked drive just ahead. "There it is."

"Ugh." She grimaced, turning into the lane leading to the abandoned lot. Which wasn't much of a lane at all. Fallen dead tree limbs snapped under the tires, and an assortment of tall grasses and brush scraped the undercarriage. "It's probably chigger city out there."

"In November? Let's hope not. Now, the ticks, on the other hand . . ." He grinned at her, teasing to dispel the queasiness.

"Well, thanks for the lovely thought."

"Any time. But hey, I'll help you look for the little critters later, like the song says."

Kat laughed, and he let the sound wash over him. Prayed it would overtake the oppressive weight settling on his chest, stop the trembling in his hands.

It didn't.

"There's not much to see, that's for sure." Kat arched a brow at the sagging, rotted heap of lumber he used to call hell. The house squatted in the undergrowth, weeds and bushes sprouting from the windows and front door, looking for all the world like an ancient, hairy, butt-ugly witch gaping at them from a stand of trees.

"Charming, huh?" He curled a lip in disgust.

"Doesn't appear we'll be going inside."

"Best news I've heard all day." In truth, no one could've forced him at gunpoint.

Together they walked toward the collapsed front porch, boots crunching in the dry foliage. He halted a few feet from the structure, a flood of awful memories assailing him. Ghosts everywhere, film reels of terror that would never die. The stress must've shown on his face.

"What are you remembering?" Kat linked her arm around his waist, hugging him close.

He draped his left arm over her shoulders, nodding at the porch. "Our dog used to hide under there when my father started yelling. He'd slink off when the bastard wasn't looking, crawl underneath to the darkest corner and wait out the storm. Chex was smart. Smarter than me."

"Chex?"

"His favorite snack. Mom and I would sneak squares of Chex cereal to him on the sly." A rare good memory, and those few always involved his mother.

Why did you leave me?

"How was he smarter than you?"

"Because he knew exactly how to live in a war zone and stay under the radar. If it weren't for me, he would've fooled the old man for years." His larynx seemed to shrink to the size of a pinhole. Even after more than three decades, God, it still wrenched out his heart.

"What happened?" she asked softly.

"During one of my father's drunken rages, I decided Chex's hiding place would work for me, too. But he caught me. I thought I was in for another beating." A bitter, hoarse noise escaped his throat.

"Instead, he broke my dog's neck while my mom and I screamed. Nothing he ever did to me, even that last night, ever hurt so damned much."

That's not true, a voice whispered. *He destroyed you in the garden.*

Removing his arm from Kat's shoulders, he pressed trembling fingers to his throbbing temple. Where had that stray thought come from?

"That's evil!" Kat shuddered. "I don't know what I thought to accomplish by making you do this, and you don't look well. Why don't we go?"

"You didn't force me, sweetheart. To be honest, I should've done this long ago. If I had, maybe I wouldn't have nightmares."

Even as he said it, he wondered whether this was the case. He might've simply had them sooner.

"Maybe," she said, clearly not believing it herself. "Let's finish up so we can go home and have some hot chocolate."

Home. The woman he loved referring to his house as "home" warmed some of the cold spots. "It's a plan."

"Where to?"

"Around back."

Which was the absolute last place he really wanted to be. As they rounded the corner of the old house, the pressure in his chest increased to the point of sharp, twisting pain, and his heartbeat slammed against his rib cage.

"Where was your mother's garden?"

Howard gestured toward an area about thirty yards straight out from where the back door hung open and loose on its hinges. "Over there, I believe." His voice sounded strange and thick to his own ears.

Nothing there now except more of the same. Just a dense tangle of weeds and brush, his mother's once neat, lovingly tended haven overtaken by decades and the elements. In no way did the area resemble anything familiar, but he was drawn toward it, anyway. The moth to the proverbial flame, his legs propelling him forward of their own accord.

He stopped at the center of where he recalled the garden being located, rubbing his aching chest. Dimly, he was aware of Kat behind him, waiting, allowing him a few moments to himself.

Right here, life ended as I knew it.

For the better? Yes, in most respects. And yet . . .

The yawning emptiness left in the wake of his mother's departure, of a long-ago night of confusion and horror, ate at his soul. "Why?"

"Why what, sweetie?"

Absently, he shook his head. The answers were here. Answers too hideous to contemplate. He ought to run, like he did so many years ago. Run as though the devil himself was in hot pursuit. Get away.

Get away.

Voices. Angry. Shouting. Disturbing the peace of his magical forest.

A sickening, soggy thump. A bad curse word.

He went to see, although he knew he shouldn't. Hid behind the tomato plants, peered around the stalks, ripe with lots of tomatoes. And he saw . . . he saw . . .

"Noooo."

Howard sank to his knees, holding his head in both hands, heedless of the sling on his right arm. His skull was splitting in two, the agony unbearable. The memory wanted out, clawed his brain like a crazed demon in a cage. Maddened and screaming.

He ran, crashing through the trees. Ran away from— what?

What had he seen?

But he'd shut it out, his world reduced to fleeing for his life. His mind blank as a sheet of paper, no other motive but survival pumping his legs.

I'm gonna catch you, worthless little bastard!

No, no! Mommy!

His father, tackling him. Hitting, kicking. Pummeling his small, starving frame until he couldn't move.

Gonna die.

"Howard! Oh, God, honey!"

Hands, shaking him. Grabbing his face.

"Howard, breathe! Come on, baby, where are you?"

He wasn't breathing? He gulped a deep breath, struggling from the abyss.

"Kat?"

"Thank God! I'm right here." On her knees, she threw her arms around him, pulled him in. Held him close, tight as a vise. Rocking and kissing him in turn, the salt of her tears on his lips. "I'm sorry, I'm sorry, I'm sorry . . ."

They might've stayed locked together ten minutes or an hour. He didn't know. Only knew that the lush curves pressed against him, the heat of her sweet body, her gentle crooning, brought him out of the nightmare. Quieted the demon in the cage.

Inside, anyway. Outside, he couldn't stop shaking. The devastating aftereffects of terror-induced adrenaline. An electrical storm moving farther and farther into the distance, until his world stilled once more.

And there was only Kat.

Loving him.

"Did you remember all of it?" Leaning back some, she searched his eyes.

"No," he croaked. "I can't do this, Kat. Take me home, please."

"You've got it, big guy."

He let her take his arm, help steady him as he pushed to his feet. They walked back to his truck without a word or a backward glance.

As Kat put the old place behind them, he knew whether he spent the rest of his life in Tennessee or not, he'd never return. If the past wanted to stay buried, fine by him.

His future was sitting at his side, in the form of an angel.

From the dining table, Kat surreptitiously watched Howard over a stack of her students' handwriting samples. He was dressed in his favorite lounging attire of dark blue sweats and a white T-shirt, cranked back in his favorite recliner, flipping channels on the television. Normal, peaceful.

Except for the wistful melancholy in his beautiful brown eyes, the pain he covered with a sexy smile when his gaze landed on her. Emotional pain more than physical, though he still groaned when getting up to move around.

His bruises, shoulder, and cracked rib were healing, and he didn't appear to be in nearly as much discomfort as he had been three days ago when they'd driven to Clarksville. In spite of her fussing, he'd ditched the sling early and thumbed his nose at the pain medication. No, the worst of his bruises were inside.

She didn't know how to heal them. Her one attempt at armchair psychology had backfired, big time. She'd had no business encouraging him to try and lift his mental block without the benefit of professional help. And that step, he absolutely refused to discuss.

Straightening the papers, she placed them in a neat stack on the table and laid her purple checking pen on top of them. "Sweetie?"

"Hmm?" His thumb was getting quite a workout, the dizzying montage of channels making her a little nuts.

"What do you want to do for dinner? I can make spaghetti, or there are pork chops in the freezer."

He laid the remote on the end table next to him and stretched, turning his head to look at her. "Nope, I won't have my girl slaving in the kitchen when she has to work all day," he said, pushing out of his chair with a moan.

"I miss your cooking, but I don't think you're up to standing over a stove yet, buddy." Howard didn't just cook; he created culinary art. Not easy stuff like soup and spaghetti.

"Tell you what. I'll make a run to Beer Bellies and

pick us up some burgers, and you can finish checking your papers."

She frowned. "Sounds great, but maybe I should ride along. You haven't driven since you were injured."

"And I'm about to go stir-crazy, angel." He walked over to the table and bent, stroking her cheek, giving her a slow kiss. "I just need to stretch my legs for a bit. Maybe by the time I get back, you'll be done and we can eat dessert. Before dinner."

"You are such a sex fiend!" She tried to scowl into his smug face, but failed.

"You wouldn't have me any other way."

Her anticipation matched his. "Hurry back."

"Twenty, thirty minutes tops. I'll set the alarm on my way out." He gave her a stern frown. "Don't open the door for anybody—I don't care who it is."

"I'm not ten, Howard." The man still wanted total control, and it didn't look like that would ever change. Her lips twitched, a grin threatening, but seeing the worry in his eyes, she stifled it. "I'll be fine. We can't live our lives joined at the hip or be afraid to venture from the house apart."

"I know, but . . . you're right. Maybe you should come along."

"Go," she urged with a shooing motion. "I've got plenty to keep me busy. If I need you, I'll call your cell."

He hesitated, less certain than before, but finally relaxed. "Okay. Call if you so much as hear a flea fart."

This time, she did grin. "You have such a way with tender words. Must be why I love you."

Howard cocked his head, an arrested expression on his handsome face. "Kat . . ."

"Yeah?" She held her breath.

He shook himself, grabbing his wallet and keys off the counter. "Be back soon."

As he headed out through the door leading to the garage, pausing to set the alarm, she blew out the breath she'd been holding. The moment may have been lost for now, but the L word was hovering on those gorgeous lips. She knew it—and she got the distinct impression he did, too. A definite step forward.

How would he tell her? With flowers at dinner? After they'd made sweet love? Or during? She shivered, imagining how lovely it would be. Fantasizing about making things official with Howard was much more entertaining than checking papers. Before she knew it, the phone was ringing. She'd been sitting in her chair, daydreaming for twenty minutes, work untouched.

Plucking the phone out of its cradle on the counter, she spied Howard's cell phone number on the display and answered. "Hey, handsome. What's up?"

"Well, I've got the food, but I'm going to be a few minutes later than I thought," he said, sounding annoyed.

"Why?"

"Detective Ford called, and he wants me to swing by and take another look at the ring. On top of that, the police discovered something else in the wreckage from the explosion."

"What'd they find?"

"He didn't want to get into it on the phone. Said just to come take a look. Sorry, babe. I'll be there before the burgers get cold, I promise."

"No problem," she replied, striving to hide her worry. The last thing Howard needed after Sunday's trip to nightmare hell was more stress. "I'll be waiting. Naked."

He groaned, a hint of amusement in his tone. "That's *so* not fair."

"Bye, Howie."

She hung up, smiling. Hopefully, she'd given him something to see him through his meeting with Ford.

With any luck, that something would lure home one very hungry man.

And not for hamburgers.

Bye, Howie.

Kat hung up with a decisive *blip*, not giving him a chance to fire back a retort.

Chuckling, he flipped his phone shut and slipped it into the front right pocket of his sweats. His shoulder gave a stab of protest at the movement, but he'd hated being restricted by the sling and had taken grim pleasure in tossing the contraption onto the dresser, in spite of Kat's scolding.

On a side street off the main square, he parked in front of the modest one-story building housing the Sugarland PD. He stepped from the truck with a grimace, questioning whether he ought to have quit the painkillers. On the other hand, he preferred being clearheaded and able to drive. Gave him back a measure of control.

Inside, an attractive, uniformed woman at the front desk pointed him toward Ford's office, eyeing him with undisguised interest. He thanked her politely and made himself scarce, startled to realize he wasn't even the least bit tempted. One year ago, the old Howard might've investigated the vibes she was throwing his way. But the poor lady couldn't hope to measure up to his Kat.

Yep, he'd been tamed, and good.

At Ford's partially open door, he knocked and was greeted by, "Come on in and shut the door."

The detective stood behind his desk, flashing Howard a brief smile and shaking his hand before resuming his seat and getting down to business.

"I'm glad to see you up and around, Lieutenant," he

said warmly. "A hell of an improvement over last time we talked."

"Thanks." With a grunt, Howard lowered himself into a sturdy chair facing the desk. "I won't run any marathons for a while, but yeah. At least I'm vertical. What do you have for me?"

Ford lifted one of two small brown envelopes on his desk and shook the contents into his palm. "I'd like you to look at this ring again. Study it closely, see if anything about it seems familiar. Go ahead, you can't mess up evidence. We couldn't get a print, and the dried blood has already been tested, what there was of it."

Reluctant, Howard took the tiny object from Ford's outstretched hand, grasping the bottom edge of the gold loop between his thumb and forefinger. "Any DNA results?"

Ford barked a short laugh. "Are you kidding? The lab we use is so backed up, I'll be lucky if I don't have to sleep with the tech to get them before I'm ready for social security. We do know it's type A, which doesn't help much outside of proving the blood wasn't Pearce's or Miller's."

Half listening, Howard frowned at the simple solitaire diamond. The swirling etched pattern engraved in the gold on either side of the setting he'd been too upset to note before. Old-fashioned, he mused, though this was more of a perception. What he knew about jewelry could fit on the head of a pin.

Ford crossed his arms over his chest. "Impressions?"

"The ring isn't new. And it's not what I'd imagine someone buying for his lady if he had money for something nicer." As those words left his mouth, a strange prickle stood the hairs up on the back of his neck. An uneasy shadow crept in, unseen hands wrapping around his throat.

Was it cold in here?

"You okay?"

"I'm good. Just a little cold. Forgot my jacket." Quickly, Howard scanned the inside of the band, then handed the ring back to the detective. "No engraving. Nothing helpful. I'm sorry, but I still don't recognize it. I have no idea why he'd leave this for me."

"That's what I figured." Ford slid the ring into the envelope, then laid it aside and picked up the second one. "What about this?"

Reaching inside, the detective removed a silver necklace and held it aloft by the clasp. A thin silver cross about two inches in length dangled from the chain, the surface blackened, smudged, and dirty.

Howard's gut clenched as his fingers closed around the cross. He felt suddenly, desperately sick. "Where did you find this?"

"Combing through the wreckage has taken a while. Some of my homicide guys discovered it yesterday in the rubble of what used to be the victim's closet."

"What's so special about it?"

"The necklace was duct-taped to a shard of the detonator. He wanted to make sure we knew he'd left us a little gift."

"Jesus." Howard closed his eyes. "Jesus Christ."

"What could he possibly think these items mean to you?"

Howard opened his eyes again, staring at Ford. "I don't know. The cross might've belonged to Janine, but I never saw her wear it."

But something niggled at his memory, a black worm tunneling through the rot of his past. Digging to the root of the evil.

A wedding ring. A silver cross.

A wisp of recollection. His mother's rare smile, the sun catching on the chain around her neck.

Ford spread his hands, frustrated. "Give me something. Anything. This bastard's screwing us all up the backside, and the city brass is about to go nuclear. He's a frigging ghost."

Ghost.

Blood rushed from his head, replaced by the piercing headache. Again. Throbbing at his temples, a drumbeat, threatening to detonate his brain like the bomb had done to Janine's home.

To her corpse.

He shoved to his feet, the chair screeching backward across the linoleum, and tossed the necklace onto Ford's desk. "I have to go." Or he was going to vomit. "Kat's home alone and I don't like leaving her for long."

The detective stood, palms braced on his desk top, eyes round. "Paxton, what—"

"I'll call you."

In a daze, he stumbled for his truck. His need to return to Kat fast bordered on panic. A wild, inexplicable urge jolting his system into action, setting his pulse to a gallop.

The aroma of the cooling burgers assaulted his nose as he climbed into the truck. No longer tantalizing, the smell made him swallow in reflex, trying not to get sick.

Intuition. As a firefighter, he'd learned to appreciate it, had survived more than one hairy situation by paying attention to the knot in his gut.

He was being ridiculous. Probably.

They could laugh at his overprotective instincts later. Much later, after he'd made love to her and held her in his arms.

After he told Kat how very much he loved her.

With a grateful sigh, Kat finished checking the last of her students' writing exercises, tossed her pen onto the table, and stretched. Her stomach rumbled in anticipation of a fattening, juicy burger, despite her plans to dine on a mouthwatering man first.

How long had Howard been gone? Her eyes strayed toward the wall clock. Forty-five minutes. He ought to be home any minute, provided the detective's business was brief.

Almost in direct answer to that thought, she heard a scrape from the direction of the kitchen. The telltale whoosh of a door opening, and the high-pitched steady tone of the home entry system, giving Howard thirty seconds to punch in the code before the thing began wailing.

Smiling, she vacated her chair and took a step toward the kitchen entry. "What took ya? I'm starving—"

Her greeting was interrupted by the phone, ringing from its place on the table. She'd laid it there after Howard called from Beer Bellies. Glancing toward the kitchen, she called, "Howard? I'll get it."

Turning around, she stepped back to the table and stared at the number on the caller ID.

Howard's cell phone.

Confused, heart racing, she grabbed the handset and punched the Talk button. "Howard? Why are you calling from the kitchen? That's *so* not funny—"

"What?" he barked. His voice rose. "What do you mean *from the kitchen*? I'm on my way home. Kat?"

Oh, God.

"Howard?" Her voice shook. Her hands began to tremble so hard, she almost dropped the phone. Slowly, she began to back away from the table, eyes glued to the doorway in front of her.

"Katherine, tell me what's going on," he yelled.

"Howard, if you're not coming in through the kitchen . . . then who just set off the alarm?"

20

Fear blasted a trillion megawatts of electricity through his body.

Who just set off the alarm?

How he managed to keep his truck on the road or avoid running over anyone as he blew through every light downtown, Howard didn't have a clue.

"Get out of the house!" he shouted, swerving to keep from sideswiping another vehicle. "Get out now!"

"Howard, there's a man here," Kat whimpered, voice breaking with terror. "The man from the party."

The sound tore him apart, filled him with rage. "Run! Go out the front door!"

"He has a gun! Oh, God!" she cried, fumbling the receiver. "What do you want?"

A gun. Mother of God, he was too late.

His foot pressed down on the accelerator, his chest ready to explode with fear. "Kat? Sweetheart, talk to me!"

"I'm afraid she can't do that right now," a man said. *His* smug voice, the killer who'd called from Janine's house.

"What do you want from me?" Howard demanded. "What the hell is this all about? Take me and leave her alone!"

He laughed as though this was a humorous request. "Don't you wish. Listen closely. First, you're going to call your illustrious chief and have him send in the troops. Your team, the police, snipers, whatever. I don't give a shit who they send, as long as Bentley Mitchell's holier-than-thou ass is present and accounted for. Got that?"

This man's hatred for Bentley practically dripped blood through the phone. What in the name of God was going on?

In the background, Howard's house alarm began to shriek.

"Yeah, I got it." He got that the murdering lunatic was grandstanding.

And there was nothing more dangerous than a man with nothing to lose.

"Good. Next, you tell all of them to stay clear, especially the fuckin' cops, since they're probably on their way. You come in alone, or your bitch dies. Got that, too?"

Howard's hands tightened on the steering wheel, turning his knuckles white. If he could reach the son of a bitch, he'd rip his lungs out through his throat. "I understand."

"You know," his tormentor said cheerfully, "I'm really looking forward to our reunion."

His blood ran cold. His head pounded.

"Reunion? I don't know you. Nobody I know would do this to me. To those innocent women."

"Oh, you know me, all right. But I'm not surprised you need a little nudge. What's it been, about thirty-one years?"

The monster from his nightmares chuckled.

"Drive careful, boy."

Kat stared at the man taunting Howard on the phone—the man from Bentley's party. The gun in his hand was pointed straight at the center of her chest. If she attempted a break for the door, he'd shoot her before she took two steps. So she tried to tamp down the mind-numbing terror and study her captor as she hadn't before. His features, mannerisms, mood. Any detail she might capitalize on to help delay him from killing her.

He wasn't overly tall, perhaps five-ten or five-eleven. He was built lean and tough, tanned, his brutally handsome face weathered. He'd lived hard, if the grooves carving lines on either side of his mouth, the dead hollowness in his icy blue eyes, were any indication.

Age hadn't yet taken his looks. She guessed him to be in his mid- to-late fifties. His black hair was liberally threaded with gray, a bit scruffy over his ears, but attractive enough if a woman met him on the street and didn't know he intended to mete out a gruesome end. Sort of like Al Pacino in *The Godfather*, before he started blowing people away.

Forcing her attention back to what he was saying, she caught the tail end of his verbal game. Reunion?

"What's it been, about thirty-one years?" His low chuckle was one of malicious pleasure. "Drive careful, boy."

Oh, please, no. For Howard's sake, please don't let it be true.

He hung up and returned her scrutiny, raking her up and down with his steely gaze. Those eyes were the key. Barren of the slightest scrap of humanity. Flat and fathomless, a writhing snake pit of evil.

"Turn off that fucking alarm," he ordered, waving the muzzle toward the back door. "Don't even think of running unless you want a hole in your spine the size of my goddamned fist."

Her legs the consistency of noodles, she walked as slowly as she dared to the box beside the door leading to the garage. Hand shaking violently, she punched in one of the codes Howard made her memorize—the one programmed to silence the alarm, but send a 911 call to the police.

"Stupid slut, I know what you did," he laughed, as though reading her mind. "Your boyfriend's already calling the cops—like I give a shit. Won't make any difference to either of you soon enough. Move toward the bedroom. Now!"

Dropping her gaze, she spied the edge of a pair of handcuffs sticking out of his front pocket. Her stomach lurched. If she let this maniac shackle her without a fight, not only would she be vulnerable, but Howard would be at his mercy, handicapped by fear of not being able to help her in time. *Like hell.*

"I know who you are," she said, stalling.

"Do you?" He cocked his head, lips curving upward. "Think you're so smart? The real question is, who is Bentley Mitchell?"

Her insides froze. God, Bentley couldn't have anything to do with the murders. That would destroy Howard. "Suppose you tell me."

"And spoil the surprise?" He waved the gun. "Move it!"

As she turned to walk back into the kitchen, she saw the sliding glass door to the deck open about a foot. She guessed he'd entered there, jimmied the lock somehow. On the counter to her right sat a water glass. A poor weapon, but better than nothing. On the way past she snatched the glass and spun, catching him off guard.

With all her strength, she smashed it into the side of his head. He bellowed as the object shattered, slicing her hand and, hopefully, taking off half his face. Bending double, he grabbed his cheek, howling as she sprinted for freedom.

And she almost made it.

His body crashed into her from behind, sending them both into the breakfast nook table with a noisy clatter. The impact knocked the wind out of her, sent a bolt of pain shooting through the wrist that smacked the table's edge. She cried out as they bounced, overturning chairs and landing in a heap of tangled limbs.

She scrambled from under him on her hands and knees, then pushed to her feet and leapt over the fallen chair. He caught her waist in midleap, tackling her to the floor. Her ankle gave a sickening twist and her chin bashed the hardwood flooring, clapping her teeth together. Blood gushed into her mouth and she thought she must've cut her tongue. The least of her worries.

Heaving a great gulp of air into her lungs, she screamed fit to raise the dead, and immediately found herself flipped onto her back, staring into her attacker's furious, bloodied face.

Score one for me.

The satisfaction of cutting the asshole barely had time to register. Drawing back the hand with the gun, he leveled a blow to her temple in a lightning strike that shattered her vision and spun her brain into orbit.

"Whore," he snarled, delivering another blow, this one catching her ear. "You're gonna burn, and your lover's gonna watch. Then I get to kill him, too. At long fucking last."

Dimly, she was aware of being dragged. By her hair.

Howard.

Despite her best efforts, the vortex sucked her into darkness.

Howard slammed on his brakes and hit the garage door opener, truck screeching to a halt in his driveway just ahead of a police cruiser.

He was out and running for the garage even as an authoritative voice shouted for him to halt. Spinning around, charged with adrenaline and terror, he yelled, jabbing a finger at the officer. "I live here! I'm Lieutenant Howard Paxton, and you all need to stay the hell out or he's going to kill her! His orders!"

The wide-eyed cop hesitated, pistol in hand. "The hostage—"

"Is dead if you interfere. He wants me inside, and that's where I'm going, unless it's your policy to shoot an unarmed man in the back."

End of conversation. He'd wasted enough time.

Leaving the hapless cop to deal with what would surely escalate into a circus, Howard sprinted for the door leading into the kitchen from the garage.

The sight greeting him filled him with dread. Shards of glass littered the floor, and a trail of crimson droplets led to the small breakfast table, which had been knocked aside, the chairs overturned. The droplets became smears of blood. Signs of a struggle, and he knew without a doubt Kat hadn't gone down without a fight.

"Oh, baby, no." His fists clenched, the need to pummel the monster who'd hurt her washing over him like a red tidal wave.

Calm. Focus, or you won't get her out alive.

Every one of his senses on alert, he stalked slowly through the living room, searching every shadowy corner. Without his noticing, the afternoon had quickly become evening, the days much shorter now with winter coming on. Dying rays of the last sunlight hardly filtered through the drapes.

He moved down the hallway, half expecting an ambush. None came. He didn't turn on the lights, didn't care to announce his exact whereabouts sooner than necessary. Stupid, since he had no doubt that his nemesis knew he was here. He felt the other man's awareness singing along an invisible connection, charged with tension.

Drawn to his bedroom, he crept to the doorway.

Stepped inside. The stench of gasoline assaulted his nose.

"Paxton here," he said, trying to keep a leash on his seething fury. He peered into the room, taking in the silhouette of a man standing on the other side of his bed. Kat lay on her back, motionless, one wrist hand-cuffed to a slat in the headboard. "I'm unarmed and alone. I did what you said."

"How noble," the figure sneered. "And dumb. Then again, you always were a sniveling little bastard."

The bedside lamp was switched on, bathing the room in a soft glow. Their captor stood behind the lamp, using its protective glare to his advantage. Blinking, Howard swung his gaze to Kat, studied her anxiously as his vision adjusted. She stared at him through wide, terrified green eyes, silently beseeching. A livid red welt marked the left side of her face, al-ready forming an angry bruise, her eye swollen half shut. Her right hand was sliced and bleeding.

He could only thank God she was fully clothed, that the murderer's plan hadn't included time to violate her. His fists clenched at his sides, a muscle in his jaw jumping.

The monster wasn't dead.

He was *fucking* dead.

"Baby, are you all right?"

After a brief pause, she nodded at Howard, eyes glittering with unshed tears. "I'm okay."

The man stepped into the pool of light, a lighter in one hand, a gun in the other, pointed at the center of Howard's chest. Blood dripped from a long, nasty gash down the side of his face. An older man, maybe not quite Bentley's age. Salt-and-pepper hair. Fit and hard. Cold.

Death incarnate.

He'd stared into those steely blue eyes before. His heart shrieked in protest even as his mind warred with itself. Struggled to suppress the night of horror that had nearly destroyed him. Had altered his life forever.

"Cat got your tongue, boy?" A corner of his mouth hitched up. Smug asshole. "You look like you've seen a ghost . . . Howard Paxton Whitlaw."

A fissure. A crack in the dam, growing wider, wider . . .

Until he didn't have a prayer of holding back the flood. Washing in with the truth to spill like toxic waste into every corner of his mind. The unspeakable tragedy.

A moonlit garden stroll through his magic forest, tomatoes ripening on the vine.

A loud argument. A soggy thump.

The dirt squishing through his toes as he went to investigate and saw . . . and saw . . .

"No." Howard felt the blood rush from his face. His knees turned to water and he had to concentrate to remain upright.

His mother, crumpled on the ground. An oily puddle forming around her dark head.

A man, standing in the darkness with a shovel.

This man.

Digging a hole to bury his sweet mother in the garden she'd loved so much.

Oh, God. Sweet mother of God.

"Frank Whitlaw," Howard choked out. The agony was almost too much to bear. The horror of the truth too great. Only his desire not to fold in front of the man he hated more than anyone on earth kept him standing firm. "*You.* You killed my mother. Buried her in the garden."

"Oh, honey," Kat whispered. He felt her love reach out, try to soothe his pain despite her own.

"With the greatest of pleasure." The devil grinned. "Did ya like the little gifts I left for you with the other whores? Took the ring and necklace right off Liz's dead body before I planted her like a seed in her own tomato patch."

Howard took a step forward. "You sick sono-fabitch—"

"Back off," he growled, tensing, raising the gun higher.

"You were dead. The police said so. They found your body in your truck."

"A body," he smirked. "Burned beyond recognition, with my wallet conveniently lying nearby. Nobody missed the drifter who played my role. Frank Whitlaw was dead, and who wasn't happy as shit about that? They didn't *want* to know any different. Besides, no DNA back then. All told, I got the last laugh."

"Where have you been all these years?" Not that he cared much, except talking might give Howard precious minutes to figure out what to do.

Frank waved the gun, bragging. "Drifting from state to state. Mostly putting cheating whores out of many a man's misery. A game of stealth and a public service all in one." He snickered at his own joke.

"But after thirty years, the game sorta lost its challenge. Got curious about the old stomping ground a few months ago and blew in to investigate. Imagine my unpleasant surprise to learn the little bastard I'd left for dead hadn't died after all—and you'd been adopted by Bentley Mitchell, no less. Oh, that's rich."

"You've been here for months?" The idea made him sick.

"Yep. Watching, learning your routine at the station and at home. Planning." His eyes shone with wicked glee. "You're a loose end, boy. The one who got away, and that just ain't acceptable. So I mapped out the perfect game of revenge. It's only fair, considering how you ruined my life. I loved Liz once, and you took her from me."

The nightmares. Somehow, on a subconscious level,

he must've sensed Frank's presence. Nothing else made sense.

Still, the whole scenario was incomprehensible. Why would Frank go to such extremes to kill him, now a grown man and a virtual stranger?

"I want to know how you could murder the mother of your child. How you could try to kill your own son. Murder defenseless women. What revenge are you raving about?"

Frank's gaze hardened. "How? Easy. Your whoring bitch of a mother got exactly what she deserved for spreading her legs for another man, then pawning off her bastard son as mine for five fucking years! Like I didn't know. Then she planned to run off and leave me, taking your sorry hide with her. After everything I did for her!"

Bastard son. The room tilted.

"Wh-what?"

Frank's finger tightened on the trigger. "You not having a clue makes this extra sweet. You're not my son," he snarled. "You're Bentley Mitchell's bastard."

In an instant, his world shattered. Howard swayed on his feet, struggling to comprehend.

Why had Bentley kept the truth from him? To protect Georgie? There was no way Bentley hadn't known, or at least suspected.

Suddenly, he was out of time for answers.

"My plans have been realized. Bentley gets to watch his only son burn. Trial by fire, the ultimate, most satisfying judgment," he said, holding up the lighter, eyes gleaming with malice. "After I make my escape in the chaos, I'll return to get rid of his sanctimonious ass and his precious wife, too."

Yeah, that wasn't going to happen. Not while Howard had breath left in his body.

"You won't get away from here undetected. By now,

the neighborhood is cordoned off and the house is sur-rounded."

"You'll never know, will you?" Flicking on the lighter, he took a couple of steps backward, keeping the gun trained on Howard. Held the flame toward the gasoline-soaked curtains.

A voice blasting from a megaphone outside identi-fied himself as Detective Shane Ford. "We've got the house surrounded. Let's talk about this."

Ford said something else, but Howard focused on Frank. Their captor hesitated, distracted for a moment by the cop's voice. The man turned his head the barest fraction, glanced out the window, though he couldn't see the front of the house from here.

It was the split second Howard needed.

He launched himself at the other man, putting his body between Frank and Kat. His nemesis snapped his gaze back to Howard with a vicious curse, and fired.

The bullet punched Howard's side as he barreled into Frank, taking him to the floor. *Shot.* The sting barely registered. His sole focus was winning the fight for their lives. They rolled, knocking into furni-ture, each battling for the upper hand. Frank was quick, wiry. Much stronger than he appeared. He bucked, throwing Howard to the side, scrambling for the curtains. With a flick, he set the fabric ablaze, then tossed the lighter.

The curtains went up like a blowtorch. Howard had less than two minutes to get them out of here before the rest of the room ignited.

Howard fell on him once more, grabbing at the wrist holding the weapon. Frank kicked and with his upper body, lurched sideways, smacking Howard's skull into the wall. Seeing stars, he fought to keep his attacker from bringing the muzzle of the gun between their bodies and finishing the job.

Desperate, he levered his torso across Frank's, using

his full weight and sheer strength to pin the other man. Getting a good hold on Frank's wrist, he slammed the man's gun hand into the floor twice. Hard. Bone cracked and the asshole howled, the weapon tumbling from his fingers.

"Howard, hurry!" Kat screamed. The blaze licked at the ceiling, the walls, spreading rapidly outward to his dresser and a stuffed chair.

Grabbing the gun, Howard flipped it and smashed the butt into the killer's head. Relief and gratitude swamped him when the man went limp, unconscious.

For one moment, as he rose on trembling knees, he considered putting a bullet in Frank Whitlaw's prone body. Making damned sure he'd never pose a threat again.

But Bentley—no, *Dad*—hadn't raised him to be cold and ruthless. For the first time in his life, he was proud to be his father's son.

Leaving the murdering bastard to face the flames would have to be justice enough. Pitching the gun aside, he crouched by the fallen man.

A quick search of Frank's pockets produced no key for the handcuffs. No more time. He lurched for the bed, dizzy.

"Hurry! Oh, God, you're bleeding!"

"I'm all right." He wasn't, but it didn't matter now. "Scoot over."

Kat made room for him as he knelt and grasped the links between her wrist and the cuff attached to the headboard slat. He pulled with all his might, but no use. He needed leverage.

"H-Howard, the fire!"

The edge of the bedspread ignited. Jumping off the bed, he stripped the cover and hurled it into a corner just as the material was engulfed.

The smoke began to thicken. Kat coughed, shaking her head. "Get out!"

"No!"

He redoubled his efforts, this time leaning back and planting one foot against the headboard as he pulled. Muscles bunching, straining with the effort. The slat bowed, and he heard a crack as the wood began to give.

Careful not to smash her hand, he kicked the weakened slat. The wood snapped and she was free, cuffs dangling from her wrist.

"Let's go!" Grabbing her arm, he yanked her off the bed just as it went up in flames.

He pulled Kat for the door, but she was limping badly. Without breaking stride or sparing a glance for their would-be killer, he swung her into his arms. Cradling his precious burden against his chest, he moved quickly down the hallway, toward the front door.

Toward freedom.

Shifting her, he unlocked the door and pushed outside. Into the clean, cool air. Vaguely, he was aware of the sticky warmth saturating his middle, the front of his sweats. Blood pumped with every staggering step, every heartbeat, flowing steadily.

Her fingers twined in his hair. "You can put me down," she whispered, raising her head to kiss his cheek.

"Never," he vowed, hugging her tighter.

He managed the steps and started across the lawn, dazed by the sight of dozens of vehicles and flashing lights. Cops and men in SWAT gear on the perimeter, lowering their weapons. Behind the police line, several fire engines blocked the street and a couple of ambulances waited.

He spotted his team, waving, joining the chorus of cheers. Bentley, who'd been standing with them, began making his way through the crowd toward his son.

Strangely, as he carried Kat toward safety, the cheers became yells. Frantic shouting. A look of sheer panic bloomed on Bentley's face. Sean and his team were waving now, but not in joy.

"Get down, get down!"

A loud *pop* split the air. Howard jerked, gasping, trying to retain his hold on Kat. His legs gave out and he sank to his knees. He fell forward onto the ground, curling his body around Kat, protecting her.

A volley of gunshots peppered the evening like firecrackers. Over and done in a few seconds.

"Howard?" Kat wriggled underneath him, eyes wide with fear. "What happened?"

"Kat . . ." His breath left him in a wheeze. He thought he'd known pain. He was wrong.

White-hot talons of agony spread through his back, wrapped around his chest to constrict his lungs. Setting them ablaze. Dazed, he saw the Pez candy from his front pocket scattered on the grass like confetti. What a stupid thing to notice.

More shouting. People running toward them. Hands pulling them apart. Taking Kat from him.

"No," he moaned.

"Let me go, dammit!" Her anguished face appeared above his, her soft hands cupped his cheeks. Tears streamed unchecked down her cheeks. "Oh, God, no. Don't you leave me, not now. Do you hear me, Lieutenant?"

He reached for her, determined. She took his hand and he squeezed, hoping to reassure her. "I love you," he whispered. "Should've told you . . . before . . ."

"I love you, too. So much." Her face crumpled. "You're not going to die. I won't let you."

"Kat, move aside so we can help him," Julian said, gentle but firm. "You can stay where he can see you."

A distinct crackle reached his ears. "My house . . ."

"Can be rebuilt, son," Bentley said, expression grim. To Sean and Jules, he ordered, "Help me turn him."

Howard's T-shirt was hiked up and he was rolled to his side. Something slapped onto his back. Pressure bandage. They laid him flat again, repeating the procedure on the wound in his abdomen, then started an IV.

His gaze collided with his father's. "Is he . . . dead?"

Bentley nodded. "Cops finished him."

"Good. Dad . . ." He had to tell his father, wanted him to know. . . .

"Don't talk, son." His dad's lips trembled and he made a visible effort to get hold of his emotions. "We've got plenty of time."

Howard wasn't so sure. As they lifted him onto a stretcher and loaded him into the ambulance, he began to shake, chilled to the bone. No one had to tell him his injuries were bad. He fought for every breath, with every ounce of willpower in him.

A losing battle. His lungs were iron heavy, taking in air almost impossible. He knew the signs. Collapsed lung, internal damage. Shock. He coughed, blood bubbling to his lips. Filling his mouth, choking him.

"Howard," Kat sobbed. "Please don't leave me."

The mournful cry of the vehicle's siren faded into the distance, like his ears were stuffed with cotton.

"Love . . . you . . ."

Despite his monumental effort to stay with his angel, his vision dimmed. His tenuous grip on life slipped.

And he fell down, down into a deep well.

Like the end of a movie fading to black, his world disappeared.

21

Kat hadn't believed it possible for a person to cry so much without doing themselves physical harm.

Howard couldn't be gone.

In the ambulance, as Julian worked desperately to save him, she'd seen the spark in his beautiful brown eyes dim until they were nothing more than blank marbles. No hint of life, of the man who used to reside there. Her best friend and protector.

The man who loved her.

His heart stopped beating. And so had hers.

Julian did his best, laboring feverishly, restarting the organ several times. But when the doctors and nurses rushed Howard into the OR, he'd been clinically dead.

Dead on arrival.

Three impossible, cruel words stripping her soul raw. The sedative a nurse jabbed into her arm to calm her and stop her frantic screaming had succeeded—but only on the outside.

She sat huddled in a chair in a corner of the waiting room, arms wrapped around her knees, shell-shocked. Every fiber of her being cried out for him. To know what was going on behind closed doors. To touch and hold him.

A slender arm encircled her shoulders, pulled her close. "You sure you're okay? Physically, I mean."

She inhaled her sister's familiar scent, battling a flood of fresh tears. "Yeah, they checked me out. A black eye and a twisted ankle. Small potatoes compared to what Howard . . ." Her throat burned.

"Shhh, I've got you, sweet pea."

Grace's pet name for her did her in. With a low, animal moan of grief, she buried her face in her sister's shoulder and sobbed. Cried until she slumped in exhaustion, certain she'd shrivel from lack of moisture like a dried plant. Grace stroked her hair, patted her back as she dissolved into hiccups.

"I tried to reach Mom and Dad, but I think they went to dinner with Joan and Greg," Grace murmured. "They're not answering their cell phones. I'll try again later."

"That's okay." Kat loved them dearly, but she couldn't deal with her parents, their thousands of horrified questions when they learned what had happened. Not right now.

Grace pulled back a bit, smoothing Kat's tangled hair out of her damp face. "How did your talk with Detective Ford go?"

"Fine. He's really nice. I told him what happened and everything Frank Whitlaw admitted." She sniffed, shredding her mangled tissue. "He's going to get a team together to search behind the old Whitlaw place for Liz Whitlaw's remains. If the monster wasn't lying, they'll find her. It's all I can do for Howard right now. Give him some peace, you know?" Her voice broke, but she retained control.

"Yeah, I know." Grace pulled her close again.

Earlier, the Mitchells had disappeared down a corridor off the ER, and Kat assumed they'd been whisked to a private room to await news. The main ER waiting area was packed to the brim with firefighters and cops. All of Howard's friends, praying for his survival.

When a somber doctor emerged and announced to the gathering that Howard made it through surgery, her hopes leapt. They were quickly tempered when he cautioned that the lieutenant's condition was extremely critical. His chances were being measured, literally, in hours. If he hung on until morning, he might live.

"I'm not leaving," Kat informed her sister, just in case she thought to force her to go home and rest.

And where is home?

"Then neither am I, sweet pea." Grace hugged her tight. "Neither am I."

He was buried.

Suffocating in a deep, dark grave. Alone. Food for the worms.

Like his mother.

No! He refused to go down easy. Too many loose ends. Too damned much to live for.

Had to reach his angel. How?

Howard? Baby, come back to us. I love you.

Where was she? He strained, but could feel nothing. Not his fingers or toes. He had no voice.

Maybe he was already dead. A ghost who refused to leave her. Unable to accept his demise.

You have to live. I need you. . . . Your parents need you.

Not dead, but close. Perched on the precipice of eternity, his soul torn between two worlds.

But his heart was in this one, with her. So he struggled long and hard to emerge from the void.

So tired.

Exhaustion took him against his will, and consciousness dissolved into black mist.

The lieutenant was alive because he wanted to be, the doctors observed. Despite the fact he kept his body in extraordinary physical condition, his survival defied any other explanation. For days he'd been as near to death as anyone could be and not succumb.

Kat wiggled in the uncomfortable chair beside his bed and laid aside her magazine to study him. Dark lashes curled against his stubbled cheeks. His face was gaunt, waxen. If it weren't for the gentle rise and fall of his chest, she'd believe he was dead. Due to his incredible willpower, however, he was on his way back.

Today was the first day she'd been able to let go of the terror that he would die. Finally, he was breathing on his own, and yesterday he'd shown signs of waking. He'd opened his eyes the tiniest bit and tried to speak, but quickly went under again.

A wonderful improvement. Better than any of them dared to hope for a few days ago.

Howard shifted, turned his head on his pillow toward her with a groan, something he'd been doing a lot. She leaned over and propped her arms on the mattress by his head, raking her fingers through his funky two-toned hair. He'd always loved when she did that, and she liked to think the stimulation helped him stay connected to life. To her.

"Kat?"

The rasp of his wonderful, deep baritone voice startled her after so many agonizing days of ominous silence. Bending to him, she checked the surge of excitement bubbling in her breast. He had so very far to go; this spurt of wakefulness might not last.

"I'm here, baby. Come on, handsome, open those gorgeous eyes for me."

And slowly, a millimeter at a time, he did. He stared at her through spiky lashes, looking dazed and lost, but wonderfully alive. A miracle.

"Well, hi there," she said softly, caressing his cheek. "Good to have you back."

He blinked in response, awareness returning to his gaze. Knowledge flooded his features. Relief. And love.

"You're really here," he murmured, groggy.

"I really am. I'm staying, too, until you get out of here."

"Only that long?"

"Of course not, silly," she teased. He smiled back, the effort tired and lopsided. And beautiful.

"I love you."

"I know, and I love you more."

Howard reached for her but didn't quite have the strength to lift his arm, so she took his hand and brought it to her face, rubbing it against her cheek. "Better?"

"Yeah." He sighed, as if he needed her touch to exist. He studied her, sharper now. More and more aware. "Your bruises are healing."

She grimaced. "The puffiness is gone around my eye. Now, if all these interesting colors will fade, I'll be happy."

"You're perfect to me."

"You're biased, but thanks."

"Your ankle?" He frowned.

"It's fine. Stop worrying about me and concentrate on getting well." Good Lord, the man had taken two bullets and almost died, and he was worried about her bruises and turned ankle.

Exhaling a deep breath, he closed his eyes. After a few minutes, he opened them again, looking at her with surprising intensity.

"I thought you'd gone back to sleep."

"No, just thinking."

"About your mother?" she guessed, hating the flash of sorrow the question caused.

"Among other things."

"Sweetie, I'm so sorry about what truly happened to her." She kissed his fingers, clenched his hand to her breast. "I'm sorry you had to find out the way you did."

"Me, too. Or I was, at first." His jaw tightened and his voice broke. "Now I know the truth. She never left me, Kat. She never would have."

"Howard . . ." What she must tell him next might be the hardest thing she'd ever had to say to anyone. And the toughest for him to hear. "I told Detective Ford everything Whitlaw said. What he claimed he'd done with your mom's body. They searched for days."

She paused. God, this was tearing her apart. She could only imagine how he'd feel.

"Tell me."

"She was there in the garden. I'm so sorry."

"All this time," he said in a small voice.

"Yes. Dental records confirmed her identity."

Falling strangely silent, he appeared lost in his thoughts. "I'd like to hold a funeral for her. Something small and nice," he said after a while.

"Your parents and I figured as much. We'll help you plan it as soon as you're feeling better."

"Thank you." He shook his head. "I can't cry for her, angel. Why can't I cry?"

"Too much shock all at once. You're tired." *But you will.* "Why don't you rest, okay?"

"Kat?"

"Hmm?" The intensity was back.

"Stay with me forever? Please?"

Forever. Her heart lurched with hope, but that didn't mean a literal commitment. She gave him a playful grin. "Just try to ditch me, buddy. I might have to use the fishing pole again."

His lips hitched up. "Can't promise you won't want

to at times. But if you can stand me . . ." His voice faded. He was worn out, depleted.

"Oh, I think I can manage." Not a proposal, but she'd take his request as a giant step. Scooting right up onto the bed next to him, she pressed a soft kiss to his mouth. Then she snuggled into his side, careful not to jostle him.

Content, happier than she'd ever been, Kat finally gave in to days of nail-biting terror and joined the man she loved in slumber.

When Howard next awoke, he'd expected to find Kat at his side. Instead, Bentley sat in the chair by his bed, watching the television mounted on the wall of his private room.

My father. Not the piece of feces who'd nearly destroyed him, but this man. A man of integrity and honor.

A man he should've called Dad long before he knew the truth.

He'd spend a lifetime making up for the pain he'd caused.

Howard cleared his throat. "Hey."

His father's head whipped around, expression swamped with relief. "Thank God!" He swiveled in his chair, laying a big hand on his son's arm. "Kat told us you woke up for a bit yesterday and talked with her. We were afraid you'd relapsed."

Yesterday? "No wonder I feel rested," he joked. The older man didn't smile.

"I'm so damned glad to see you awake. When that sonofabitch stumbled onto the porch and shot you in the back and I thought we'd lost you . . ." Visibly shaken, his father gathered himself. "I'm not sorry Whitlaw's dead."

"Me, either."

"I suppose you want answers." He looked uncomfortable. Afraid.

"Kat told you Frank revealed that you're . . . my real father." There. Now the issue was on the table.

"Yeah. She's a special lady, your Katherine."

"Yes, she is. Don't change the subject."

"Wasn't going to." His father blew out a harsh breath, swiping a hand down his face. He looked like he'd aged a decade since his son almost died.

"Start at the beginning. Please," he amended, softening his tone. He didn't want Bentley—Dad—to believe he harbored any anger or blame.

"All right." Settling back in his chair, he crossed his arms over his broad chest, a faraway look in his eyes. "I was intimate with Liz once, before I met Georgie. Only once. I had no idea Liz was married. When I saw her in Sugarland ten months later carrying an infant, I was stunned."

Howard could imagine. "Did you confront her?"

"Of course I did. She was clearly terrified, kept looking around to see who might overhear. That's when she told me she was married to Frank Whitlaw. Hell, everyone knew that sorry, drunken asshole. Always stirring up trouble, mean as the devil. But nobody knew his wife because he kept her at home on a tight leash most of the time."

"I remember." The sadness behind her pretty smile. The deep cuts and bruises. But he didn't say this to his father. The man carried enough guilt already over not realizing the extent of his mother's horrible situation at home.

"When I demanded to know if you were mine, her fear was a palpable thing. She begged me to drop the matter. Pleaded. She never admitted you were mine, and I understood she couldn't without incurring Whitlaw's wrath. In the end, I agreed to stay away because it seemed to bring her peace."

"You didn't know how bad things were for us."

"No, I swear," he said sadly. "As God is my witness. I wasn't in love with her, nor she with me. She came to town one night, a rare reprieve, she said, though I didn't know from what at the time. We were lonely and spent a few hours together, then parted ways. But if I'd suspected that monster was brutalizing my son, he'd have been buried in that garden instead of your mother."

This explained so much of Frank's cruel torture, his hatred. He'd known of Liz's betrayal, that Howard wasn't his, and it drove him over the edge. From meanness to active, wicked cruelty, to something far more evil.

"She loved you madly," his father went on. "The few times I saw her bring you to town in those five years, anyone could see how she doted on you. I should've known she'd never leave town and not take you with her. But the authorities claimed she'd split and couldn't be found, so I dropped it."

And I loved her. She was my whole world.

Howard fought back a wave of sorrow. "Now we know she didn't. Strange, but knowing what really happened makes the hurt less. Is that wrong?"

"No, son." Bentley shook his head. "It's only natural for you to feel a certain release in knowing your mother didn't abandon you to be beaten half to death by Whitlaw. She was going to leave him and escape with you, and she got caught."

Now for the tough stuff. The main question burning a hole in his heart. "Why didn't you tell me you're my father? Why?"

Bentley's face paled. "I don't have excuses, but I had some valid reasons in the beginning. Do you remember how you came to me and Georgie? You were frightened. You didn't speak. You trusted no one, and had nightmares for years. We thought we'd never reach you, and by the time we finally did there was no way I'd risk harming your progress in any way. Your world had already been shattered once. I thought I'd tell you . . . someday. Then someday came and went. What was the point in dredging it all up later?"

Oh, there was more. So much more to his father's reasoning than he'd admit. So Howard did it for him. "You thought I'd blame you for the years I suffered with Whitlaw. That you'd lose me if I found out." He hesitated, then laid bare the real issue.

"You believed I didn't love you like a son ought to love his father."

"God help me." Bentley's chin dropped to his chest. "Can you ever forgive me?"

"There's nothing to forgive . . . Dad." Swallowing hard, he opened his arms. "I love you. Always have."

With a hoarse sob, his father returned his embrace. Carefully, though, so as not to hurt his son. Howard hung on to his own emotions by a slim thread. He hadn't known it, but he'd been waiting for this moment his entire life.

"Say, do you think Georgie would mind too much if I call her Mom?"

Giving a watery laugh, his dad straightened, wiping at his eyes.

"Son, I think that would make her just about the happiest woman in the world."

Howard smiled, unable to squelch a spurt of smug, manly satisfaction. "Except for Kat, of course. I'm going to ask her to marry me."

Bentley tried to pull a somber face and failed. "There will be no living with them now."

"But it'll be fun to try, huh?"

"Most of the time." His father laughed, arched a brow. "But you might want to hide that fishing pole."

The day of Liz Whitlaw's funeral dawned sunny and mild for late December. Exactly the kind of day his mother would've loved, Howard said wistfully that morning as they'd dressed in Kat's apartment.

Six weeks after the shooting that had nearly killed him, Howard stood tall and breathtaking in his dark suit. Sunlight glinted off his spiky sable hair, which had regained its healthy shine. His skin was no longer pale, and his cheeks had filled out from the weight he regained after losing so much while in the hospital.

His recovery had been slow and painful, yet through sheer determination and hard work, he was regaining strength. Bentley and his friends had been forced to bribe, plead, and finally threaten him to make him stay home another two weeks.

In January, he'd rejoin A-shift. Kat had never known a more amazing, incredible man.

Beside her, Howard thanked the last of the small gathering as they departed the cemetery. His parents had already said their good-byes after hugging the stuffing out of him. His friends had come to support him, and as grateful as he'd been for that, she could tell how tired and glad he was to have this day over. To find closure at last.

Yet in six weeks, he still hadn't shed a tear over the death of his mother. Even today, of all days. Kat was more than a little worried about him.

"The service was lovely," she said, taking his hand.

He nodded, squeezing her fingers. "Yeah, it was. I'm glad I gave her back the silver cross. She used to wear it every day."

Her wedding ring, he'd put away without a word.

He stared at the white casket not yet lowered into the ground. Tentatively, he reached out, laid his free hand on top of the smooth surface, brushing it with his thumb.

"She never left me," he whispered, repeating the

stark, heartbroken words he'd uttered in the hospital six weeks ago. His mouth trembled. "She never left me, Kat. She was all alone, abandoned in the ground all those years, and I thought . . . I believed the worst of her. . . ."

His big body shuddered, and she thought, *Here it comes. The breaking of the dam.* She moved to stand in front of him.

"No, baby. Look inside your heart and you'll find you never really believed your mother would've done that to you. Not for one second."

"I . . ." His face crumpled. "Oh, God."

Wrapping her in his arms, Howard crushed her against his chest. He began to shake all over.

And the dam broke. A sob tore from his throat, and another. The flood came and he cried as she'd never seen a man cry before. A great torrent of grief cleansing his soul. As much as his pain tore her apart, he needed to get it out. This day had been more than thirty years coming. He was due.

He continued to cling to her long after he'd quieted. He silently asked for her strength, her reassurance, and she readily gave. Anything for him to finally be at peace.

"Honey, are you all right?" She rubbed his back, loving his heat pressed against her.

"You know, I am." He kissed the top of her head. "Better than all right for the first time ever. Ready to go?"

"You bet." Turning, he kissed his fingers, then pressed them to the casket. "I love you, Mom. Goodbye for now."

Hand in hand, they walked to his truck. Kat observed him from the corner of her eye. He seemed lighter. More relaxed than he'd ever been.

When they arrived at her apartment, Howard stripped off his coat and tie with relish, tossing both into a corner of her bedroom. Next he unbuttoned his white dress shirt, yanking the tails out of his pants. "Jeez, that feels good."

Naked would be better, but saying so right now hardly seemed appropriate. Instead, she kicked off her evil heels. "Does it ever." She moaned, wiggling her toes.

Flopping onto the bed, he patted the covers. "Come lie down with me for a while."

"With pleasure." Without bothering to remove her dress, she snuggled in, pillowing her head on his shoulder as his arms went around her.

"I've been thinking this place is pretty small for a guy like me," he began, his tone casual. "I take up a lot of space."

"You won't be stuck here for long. The carpenters will be finished fixing your house soon and you can go home." Hardly daring to breathe, she left the statement hanging. In the hospital, he'd asked her to stay with him forever. Had he changed his mind?

"Yeah, but the deal is, after what happened . . . I don't want to go back there. I'm afraid the taint of Whitlaw would always hang over us there."

"Us?"

"Look at me, sweetheart." He tipped her chin up, gazing down at her through his lashes. "I need you with me wherever I go. In my life, at my side. I've decided to put my house up for sale. What do you say we look for a new home? Our home, together. Here in Sugarland, or close by so we can both keep our jobs."

"Y-you want us to live together? Permanently?" Her heart pounded. She wanted so much more.

He gave her a beautiful, dazzling smile. Took a shaky breath. "Katherine McKenna, would you do me the honor of becoming my wife?"

"Oh," she squeaked. "Oh, God. Yes! Yes, yes, yes!" Pouncing, she hiked her dress and straddled his hips. She took his face in her hands, peppering him with kisses. Nipping and teasing. His booming laughter rang out under her assault until the sound dissolved to a raspy wheeze. Contrite, she drew back. "Oh, gosh! Did I hurt you?"

"No," he gasped. "I prefer this to the fishing pole."

"Funny guy." Relieved, she captured his mouth in a slow, sensual kiss, careful not to jostle him.

"Angel?"

"Hmm?" Her fingers parted his shirt and began a thorough investigation of his muscular chest.

"We'll go shopping for an engagement ring tomorrow."

Yessss! her inner female shouted with glee. Howard Paxton was all hers. Instead, she murmured into his lips, "I don't need a ring. All I need is you."

He chuckled. "Liar. You know you want a big fat one."

Busted. "One that'll set your savings back into the Dark Ages." She tickled a taut male nipple with her tongue.

"You got it, sweetheart," he agreed, voice drugged with desire.

Encouraged, she scooted back. Reached for his zipper. "Diamonds aren't the only thing I prefer extra large, Lieutenant. Are you too tired to celebrate properly?"

"Oh, it takes a lot to bring a big guy down." He flashed a wicked grin. "See?"

She freed his long, thick erection and wrapped her fingers around the hot shaft. His moan of pleasure was sweet music.

"I most certainly do." She helped him off with his pants and boxers, then quickly undressed. "I want to ride you."

"*Please.* Do me, babe."

Straddling him once more, she guided the head of his cock to her moist opening. Needing him so much, this man who would be her husband. Sharing more than sex. A true joining between a man and his woman.

Bracing her hands on his chest, she impaled herself on him. Seated him deeply, fully inside.

"Ahhh, yeah. Ride me, sweet angel."

Leaning forward the slightest bit, she pumped his shaft. In and out, their slick heat melding together, creating sparks of fire. Building higher to lick at them both. Slow and delicious, her clit stroking his length. Driving them mad.

When Howard couldn't take any more, he rolled her onto her back without ever leaving her sheath. He moved his hips in perfect rhythm with hers, unhurried. Soaring with her, kissing her deeply and with heartfelt passion. This was different from the scalding sexual heat they'd shared before. More complete. More everything.

No doubts, no questions left between them.

This was making love.

They reached the summit together and he spilled into her, burying his hands in her hair, whispering, "I love you so much. God, I love you." Again and again, this moment etched in her soul forever.

"And I love you." She buried her face in his neck, inhaling his scent, drinking him in.

Propping up on his elbows, Howard gazed down at her with those gorgeous brown eyes she could drown in.

"I'm yours, for always."

"Promise?" She traced his sexy lips with one finger.

"Even better, angel. I'll show you."

He did. Holding her close, Howard began to move inside her. Taking his lady to new heights, making good on his vow.

Again.

And again.

Turn the page for a special preview
of the next book in the
Firefighters of Station Five series,

UNDER FIRE

Coming from Signet Eclipse in May 2009

The back end of the SUV filled Zack Knight's windshield before his exhausted brain jolted to awareness, screaming the belated message to slam on his brakes.

Too late, he jammed his foot hard to the floorboard. Only a split second to realize he wasn't going to be able to stop on the rain-slickened pavement, for his stomach to plunge to his toes. One heartbeat to curse his stupid mental lapse and recognize the very real irony of a firefighter/paramedic causing a traffic accident.

A brief, muffled squeal of tires sounded in his ears. His classic 1967 Mustang was low to the ground, built like a sleek silver bullet, and the car hydroplaned right into the tail of the SUV with only slightly less force than a shot from a gun.

A loud, sickening crunch of metal, and the bone-jarring impact was over before he could blink. Just like that. One millisecond of inattention. On the job, he'd seen the tragic results often enough.

Fortunately, he was alive and seemingly unhurt, if a little dazed and breathless.

Mortification cut through the shock. Good God, he'd just rear-ended someone! "Oh, Jesus."

Unfastening his seat belt, he glanced behind him to check for oncoming traffic in the left-hand lane, then threw open his door and slid out. Taking a couple steps, he grimaced in pain. The impact had wrenched his back and neck. The pain wasn't too bad right now, but by tomorrow he'd be damned sore. Putting aside his discomfort, he limped to the driver's side. The sight that greeted him made his heart lurch. A woman sat behind the wheel, face buried in her hands, expression hidden by long honey brown hair.

"Ma'am?" She didn't move, so he knocked on the window, his pulse jackhammering. "Ma'am, are you all right?"

Slowly, she lowered her hands, raised her head, turned to peer at him . . . and the world did a funny little flip.

Oh, *wow.* The lady had a lovely oval face that could make angels weep and cause J-Lo to sue her parents for faulty genes. Frigging supermodel drop-dead gorgeous. She opened her door and he stepped back to accommodate her, nervous and embarrassed. On top of everything, he'd never been good at relating to women on any level—pathetic, but true—and now he had to keep from staring like an idiot at the goddess standing in front of him.

A visibly upset, wide-eyed, long-legged goddess wearing black leather pants and high-heeled boots, a snazzy black leather coat, and a fuzzy red sweater underneath. Oh, *wow.*

And, holy shit, those eyes! Golden, dark-edged irises, like a jungle cat's. Exotic. For a brief second, he allowed himself to wonder what it might be like to just throw in the towel and let himself get eaten.

Shaking himself from his stupor, he held out a hand. "God, are you okay? I'm *so* sorry, I—"

"Don't they *stop* at red lights where you're from, Forrest Gump?"

Ouch. No doubt she wouldn't believe the man who'd just plowed into her backside—now *there* was a double entendre he didn't need—possessed a so-called gifted IQ of 150.

"Like I said, I'm sorry. I'm Zack Knight, and I'm a firefighter and paramedic. Would you sit in your truck and let me check your vitals?" Oh, Christ. He'd like to check a helluva lot more than the lady's pulse, if the stirring in his poor, neglected groin was any indication.

She laughed—a bold, brassy sound, and plenty jaded. Like life was one big, unfunny joke after another, usually on her. Zack knew the feeling well.

Her smile was breathtaking, wide and full of straight, white teeth, dispelling the notion she was the frightened victim he'd first thought. No, this woman was capable of handling anything, and probably had. Twice.

"My vitals. Right. Like you haven't done enough already? Thanks, sugarlump, but I'll take my chances. Let's see the damage."

She walked to the rear of her SUV, a sporty red Explorer with the bumper and hatch door buckled inward at the bottom, the paint scratched. Wasn't his insurance agent going to be ecstatic? This ought to do wonders for his premium, which he couldn't afford in the first place.

Even the Mustang, built in an era when manufacturers didn't use plastic soda bottles for bumpers, had sustained a mangled grill and buckled hood. Hundreds, if not thousands, of dollars down the drain. Zack swayed a little, feeling sick.

Heaving a deep breath, he tugged his wallet from his back pocket and removed one of his cards. He forced himself to meet her amber gaze squarely.

"This has my work and cell phone numbers on it. I'll call the police so they can make a report, and write my insurance information on the back while we're waiting. Sound okay?"

She nodded. "Fine."

"Are you sure you're all right? I really think you should go get examined." He ought to do the same, but wouldn't. He had to get his ass to the station, pronto, before the captain served it to him roasted on a platter.

Her mouth tightened. "Let's just get on with it, hotshot. It's colder than a well digger's butt out here and the rain is getting harder." Tucking a damp strand of hair behind her ear, she started to turn.

"Wait. What's your name?"

Arching a brow, she gave him a penetrating look, as though deciding whether or not to grace him with the information. For the first time, he realized how tall she was. In heels, she topped his six feet by an inch or so. Without them, she'd still almost match his height.

Sensual lips curving upward, she stuck out a slender hand tipped with bloodred nails. "Corrine Shannon, exotic dancer. Cori, if you like."

Shit yeah, I like.

Her throaty voice flooded his mind with naughty images of her lips nibbling down his naked body in the dark—

Whoa. Down, boy. He cleared his throat and clasped her hand. "That's nice. Company or p-private?" Immediately, he wanted to slice off his tongue. What the hell had made him blurt such a stupid question?

"Private. I work birthdays, anniversaries, bachelor parties . . . whatever. Thursdays through Saturdays, six p.m. to two a.m." The smile became knowing, feral. Her tawny eyes sparkled as she reached out, pushed his gold wire-rimmed glasses higher on his nose, then trailed a long nail down his cheek. "Don't sweat it, fire boy. You can't afford me."

His eyes widened. "I—I didn't mean . . . I wasn't—"

Cori turned on her elegant heel, strode back to her vehicle, and climbed in, leaving him with his mouth hanging open, the memory of her touch scorching his skin. Until he reminded himself the woman was a pro. Seduction came natural to her, probably meant nothing more than bigger tips. And his experience with women was sadly lacking.

Just as he turned to walk off, she leaned out her open door. "By the way, are *you* all right?"

The soft question, posed with genuine concern and without a trace of her earlier attitude, almost did him in.

He managed a weak smile. "Yeah, I'm good."

She frowned. "You don't look so good, Zack Knight."

Which made today like any other.

A wave of sheer exhaustion swamped him anew. His chest felt heavy and his body ached as though he'd been beaten with hammers, and not just because of the wreck. Worse, he was now so late for A-shift that the captain would definitely chew his ass, spit it out, then devise some wicked method of punishment. And he still had to work a double shift because he desperately needed the extra money; he didn't want any of his friends to find out why.

Zack's beloved home was gone. His life savings, gone. The Mustang, his pride and joy, he'd held on to by his fingertips. All to save the hide of an unfeeling bastard who'd written off his only son as a failure.

He'd never recover from the financial blow, not to mention the physical one. God, he was so tired, most days he couldn't remember his name, and the team had started to notice. This morning's wreck had been a mere symptom of a much larger problem. They'd watch him like hawks now, ready to intervene if he started to sink.

They had no idea how easy giving up would be.

Twenty-six years old, flat broke, and at the mercy of dangerous criminals. How do you like those apples, genius?

* * *

Cori Shannon squinted through the windshield at the sleet, fighting the steering wheel in the pissy weather. Dammit, she'd missed her morning class. And right before a big exam, too. All because that guy frickin' fell asleep at the wheel. What was his name?

Zack. The firefighter.

The cutie with the blue peepers hiding behind those conservative wire-rimmed glasses. Tall, lean, and fit. He'd been young, twentysomething, with soft, coal black hair tumbling over his forehead and framing a kind face. Okay, a *gorgeous* face with a delicious body to match.

In truth, she hadn't been able to take her eyes off the way his rain-splattered shirt clung to the hard muscles of his chest. Had feasted on the sight of his wet pants plastered to his long legs and tight, perfect rear end.

Oh, he was a very sexy man all right, but . . . there'd been something vulnerable in his gaze. Something deep and sad that drew her, made her want to take him in her arms and hold him.

Because, shit, she recognized herself in his lost expression. Crazy, but for one split second, she'd fought the impulse to grab his hand and say, "Hey, let's blow this place. Jump in and we'll get the hell gone."

Funny thing was, the man looked like he might've taken her up on the offer.

Not that she would've made it, as much as the idea had merit. "You're an upstanding citizen nowadays, Corrine, my girl," she muttered to herself. "No more disastrous decisions for you."

She shivered. Alexander Gunter was dead, and she'd come damned close to paying the ultimate price for giving up her dreams the first time around the block. For marrying a man wearing the guise of a savior, only to discover the ruthless jackal underneath.

Done and gone. She was so near the realization of her dream that she could taste success. In spite of the crappy start to her day, happiness curled through her belly. May graduation was a mere four months away. By God, she'd done it!

Once the last of her school bills were paid off and she started drawing a regular check from her new job, all of her debts would be history. Best of all, she'd say "So long" to exotic dancing for good.

Brows furrowed, she wondered why on earth she'd deliberately given Zack Knight a skewed impression of herself. Why hadn't she just told him she was in nursing school? A bit of defiance rearing its ugly head, she supposed. Yeah, a secret, perverse part of her had wanted to see how Zack would react to news that would have most men panting in anticipation—however misguidedly—of an easy screw.

Not this one. The memory of his blue eyes widening innocently at the disclosure of her profession caused a weird ache in the region of her heart. No guy could possibly be so sweet and naive in this day and age.

What a refreshing change.

Rot in hell, Alex.

A crack of lightning and a drum roll of thunder made Cori jump, startling her attention back to the road. The sleet drove against the windshield in sheets, lowering visibility to almost nil. The Sugarland Bridge loomed ahead, a ghostly specter enshrouded in gray. The morning had grown so dark that she could hardly tell where the sky ended and the river burgeoning underneath the bridge began.

Glancing in the rearview mirror, she noticed a pair of headlights approaching from behind. The deluge might be distorting things, but it seemed the lights were approaching far too fast for the treacherous conditions.

Starting over the bridge, she tensed, attention divided between driving carefully and the idiot who was rapidly gaining on her. What fool needed to be in such a hurry in terrible weather like this?

The driver was closing the gap between them at an alarming clip, rushing up until the glare from the headlights was blinding. The jerk didn't try to pass, but rode her tail, no more than a few feet behind her. Too dangerous and freaky for words. Cori held steady, determined to pull off to the shoulder on the other side and let the car go around her. Just a bit farther and—

A muffled pop sounded. The SUV skidded to the right, and, panicking, she jerked the wheel in the opposite direction, overcorrecting.

On a clear day, in dry conditions, she would've been able to straighten the vehicle without mishap. But not on what might well be the last day of her life.

Crossing the oncoming lane, the opposite guardrail approached at a terrifying speed. She instinctively stamped hard on the brake pedal, sending the Explorer into a skid from which there was no stopping.

Cori screamed as the SUV rocketed into the guardrail. A deafening explosion of glass and grinding metal drowned out everything else. The airbag deployed in her face, saving her from slamming into the steering column or windshield, but the crash jarred every bone in her body. She sat stunned, unable to move, dizzy. The vehicle seemed to be rocking like a child's seesaw. She must've really shaken her brain. At least the glaring headlights were gone.

Frowning, she turned her head to look out the driver's-side window, wincing at a stab of pain in her temple. What do you know? The jerk hadn't even stopped. Unlike the rocking.

Oh, no. The motion wasn't from dizziness.

Hands shaking, she pushed the deflating airbag out of her face and peered out the shattered front windshield. Horror numbed her entire body.

"Oh Jesus . . ."

Her Explorer tottered just a few feet above the swollen, angry Cumberland River.

Nothing between her and a watery grave except the hand of God.

A-shift had worked some tough scenes over the years, had tread the razor's edge in some gut-wrenching situations. But as Zack drove the quint past the police barricade and neared the bridge's summit, Tanner let loose a few creative curses. God almighty, this one was a real bitch.

"We'll wrap the chain around something solid, like the opposite guardrail or bridge support, then hook it to the rear axle of the SUV, try to stabilize the vehicle. Extract the driver through the back hatch."

"Yes, sir." Zack frowned as the teetering Explorer came into view. Recognition dawned, hitting his gut like a fist. "Sonofabitch."

Tanner snapped his sharp gaze to his FAO's face. "What?"

"That's her. The lady I hit on the way to work."

"Keep your head in the game, kid. That doesn't necessarily mean anything."

Zack's thoughts mirrored Tanner's. The woman might've been more injured than Zack previously believed. She could have passed out. Or perhaps she was rattled from being hit, and a moment of inattention resulted in her current predicament. Either way, the idea he might be responsible for a woman's life literally hanging in the balance, even indirectly, filled him with horror.

If what happened to Cori Shannon was his fault, Tanner wouldn't have to fire him. He'd be finished.

Pulling the hat low over his eyes, Zack threw open the door and swung down from the quint, wincing at the pain in his stiffening muscles. The wind howled with frightening strength, the forceful gusts threatening to sweep man and machine right off the structure and into hell. Rain pummeled his body in icy sheets, soaking him to the skin once more and chilling him to the bone despite the thick coat, pants, and hat—in spite of the rising fever he hadn't told anyone about. He was hot and cold by turns, limbs weighing a ton. Once Miss Shannon was safe and the situation put behind them, he'd collapse on his bunk at the station.

Opening a side compartment on the quint, he and Tanner wrestled out a thick, industrial-strength chain while Eve and Tommy Skyler ran over to the Explorer. Six-Pack and Julian Salvatore hopped out of the ambulance and jogged toward Zack and Tanner.

"Get this wrapped around the guardrail over there," Tanner shouted at Salvatore above the thunder and lightning.

As Skyler helped Salvatore, Zack hurried to the side of the Explorer, watching his footing. The driver's door was positioned over open space, muddy water swirling only feet below them. To see Cori, he had to lean forward carefully without touching the vehicle and upsetting it, or losing his balance in the wind and falling off the bridge. With the added weight of his gear, he'd sink like a stone.

He knocked on the window as hard as he dared. "Ma'am? Ms. Shannon?" Slowly, she turned her head to peer at him through the rain-splattered glass. "Sugarland Fire Department. Are you hurt?"

"Hit my head," she called back, voice barely audible above the storm's racket. "Nothing's broken."

Thank God for that. He tried to sound encouraging. "All right, that's good. Listen, I promise we're gonna get you out of there. Sit tight while we secure the back end. Then we'll bring you out through the rear. Okay?"

After a pause, she nodded.

"That's my girl. I'm going around to the back and—"

"No! Don't leave me!" she wailed.

"I'm not leaving you, Cori, you have my word." He put a thread of steel into his voice, using her first name on purpose. The calm assurance, the familiarity, firefighters were taught to employ to keep a victim from wigging out. "I'm not going anywhere except through the back to meet you."

Cori was terrified. Depending on him. In that moment, Zack's problems, the sickness threatening to topple him, vanished. His whole world shrank to a laser point of purpose. Nothing mattered except getting her to safety.

As Zack hurried to the back end of the vehicle, he wondered if she'd recognized him. Probably not, with the storm obscuring her vision and the hat shielding his face. If she was in shock, she might not even consider how he knew her name.

Skyler and Salvatore had secured the chain to the rear axle by the large hook on one end. They'd wrapped the other end several times around the guardrail on the opposite side of the bridge to take out as much slack as possible.

Salvatore waved a hand at the makeshift support. "I don't like this," he said. "The guardrail can't take the dead weight if she shifts."

"It's what we've got to work with." The captain jabbed a finger at Howard. "Six-Pack, you're the heaviest. Your weight will help hold it steady while you take her—"

"No." That single, sharp command from Zack got the entire team's attention. Including Tanner's, who gaped at him. "I promised Ms. Shannon I'd go in and get her, and I'm not about to break my word. She's hanging by a thread, and we need her calm."

Tanner's face darkened with anger violent enough to rival the storm. "Knight, did you hear what I—"

"I heard, Cap, and I'm still going in. Ms. Shannon doesn't have time for us to stand around arguing about it." Dismissing Tanner, he turned to Skyler. "Tommy, get the hatch."

To his credit, Skyler turned and twisted the knob, opening the rear entry without argument. The door gave easily, despite being bent from the earlier wreck. Had to be done anyway, so Zack hoped Skyler wouldn't catch hell later. His own job, however, was probably toast.

"What's this? Look!" Crouched by the right rear tire, which was suspended a couple of feet off the ground, Eve pointed to the tread.

"Tire blew," Six-Pack observed. "That's what sent her into the skid."

"Not just a blown tire. A bullet hole."

Another wave of heat and cold swamped Zack, and he had to concentrate hard not to let his weakness show. A bullet. Jesus Christ, someone shot out her tire! Who would do such a malicious thing?

"Let's push the vehicle down, get the back tires on the ground," Tanner said. He positioned himself on the right corner of the vehicle, leaning just inside the hatch, Six-Pack on the left. The two men braced their hands on the lip above the bumper. "Slow and easy."

When the rear tires met pavement, the captain nodded at Zack. Carefully, Zack popped a latch on Tanner's side and let down the rear bench seat to clear the path somewhat. Pushing his hat back, he crawled inside. On his hands and knees, inch by inch. "Cori? You still with me up there?"

"Hurry!" Long gone was the cocky attitude of their earlier meeting.

His heart lurched in response to her terror. "I'm here, but you're going to have to meet me halfway."

"Nooo! If I move, we'll fall!"

"If you don't, we'll fall anyway. You want me to get you out, right?"

"Yes, but I can't—"

"You *can*. Listen to me. Unbuckle your seat belt. Do it now."

She did, taking the strap off her shoulder. "Okay. Now what?"

"Good. Turn your body to your right, nice and slow, so you can see me." Leather squeaked as she followed his direction, scooting around in the seat. Bracing a trembling hand on the console, she got her first good look at him. Instantly, her eyes widened in recognition.

"You!"

He tried a reassuring smile. "Kismet, huh? Don't worry. In spite of earlier evidence to the contrary, you're in good hands."

She let out a shaky laugh that didn't quite hide her fear. "So you're not a *complete* dipstick. Nice to know, Zack."

He grinned at her, glad she had some sass left, even if the barb was directed at his head. That meant she was thinking clearly, and would help him get her out of this mess.

A groan of metal reached his ears from somewhere behind him, and a ripe curse from Salvatore.

"Move it, *amigo*! She's not gonna hold for long!"

Amigo? Since when? Salvatore couldn't stand him, so he and Cori must be in deep shit. A trickle of sweat streaked down Zack's fevered cheek as he inched forward. Reached out a hand. "Cori, climb over the console."

"Zack—"

"If you don't, we're both going to die, because I'm not leaving without you. I promised."

She glanced at his outstretched hand. Read the truth on his face. He'd willingly give his life for hers. His resolve seemed to fortify her own, and she heaved a deep breath.

"All right. Here I come." Wiggling a bit, she crept forward, squeezing between the seats. One hand over the other.

"Easy does it. Just a little more."

The truck gave a sudden lurch, nose dipping downward. Cori shrieked, grabbed for him and missed. Metal squealed, the noise deafening as the truck slid, tearing the undercarriage. He didn't have to look to know the guardrail was giving way. Or that Sean and Howard were no longer holding down the tailgate. The SUV tilted toward the swollen river at a crazy angle.

With nothing to stop him, the momentum sent him into the back of the middle seats. Sweet Jesus. If he went over, he'd crash into Cori and send them both toppling through the shattered front windshield.

The vehicle shuddered and stopped.

Leaning over the row of seats, he reached for Cori once more. "Now or never."

Bracing her booted feet against the back of the driver's seat, Cori pushed herself toward him in one last-ditch effort, beautiful face totally focused. Determined. When she grabbed for his hand this time, she didn't miss.

Zack pulled Cori over the seat, practically threw her toward the open hatch. Bracing himself underneath her, he cupped her ass and shoved her hard toward his team.

Several pairs of hands hauled her to safety, and he exhaled in relief. Cori was out. Following behind, he scrambled toward the opening. His fingers wrapped around the lip and he hauled himself up—

Just as the guardrail holding the chain gave way.

The terrible sound of rending metal filled the air. Lightning split the sky as the rail snapped. The chain whipped, the backlash popping loudly, slamming into his head with the force of a shotgun blast. He flew backward from the impact.

"Zack!"

Shouts, screaming. Drowned by the storm as the truck slid free of its perch. He tumbled with it, falling, falling. Saw the bridge disappear.

The rear door banged shut as the SUV hit the river, hard. He crashed around in the interior, along for the ride, and thought, *Well, shit. There goes my brand new glasses. Will insurance cover a new pair?*

Ice-cold water rushed in, filling the cabin. Dragging at the heavy protective clothing that would serve as his shroud if he didn't get out. Before the water closed over his head, he managed to suck in a deep breath.

Zack's head throbbed with intense agony even shock and the freezing water couldn't blot out. Disoriented, he groped for a window or door handle.

Which way out? Where? Nothing but pitch black.

He searched, running his hand along the interior. Leather. A seat, but which one? The cumbersome gear weighed him down and must come off. *Stay calm. Find the windshield, exit through the busted glass, then discard the coat.* He shoved forward, hands out, but he was swimming blind. He found a side window, the edge of a door.

Zack yanked on the handle, pushed. The door wouldn't budge. Swiveling in the opposite direction, he tried another escape route. Seconds passed, maybe a minute. His chances were slipping away. He found another door, but by now his lungs burned. He needed air.

He located a different handle. Pulled, pushed. Kicked the glass. All to no avail.

His lungs screamed, his futile efforts to free himself slowing. As reality hit, horror electrified his brain.

He wasn't getting out of this alive.

Two hours ago, he'd actually entertained giving up.

Now he wanted desperately to live. Get involved with life again. To find out who'd taken a shot at Cori Shannon, and why. Maybe get to know her and . . . what?

But fate had stolen those options from him.

Please, God, I don't want to die! Help me. . . .

Precious air exploded from his lungs. Unable to stop the inevitable, he sucked in great gulps of brackish water. Clawed at the glass, the door. No use.

His limbs grew heavy, refused to function any longer. His struggles ceased, the fight over. Consciousness began to fade, along with the pain.

Besides his team, who would mourn his loss?

Nobody. Not even his father.

You're a disappointment, boy. Going nowhere.

If he could, he'd laugh at the irony. His father had been right after all. And he couldn't even blame his own tragic end on the old fucker's debt to his dangerous friends.

No time for regrets. No more fear. Only a strange lightness in his body as he finally accepted, let go.

Zack smiled inside, raised a gloved middle finger in defiance.

Get seven hundred and fifty thousand dollars out of that, assholes.

ABOUT THE AUTHOR

Jo Davis spent sixteen years in the public school trenches before she left teaching to pursue her dreams of becoming a full-time writer. An active member of Romance Writers of America, she's been a Golden Heart Award finalist for Best Romantic Suspense. She lives in Texas with her husband and two children. Visit her Web site at www.jodavis.net.

AVAILABLE NOW

From *New York Times* bestseller
CHRISTINA DODD

THIGH HIGH

Nessa Dahl always had the good sense to steer
clear of trouble. Then Jeremiah MacNaught
showed up in New Orleans, determined to get
to the bottom of a string of bank robberies by
two women wearing Mardi Gras masks. Little
does Nessa realize that the handsome
investigator is convinced she's involved with
the crimes—or that he's willing to do anything
to get the truth. Even if it means taking the
beautiful woman he's convinced is a liar and
thief straight to bed...

Available wherever books are sold or at
penguin.com

AVAILABLE NOW

TROUBLE IN HIGH HEELS

Christina Dodd

*One wild night can lead to all
kinds of trouble...*

When Brandi Michaels discovers her fiancé
hopping a flight to Vegas to marry his
girlfriend, she pawns her engagement ring,
buys herself a fabulous outfit, and spends one
sultry night in the arms of a gorgeous Italian
stranger named Roberto Bartolini. When
Brandi becomes the mark for a killer, she has
no choice but to turn to Roberto—a man
who's destined to be either her savior or her
downfall. But one thing's for sure: She's not
going down without a fight....

Penguin Group (USA) Online

What will you be reading tomorrow?

Tom Clancy, Patricia Cornwell, W.E.B. Griffin,
Nora Roberts, William Gibson, Robin Cook,
Brian Jacques, Catherine Coulter, Stephen King,
Dean Koontz, Ken Follett, Clive Cussler,
Eric Jerome Dickey, John Sandford,
Terry McMillan, Sue Monk Kidd, Amy Tan,
John Berendt...

You'll find them all at
penguin.com

*Read excerpts and newsletters,
find tour schedules and reading group guides,
and enter contests.*

Subscribe to Penguin Group (USA) newsletters
and get an exclusive inside look
at exciting new titles and the authors you love
long before everyone else does.

PENGUIN GROUP (USA)
us.penguingroup.com